The Captain Of The Guard

By

James Grant

Double 9
BOOKS

The Captain of the Guard
by James Grant

ISBN: 978-93-62760-10-4

Published by

DOUBLE 9 BOOKS

2/13-B, Ansari Road
Daryaganj, New Delhi – 110002
info@double9books.com
www.double9books.com
Tel. 011-40042856

ABOUT THE AUTHOR

James Grant, born on August 1, 1822, changed into a Scottish creator famend for his prolific contributions to literature, specially within the genres of historic fiction, journey, and military narratives. His early years had been steeped in a navy environment due to his father's profession in the British navy, which significantly stimulated Grant's writing. Grant's literary profession flourished at some stage in the 19th century, marked via a high-quality output of extra than 90 novels, regularly published under various pseudonyms inclusive of Harry Gringo and Lawrence L. Lynch. His works were recognized for his or her bright portrayal of navy life, regularly drawing from his firsthand reviews and historic activities. "Adventures of an Aide-de-Camp" is certainly one of his remarkable works, depicting memories of navy adventures and reflecting Grant's intimate information of military existence. His writing style changed into characterized via particular descriptions, intricate plots, and a penchant for ancient accuracy, making his narratives compelling and engaging. Grant's literary achievements solidified his reputation as a prominent figure in nineteenth-century literature, and his have an impact on at the style of military fiction stays huge to this day. He continued to jot down and publish till his passing on May 5, 1887, leaving in the back of a wealthy legacy of gripping storytelling and historic insight.

CONTENTS

PREFACE

Many of the scenes and episodes which are delineated in the following story are taken from the annals of Scotland.

Those which belong to romance I leave the reader to discover.

My wish has been to portray the state of the nation and its people during the reign of the second James, without afflicting the reader by obsolete words and obscure dialects, which few now care about, and still fewer would comprehend, but following history as closely as the network of my own narrative would permit.

In some of the proceedings of the Douglas family, and minor details, it has suited my purpose to adhere to other sources of information, rather than the "Peerage," or the folio of Master David Hume, of Godscroft, the quaint old historian of the House of Douglas.

March, 1862.

CHAPTER I
THE FOUR COFFINS

God save the king, and bless the land
In plenty, joy, and peace;
And grant henceforth that foul debate
'Twixt noblemen may cease. — Chevy Chase.

On the evening of the 22nd November, 1440, the report of a brass carthoun, or cannon-royale, as it pealed from the castle of Edinburgh, made all who were in the thoroughfares below raise their eyes to the grey ramparts, where the white smoke was seen floating away from the summit of King David's Tower, and then people were seen hastening towards the southern side of the city, where the quaint old streets and narrow alleys opened into the fields, or the oakwoods of Bristo and Drumsheugh.

Crowds from all quarters pressed towards the Pleasance, the route by which the great earl of Douglas (duke of Touraine and lord of Longoville), who had been invited to visit the young king, was expected to enter the city. Curiosity was excited, as it was anticipated that his train would be a brilliant one. All in the secluded metropolis of the north were on tiptoe to behold a sight such as they had not been gratified with since the ambassadors of Amadeus VIII., duke of Savoy, had come to ask the hand of the king's little sister, Annabella, for his son, the valiant Louis Count de Maurienne, to whom, however, she preferred a Scottish earl, with a Scottish home, on the bonnie banks of the Clyde.

The boom of the same cannon brought to the bartizan of the great tower whereon it stood four armed men, who immediately turned their eyes towards the south.

Two of these were men well up in years. They wore furred caps of maintenance, denoting their high rank or position, and had long crimson robes, with capes of ermine that fell to their elbows. Beneath these flowing garments there glittered at times their steel habergeons, and the embroidered belts which sustained their swords.

One was a man of a tall figure and noble presence, with a long, grave, and pleasing face.

The other was equally noble in bearing, but his face was less pleasing in expression, for his temples were hollow, his eyes keen, his brows knit, and there played about his thin, cruel lips a crafty but courtly smile.

"Summon Romanno, the constable; bid him display the king's standard—call the garrison to their arms—shut gates and barriers," were the orders given rapidly by both at the same moment.

The first was Sir Alexander Livingstone, of Callendar, Regent of Scotland, and governor of the young king, James II., then in his eleventh year.

The second was Sir William Crichton of that ilk, the Lord Chancellor, appointed by the Parliament, after the murder of the late King James I., in the Black Friary, at Perth.

"Red-haired Achanna, with his Judas-coloured red beard, has played his cards well for us and for the king," said the Chancellor, with a crafty smile.

"Achanna," replied the Regent, grimly; "yes, a wretch born with the stamp of hell on his forehead—a hireling clerk, as well as swashbuckler."

"But a useful man withal, and said to be a go-between of Douglas and Duke Robert of Albany."

James Achanna, the person to whom they referred, was a red-haired and red-bearded gentleman, of Galloway, outwardly a stanch adherent of Douglas, but in the secret pay of his enemies, the Regent and Chancellor. Thus he had conveyed the artful message by which the hostile earl, and the chief members of his family, were *lured* to visit the court of the young king.

"So he is in sight at last," said the Regent through his clenched teeth; "do you see his train, my lord?"

"Aye; on the road by Kirk-liberton. He is coming down the brae in his bravery, with banner and spear, but that pride shall have a fall, for he comes to his doom."

"But, Chancellor, his countess and her sister," whispered the Regent; "they—they——"

"Well; what of them?"

"Must they too perish?"

"Let the whole brood perish at one fell swoop," was the fierce response, in a husky whisper. "Had they but one neck, I tell thee, Livingstone, it should be laid on the block that awaits the Douglas in the hall below us."

"Hush!"

"And wherefore hush?" continued the elder statesman, fiercely.

"Know ye not that Sir Patrick Gray loves the earl's cousin?" said the Regent, glancing hastily at their two companions, who stood a little way from them.

"Murielle Douglas," replied Crichton, grinding his sharp teeth; "well, be it so; but I shall give her a colder gudeman than the king's liege subject, and the Captain of his Guard—will God I shall!"

The Regent waved his gloved hand to impress the caution he wished his colleague to observe, and, as if afraid to trust his discretion further, withdrew to a corner of the rampart enclosing the summit of the great tower, which then formed the donjon or keep of the castle of Edinburgh; but ever and anon, as the gleam of arms flashed in the sunlight, on the green pastoral slopes of Liberton, they exchanged a deep and bitter smile.

Two handsome young men, who had not yet spoken, but who attended them and stood apart, were sheathed in complete armour, and wore the beautiful bascinets of that reign; these had a tube for the plume, and were encircled by a camaile like the old caps of the Templars. They had gorgeous military girdles and long swords, globular corslets, and wide hanging sleeves of scarlet cloth lined with yellow silk (the royal colours), depending from their shoulders; this was a very anomalous fashion with armour, but formed a portion of the military foppery of that day.

He with the short beard and black moustache, in the prime of strength and manhood, is Sir Patrick Gray, a younger son of the lord of Foulis, and *Captain of the King's Guard*; and he, the less in stature, the junior in years, with fair hair and merry eyes, is Sir Thomas MacLellan of Bombie, his cousin and friend, and lieutenant of the same guard, which the Regent had embodied to protect the person of the young king from the perils amid which his father had perished—perils which the house of Douglas seemed about to revive.

"Do you see, gentlemen, how the lances in his train glitter, as they come rank on rank over yonder long green brae?" said the Regent, turning round; "by my soul, Lord Chancellor, he has an escort that might befit a king!"

"A train of cut-throats, swashbucklers, and scrape-trenchers; MacDouals, MacGhies, Achannas, and MacCombies——"

"Chancellor, do not add MacLellans, I pray you," interrupted the lieutenant of the guard.

"The broken men of Galloway," continued the Chancellor, wrathfully; "the bullyrooks of Thrave—outlaws, whose unchristian acts would put to shame the pagans of Argier or Cathay—of the Soldan or Prester John! and I say so, under favour, Sir Thomas," he added, turning with a sudden smile to the lieutenant, who was chief of the MacLellans of Bombie, a powerful family, whose lands were surrounded by those of the Douglases and their adherents.

"Do you include the Lord Abbot of Tongland among those rare fellows?" asked Sir Thomas, who was piqued for the honour of his native province.

"An abbot who acts as the earl's beadsman can be little better," was the sour reply.

The young man bit his moustache impatiently, but the more politic Regent, to soothe the irritation which his colleague's words were inspiring, said hastily to one who had hitherto been silent, "Sir Patrick Gray, how many followers think you, by your soldier's eye, the earl hath under his banner yonder?"

"At least two thousand men, with horse and spear, if I may judge by the breadth of the road, and the cloud of dust they raise," replied the captain of the guard, with soldier-like brevity and confidence.

"Two thousand!" muttered the Regent; "passing strong for a mere subject."

"Douglas never leaves his castle gates with less," said MacLellan; "and wherefore marvel? They are not so many after all for such an earl as Douglas, when the laird of Roslin's daughter never enters Edinburgh with less than seventy mounted gentlemen in her train, each clad in a velvet jupon, with a chain of gold at his neck."

"Two thousand lances," muttered the Chancellor also, stroking his shaven chin, for beards were only worn by soldiers at that time, and not always by them.

"And you have but three hundred men-at-arms in garrison here—billmen and cannoneers?" whispered the Regent.

"But they are all my own vassals, men bred under my roof-tree since they were boys of the belt; these, with a hundred pikes of the king's guard, are more than enough for our purpose, within a castle so strong as this," replied the Chancellor, whose pale lips quivered with the nervous fury he strove in vain to conceal from the two gentlemen who stood at the other corner of the bartizan; for a plot had been laid to destroy the mighty earl of Douglas, one of those dark, terrible, and sudden plots, which, under the name of *raids*, so frequently convulsed the kingdom of Scotland, and marked its martial annals with blood and crime, the only shadows that tinge a great and glorious past.

The soldiers, pages, and idlers of the castle who had been playing at troy, chess, or shovel-board, for the bonnet pieces and silver pennies of King James, relinquished their sport, and crowded to the ramparts to observe the approach of the now obnoxious and turbulent Douglas.

And now, for a time, these four persons described continued to observe in silence the approaching train of the great feudal peer, the lances of whose vassalage (among them were many knights, barons, and gentlemen of his surname) glinted brightly in the evening sun, as they moved down the northern slope of Liberton, past the old tower built by David Liberton, sergeant of the overward of the constabulary of Edinburgh, in the time of David II., and past the older church, the foundation of which fond tradition unvaryingly ascribed to Macbeth, though, mysteriously enough, on its demolition in 1815, there was found in its base an iron medal of the 13th century, inscribed in Russian characters, "*The Grand Prince St. Alexander Yaroslavitch Neffvskoy.*"

On the earl's train disappearing among the wooded hollows which lay between the city and the furzy slope of Braid and Liberton, the captain of the guard and his kinsman the lieutenant, with their esquires, pages, and lacqueys passed forth from the castle, to swell the retinue of the chief magistrate of the city, Sir Thomas Cranston of that ilk, baron of Denholm and Stobs, warden of the marches, and one of the conservators of peace upon the borders, for the steel-gloved provosts of those stirring times were men of a different metal from the men of words, who "twaddle" in the same place in this age of steam and electricity.

As they passed out, the king's master butcher entered the gateway of the fortress, accompanied by a peddie or foot-boy, bearing a covered bundle upon a trencher.

This covered bundle contained a *black bull's head.*

"See you *that*, Sir Alexander?" said the Chancellor, twitching the furred sleeve of his compatriot.

"The black bull's head!" said the other, with an irrepressible shudder.

"Yes; for the banquet to-morrow."

"Holy Dame!"

"It is the fatal signal, to be placed on the table the moment the king rises."

"The king! Oh, Chancellor," said the Regent, in a voice that turned almost to a groan, "after all I have urged, mean you that he, poor boy, shall share the odium of our act—a deed at which one half of Scotland, and perhaps all France, may cry aloud?"

"Let them cry; the *end* shall sanctify the means. With Douglas in his grave, the great seal will be firmer in my hands, the sceptre lighter in yours, and the crown shall shine the brighter on the head of him whose father was wronged and slain by such as Douglas in the Black Friary at Perth."

"I pray God all may end as you predict," said the Regent, doubtfully; "but yet I shudder when contemplating this lure—this snare; the mock banquet, the mock tribunal, and the bloody lykewake of the morrow."

That night, after dusk, four coffins were secretly conveyed up the rock, and through the west postern of the castle, by James Achanna and other "muffled" or masked men, and these were concealed in the chancellor's private closet, the door of which opened off the great hall of David's tower.

These coffins were covered with crimson velvet and had nails, handles, and plates of gold, or at least of richly gilt work.

The first had the name of the most potent prince William, sixth earl of Douglas, third duke of Touraine, lord of Longoville, Galloway, Annandale, and Liddesdale, *qui obit 23rd Nov., 1440*, in his seventeenth year.

The second coffin bore the name of his younger brother, Lord David, *qui obit 23rd Nov., 1440.*

The third bore the name of his countess, Margaret Douglas, so famed for her beauty as the Fair Maid of Galloway, *qui obit 23rd Nov., 1440*, in her eighteenth year.

The fourth bore the name of his sister, Lady Murielle Douglas, two years younger, with the same fatal inscription, *qui obit 23rd Nov., 1440.*

Beyond these four coffins, in the gloom of that vaulted closet, were a grindstone, an axe, and a block.

We have opened our story on the evening of the TWENTY-SECOND November; thus we shall soon see with what intent these terrible objects were provided.

CHAPTER II
WILLIAM, DUKE OF TOURAINE

Vails not to tell each hardy clan,
From the fair middle marches come;
The Bloody Heart blazed in the van,
Announcing Douglas, dreaded name!—Scott.

At this time the house of Douglas, one which in past ages had ever led the van of battle in the cause of Scottish honour and liberty, had attained the most exorbitant, and in that warlike and feudal epoch, dangerous power—a power that never ceased to menace the freedom of the people on one hand, and the independence of the throne on the other.

William, sixth earl of Douglas, and third duke of Touraine, had just succeeded to the vast possessions of his family by the death of his father, Archibald, who had been Lieutenant-General of Scotland, and Marshal of France, and who died at Restalrig, in 1439.

In his seventeenth year, William found himself master of all the princely heritage his warlike sire had left him, the earldom of Douglas, with the lordships of Bothwell, Annandale, and Liddesdale; the county of Longoville, and the dukedom of Touraine, "the garden of France."

To these he had added the principality of Galloway, the county of Wigton, and the lordship of Balvenie, by marriage with his cousin, Margaret, the Fair Maid of Galloway, a high-born girl of great beauty and spirit, who was one year his senior, and whose proud and fiery temper made her prove his evil mentor in many an act of folly and outrage; while Lady Murielle, the younger and gentler sister, whose loveliness was long embalmed in many a sweet old Galloway song, strove anxiously, but vainly, to avert them.

Even in that age of pride, vain of his lofty ancestry, which he could trace back through a long line of brave and loyal nobles to that Sholto Dhu-glas, the grey and swarthy warrior, who, in the eighth century, slew Donald of the Isles—rendered powerful by the vast number, the unity and rank of his vassalage, by the strength of his fortresses and extent of his territories, which included the richest and most important districts of the kingdom; hourly told by high-born and artful flatterers that he possessed wealth equal, and armed forces superior, to the king, this rash young noble had of late begun to assume all the state of a crowned head.

On the death of his father, he sent into France two ambassadors to Charles VII., to make his oath of fealty for the dukedom of Touraine.

These unwise envoys, Sir Alan Lauder, of the Bass, a knight of Lothian, and Sir Malcolm Fleming, lord of Biggar and Cumbernauld, were received by the French monarch with a degree of state and ceremony on which the Regent and Chancellor of Scotland, as guardians of its young king, could not fail to look with jealous eyes; thus, stifling their secret piques and heart-burnings, they resolved to coalesce for the public weal, and to watch, win, or CRUSH this warlike feudatory, whose power, ambition, and splendour overtopped the throne, and threatened to extinguish themselves.

On the other hand, flattered by the messages of Charles the Victorious, despising the Regent and Chancellor as mere knights of Lothian, the young earl became guilty of outrages, and evinced an arrogance, that made all tremble for the issue.

When he left any of his castles, he never rode with less than one or two thousand knights and horsemen in his train, all brilliantly armed and accoutred; and this haughty retinue frequently carried havoc, and always terror, wherever they appeared. His household was magnificent; he appointed his petty officers of state, and within his castle-halls of Thrave, Bothwell, and Douglas, held courts which rivalled the meetings of Parliament; while, to the many royal summonses sent him, scornful and insolent answers, dictated by his friends, or rather by those who were the friends of his father, the knights Fleming and Lauder, were returned to the Regent and Chancellor.

Under his banner and name, his followers, many of whom were nobles, thus filled the land with outrage and tumult. The people were without protection and without redress, while the court of the young king was daily crowded by suppliants who cried for vengeance.

"There were," saith Lyndessy, in his Chronicles, "so many widows, bairns, and infants seeking redress for husbands, kindred, and friends, who had been cruelly slain by wicked murderers; siclike, many for hership, theft, and reif, that there was no man but would have had ruth and pity to hear the same. Soon murder, theft, and slaughter were in such common dalliance among the people, and the king's power had fallen into such contempt, that no man *wist* where to seek refuge unless he swore himself a servant to some common murderer or tyrant, to maintain himself against the invasion of others, or else gave largely of his gear to save his life, and afford him peace and rest."

Not content with having produced all this, the young duke, or earl, urged by his ambitious counsellors, dared openly to impugn the king's title to the crown, affecting to prefer the claims of his own uncle, Malise, earl of Strathearn, who was descended from Euphemia Ross, the second queen of Robert II.; and he intrigued with Robert Stuart, the exiled son of the king's uncle, the late Murdoch, duke of Albany, to subvert the Royal succession.

Sir Alexander Livingstone, the Regent, and Sir William Crichton, the Lord Chancellor, saw that a crisis had come in the affairs of the realm; that the throne and their own position must sink together beneath the overweening power of Douglas unless a dreadful blow were struck; and thus, with all the dark ferocity and stern subtlety of the age in which they lived, they prepared to *strike it*!

James Hanna, or Achanna, one of those smooth-tongued political villains, of whom Scotland has in all ages produced a plentiful brood—a wretch who for gold contrived to be a secret adherent and deluder of both parties, was despatched with a royal message to Douglas's castle of Thrave, in the name of the Regent and Chancellor.

In this mandate, which bore the privy seal of the realm, they "professed the highest esteem for the young earl's character, and a profound regret for the petty jealousies which had so long separated them. They anxiously and earnestly solicited his august presence at court that he might cultivate the friendship of his sovereign, now in his eleventh year, and lend his great talents and influence to the administration of affairs—while the presence of the countess and her sister, Lady Murielle, could not fail to shed some rays of splendour on the court, and be a source of joy to the young princesses, the sisters of his majesty."

This document, so fulsome when addressed to an almost untutored boy, added, that on the vigil of St. Catherine, a banquet in celebration of their friendship and the extinction of discord would be royally held in the great hall of the castle at Edinburgh.

The young earl smiled scornfully on hearing this missive read by the wily Achanna on his knees; but he tossed from his wrist a hawk with which he had been playing, and replied—

"My father never yielded to James I., nor will I to James II., and his two cock lairds of Lothian, who pretend to govern Scotland. Nevertheless, we shall mount and go, were it but to flaunt our bravery at court."

Sir Malcolm Fleming, of Cumbernauld, an old and faithful friend of his father, urged him to mistrust Crichton and remain among his followers; but the desire to dazzle his enemies by the splendour of his retinue, and the *arguments* of his kinsman, the earl of Abercorn, outweighed all that the more faithful and wary could advance.

And herein lay a secret which death might reveal to him; but in life he would never discover.

James the Gross, earl of Abercorn, had loved, but in vain, the beautiful Maid of Galloway, who preferred her younger and more handsome cousin, Earl William; but James was the next heir to the latter, if he and Lord David died without children: thus avarice, ambition, and revenge spurred him on, and caused him to urge the immediate acceptance of the Chancellor's invitation, and *his* energetic advice, with the young earl's vain-glorious wish, bore down all the faithful Fleming could urge.

James Achanna was the villainous tool who worked for him in the dark; and herein was another secret; for Achanna had been a page to the father of the countess, and had loved her too.

This love had expanded suddenly, like a flower that blooms in a night under a tropical moon, and the coquette soon discovered it.

"You love me?" said she imperiously, reining up her horse, as they one day rode side by side near the loch of the Carlinwark.

"Yes," said the page, tremulously, and covered with confusion by the abruptness of the question.

"How old are you, James Achanna?"

"I am four-and-twenty, madam."

"You are but a boy," said she, laughing.

"I am six years *your* senior," he replied, gathering courage.

"And you think me beautiful?"

"Oh, madam!"

"At your age boys think all women beautiful. But, my presuming page, you must cease with this folly and learn to know your place, or it may be changed to one more exalted;" and she pointed with her riding-switch to a stone corbel called the gallows-knob above the gate of Thrave.

The cheek of Achanna grew deadly pale; he ceased the "folly;" but from thenceforth thought only of revenge, and afterwards entered readily into the scheme by which the Douglases were lured to Edinburgh.

Thus, summoning Sir Alan Lauder, his Master of the Horse, the young earl, with all the impetuosity of a pampered boy, ordered his train to be assembled, and set forth for the capital.

Achanna preceded him on the spur, and reached Edinburgh a day or two before him.

The reader will now begin to perceive why those *four* coffins were conveyed by him, under cloud of night, into the vaults of David's Tower; and why a black bull's head, the ancient symbol of sudden death and slaughter among the Celtic Scots, was concealed by the King's master-butcher in the cabinet of the Chancellor.

CHAPTER III
THE ENTRANCE

So many and so good
Of the Douglases have been;
Of one surname in Scotland
Never yet were seen.—Old Rhyme.

Mounted on fine horses, the bridles and saddles of which were covered by elaborate steel and silver bosses, Sir Patrick Gray, Captain of the King's Guard, with his cousin and Lieutenant, Sir Thomas MacLellan, of Bombie, fully armed and equipped, rode down the steep path from the castle, and, traversing the town, proceeded towards the street by which the earl of Douglas and his train were expected to enter.

For small bonnets of fine blue Flemish cloth, they had relinquished their heavy bascinets, with their large plumes and velvet tippets, which were borne behind them by pages.

The Captain of the Guard was preceded by a mounted esquire, Andrew Gray, of Balgarno, bearing his banner *gules*, a lion rampant, within a border engrailed.

Save the black or grey-robed Dominicans or Franciscans, and priests of other religious orders, all the men of every rank who crowded the thoroughfares that led towards St. Mary's Wynd and the straggling street which ascended from thence to the convent of St. Mary de Placentia (whence to this day it is still named the Pleasance), were well armed with habergeons and caps of steel, swords, daggers, knives, and Jedwood axes—for the paths of life, even for the greatest and noblest in Scotland, were not strewn with roses in those days, but rather with briars in the shape of blades and spears, woes, wars, tumults, and turmoils, such as their descendants cannot realize in these our days of peace and good order.

Parting on all sides before the esquire, who bore the banner, the people made way for the Captain of the Guard, who with his kinsman joined the attendants of the chief magistrate, Sir Thomas Cranstoun, who was sheathed in complete mail—all save the head—and wore at his gorget a massive chain of fine gold, the links of which glittered among the white hair of his flowing beard.

He was bravely mounted on a great Clydesdale battle-horse; he wielded a heavy steel mace and wore a glittering jupon, on which were embroidered the arms of his family quartered with the triple castle of the city.

He was accompanied by all "the honest men" of the city (*honest* men meant tradesmen—but this was in 1440), preceded by the four baillies, the treasurer, the older corporations, such as the fleshers, the furriers, the cordiners, the candlemakers, and others, under their several devices and banners, and all armed to the teeth. These martial craftsmen lined the narrow and crowded wynd, and from thence up the broader High Street, by which the earl was expected to proceed direct to the castle.

And now, to swell the multitude, came several officers of state, accompanied by the heads of all the religious houses and the heralds of the king. Among them were William Lord Hay, the High Constable; Walter Halyburton, the Lord High Treasurer, and William Turnbull, a canon of Glasgow, who was Lord Privy Seal. Amid the buzz of the assembled multitude, on the varied colours of whose costumes the bright evening sunlight fell in flakes between the broken masses of the picturesque old streets, there were occasionally heard half audible expressions of anxiety for the issue of this noble's visit, as his family and vast retinue of military retainers were so dreaded for their petulance and turbulence, that all the booth-holders and craimers had closed their places of business and buckled on their armour to be ready for any emergency. In the same spirit the baillies wore shirts of mail under their velvet gowns, and the alarm increased rather than diminished when the Provost was heard to say to Sir Patrick Gray—"I am glad the King's Guard are in readiness, for the wild men of Galloway and those scurvy thieves and bullyrooks of Annandale who follow the banner of Douglas, are certain to work mischief in the town."

Such was the state of feeling in Edinburgh when the long, glittering, and steel-clad train of the mighty Douglas was seen descending the slope past the convent of St. Mary, of which no relic now survives save a fine alabaster carving which represents our Saviour brought before the Jewish High Priest; and the excitement reached its height when the Provost put spurs to his horse and courteously rode forward to greet the noble visitor and bid him welcome to the city with fair words of peace, and to place himself upon his right—a condescension at which the surlier burghers murmured under their beards; for the Provost of Edinburgh, when within its boundary, takes precedence of all nobles, and rides on the right hand of a crowned sovereign only.

When the Provost rode forward, Sir Patrick Gray touched his horse involuntarily with his spurs to follow him; but MacLellan, who was chief of a Galloway clan at variance with the Douglases, arrested the impulse by grasping his bridle and saying hurriedly,—"Stay, kinsman, be wary."

"Wherefore?" asked Gray, with an air of annoyance; "for many months I have not seen Murielle."

"Then the greater reason to stay and make no advance at present."

"The greater reason!" reiterated the other, with increased surprise.

"Bear with me—but women often change their minds."

"Thou art a libeller; she will never change, at all events, and I shall risk—"

"The Regent's displeasure—the Chancellor's suspicions?" interrupted MacLellan, with a smile.

"You are right," replied Gray, checking his horse, while his nether lip quivered with annoyance.

"Listen, kinsman," resumed MacLellan, "this Provost may leave his place, knight and baron though he be, to speak well and fairly this great lord, whose train of lances fill his burgess-wives with fear lest latches be lifted, booths broken, and goods and gear be harried in the night; but *you*, who bear the king's colours on your surcoat, must not make any such advance, especially at such a time as this, when Douglas, like his father before him, hath acted the bullyboy to all Scotland."

"The advice is good, MacLellan," said the captain with a sigh; "but still, will not Murielle expect that I—I should—"

"Approach her?"

"Yes—it is the merest courtesy."

"No; she must be aware that your place is beside the High Constable, who, after our politic Provost here, represents the King."

"Hush! here come the archers—some of your wild Scots of Galloway."

"Wild though you term us," said MacLellan, laughing, "we rough Galwegians lead the line of battle—our privilege long before the field of Northallerton became the grave of ten thousand Scotsmen."

The archers who headed the earl's train were now passing among the crowd, and a band of most picturesque looking desperadoes they were. In number about eighty, they had short bows in their hands, with swords and axes in their broad leather girdles. They were bare-kneed and bare-armed, with long bushy beards and thick matted hair (which had never known a comb) falling in shaggy volumes from under little helmets of steel. In some instances they wore caps of boiled leather, fashioned to the shape of the head, and crossed with a wicker work of iron bands for defence. They wore socks of untanned deerskin, and pourpoints of coarse grey stuffs, with kilts and mantles; and here and there might be seen one, who, by the eagle's wing in his cap, claimed to be of gentle blood; for these hardy and rudely clad warriors were the lineal descendants of those *wild* Celts of Galloway, who, since Corbred Galdus, king of Scotland, was slain by the Romans at Torhouse, had the privilege of leading the van of the Scottish hosts in battle.

After them came the earl's confessor, John Douglas, Abbot of Tongland (accompanied by his crossbearer, his chaunter, and three priests), a learned old churchman who had long favoured a very strange project for the especial behoof of his Satanic majesty; but of this more anon.

Next came James Douglas (by his habits surnamed *the Gross*), earl of Abercorn and Avondale, a powerfully formed but bulky and obese man, with eyes and mouth betokening cruelty, pride, and wickedness. He was in full armour, with his barred visor up. He was surrounded by esquires, pages, and lacqueys, and his horse was led, for in his hands he bore aloft a vast cross-handled sword, with a broad wavy blade.

This was the weapon whilome wielded in the wars of Bruce by the Black Knight of Liddesdale, "The Flower of Chivalry;" and now it was borne as a palladium, or sword of state, before his more aspiring descendant.

Hugh Douglas, earl of Ormond, similarly accoutred, but in black armour engraved with gold, bore the banner of his chief, a wilderness of heraldic blazonry—azure, argent, or, and gules; but above all, over Galloway, Avondale, Longoville, and Touraine, shone the bloody heart of glorious memory—the symbol of that god-like heart which beat in victory at Bannockburn, and lay cold with the "Good Sir James," amid the Moorish host of Teba. It was topped with an imperial crown and the three stars; the paternal coat of Douglas, with the motto—"*Jamais arrière*."

By his side rode Sir Malcolm Fleming of Cumbernauld, and Sir Alan Lauder, of the Bass, who had borne the young earl's vain-glorious and unwise embassy to France.

Eight knights of the surname of Douglas, who had won their spurs where *then* spurs only could be won, in battle, to wit, the Lairds of Glendoning, Strabrock, Pompherston, Pittendreich, Douglasburn, Cairnglas, Braidwood, and Glenbervie, all horsed and armed alike, the sole difference being the heraldic cadence of descent on their splendidly embroidered jupons and horse-trappings, bore on the points of their lances a canopy of blue silk tasselled and fringed with silver.

Under this princely canopy, the earl and countess—so the people preferred to call them, rather than the duke and duchess of Touraine—rode side by side on white horses.

They were very youthful, for the husband was only seventeen, and his wife a year older; but they had a stature and a bearing far beyond their ages.

"The Fair Maid of Galloway," as she was still named, though a wedded wife, was a dark-haired, black-eyed, and beautiful girl of a proud and imperious aspect, nor could the grace of her lovely head and neck be hidden by the grotesque horned head-gear which towered above her young brow and waved upon her shoulders, glittering with gold and spangles. She wore a long dark yellow riding robe, trimmed with black wolf's fur, and having hanging tabard sleeves, under which could be seen the sleeves of her inner dress, which was cloth of silver, for this was the age of profusion.

The boy-earl, her husband, wore a suit of light-tilting armour, which, though polished as bright as new silver, was almost concealed by his jupon, which was cloth of gold. His helmet was borne by the page who led his horse; and his dark curls and swarthy visage glowing with youth, pride, and satisfaction, his dark sparkling eyes and haughty bearing evinced, how, like his cousin and wife, he inherited the blood of the Black Lord of Liddesdale.

When the people saw this handsome young noble and his lovely countess riding thus side by side in all the flush of youth, the pride of rank, and feudal splendour, under that gorgeous canopy upborne by those eight gold-belted and gold-spurred knights of high degree, they forgot and forgave all the wrongs and oppressions they had committed, and prayed aloud "that God and St. Mary might sain them and bless them;" but when young Lord David came, riding beside Lady Murielle, and holding the bridle of her pretty bay palfrey, the hushed applause broke forth, for, as a younger sister and unwedded maid she had no canopy over her charming head, so the sunshine of heaven fell freely on her fair young brow, which had no horned head-dress to conceal it, but only a little blue silken hood and a golden caul to confine her beautiful hair.

Gray and MacLellan bowed low and kissed their ungloved hands to the sisters as they passed.

Both ladies changed colour for a moment, but the youngest most deeply and painfully, for she at first grew very pale. Those who were acute in noting such indications of inward emotion might have discovered nothing save vexation or annoyance in the eyes of the countess, and the flush of tremulous pleasure in the returning blush of Murielle, on suddenly meeting a lover whom she had not seen for many months. But the pallor of one and the flush of the other were keys to greater secrets. "Thank heaven, her companion is only that simpleton, little Lord David," said Gray, as his eyes followed hers; "when I saw by her side a gallant so bravely apparelled, I thought your croak about fickleness was about to prove prophetic, MacLellan."

CHAPTER IV
THE SISTERS

Her lips were a cloven honey cherrie,
So tempting to the sight;
Her locks owre alabaster brows
Fell like the morning light.
And, oh! the breeze it lifted her locks,
As through the dance she flew;
While love laugh'd in her bonny blue ee,
And dwell'd in her comely mou'.
The Lords' Marie.

A long train of nearly two thousand mounted spearmen, drawn from the Douglas estates in Lanarkshire and Galloway made up this splendid "following," as such a retinue was then termed; and as they wound up the long vista of the crowded street, Gray contrived to place his horse close to the bay palfrey of Murielle, and in a moment they exchanged a deep glance and a pressure of the hand, which explained what—in that age of little writing and no post offices—they had hitherto been unable to tell, that both were steadfast and true to the troth they had plighted at the three thorn trees of the Carlinwark on a moonlit St. John's Eve, when the countess thought her little sister was asleep in her lofty turret at Thrave.

"Do you pass forward to the castle to-night?" he asked Lord David, while fixing his glance on Murielle, for the question related to her.

"No!" replied the little lord, with haughty reserve.

"Whither then?" asked Gray, while a shade of annoyance crossed his handsome face.

"To the house of our kinsman, the abbot of Tongland; does that please you?"

"Good, my lord, I shall there pay my respects to the earl—and make all speed."

"Oh pray Sir Patrick, do not hurry yourself," was the jibing reply.

"Till then, God be wi' you," said Sir Patrick, checking his horse.

"Adieu," added Murielle, with another of her quiet glances; but the lord, her cousin, turned bluntly away, as the king's soldier wheeled his horse round, and with mingled love and anger in his heart remained aloof till the brilliant train passed on.

A group of handsome girls, nearly all of the surname of Douglas, Maud of Pompherston, Mariota of Glendoning, and others, accompanied Margaret and Murielle, as *dames d'honneur*, or ladies of the tabourette, to be educated and accomplished for the positions they were destined to fill in the world: "To be reared to gifts and graces, to silk embroidery, to ritual observances," and the courtly art of winning high-born husbands, in the household of the duchess of Touraine.

These girls managed their horses with grace, they were all beautiful and gay, but the two sisters of Thrave far exceeded them, though their loveliness differed like the tints of spring and summer.

Murielle's beauty was in some respects inferior to that of her proud and imperious sister, but it was of a more winning and delicate character. Though there were scarcely two years between them, Margaret seemed quite a woman, while Murielle was still girl-like, and in her merrier moods at times almost childish.

The abbot of Tongland relates in his writings, that when Lady Murielle was born at Thrave, she was so lovely a child that lest the fairies might steal her away, and leave in her cradle a bunch of reeds in her likeness, her mother secretly consecrated her to God; but convents were already on the decline, and old Earl Archibald of Douglas and Touraine, as her tutor, could not brook the idea with patience.

"And what news had Sir Patrick Gray?" asked the countess, coldly, as her horse came close to Murielle's during a stoppage caused by the pressure of the crowd.

"No news; nothing," replied Murielle, timidly, for her sister, from infancy, had insidiously usurped an authority over her, which habit had confirmed.

"Did he not speak?" asked Margaret imperiously.

"He merely made cousin David and me a reverence; little more, and passed on."

"After assuring himself, however, where he might be able to see *you* to-night," added cousin David.

"Are you not happy, Margaret, to find these citizens of the king receive us so well?" said Murielle, to change the subject.

"Dare they receive us otherwise?" asked the countess, while the eight bearded knights who bore her canopy exchanged approving smiles under their uplifted visors.

"Sister!"

"Well, sister! These baillies and deacons in their holiday gaberdines and worsted hosen—these websters and makers of bonnets and daggers—these grimy fourbissers, lorimers, and dalmaskers of iron, with their carlins in curchies and plaids, do well and wisely to cringe and vail their bonnets to-day."

"Wherefore?"

"Have we not two thousand horse marshalled under our banner?" said the young earl, who shared to the full the emotions of the haughty girl, his wife.

"True, my lord and cousin; but they might, like dour carles, bite their thumbs, and scowl at us from under their bonnets, for all our bravery," replied Murielle.

"'Tis a beautiful horse that roan of Sir Patrick Gray," said the earl; "and its housings are——"

"Gules and or," interrupted Murielle, for then all well-bred people knew the science of heraldry.

"His own colours, of course, and *not* the king's," said the countess, with an artful smile; "you laugh lightly, Murielle, because you love that man."

"Is it a sign of love to be merry?" asked Murielle, softly, while her fine eyes dilated with wonder.

"Nay, sister, 'tis more often a sign of love to be sad, and sad enough you were at times in Thrave. But please God and St. Bryde, dear Murielle, even in these stormy times, no cloud shall cast a shadow on any love of yours."

"Even if he be the Captain of the King's Guard," said little Lord David, with the spirit of a mischievous boy. His cousin coloured with an air of annoyance, but said smilingly, while holding up a tiny finger, "Oh fie, Davie, you had almost said——"

"The captain of our enemy's band of hirelings," said the fiery young earl, interrupting her; "and, under the royal favour, he would have said right. I know, sweet cousin, what my brother *thinks*, however he may speak, or not speak."

This unpleasant turn to the conversation caused the timid Murielle to shrink within herself, and the little lord was beginning to laugh maliciously when a sudden brawl ensued in the crowd, and Sir Malcolm Fleming, of Cumbernauld, on finding his horse incommoded by a group of magistrates and deacons, daringly struck one of the former on the head with the shaft of his lance, exclaiming, "Back, sirrah, back! By St. Bryde, I will rend the auld carle's beard frae his jaws!"

"A Douglas! a Douglas!" cried a horseman in a *closed* helmet, pressing briskly forward.

This man was Abercorn's creature, James Achanna, who, with his poleaxe, was ready to strike on *both* sides to ferment a brawl, by which the grand *coup* in the castle on the morrow might be anticipated.

"Armour—rescue!" cried a number of the armed craftsmen, pressing also forward with swords drawn and partizans lowered menacingly, as they were justly indignant at an affront offered to one of their magistrates.

A tumult would undoubtedly have ensued, for Lord David had drawn his little sword, and the young earl only laughed as if it were sport to see his knights maltreat the burghers, but the rising fray was quelled by his confessor, the politic old abbot of Tongland, who pushed his horse between the belligerents, and while waving a benison to the people with his right hand, by his left arrested the threatening lance of the irate laird of Cumbernauld. So thus the matter happily ended, and with this single untoward affair the earl and his train reached the town mansion of the abbot, which stood within spacious gardens on the southern slope of the Canongate, the way that led to the abbey of Holyrood; for as yet, the latter was simply an abbey house and church, and not until sixty-four years after was a royal residence added to the sacred edifice which King David (in honour of the fabled miracle by which his life was saved) founded of old, in the wild part of the forest, which was then nameless, or simply described as "the hollow between two hills."

"You look weary, sister," said the countess, as the earl kindly and gallantly lifted Murielle from her saddle in the court-yard of the abbot's house.

"The long journey of the day has tired me, but after a sound sleep I shall be fresh for morning mass in St. Giles to-morrow; for is not to-morrow the vigil of St. Catharine?"

"And the day of our banquet with the King, the Regent, and Chancellor."

"Alake that such trust should be!" muttered Sir Malcolm Fleming under his long white moustache.

"What, art croaking again, stout Cumbernauld?" said the earl, laughing; "who can say but the young king may fall in love with our Murielle, and make her queen of Scotland?"

The Douglas knights loudly applauded the surmise.

"How bright the sunset falls on yonder hill," said Murielle, colouring with annoyance; "how is it named?"

"Arthur Seat," replied Lord David.

"See how the rays fade upward, from rock to rock and rift to rift, as the sun sinks. It makes me think o our Galloway song," said Murielle, always a creature of impulse, as she kissed her sister and sang:—

"A weary bodies blythe when the sun gaes down,
A weary bodies blythe when the sun gaes down;
To smile wi' his wife and to dawt wi' his weans:
Wha wouldna be blythe when the sun gaes down?"

"Are you crazed, Murielle," said the Countess, with a smile of disdain, "to lilt thus before grooms and lacqueys?"

But the bearded knights of Galloway, who had now relinquished the silk canopy to their pages, laughed gaily and praised Murielle, whose charms and playfulness ever won the hearts of all.

The earl's numerous retainers stowed themselves away in the city, where they filled with noise and tumult all the hostelries which had been established by the late King James I.; while the buffoons, in parti-coloured caps and doublets, the plaided pipers, and bearded harpers, who had followed them, made the streets, which, after vespers, were usually quiet, a scene of continual mumming, with alternate music and discord, as they danced by torchlight before groups of citizens, who loitered at their forestairs, galleries, and arcades; and so the night of the 22nd November closed in, while the Regent's followers kept the gates of the castle securely guarded.

CHAPTER V
THE ABBOT'S HOUSE

Now gleams the moon on Arthur's mighty crest,
That dweller in the air abrupt and lone;
Hush'd is Edina in her nightly rest,
But hark! there comes a sweet and solemn tone,
The lingering strains that welled in ages gone.

The mind of Sir Patrick Gray was oppressed by vague doubts and apprehensions of—he knew not what. That the earl and countess were colder to him than when last they met he was painfully conscious by their absurdly haughty bearing, by the increased timidity of Murielle, and the undisguised petulance of her kinsman, perhaps her lover, the young Lord David.

Gray's love for Murielle was now no secret to the earl's powerful family, but being a poor younger son of the baron of Foulis, it was, as he bitterly knew, a matter of jest among the Douglases; for his whole inheritance were his sword and spurs, which he had won at the battle of Piperden, where the English, under Henry, earl of Northumberland, were defeated by the Scots under William Douglas, earl of Angus.

Moreover, Sir Patrick, by education, habit, and thought, was a staunch and loyal adherent of the young king, James II., as he had been of his father, who was so barbarously murdered at Perth; and thus, inspired by love and doubt, hope and fear, presuming upon the friendship of the abbot of Tongland, with whom he could "count kindred," through the MacLellans of Bombie, he presented himself at his mansion in the dusk, and was immediately ushered into the hall, or chamber of dais, where, as supper was over, a brilliant group, or rather several groups, were assembled.

The house of the abbot of Tongland (a wealthy monastery on the banks of the Dee, founded during the reign of David I., by Fergus, lord of Galloway, on his wedding the daughter of Henry, king of England,) was a quaint edifice, one portion of which had crow-stepped gables, and the other a battlement with singularly grotesque gurgoils, through the gaping mouths of which the rain had been disgorged upon the passers-by for centuries. An arch and great oak gate, furnished with a giant risp or tirling-pin of iron, guarded by six loopholes of warlike aspect, gave access to the house and its gardens, which sloped south towards the craigs of Salisbury.

The usual quiet and seclusion of the abbot's mansion were changed on this night for bustle, noise, and light; a crowd of pages, grooms, lacqueys, and armed men led saddled horses to and fro, or loitered about the entrance, while flakes of ruddy light fell through the deep windows of the chamber of dais upon the green shrubbery and the few flowers which still lingered since the last days of autumn.

This chamber was a veritable hall, such as might have graced a baron's castle. It had many niches or ambres of carved stone, a vast gothic fireplace, to the clustered pillars of which the fire-irons were *chained* in the old Scottish fashion, to prevent their being too readily used in brawls, and on the lintel was inscribed, in antique letters, the legend,—

(Laus et honor Deo.)

On the hearth a fire of coal and oak-roots from the Figgate-muir was blazing cheerily.

In this chamber, the lordly abbot had feasted four years before the papal legate, Æneas Sylvius Piccolomini, bishop of Trieste, afterwards Pope Pius II., and it was on that occasion that the latter so wittily remarked, with an irreverent wink to the abbot of Melrose, "that if there was a great reason for prohibiting the marriage of priests, there was a much greater for *permitting* it."

The doors were oak carved with legends and monograms; the floor also was of oak, roughly dressed with the hatchet and secured with broad-headed nails, all the bright heads of which were visible, as it was not carpetted, but only strewn with fresh rushes from the Hunter's Bog. The walls were comfortably wainscotted up to where the vaulted roof rose in the form of an arch, and there the stone-work was covered by distorted figures, representing old legends connected with the abbey of Tongland.

The sleek and portly abbot was seated near the fire in a lofty chair, the back of which bore a carved mitre, and he was conversing easily and pleasantly with all his guests in turn, for he was a benign and amiable old prelate with a bald head, a rubicund and somewhat unmeaning visage, and twinkling eyes half hidden by wrinkles and fat.

Two chairs of state opposite were occupied by the earl and countess of Douglas. On tabourettes near them were seated Murielle and a group of ladies. Several gentlemen all richly dressed were loitering near them, for they were conversing gaily and variously employed—at chess, or the game of Troy; and on the silks, velvets, jewels, and cloth of gold and silver, of which their costumes were composed, the glow of the fire fell brightly, together with the light of twenty great candles, which flared in sconces of brass hung round the walls on tenter-hooks.

The stomacher of the countess-duchess was entirely covered with native pearls, for those found in the Scottish streams were held to be of great value. Among the costly jewels lost by Henry V., when his camp was plundered at Agincourt, Rymer mentions *una perula Scotiæ*; and only a few years before the date of our story, James I presented to Æneas Sylvius, the Roman legate, *one*, which is now in the papal crown.

Before her sweet face, pretty Murielle was manœuvring her fan, quite as skilfully as any of her countrywomen might do at the present day; and through the sticks of it, her merry and soft violet eyes peeped from time to time at a handsome and soldier-like man, who wore a crimson velvet pourpoint, with a steel gorget, a gold belt, and hanging sleeves of yellow silk. He was Sir Patrick Gray, the captain of the guard. While talking gravely of "the growing heresies of John Huss and Paul Crawer," he seemed to be entirely occupied with the countess of Ormond, before whom he knelt on one knee, and for whom he was winding and unwinding several balls of brightly coloured silk and golden thread, which she was using while embroidering a missal cover, for the ladies of those days were never idle; but in his abstraction, or pre-occupation with Murielle, he made many a provoking knot, which the little white fingers of the lovely countess required all their cunning to unravel.

His love for Murielle had brought him hither uninvited; and he felt (like his kinsman, MacLellan) that he was among the enemies of the king his master, and of the government; while the coldness with which the boy-noble and the girl-countess treated him filled his heart with sorrow and anger.

The scraps of conversation he heard all savoured of hostility to James and to his ministers, with dark hints of daring and ulterior political projects, as yet undeveloped and apparently obscure.

He was aware that Earl James of Abercorn, Earl Hugh of Ormond, Sir Malcolm Fleming, Sir Alan Lauder, and other kinsmen of the Douglases viewed him with undisguised aversion; and while he continued to play with the balls of thread, and utter pleasant commonplaces to the ladies near, those four personages were standing aloof in a corner, leaning on their swords, which were somewhere about five feet long, "nursing their wrath to keep it warm," and wishing they had the captain of the king's guard on a solitary hill-side, or even in the street without.

"And this Livingstone—I beg pardon, *Sir* Alexander Livingstone, Laird of Callender—a mere baron," he heard the earl of Douglas say to the abbot; "by what warrant or right is such a man as *he* regent of the realm?"

"I have heard your noble father ask the same question often, with the same tone—ay, and with the same sombre gloom in his eye, my lord," replied the abbot evasively.

"Well—know you by what right?" reiterated the young noble bitterly, giving vent to the hatred his dead father had carefully and unceasingly inspired and fostered.

"Is it hereditary?" asked the abbot gently.

"Assuredly not."

"Then how came Livingstone to have the regency?"

"'Twas given by parliament and the nation."

"Hence his *right*," said the abbot, smiling at obtaining the very reply he wished; but the petulant young earl rasped the rowels of his gold spurs furiously on the hearth, for these quiet answers from the "keeper of his conscience" galled and fretted him.

"Well, the time is come for the nobles, the barons, and others to reconsider that too-hastily given right," said the countess; "for what is he, or what is this Lord Chancellor, that earls and chiefs are to veil their bonnets in their presence?"

The abbot, who dreaded the violence of the young countess more than the temper of her husband (who was not exactly a lamb), was prudently silent; but she was determined to force an answer from him, and said bluntly, "Speak, abbot, you are silent!"

"Pardon me, lady, I was thinking of Plutarch. Know you what he said?"

"How should I know, Lord Abbot," said Margaret, while her black eyes sparkled with annoyance; "was he a heretic like Paul Crawer, or a magician like Michael Scott, with an urchin or prickly hedgehog for a familiar?"

"Why ask you all this?" "Because the name sounds cabalistic to a Scottish ear," said Margaret, crossing and fanning herself.

"He was a scholar—and yet an unfortunate pagan, for he knew not of St. Nicholas, the patron of scholars."

"But *what* said he?"

"That '*love and hatred corrupt the truth of everything*,' and he thought profoundly, madam, for verily they do. Yet if our holy father at Rome will but listen to my prayer, ere long hatred and evil shall exist on earth no more; but all men shall live and die in peace and goodwill one with another—even unto the end of time."

The young earl smiled disdainfully, and relapsed into gloomy silence, for he knew that his father confessor referred to a strange project which he had long cherished, and concerning which he had seriously pestered the late Roman Legate, Æneas Sylvius—that the Pope Eugene IV., as head of the Church and "vicegerent of heaven upon earth," would intercede for the fallen angel, to have him forgiven and received once more into divine favour, to the sublime end that all evil in the world would henceforth cease; for the good old clergyman, in his largeness of heart, like his poetic countryman in after years, felt that he could even forgive the devil, when he thought

> Auld Nickey Ben,
> Maybe ye'll tak a thocht and mend.

But poor Pope Eugene was too much bothered and embroiled by the untractable council of Basle, to attend at that time to the mighty crotchets of the abbot of Tongland.

"Patience yet awhile, my son," said the benevolent abbot, crossing to the young earl and caressing his curly black hair; "when I have the Master of Evil forgiven, and restored to the place from whence he fell, the lusts of the flesh will be effectually prevented from warring against the spirit of grace. *Sit nomen Domini benedictum!*"

But the earl remained obstinately silent, with his dark eyes fixed on the fire, as if the gloomy future might be traced amid its glowing embers.

His kinsman, John of Abercorn, smiled coldly, for by *his* secret connivance many said this visit to the court had been planned; while the grim and turbulent lairds of Biggar and the Bass grasped their long swords with an air that seemed to say, the peaceful and holy days of the abbot's hopes were yet a long way off, and that the devil was likely, as he has ever done, to poke his nose for a long time in Scottish affairs; but a sad and sombre frown was in their eyes, for this journey of their chief to Edinburgh had been undertaken in direct opposition to all their entreaties, advice, and forebodings.

CHAPTER VI
MURIELLE

Sweet love! sweet lines! sweet life!
Here is her hand, the agent of her heart;
Here is her oath for love, her honour's power:
Oh that our fathers would applaud our loves,
To seal our happiness with their consents.
Two Gentlemen of Verona.

An hour passed without Gray finding an opportunity for addressing more than the merest commonplaces to Murielle, yet his mind, even when conversing with others, was so full of her image, that the very rustle of her dress made his heart beat quicker; and he could see her form, face, and expression as distinctly as he heard her voice in fancy for ever, when she was absent; and the ribbon she had taken from her breast, and given him to wear in his bonnet, was a gift more prized than a royal crown.

Their eyes were eloquent although their tongues were mute, for "their natures had so gradually blended into each other that, like two tints of the rainbow, the lines between them would soon become so extinct, that a separation would be the destruction of both."

But the Countess Margaret had a secret grudge at our captain of the guard, and it arose from this circumstance.

Prior to her marriage, and almost from her childhood, she had been a practised coquette, who had won many a brave and noble heart with a facility which her rank increased—but won only to cast them from her when tired of them, as she had done her dolls and toys when a girl, or her jewels, dresses, flowers, and baubles in riper years. They had served to beguile a day, a week, a month, those human playthings, and that was all she cared for.

Sir Patrick Gray had proved rebelliously insensible to her beauty of form, her gaiety, and brilliance of conversation, for he loved little Murielle, and hence the more gorgeous Margaret had an additional cause to treasure a pique at him; and having *other* views regarding her sister, she now, in revenge, permitted him to fan his love with hope, ere it would be crushed for ever, by her marriage to one as yet unnamed. Hence the malicious smile, which curled her beautiful lip, as she looked at them from time to time, on the night we are describing.

Gray and MacLellan confessed to each other that two sisters more charming could scarcely be met.

Murielle's face was pale, her features were delicate, and her eyes of that deep hue, alternating between hazel and violet, which seemed black at night. Her hands and arms were lovely in their form and delicacy.

Then Margaret was so stately and queen-like, pure and cold as marble, save when excited (which was not unfrequent), distant and proudly reserved at one time—full of fire and passion at another. Tall and beautifully formed, her hair and eyes were of the deepest jet, to which the purity of her complexion formed a singular contrast; while a softness was imparted at times to her otherwise haughty expression by her long and thick eye-lashes, which she could drop with the most skilful coquetry.

The face and eyes of Murielle, though less striking, had a strange charm, as they brightened, deepened, and seemed to *grow* in beauty, one knew not why or how; but it was the indescribable charm of *expression*.

The old abbot, finding his efforts to amuse his fiery and feudal friends a somewhat arduous task (as they were all inspired by jealous, ambitious, or angry thoughts), came in despair to Murielle, who was his favourite, and who loved him as a daughter would have done.

"Your harp is here; sing us something, my lady daughter," said he; "a song of our wild Galloway hills—or a Lowland ballad, if you prefer it; but do so, I pray you, for clouds are gathering in your kinsmen's faces, and I know that your sweet voice can best dispel them."

Murielle assented with a kind smile, and in a moment, Gray, anticipating Lord David Douglas, handed the harp to her, and in doing so, contrived, quick as lightning, to touch and press her hand, which made her colour slightly, as she bent over the instrument, and ran her rapid little fingers among the strings.

It was a clairsach, or harp of the old Scottish form, being only thirty inches or so in height, and furnished with thirty string holes. In front of the upper arm was the crowned heart (the Douglas cognisance), formed of precious stones, and surrounded by minute inlaying of mother-of-pearl.

"I thank you, child, for your readiness," said the abbot, patting her pretty shoulder, "and in my turn, though I may not sing now at my years, I shall tell you a legend of the olden time, which was told me by an aged monk of Tongland, now asleep with his fathers in the abbey kirkyard."

"A bribe, my lord, to make me hasten with my song," said Murielle, smiling in the old man's face.

"And to make it as brief as possible," added the impatient Margaret.

"Say not so, countess," said the abbot, "we will not tire readily of Lady Murielle's voice."

"A churchman turned a gallant in his old age!"

"Your sister is fortunate, lady, in the best gifts of heaven," continued the abbot, "and must have been born—"

"Under a fortunate star, you would say?"

"Yes, countess, if such things exist."

"Nay," said Murielle, laughing, "I had a kind fairy for a godmother, like the good princesses of the old romance."

Then in the chaunting cadence adopted by the singers of those days, she sang the four-and-thirty verses of the old ballad of "Sir Hugh le Blonde," a knight of the Mearns—but with these we will not inflict the reader.

It told of how the subtile Rodinghame made love to a fair coquette, who was queen of Scotland; and how, when she repelled him, in revenge he put a leper man in her bower chamber. Then came the proud and jealous king, who, on finding him in such a place, ordered the queen to be burned at a stake, unless she could find a champion to do battle with Rodinghame, her traducer, but such was the terror of his prowess that none appeared; the day of doom came; the hapless queen was bound to a stake, and the torch was about to be applied, when Sir Hugh le Blonde, in his armour, sprang forward, and lifted the gage of Rodinghame.

They fought long and desperately, but Sir Hugh slew the accuser, after forcing him to confess his treachery. Thus the queen was restored once more to favour and honour, to the joy of her husband and all his court.

In gratitude to her preserver,

> Then said the queen unto the king,
> "Arbuthnot's near the sea;
> Oh yield it to the northern knight
> Who fought this day for me!"

> "Yes," said our king, "and thou, Sir Knight,
> Come, quaff this cann of wine;
> Arbuthnot's but a baronie,
> We'll to it Fordoun join."

Thus the descendants of Sir Hugh became lords of Arbuthnot and Fordoun; the sword with which he defended the queen was long preserved by the viscounts of his family, and his helmet was hung in the church of Garvoch, which, in 1282, he bestowed upon the monks of Arbroath for the safety of his soul, and in memory of his victory.

"How like you the song?" asked Abercorn of the countess.

"Well," she replied, with a dark smile; "because it acts as bird-lime."

"Bird-lime," said he, with a perplexed smile; "how?"

"For the king's popinjay," replied the countess, waving her fan towards Sir Patrick Gray; but the ballad was suited to the fashion and spirit of the age, and as Murielle's voice was soft and low, it mingled sweetly with the rippling notes of her little harp.

In the olden time, by ballads and stories the nights were usually passed before bed-time; and thus, after some well-bred compliments had been uttered on her performance, Murielle relinquished her harp to Sir Patrick (who achieved one more pressure of a pretty hand), and turned to claim from her venerable friend the fulfilment of *his* promise.

"My story," said the abbot, smoothing his cassock over his ample paunch, "relates to a time when the Spirit of Evil, he whom I hope to turn one day to a spirit of goodness and purity (here the earl gave a sigh of impatience), had more power in the land even than he hath now. Yet he was conquered and put to flight by our blessed apostle St. Andrew; and now I shall proceed to show you how the cross on which the latter was martyred became the symbol of the Scottish nation, and why it has been borne on our breasts and on our banners in many a righteous battle."

"'Tis well, Lord Abbot," said Earl James the Gross, bluntly; "I like your ending better than your beginning, which savoured somewhat of a sermon, and the night waxes apace."

Then the abbot related the following miraculous story, which we give more correctly than it will be found in the Bollandists, in the "History of the Blessed Regulus," which was written at St. Andrew's in 1140, in the "Golden Legend," or even in the old Gothic "Legenda Sanctorum, post Longobardicam Historiam," because we had it from the writings of the abbot himself.

CHAPTER VII
THE LEGEND OF ST. ANDREW'S CROSS

> Some seek the Edens of the east,
> Some Carrib isles explore;
> The forests of the far-off west,
> And Afric's savage shore.
> *Still* charms of native speech and spot,
> And native springs for aye,
> Will band like brothers Scot with Scot
> Upon St. Andrew's day!—Scottish Song.

In the year 370, St. Regulus, or Rule, a holy Greek monk, who dwelt in Petræa, a city of Achaia, and who had preserved in secret the reliques of St. Andrew the apostle and martyr, was strangely warned by a vision, which was repeated three nights in succession, to secure them from the Emperor Constantius, who was coming to deprive him of his charge, and Regulus was commanded to take them elsewhere.

A deep and melodious voice, that seemed to come from afar, desired him to go to the shrine wherein the reliques lay, to take therefrom an arm, three fingers of the right hand, a tooth, and a kneebone; these he was carefully to preserve, and to convey into a distant land in the west, "*a region situated in the uttermost part of the world.*"

After the third vision St. Regulus obeyed.

He placed the reliques in a box, and embarked in a small ship, taking with him Damianus a priest, and Gelasius and Tubaculus, two deacons, eight hermits, and three devoted virgins.

After great toil and suffering, and after encountering many storms, they passed Melita, where, as the Scripture tells us, St. Paul had been of old, thence between the Pillars of Hercules, along the coasts of Gaul and Celtiberia; and, after traversing the sea of Almainie, were cast on a bleak and rocky promontary of Caledonia, near where now the spires of the fair and stately city of St. Andrew form a landmark to the mariner.

Then the coast was wild and desolate, and was named by the painted Picts, who dwelt there, Muick-rhos, or "peninsula of fierce boars."

Wild woods, pathless and dense, covered it, and a stormy sea beat drearily on its rocky shore.

But these pilgrims having now reached, as they thought, "the *uttermost* part of the world," built their cells, and began to preach and baptize, uniting their labours with those who had landed elsewhere on Scottish ground, and so, in the fulness of time, that peninsula became a bishopric.

In the beginning of the ninth century, Adrian, a holy man, became first bishop of this see of St. Andrews, where in days, then long passed away, St. Regulus and his kuldees had founded a cell dedicated to the Holy Virgin, about a bowshot westward from the shore, upon a sea-weedy rock named unto this day, Our Lady's Craig. But no vestige of the edifice remains, and the wild waves of the German Sea sweep over it with every rising tide.

There, in his own chapel, did St. Regulus serve God devoutly for two-and-thirty years, and there also died Constantine III., King of Scotland, after spending the last five years of his life as a kuldee of Kirkrule, for so the place was also named.

In those, the days of Adrian, Hungus, the Pictish king, granted to God and St. Andrew that the place where the bones of the latter lay "should be the mother church of all the churches in his kingdom," which comprehended the entire Lowlands of Scotland, and much of what is now called England. He laid, in proof of his gift, a *turf* of the ceded territory upon the high altar, and it was the *first* instance of the symbolical transfer of land by enoffment in Scotland.

Adrian, the bishop, was a man full of goodness and holiness; none excelled him in devotion to St. Andrew, and when not preaching to the people, he usually secluded himself on the little Isle of May, at the mouth of the Forth, and there he always spent the forty days of Lent, living on herbs, pure water, and fish, which he caught from the rocks overhanging the sea.

There he said so many prayers daily, that when he had attained his fortieth year without having committed a single sin, the devil spitefully resolved to work him some mischief, if such were possible; but the entire isle whereon he dwelt had become as it were so holy, that all the powers of hell could not prevail against him.

Ere long the fallen angel had an opportunity, when fires were lighted on the hills of Fife and Lothian, summoning the people to arms, when, in the year 870, Athelstan, king of the western Saxons, a savage warrior, who had cloven the head of his father by a single stroke of his sword, and had committed many other inhuman atrocities, but to whom Alfred the Great had ceded the territory of Northumberland, marched northward with a mighty host of barbarians, intent on conquest.

Athelstan had placed his dagger on the altar of St. John of Beverley, as a pledge that if he conquered in the north he would enrich that church, in testimony of his belief in the saint's patronage; and so, after laying waste the southern portion of the Pictish territories, he halted on the banks of the Tyne, near Haddington.

After long vigils in the Ocean cave, where the humble and rude altar of St. Regulus is still to be seen, the holy Adrian joined the host of King Hungus, which numbered thirty thousand warriors, a thousand of whom wore torques of beaten gold. He came to add the influence of his presence, and by his prayers and ministry to propitiate heaven that these yellow-haired invaders might be repelled.

By a blow of the same sword with which he slew his father, Athelstan cleft a rock near the castle of Dunbar, as a symbol that he would conquer all the northern land; the mark, a yard in width, remains there to this day, and was oddly enough referred to by Edward I. before Pope Boniface, as his *best* claim to the kingdom of Scotland!

For aid, Hungus applied to Achaius, king of the Scots, who sent his son Alpine with ten thousand warriors, to assist in repelling the dangerous invaders who had now possessed themselves of all South Britain, and founded the petty kingdoms of the Heptarchy; and thus, on the 29th of November, the eve before St. Andrew's day, the three armies came in sight of each other, on the banks of a little stream which flows through a narrow, deep, and stony vale, near the pastoral hills of Dirlton.

There, on the eastern slope of these hills, Adrian, the bishop, set up an altar, and said mass solemnly, with supplications for victory, while the wild bands of King Hungus, and the wilder warriors who came from the western mountains of the Dalriadic Scots, all clad in hauberks and byrnes of ringed mail, were hushed in prayer, as they knelt with bare knees on their bucklers or on the green sward, bowing all their helmeted heads when Adrian stretched forth his hand and blessed them in the name of his master who was in heaven.

So night closed in, and, worn with toil, the bishop retired from the tumultuary camp to a lonely house which was near, and there sought repose.

And *now* the master of evil thought his time was come to attempt the good man's downfall.

Assuming the form of a beautiful woman, he appeared at the house of St. Adrian, and sent in a messenger, saying, "there was one without who desired to make confession."

St. Adrian, who was at supper, sent one of the little boys who served at his altar to say that "Killach, the Penitencer, would hear her, having full power from himself to hear all confessions, to loose, or to bind."

But, although Killach was a man of great sanctity, who afterwards succeeded Adrian in his see, she said loudly that she would reveal the secrets of her soul to none but his master.

St. Adrian therefore desired her to be admitted.

On entering she, for so we must style the spirit for the time, fell at his feet, and on being blessed by him trembled in her guilty soul; but, on raising her veil, Adrian could not repress an exclamation of surprise at her marvellous beauty. Her skin had the purity of snow, her eyes were of the deepest blue, and shaded by long dark lashes, though her hair was of a wondrously bright golden tint, and glittered like a halo round her head. Her face and form were faultless, her stature tall, and her motions full of grace.

"Whence come you, daughter?" asked the saint,

"From the land of the western Saxons," replied the spirit, in an accent that was very alluring.

"And *who* are you?"

"I am the daughter of Athelstan," she continued, weeping.

"Of Athelstan the wicked king!"

"Yes," and she bent her lovely face upon her hands.

"He whose host we are to combat on the morrow?" continued the saint with growing surprise.

"The same."

"How and why came you to me?"

"He proposes to bestow me in marriage upon one of his chiefs, who is a Pagan; but I have devoted myself to the service of Heaven, and, escaping from his camp in secret, have cast myself upon you, as a man of holiness and of God, to succour and to protect me against the evils and perils of the world."

She wept bitterly, and as she seemed faint and almost famished, the kind bishop led her to a seat, and pressed her to join him in his frugal supper, to take food and refreshment, and thereafter repose.

Then the evil spirit, perceiving the advantages so rapidly won, cast aside her head-gear, and appeared only in the long flowing weed of a Saxon woman, with loose sleeves, which revealed the singular whiteness of her arms and bosom; and, as supper proceeded, and the conversation became animated, she clasped again and again to her beating heart and her warm lips the wrinkled hand of St. Adrian with a fondness which, with the growing splendour of her beauty, bewildered him; Adrian became troubled, he knew not *why*, his soul seemed to tremble within him in unison with the heart that beat in the snowy bosom beneath his fingers, and he prayed inwardly to God and to St. Andrew, his patron, against this new temptation, but apparently without avail.

He had a silver cup, the gift of King Hungus, and each time, say the legendaries, he signed the cross above it, red wine of Cyprus filled it to the brim, but of this miraculous cup his fair guest declined to drink, affirming that she "preferred pure water."

Incited by her, the saint filled and emptied his cup more frequently than was his wont; till, dazzled alike by her beauty, which seemed strangely to increase in radiance, her wit and helplessness, he felt as if madness were coming over him, for his inward prayers availed him nothing, and ere long he seemed to lose the power of remembering them.

Suddenly a loud knock rang on the door of the house, and Killach, the Penitencer, came hastily to announce that an aged pilgrim, who had come from afar, desired to speak with the bishop of St. Andrew's.

"How far hath he come?" asked the lady, laughing.

"From Bethsaida, a village by the sea of Galilee, where he and his brother Peter were fishermen."

On hearing the birth-place of the apostles named, the evil spirit trembled; but the bewildered bishop said, while turning to his beautiful guest—"Tell the palmer I shall see him at some other time; after so long a journey he must need rest."

But again the pilgrim knocked and became more importunate; then Adrian, fired by the wine he had taken, and dazzled by the beauty at his side, seemed to lose alike his charity and humility amid the snares of the devil, for he commanded the insolent pilgrim to be cast forth upon the highway.

"Nay, nay," said the golden-haired damsel, running her white fingers through his snowy beard, "let us amuse ourselves with him, for these palmers are quaint fellows."

"Is it your pleasure, fair lady," said Adrian, taking her hand in his, "that I should permit him to interrupt us?"

"No—but let us jest with him; for I know well that these palm-bearing pilgrims are sad rogues at times. Ask him some puzzling questions, and if he answers them, admit him."

"Agreed," said the bishop, draining another goblet, and as her laughter seemed very infectious, he joined her in a peal of such merriment, that old Killach, the Penitencer, trembled in his cassock; "propose a question, sweet lady, for you surpass all in wit as well as in beauty."

"Inquire of him what is the greatest marvel in the smallest space made by God."

Killach went forth and propounded this strange question.

"The faces of mankind and the leaves of the trees; for no two of either are alike in the world," replied the poor pilgrim, who stood without the door of the chamber, bending wearily on a knotted staff, and shivering in the night air, though clad in a long blackweed, his cowl hung over his eyes and his white beard flowed over his breast.

"A fair response," replied the beautiful lady, gaily, caressing more tenderly the bishop's hand with her velvet-like fingers, while her bright eyes beamed into his, and the night currents blew her perfumed hair across his face; "pray ask him next, what is higher than heaven."

"He who made it," replied the pilgrim, bowing low. Then the evil spirit trembled, but again asked merrily:

"What is the distance from heaven to the base of the bottomless pit?"

"Ask that question of *thyself*, who hast measured the distance to the full, which *I* never did—thou accursed spirit!" replied the pilgrim furiously, beating thrice on the door with his staff, whereupon, with a shrill shriek, the Devil vanished from the side of the terrified bishop; but his conqueror remained for a time unmoved, and then quietly disappeared, seeming to melt away before the eyes of those who saw him.

Then Adrian fell upon his knees and returned thanks to heaven, and to his patron, St. Andrew, for escaping this last and most subtle snare of the evil one.

But now he found that the morning was far advanced; that already the combined armies of the Northern kings were meeting the hordes of Athelstan in the shock of battle; and so the sainted bishop came forth with a more than usually humble and contrite heart, and, attended by his crossbearer and followers, ascended an eminence in view of the field, and then he knelt down to pray for victory over the Saxons.

There in the hollow, through which the Peffer flowed among groves of oak towards the sea, the roar of battle rang—the tumultuous shouts and yells of triumph or agony, as Scot and Pict, or the yellow-haired Saxon, closed in mortal strife; the twanging of bows, the trampling of horses, the clash of axes, swords, and maces swung on ringing bucklers; or, as the ghisarma of the Saxon, the long tuagh of the Celt, clove hauberk of rings, or helmet of steel; and amid the carnage, wherever death and slaughter were deepest, rode the royal parricide, the terrible Athelstan; "of earls the lord, of heroes the bracelet giver," as the harpers who sang his praises styled him; but he was fated never again to hear their adulous strains, or see his wooden halls of Jorvik, or York as it is named now.

Despite the valour of King Hungus and his auxiliaries, the Saxons, among whom were many thousand southern Britons, forced to military service and slavery, were gradually gaining the victory, and the Scots and Picts were giving way, when lo!

Across the eastern quarter of the blue firmament there suddenly came a thunder cloud, the hues of which alternated between deep black and brilliant purple, though its ragged borders gleamed with golden tints. Lightning was seen to flash behind it, while hoarse thunder hurtled athwart the noonday sky, and sank growling into the estuary of the Forth, beyond the Isle of May.

Then the cloud opened, and amid a blaze of such light as that which dazzled Saul on his way to Damascus, there shone above the Scottish host, with an effulgence that made their serried helmets outshine the rays of the sun, the figure of St. Andrew the Apostle, on his cross, the two trees tied like the letter X, to which he had been bound, when scourged to death at Petræa, in Achaia.

Then St. Adrian lifted up his eyes, and knew in him the pilgrim of the blackweed; the same stranger who on the preceding night had saved him from the snares of the evil one, and falling on his knees, he bowed his silver hairs in the dust.

When he looked again, cloud, figure, and cross had passed away; but inspired by this miraculous omen of victory, the Scots and Picts rushed with new vigour on the Saxons, who were soon defeated, and with dreadful slaughter.

Athelstan was unhorsed by King Hungus, who slew him on the north bank of the Peffer, at a place named unto this day Athelstansford. The Picts buried him on the field; but his head was borne upon a spear to an islet of the Forth, where it was fixed for a time, and the place was long named, from that circumstance, Ardchin-nichun, or "the head of the highest." [1]

From that day St. Andrew became the patron of the Scots and Picts, who put his cross upon their banners, and the badges of the former, the *thistle*, and of the latter, the *rue*, were interwoven in the collar of the Knights of the most Ancient Order of the Thistle, instituted in honour of this victory; and in memory of the apostles their number is restricted to the reigning sovereign and twelve companions.

Upon the cathedral of St. Andrew, Hungus bestowed "a case of gold for preserving the reliques of the saint, many chalices and basons, the image of Christ in gold, and those of the apostles in silver," and the bishop Adrian toiled more than ever in the service of God and his patron, until the year 882, when some Danish rovers attacked his hermitage on the Isle of May, and barbarously slew him with all his followers.

His coffin, of stone, is still lying there, and the fishermen of the Forth aver that at times a wondrous light shines from it. He passed away in the odour of sanctity, and Killach the Penitencer succeeded him as second bishop of the see.

Such is the legend of the cross of St. Andrew, and how it became the cognizance of the Scottish nation.

FOOTNOTES:

[1] Now Inchgarvie. Athelstan's grave was opened in 1832. His coffin was composed of five large pieces of freestone, and his bones measured six feet in length. The coffin was thirty inches in breadth, but only four in depth. The farm of Miracle, corrupted into *markle*, indicates where the vision is said to have appeared; and, with the adjacent lands, it was assigned to the culdees of St. Andrew's in gratitude for the victory.

CHAPTER VIII
I LOVE YOU

I do not seek to quench your love's hot fire,
But qualify the fire's extreme rage,
Lest it should burn above the bounds of reason.

Shakespeare.

By the time when the garrulous old abbot had concluded his story the night was far advanced. The lights in the sconces and the fire had burned low, while the ladies looked pale and weary, and all who were not in immediate attendance upon the earl and countess of Douglas, prepared to seek their habitations in the city.

As these were paying their several adieux, Sir Patrick Gray came close to Murielle, and tenderly pressed her hand; but she gazed upon him with a sad and foreboding expression.

"Courage, Murielle, courage!" he whispered; "with strength and bravery on my side, with equal love and goodness on yours, our mutual stedfast faith and hope, we may yet overcome everything."

"Even the prejudices of my sister?"

"Ay, even the hatred, for such it is, of your sister,—the sombre pride and wrath of that fierce boy her husband."

"Oh, that it may be so!" she whispered, breathlessly; "but there are times when I have strange fears."

"Murielle, tide what may, remember that while life lasts I love you!"

All they could desire to say was comprised in these three very little words. Little they are, yet how much do they contain! The essence of all the love speeches, love-letters, and sonnets that have been written since the invention of letters,—since Cadmus brought his alphabet from Phœnicia into Greece. When two lovers have said these words they can only repeat them.

"*I love you!*" They have nothing more to say. The countess, ever watchful, had observed this brief conference, and though anger sparkled in her deep, dark eyes, she veiled it under a bright smile, and, closing her fan, gave her pretty hand to Gray, who bowed and kissed it, though the petulant earl coldly turned from him, saying:—

"Sir Patrick, fare you well until to-morrow."

"*Until to-morrow*," added the earl of Abercorn, with one of the strange smiles which curled his thin white lips at times, as Gray and MacLellan retired together, after gaining golden opinions in the ranks of the enemy,— to wit, the ladies of the hostile faction.

The young Captain of the Guard had the art of pleasing all—the ladies especially; and at such a time, when family feuds, pride, and hatred, were rampant passions, the art was one of no small value, though in Scotland few cared to cultivate it, for chivalry was already on the decline.

In society such as that in which we introduce him to the reader, he contrived to be, or appeared to be, friendly with those who were most averse to each other in politics and ambition; yet he neither condescended to flatter nor dissemble, but often was prudently silent, where to differ would have brought swords from their scabbards; and he assented with grace and pleasure wherever he could do so with honour.

By this system, acquired amid the dark intrigues of a turbulent court, rather than in the camp, Sir Patrick Gray was a general favourite, especially of the young king, who was then, as before-mentioned, in his eleventh year, and whose preceptor he became, in all military exercises and the sports of the field. Gray had natural tact, a knowledge of the then limited world, and the great art of occasionally conquering himself.

Murielle was the stake he played for, and he never lost sight of her.

The moon had waned, and not a star was visible in the dark November sky, as he and MacLellan proceeded through the gloomy city towards the fortress.

"A moonless night, but a fine one," said Gray, wrapping his velvet cloak about him.

"For shooting bats or owls," added MacLellan, as he stumbled over the rough and unpaved street. "Ay, and a night to try men's mettle if there be witches abroad."

"Soho!" said Gray, gaily; "we have left the most perilous witches behind us, with old Abbot John, of Tongland; but assuredly one is safer in a gaberlunzie's canvas gaberdine than a velvet pourpoint to-night, when so many Douglas troopers and Annandale thieves in Johnstone grey are abroad; and the sky is so dark that the devil, were he here, could not see his own tail behind him."

Unmolested, however, they reached the castle, where the portcullis was down and all the gates secured; and where the garrison, which was almost entirely composed of the lord chancellor's vassals, kept watch and ward as warily as if a foreign army, and not the Douglases, had been in the sleeping city below.

As they entered a man passed out: he was muffled in a cloak, with an iron salade on his head—a species of helmet, which effectually concealed the face, but had a horizontal slit for the eyes.

Recognizing the voice of Gray, he rubbed his thin hands together, and smiled maliciously; for this nocturnal rambler was James Achanna, who had just been depositing the four coffins in the vault of David's Tower, and who seemed still to see before him, as the unconscious lover passed gaily into the fortress, a gilt plate inscribed: *"Murielle Douglas, qui obit 23 Novembris, A.D. 1440."*

CHAPTER IX
THE TWENTY-THIRD OF NOVEMBER

Now like a maiden-queen she will behold
To her high turrets hourly suitors come;
The East with incense and the West with gold,
Shall stand like suppliants to receive her doom.
The silver *Forth* her own majestic flood
Shall bear her vessels like a sweeping train;
And often wish, as of their mistress proud,
With longing eyes to see her face again.

In sunny beauty, the 23rd of November, 1440, dawned on the green hills, the old grey city of the Stuarts, and on the distant sea; and, as the morning advanced, a man, who by his pale and anxious face seemed to have passed a sleepless night, walked slowly to and fro on the paved bartizan of King David's Tower.

He was Sir William Crichton of that ilk—the lord chancellor of Scotland—no sinecure office, under James II.

The first object on which his keen eyes rested, was the slated roof of the abbot of Tongland's lofty mansion. There pretty Murielle was doubtless still asleep, and dreaming perhaps of her lover.

As the time drew slowly, but surely on—the time when Crichton's terrible project, the destruction of the leading members of the house of Douglas by a formal yet mock trial, after luring them from their distant stronghold into a royal fortress—his soul, though it felt neither remorse nor wavering, could not fail to be appalled, on a full contemplation of what *might* be the sequel to the banquet of blood, which he and the regent would that day hold in the great hall of the king's principal castle. To him it seemed as if the live long night, the wild shriek of

"The owle eke that dethe and bode bringeth,"

(as old Chaucer has it) had rung about the castle rocks, filling the minds of those who heard it with unpleasant forebodings—and of this emotion Crichton was especially sensible.

A civil war might rage around the throne, and by weakening the nation would lay it open to the aggressive spirit and ambitious designs of the English, who were ever wakeful to take advantage of their neighbour's troubles. Crichton's own power, his old baronial family and numerous kinsmen, might perish in the contest; but still the king's authority and the dignity of the crown, which the overweening power of the earl of Douglas, and the evil advice of his friends, endangered, would be secured, and a final blow might be struck at the terrible Red Heart for ever.

As the chancellor thought of these things, his hands trembled under his furred robe, and crystal-like beads of perspiration gathered on his pale and prematurely-furrowed brow; but the grim preparations had been made, even to the most minute particulars. Douglas, with his formidable train, was already in the capital, and all parties had gone too far in the desperate game to recede now; so Crichton prayed in his heart that the great *end* he had in view might sanctify the awful measures he was about to take; and, seating himself on a stone bench, he seemed to sink into reverie—almost prayer—while, turning to the east, where the sun, through alternate bars of saffron and dun yet shining clouds, was ascending in all his morning glory from the sea.

From time to time the pale chancellor glanced at a piece of green sward called the Butts, where the archers and the king's guard were wont to shoot, and which was inclosed by the cordon of towers and walls which girt the summit of the castle rock.

On that sward a tall lady, wearing a long robe, with tabard sleeves, and a horned head-dress, which added to the effect of her great stature, promenaded to and fro, with her missal and rosary, while watching a little boy, who was clad in a bright-green velvet pourpoint, laced with gold, and whose yellow hair glittered in the morning sunshine, as he alternately tormented and played with a pretty goshawk, which had silver bells at its head.

Let us, for a time, suppose ourselves there.

That tall lady is Isabelle Ogilvie, of Auchterhouse, wife of Patrick Lord Glammis, master of the royal household, whose son, Alexander, has married Crichton's youngest daughter, and her young charge is James II., king of Scotland, who laughs with boyish glee as he tosses and plumes his pet hawk, and, all unwitting of the dark thoughts which agitate the soul of his faithful but scheming chancellor, trains it to pounce upon and rend a lure—a toy like a stuffed bird—which, ever and anon, he casts into the air with a shout of merriment.

The morning draws on apace; bells ring in spire and tower, and the little city below (for, though a capital, it was a *little* city then) awakens into general life and bustle; but the chancellor still sits there.

Let us look, with him, over the rampart of this great tower, where his eyes survey a scene so different from what is there to-day; and yet Arthur's rocky cone, the hills of Fife, the fertile shores, the sandy bays and green islets of the Forth, are all unchanged as when the first Celtic settlers so truly named the great ridge that overlooks them all, *Scealla-bruach Craig*, or "the rock of the beautiful view," now corrupted into Salisbury Craigs.

The month is November.

The last leaves have fallen from the oak woods of Bristo, of Coates, of Inverleith, and Drumsheugh; but the voice of the antlered stag, "the wild buck bell," is borne at times on the passing wind that whirls the red leaves along the grassy hollows.

In the glen below the castle rock lie the royal gardens, where tournaments are held, and where, in after ages, the railway train shall send up its shriek to the ear of the sentinel five hundred feet above. There comes no sound from it now, save the note of the plover, or amorous coo of the cushat dove. On the long ridge, where a new city shall spring in the eighteenth century, the farmers are finishing their ploughing; the lowing cattle are in their yards; the sheep in their pens, and the pigeons are clustering on the dovecots.

Allhallow mass has been said and sung in the great cruciform church of St. Giles the Abbot, and of St. Cuthbert in the pastoral glen below the castle wall; and in every thatched grange and farmtown, apples have been duly bobbed for and nuts cracked about the blazing ingle; and now it is the vigil of St. Catharine.

Turn with me still eastward; there, the same as ever, is the backbone of old Edina, the High Street, covering the long ridge which terminates at the three square Gothic spires of Holyrood Church—a broad line of fair stone mansions, as yet undisguised by the quaint Flemish fronts and timber galleries which came into fashion about the time of Flodden Field. Southward descends the narrow Bow, and its tall dwellings, with their dovecot gables and clusters of smoky chimney-stacks, many of them bearing the iron cross of the Temple and St. John, its doorways incrusted with legends, dates, and coats armorial of races past and gone; its iron door-risps, with here and there a cloth tied round them, to show that there was illness, or a woman "in travail" within.

That grated and fortified edifice which occupies the centre of the main street is the Prætorium of Edinburgh—a rallying point for the citizens in time of war and tumult; and on its vaults shall arise the grim Tolbooth of future ages.

The bare-headed and bare-legged children that nestle on the steps of the cross are stringing necklaces and rosaries of the red rowan berries (that whilom grew in St. Giles's churchyard), to save them from fairies and elves; and now they all rise in reverence to yonder cowled friar, who hastens down to see the train of Douglas pass from the abbot's house.

That green slope on the south of the great church is the burial-ground of St. Giles's: —

"There lie
Those who in ancient days the kingdom ruled,
The councillors of favourites of kings;
High lords, and courtly dames, and valiant chiefs,
Mingling their dust with those of lowest rank
And basest deeds, and now unknown as they."

There sleep the great, the good, the peaceful and the turbulent, the faithful and the false, all bent together in their quaint old coffins and flannel shrouds, with money in their dead hands, and crosses or chalices on their breasts. Old citizens, who remembered the long-haired King David, passing forth with barking hound and twanging horn, in that Rood-day in harvest, which so nearly cost him his life; and how the fair Queen Margaret daily fed the poor at the castle-gate, "with the tenderness of a mother;" those who had seen Randolph's patriots scale "the steep, the iron-belted rock," — Count Guy of Namur's Flemish lances routed on the Burgh-muir, and wight Wallace mustering his bearded warriors at midnight by the Figgate-burn, ere he marched to storm Dunbar.

That white spot above the gate of the Portsburgh is the bleached skull of Sir Robert Graham, who was the first to plunge his dagger in the heart of James I. It has been there since 1436, when those awful tortures took place before the Roman legate, and filled even him with horror.

The lofty old mansion on the south side of the long street down which we look from the ramparts, is the residence of the princely abbot of Cambus Kenneth; the gilt vanes in the distance are those of a similar edifice where dwells John Fogo, abbot of Melrose, author of a work against the heresy of Paul Crawer, who, in 1432, was sent hither from Bohemia, by John Huss, to preach the gospel, undeterred by the flames to which Fogo had consigned Resby, the Englishman, thirty-two years before.

In the centre of the street are wooden booths, where the country folks, in their canvas gaberdines and hoods of hodden grey, or the burgesses in their pourpoints of good Flemish cloth, may "cheapen" ale at sixteenpence per gallon; otherwise, the brewster or tapster shall have a hole punched in their measures at the market-cross, where now the women of the adjacent villages and farms are arranging their baskets of butter and poultry for sale; and see! there, at this moment, come the town officers, with their halberts and helmets, and the common headsman, in the provost's livery, with a cresset full of blazing coals. Now a crowd gathers: the halberts flash as they are swayed to and fro by the pressure of the people. Then a shriek rises!

They are publicly branding on the cheek a poor woman, a leper, who has rashly ventured within the burgh; though yesterday, by sound of trumpet, at this same old market-cross, the people of the city, and the villages called Leith and Broughton, were forbidden to attend the fairs of Anster and St. Monance, under pain of pit and gallows, as the plague called the *het-sickness*,—the same disease of which Archibald earl of Douglas died at Restalrig,—rages in Fife.

If the reader, in fancy, can realize all this, he will see the quaint old Edinburgh of 1440 clustering on the steep ridge,—

"Piled deep and massy, close and high;"

the same city over which the haggard eyes of Crichton wandered, and through which, preceded by trumpet and banner, the haughty young lord of Douglas and Touraine was passing to his—doom!

Edinburgh, a village then in size and opulence, was, nevertheless, a capital city. *Now*, when in aspect and magnitude it is one of the most magnificent in Europe, by a strange anomaly it is, in reality, when its narrowness of spirit, in religion, politics, and patriotism are considered, the most provincial village in her Majesty's dominions, perhaps in the world.

By the time the trumpets were heard, the sun was at its zenith, and Crichton, with a shirt of mail under his velvet pourpoint, came forth to meet the regent in the court-yard.

Livingstone had assumed a similar steel shirt under his shortcoat, which was of red damask, laced with silver, and over which he wore a long flowing gown with open sleeves, revealing those of his ringed defence, which, being a man of more open character than his compatriot, he cared not to conceal, especially in these perilous times.

These two statesmen met, sternly and gravely, without a smile or bow.

"Is all prepared?" asked Livingstone of the chancellor, in a low voice.

"All," was the brief and emphatic reply.

"Your men-at-arms?"

"I have a hundred concealed in the tiring-room, which opens off the great hall."

"Only a hundred! Are you not most rash?"

"But they are men whose forefathers for ages have eaten the bread of mine."

"You, then, deem them stedfast?"

"Stedfast and true as Rippon steel; unyielding as flint. They are to rush forth under Achanna, when the signal appears."

"Achanna," said the regent with contempt; "always Achanna. I know not how it is, but that man makes my blood to curdle."

"He is a faithful——"

"Villain," interrupted the regent, with irritation.

"True—but such villains are useful," said the chancellor quietly.

"And the signal is the black bull's head; but does not Achanna dine with us?"

"Dine!" reiterated the chancellor, with a flashing eye and a quivering lip. "He will share the banquet at all events."

"And the four bodies," said Livingstone, gnawing the ends of his grisly moustache, and looking aside, "how mean you to dispose of them?"

"Under that green turf, where even now the king is playing with his goshawk, they will sleep as soundly as if below a ton of marble in Melrose Abbey Kirk, among their lordly kin," replied the chancellor in a low whisper, and with a ghastly smile; "but hark! I hear trumpets in the streets; and here comes Gray, the Captain of the Guard."

Accoutred as we saw him yesterday, in his plumed bassinet, with its camaile and chaplet, and his rich mail with its hanging sleeves of scarlet and yellow silk, Sir Patrick Gray, happily ignorant of the dire preparations of the two statesmen, and the mine they were about to spring, made a low bow to each, with some passing remark on the auspicious beauty of the day—for the weather was as common a topic in the time of James II. as in that of his descendant, Queen Victoria.

"A cloud is coming anon, that may darken its close," said the regent, thoughtfully.

The Captain of the Guard looked upward, but the sky was cloudless, then his eye swept the horizon in vain.

"Yea, Sir Patrick," added the chancellor, who is reported to have used the same figurative language, "have you never observed that there are periods—times of our existence, when past, present, and future hopes seem to culminate in one?"

"Under favour, my lord, I do not comprehend," replied the puzzled soldier, as he played with the buckle of his belt, and thought of Murielle Douglas.

"Yes—when we seem to hold them all—the past, the present, and more especially *the future*, in our grasp, and yet may throw them all away. Now dost comprehend?"

"Do you mean in affairs of love, my lord?"

"Love!" reiterated the chancellor, scornfully, "nay, I think but of *death*," he added in a voice so stern and hollow that the soldier started, "but ere long you may, nay you *shall* know all I mean. Till then, God be wi' you—adieu."

And with his hands behind his back, and his eyes bent thoughtfully on the ground, Crichton slowly followed the regent into David's Tower, while the Captain of the Guard, bewildered by their strange remarks, hurried to join his hundred pikemen, who were drawn up in two ranks at the gateway which opened under the Constable's tower.

Sir John Romanno of that ilk, who commanded the fortress, had now all the king's garrison at their posts, with bills and crossbows, and the cannoneers by their guns, with lintstocks lighted.

CHAPTER X
FOREBODINGS

She was mounted on a milk-white steed,
And he on a dapple grey;
And a bugle-horn hung by his side,
When he lightly rode away.
Lord William looked over his right shoulder,
To see what he could see;
And lo her seven bauld brethren
Came riding owre the lee.
The Douglas Tragedie.

"How often is a straw, wafted by the wind, the turning point in our destiny!" says an author; "a stone cast into the water causes a ripple on the most distant shore; so the most trivial event of our lives, after a thousand ramifications, leads on to some great climax."

When the train of Douglas mounted in the court-yard of the abbot's house, Sir Malcolm Fleming of Cumbernauld came hastily from his chamber, clad in complete mail, with his helmet open; thus it revealed the pallor of his face, with the sombre gloom of his dark grey eyes, whose restless and wandering expression bore evidence of a sleepless night.

"How now, Cumbernauld," said the earl of Abercorn, "is this thy dinner-dress—art going to dine with all this old iron about thee?"

"Yes—when I dine with enemies."

"Soho, man—go to! we have no enemies," said the sneering noble; "we are all friends now, and must drink to-night to the extinction of all feuds."

"Do the countess and Lady Murielle go to this banquet?" asked the old knight, with a voice rendered husky by sorrow and surprise, as Margaret and the ladies of her train came forth with all their gorgeous dresses glittering in the sunshine.

"Of a surety they do. James Achanna bore them each a special message from the Lord Regent in the young King's name; but what in the name of old Mahoun ails thee, Sir Malcolm Fleming—art ill?"

"Ill indeed at heart, lord earl."

"And wherefore?" asked Earl James, angrily.

"Come this way apart," replied the other, drawing Abercorn aside from the throng, while his voice and expression became more sad, his lips more pale, and his manner more excited. "Listen. Last night I was in my chamber disrobing for bed; my mind was full of the doubts and misgivings that have oppressed me since we left the walls and shelter of Thrave; and just as Silver Mary—that great bell which hangs in the tower of St. Giles—tolled the last stroke of the hour of twelve, I heard a deep sigh near me."

"A sigh!" repeated the earl, becoming interested in spite of himself; "was it not the wind in an arrow-hole?"

"A sigh, loud almost as a sob! I turned—there was no one near me; but the old and gloomy arras which covered the walls was violently agitated and shaken, so that the brown moths flew out of it. The sigh was repeated; and though I know myself to be brave as most men, I felt—yet knew not why—the life-blood curdling in my heart, and, as the Scripture hath it, the hair of my flesh stood up. Then an emotion which I could not resist, like the strong power we obey in a dream, led me on. I raised the old mouldy arras—and then—then—oh what a sight saw I there!"

"What?" asked the earl, in a low voice.

The perspiration rolled in bead-like drops from the pale forehead of the old baron upon his white beard and polished cuirass, as he replied in a solemn and husky whisper, "As I live by bread which the blessed God yields, and hope to die in the faith of our fathers, I beheld a decapitated corpse, the head of which rolled past me, with winking eyes, with chattering teeth, and with features livid and convulsed, as when the headsman's axe has just severed the neck! I knew those ghastly features—knew that curly hair—I knew that comely form——"

"And," said Abercorn, growing very pale in spite of himself; "and this head was——"

"Your kinsman's—the earl of Douglas!"

"Pho!" replied Abercorn, seeming suddenly to experience great relief; "by St. Bryde, I thought you were about to say 'twas *mine*. Did this grim vision speak to you!"

"No—but straightway vanished—melted away, and I was left in the chamber to solitude, to fears and prayers, but not to sleep."

"'Tis well you did not see any *more* heads roll past in this odd fashion," said Abercorn, jibingly.

"Lord James of Abercorn," said Fleming, solemnly, "I was long your father's comrade and most trusted friend. For forty long but stirring years there came no jar between us, though ever engaged in war and tumult. Together we were wounded and taken prisoners at Homildon; together we defended this castle of Edinburgh against Henry IV. of England, and repulsed him; together we fought in France, and fell wounded side by side at Verneuil—but he, alas! mortally, when attempting to save *me*, and now he sleeps the sleep of death in St. Gratians of Tournay—for there I closed his eyes, and laid his well-notched sword beside him——"

"All this, and much more, have I heard a hundred times, by the winter fire, at Douglas, at Thrave, and in your own hospitable house of Cumbernauld," said Abercorn haughtily and impatiently.

"Then hear it once again, to fire your lagging zeal, mistaken man!" said Sir Malcolm, with growing excitement in his tone and suspicion in his heart; "hear it once again, to bear witness of my faith, when I feel assured that this day no banquet, no wassail, no honour or hospitality, but death and life are in the balance!"

"What a-God's name seek you?" asked James of Abercorn, through his clenched teeth; for this animated and protracted discussion had drawn about them the abbot, their host; the earl of Douglas; little Lord David, his brother; even the Countess, Murielle, and other ladies, who threw up their veils, and listened with surprise. Sir Malcolm resumed:—

"Ay, ay, young lord; since first I learned to make the sign of the cross at my auld mother's knee in the hall of Cumbernauld, among the wilds of Dunbarton, true have I been, Abercorn, to Douglas and his race; so listen to me, if you can, without that cold sneer in your eye, on your lip, and in your heart! Trust not Crichton, and trust not Livingstone, or dool and woe will come on thee and thine! Oh, if you have one drop of warm blood in your heart, join with me in urging your kinsman and chief to share my doubts of these men."

"What in the name of Mahoun am I to say?" exclaimed Abercorn, whose eyes glared with anger, while he tugged his black beard in his vexation.

"Beware ye all!" resumed the earnest old laird of Cumbernauld! "I know what a city and a court are, with their rakes and high-born harlots; their carpet-knights and fawning cut-throats; their bullies and swashbucklers— with servile bows and smiling faces—their black, bitter, false, and cowardly hearts! So here, at the eleventh hour, as it were, I, Sir Malcolm Fleming, of Biggar and Cumbernauld, the soothfast friend of Douglas, say unto ye all, go not this day to the castle of Edinburgh."

Lord Abercorn listened to all this with rage in his eye, a sneer on his lip, and perplexity on his brow; and these mingling emotions deepened when the usually haughty countess requested the old knight to rehearse the story of the midnight vision. It certainly had a serious impression upon all, for the age was full of superstition, of omens, spectres, and supernatural terrors, when the bravest men would occasionally tremble at their own shadows. Thus for a few minutes even the young earl of Douglas seemed silent and oppressed, while Murielle burst into tears, and drew down her veil.

"It is as great a pity to see a woman weep as a goose go barefoot," said Abercorn, furiously and coarsely, using an old proverb: "by our Lady of Whitekirk! I think you are all demented. Lord abbot, talk to this old ghostseer, and assure him there can be no such thing in nature as the spectre of a living man."

"But there are wraiths," said Sir Alan Lauder; "and who can deny their existence, when Scotland is filled with tales of them."

"Lord abbot," resumed Abercorn, more irritated than ever, "speak and say, I charge you, that no such things can be."

"I can assure him of no such fallacy," replied the pedantic abbot, with displeasure, as he adjusted his long-flapped calotte cap over his thin, white, silvery hair. "History, ancient and modern, teems with tales of terrible appearances. Does not Pliny the younger, in his letters, affirm, as an incontrovertible fact, that Athenodorus the philosopher, the disciple of Zeno and keeper of the royal library at Pergamus, once saw a dreadful spectre?"

"When—how?" asked the countess, impressed by the strange names which the abbot used so glibly.

"Pliny relates that Athenodorus purchased an old house in Athens, which many had refused to occupy, because it was haunted by an unquiet spirit. So Athenodorus waited courageously to see it."

"What—the house?" asked Abercorn.

"No—the spectre. Dragging a massy chain, it came at length in a shapeless and dreadful form, and commanded him to follow it. The philosopher, who, though trembling in his soul, affected to be busy at that moment, said 'Wait a little;' but the spirit rattled its rusty chain furiously, so Athenodorus arose and followed it to the marble court near which his villa stood, and, on reaching a certain spot, the apparition vanished. Athenodorus, saith Pliny, marked the place that he might know it again. On the following day he assembled the magistrates of Athens, and on digging up the soil the bones of a man with a rusty chain were found. They were publicly interred elsewhere, and from that hour his mansion was disturbed no more. Shall we question that which such men as Plutarch and Pliny have asserted to have been? Like the foul heretic Paul Crawar of Bohemia, dare you impugn that which you cannot comprehend and which you know not? Can you deny or doubt the existence of a spirit, when you cannot prove your *own*? In all past times, in all lands, among every kind of people, however highly civilized or however lowly savage, apparitions have been seen as warnings for good or for evil; and such will be permitted until that fell spirit whose hapless state I shall one day lay before our Holy Father be forgiven, and fear and hate and war shall be no more."

Enraged by this pedantic rebuke, the earl of Abercorn twisted his moustache, and spurred and checked his horse till it almost sprang into the air.

"Then what do you advise, my lord abbot?" asked the countess, in evident perplexity.

"That my lord your husband should hearken unto the advice of his counsellors, whom his father never slighted, but ever held with reverence."

"I thank you, lord abbot," said Fleming, pressing the abbot's hand. "Let the earl at least leave behind him the two ladies of his house, his brother Lord David, Earl James of Abercorn, and Hugh of Ormond."

"To what end?" asked the earl of Ormond.

"To gratify the prayer and anxious heart of an old friend, and that the house of Douglas may not be in an evil hour laid open to the stroke of fortune, — your father's last injunction when he lay dying at Restalrig," added Fleming to the young earl.

His marked energy and anxiety, together with the entreaties of Sir Alan Lauder and those of the Douglases of Pompherston, Strabrock, and Glendoning, made the chief pause and waver in his purpose. He said, —

"Shall I return now after having ridden to his very gates, as it were? Impossible! And the young king — what will he, what will the people say? and then the chancellor's letter flattered so suavely."

"The greater reason to distrust him," muttered the bearded knights to each other under their lifted helmets.

"Wherefore, why?" said Abercorn, burning with a rage which he could no longer dissemble, as a long-projected and carefully-developed plot seemed on the point of dissolving into air.

"Take counsel of your own brave heart, and good, my lord, run not your chief and his brother too into the lion's den. Crichton flatters to deceive!" replied Sir Malcolm Fleming.

"It may be wise, when so many seem to think so, that you should remember the last words of your father at Restalrig," said Murielle, softly touching the hand of Douglas.

"True, sweet cousin. My brother David——"

"Will go wheresoever you go," replied the brave boy, with a hand on his jewelled dagger; "neither imaginary nor real danger shall cow me."

"And I too shall go," added the earl of Ormond; "but as policy seems necessary here, let our kinsman, James of Abercorn, remain behind with the countess and Lady Murielle. Then, come what may, we leave a man able and willing to avenge us."

"Ormond speaks well and wisely," said the abbot, while a close observer might have seen the gleam of joy which passed over Abercorn's white, malignant face, on hearing a proposal so exactly to his secret wishes.

"So be it, then; I am weary of this loitering; let us begone, or the chancellor's good cheer will be chilled by the November air," said Douglas.

"'Tis well to jest," began Abercorn——

"But if Crichton wrongs me, woe to him!" cried the fiery young earl, shaking his clenched hand aloft; "he dare not—*he dare not!* If he doth, by my father's grave in Melrose kirk I shall level his castle of Crichton to its ground-stone!"

"William Douglas," said the countess, who had been conferring for a moment with Abercorn, "you speak as your father would have spoken; yet act warily, as he would have acted. We know not what may be the issue of a day which has commenced so ominously, and, if swords are drawn, women would but encumber you. Murielle, Lady Ormond, and I will tarry here until the banquet is over. Make fitting excuses to the regent and chancellor—say we are indisposed by our long journey, or what you will; and now let it be known, gentlemen, kinsmen, and friends, that in this matter I yield neither to the advice of my loving lord and husband, who is ever rash; nor to the advice of Sir Malcolm Fleming, who is so wary; nor to that of our lord abbot, who is ever good and true; but to the wish of Earl James of Abercorn."

Whether these words were spoken heedlessly as a sneer at the ready manner in which that noble agreed to remain behind, or in mere politeness, none could then divine; but there came a *time* when they were remembered by many to the disadvantage of the proud and wilful young beauty.

At that moment a man in armour with a closed helmet rode hurriedly through the archway. He was James Achanna.

"Lord earl," said he, "the chancellor awaits you without the castle gate."

"Enough, then—let us go; we should have been ringing glasses and exchanging kissing-comfits with our *beloved* friend the chancellor an hour since," said Douglas, lifting his plumed bonnet as he courteously kissed the hands of his wife and her sister.

He then put spurs to his horse and rode off, accompanied by his brother David, Sir Malcolm Fleming, Sir Alan Lauder, the abbot, and five hundred men led by the earl of Ormond—all completely armed and horsed.

As the clatter of their hoofs died away, a foreboding sigh came from Margaret's breast; but there was a cold though courteous smile on the lips of Lord Abercorn, as he gave her his ungloved hand and led her, with Murielle, back into the almost deserted house of the abbot.

Why was it that Margaret's heart upbraided her? She seemed still to see before her the face of that proud and handsome, noble-hearted and high-spirited cousin with whom she had shared her heart and the revenues of her princely house!...

Why was it that, as the day passed slowly on and the November sun sank in masses of foggy cloud, the earl of Abercorn, pale, excited, and abstracted, shunned his friends and paced to and fro in the abbot's garden, casting his eyes ever and anon to the summit of the fortress, which was visible above the adjacent streets?

He started! a distant hum became a confused clamour of many voices; then the galloping of horses and a rush of feet were heard.

He looked again to David tower, and from its rampart the national cross had disappeared. A *black* banner was floating there, and only half hoisted on the staff,—a double symbol of death!

CHAPTER XI
THE VIGIL OF ST. CATHARINE

The nobles of our land were much delighted then,
To have at their command a crew of lusty men;
Who by their coats were known of tawny, red, or blue,
With crests their sleeves upon, when this old cap was new.
The Roxburgh Ballads.

At the outer gate of the fortress of Edinburgh (a barrier which then crossed the narrow street of the Castle-hill) the lord chancellor was on horseback, attended by a brilliant retinue of men-at-arms, with many lacqueys and liverymen on foot, wearing cloth hoods of the same fashion then worn in England, buttoned under the chin, and having deep capes, with scolloped edges, falling over the shoulders. These hoods were usually of scarlet cloth, and were worn with a cock's feather, placed jauntily on the left side as indicative of some pretension to gentility.

The gaberdines of these liverymen were of blue Flemish cloth, and all had embroidered on their breasts, on escutcheon, *argent*, charged with a lion rampant *azure*, the arms of Crichton, with his motto "God send grace;" and all were accoutred with swords, daggers, and partisans.

On foot beside the chancellor were his pages; one bore his sword, the other held his horse's bridle, a third his cap of maintenance upon a velvet cushion.

A little way within the barrier were Sir Walter Halyburton, lord of Dirltoun, who was then high treasurer; John Methven, the secretary of state; Sir James Crichton of Frendraught, great chamberlain and third officer of the crown; with Patrick Lord Glammis, master of the household. All these, like their immediate followers, were well armed; but that circumstance excited no notice, as it was always the custom to be so in Scotland; and a gay group they formed, as the noonday sun streamed through the old archway, whose front was blackened by smoke and time, upon their tabard-like jupons and hanging sleeves, the heraldic devices on their breasts, their glittering bassinets, waving feathers, rich sword-hilts, jewelled daggers, and gold neck-chains.

Beyond these were the hundred pikemen of the king's guard, under Sir Patrick Gray and Sir Thomas MacLellan; and high over all this array towered the castle rock, crowned by its old *enceinte*, or wall of defence, and its bastel-houses, in the *three* greatest of which, to wit, the Royal Lodging, King David's Tower, and that of the constable, originated the heraldic triple-towered fortress which, from time immemorial, has formed the arms of the city.

As Douglas and his train approached, bombarde, moyenne, and culverin thundered from the ramparts; loud and shrilly twanged the trumpets and horns, and the great crowd assembled in the narrow street made an immediate and simultaneous movement towards the guarded archway.

When the earl's train came near, the quick eyes of the chancellor, as readily as those of our lover, detected the absence of the countess and Murielle. Gray could scarcely repress his anxiety and natural surprise at a circumstance so unexpected; but the chancellor bit his nether lip with vexation, for Margaret, as heiress of Galloway, was the second head of that mighty house which he had sworn to humble for ever. Then a strange smile flitted over his usually impassible face when next he missed the sardonic visage and stealthy eyes of James Douglas, earl of Abercorn.

"Traitor lordling," he muttered, "thou too, in time, shalt dree thy destiny!"

At the distance of thirty paces from the gate the earl of Douglas alighted from his horse, and relinquishing the bridle to a page, advanced bonnet in hand towards the chancellor, who also dismounted, and approached in the same manner, while all present who were not men-at-arms also quitted their saddles, or as the abbot of Tongland says in his MSS. "*lichted down.*"

They greeted each other with a cold formality, over which Crichton, the elder by many years, and the more politic, endeavoured to spread the shallow veil of friendly warmth and courtly dissimulation.

"Welcome, lord earl, most welcome; or shall I say, duke of Touraine?"

"I am prouder of my father's name of Douglas than of any foreign duchy, Sir William," replied the haughty boy as he presented his hand with cold politeness. "Here I am but a Scottish earl."

The chancellor bowed, and stifled his indignation, for in this reply three things offended him; the earl's avowal of family pride, addressing him plainly as Sir William instead of lord chancellor, and then presenting his hand *gloved* — a token of mistrust.

"And this young gentleman," began the chancellor,—

"Is my brother Lord David Douglas," said the earl.

"Most welcome too; but the countess, once the Fair Maid of Galloway," said Crichton, with a bland smile; "will she not grace our young king's board to-day?"

"The king's grace, and you, Sir William Crichton, must hold the countess, her sister, and likewise the Lady Ormond, excused to-day; the ways are rough and the journey long from Thrave to Edinburgh."

"True; but the measure of—of my happiness (he had almost said *vengeance*) will be incomplete without them."

"There are Douglases enough here to supply their places," said the earl, glancing at his mail-clad followers with a significant smile; and Crichton said,—

"Enter, lord earl, the king's grace and the regent await you in the great hall."

After each declining to precede the other, the wily chancellor, while making a sign previously agreed upon and understood by James Achanna and Romanno of that ilk, constable of the garrison, gave a hand to each of the brothers, and led them within the gate.

There was an immediate rush among their rough and tumultuary followers to press in after them, but the king's guard and the chancellor's vassals, with levelled pikes, bore back alike the excited multitude of citizens and the wild Scots of Galloway, bare-kneed and bare-armed, with their habergeons of jangling iron rings, and the strong barrier-gate was closed with haste and difficulty. Lord Ormond, Sir Malcolm Fleming, Sir Alan Lauder, and a few others, in virtue of their rank, being alone permitted to enter.

This *coup* was the more easily effected, as at the moment of the earl's entrance Douglas of Pompherston, his purse-bearer, cried "largesse! largesse!" and to add to the incidental popularity of his lord, scattered several handfuls of silver coin among the people, who scrambled in pursuit of them, and rolled over each other in heaps, while the reckless young earl and his brother laughed and threw more, to increase the uproar and merriment.

Then the portcullis, a massive iron grille, was lowered slowly down in its stony grooves, and when its iron spikes reached the causeway, James Achanna, the double tool of Abercorn and the chancellor, exchanged with the latter one of those deep and rapid smiles by which courtly villains can read each other's hearts and convey a volume of subtle thoughts.

Unheeding, or unobservant of all these circumstances, the earl and his brother accompanied the chancellor into the fortress, and as they slowly proceeded up the steep steps and winding path, which led in a north-westerly direction, to the summit of the rock, Crichton expatiated on the joy this meeting occasioned him, as being the precursor of domestic peace, of good will and unity, between his master the king and the great house of Douglas; but while speaking he could perceive the haughty young peer exchanging secret smiles with his brother; so, nothing daunted, the chancellor continued to flatter, and secretly smiled in his turn.

"Great as the house of Douglas has been— —"

"*Is*, my lord," interrupted the earl, haughtily.

"Pardon me," stammered Crichton, reddening with anger to find himself thus addressed by a boy; "I was about to say, that in ages past, its chief glory was ever in its obedience to the crown, from whence its greatness and its honours sprung."

"Well?" observed the boy-noble impatiently.

"Enemies have accused you of treason— —"

"Yourself, for instance, Sir William."

"True—as first officer of the crown," continued the chancellor, with a severity that increased with the bitterness that grew in his heart, "I have blamed you deeply and frequently; but this day will free you of all those suspicions which that unwise embassy to France occasioned."

"Sir William Crichton!"

"I am a man four times your age, lord earl," interrupted the chancellor, speaking very fast to avoid explicit or excited answers, "so pray excuse my grey hairs if they permit me to assume a monitory tone and venture to yield advice. I would but pray you to execute justice on your vast estates of Galloway, Annandale, and Balvenie with impartiality and gentleness; and not to protect from the just vengeance of the king, our lord and master, those lawless barons who levy feudal war and destroy each other's towers, villages, and territories, and by so doing impoverish the realm and oppress the people. Disobedience to the king has been the ruin of the most ancient and noble families; thus, I would pray you, my lord, to content yourself with the splendour attained by your house, and the glorious name it has borne for ages in peace and in war, nor seek to raise it above that throne in defence of which so many of the Douglas name have died in battle. *Ave Maria!* If you would surpass your king in anything, let it be in religion, in bounty and charity to your countrymen; surpass him thus, and I, whom you have long deemed your enemy, will pray with my latest breath for the glory and prosperity of the lordly line of Douglas, and that Scotland may long have cause to remember with joy the vigil of St. Catherine."

To all these remarks, which so well became the station and superior years of the chancellor, the petulant young earl disdained to reply, save by a cold and disdainful smile or so forth; and as Crichton concluded, they found themselves in the banquet-hall of the castle, and in presence of the king and the regent of Scotland.

CHAPTER XII
THE BLACK BULL'S HEAD

Edinburgh castle, town, and tower,
God grant ye sinke for sin;
And yat even for ye black dinour
Erle Douglas gat therein.—Old Rhyme.

The hall in which this banquet was given, was the upper chamber of David's Tower.

Our novel of "Jane Seaton" contains a description of this gigantic edifice, which was the chief of the bastel-houses which crowned

"The height
Where the huge castle holds its state;"

but the MSS. of the abbot of Tongland throw some additional light upon its history.

This tower rose to the height of more than seventy feet above the summit of the steep rock. It contained a great hall and many lesser chambers, and was founded by David II., about 1360, upon the basement of a still older tower, perhaps the same edifice which vulgar tradition ascribes to the painted Picts, who are alleged to have conveyed from hand to hand the stones from the sandy quarry of Craig-mohl-ard (or the rock of the plain), [2] and at the gate of which the first David—the Scottish Justinian—was wont to sit, as his biographer, St. Ælred, tells us, dispensing justice, and hearing the complaints of the poor, even as St. Louis of France sat under an oak in the wood of Vincennes.

All the masons who built this tower died in the year it was completed; as if, says the abbot of Tongland, fate ordained that the secrets of its stairs and construction should die with them; and within it hung a bell, which, when a king of Scotland died, tolled of its own accord, like that great bell of Arragon, which always announced when "fate was nigh" the line of Ramiro.

In this old tower dwelt a brownie, who was believed to come at night to sleep near the embers of the hall fire, after plaiting the frills, pinners, and ruffs of the queen and her ladies. Some alleged that the cannon of the siege in 1573 put this useful household spirit to flight; others, that he was baptized by the priest of St. Cuthbert's Kirk, who concealed himself in the dusk within the hall ingle, where, when the brownie, in the form of a lean and withered little man, wearing a short yellow cloak, and red hosen (the royal livery), came at midnight to resume his nocturnal avocations, a handful of holy water was dashed in his face by the priest, who cried with a loud voice,—"In nomine Patris, et Filii, et Spiritus Sancti! Amen."

On this, the brownie wept bitterly, and vanished, to return no more.

The hall was hung with banners and trophies. The noonday light of the November sun, varied by many a passing cloud, poured through its arched windows upon the long table, which was spread with all the plenty and massive magnificence of the olden time; upon the rows of high-backed chairs for the guests; upon the throne for the young king, with its steps and purple velvet canopy; on the rich liveries of the trumpeters who were to announce the feast; and on the steel armour of the guards, who stood near the royal seat in honour of the guests; on each and all fell the slant rays of the sun lighting up many a glittering ornament, for the walls of the hall were entirely covered by yellow Spanish leather, stamped by alternate thistles and *fleurs-de-lis* in gold, while in the great fireplace there burned a fire of coals, mingled with pleasantly *perfumed* wood; a curious luxury not uncommon then.

The royal cupbearer, and six soldiers of the guard armed with partisans, were posted near a recess, or ambre, under the carved stone canopy of which glittered the king's service of plate. Amid it was a long slender flask of potters' ware, beautifully fashioned by the fair hands of Jacqueline, countess of Hainault and Flanders, the boldest and loveliest woman of her time, who, after abdicating in 1433, during her seclusion in the castle of Teylingen, near Leyden, employed the weary hours in making flasks of clay, and one of these she sent to the royal minstrel, James I. of Scotland, in care of the Dyck Graf of Bommel.

Now the brass trumpets sent their sharp ringing notes along the vaulted roof; spurs of gold and steel jangled on the tiled floor, while, preceded by all the combined pomp and mummery of ancient royalty, James II., a fair-haired and handsome boy, clad in a glittering doublet, fashioned like a herald's tabard, having the lion *gules* within the double tressure on the back, breast, and sleeves thereof, was led to the throne by the tall and sombre regent, while the crafty Crichton placed the young earl of Douglas on his right-hand. Again the trumpets sounded, and the guests, in succession, were marshalled to their places by Glammis, the master of the household, who executed this delicate matter—for delicate it was in that age of fierce punctilio—with scrupulous exactness, as to rank and precedence.

The boy-earl, with his dark eyes, his swarthy face and black curly hair, his bold bearing and defiant expression, formed so marked a contrast to the boy-king, who was fair-skinned, with fair hair and gentle eyes, that many present remarked the difference of their aspect and character.

On the young king's left cheek there was a small red spot, or fleshmark, which caused the people to name him in after years, "James with the Fiery Face."

"Why tarries the countess?" asked Gray, in a hasty whisper, of Lord David Douglas.

"She is not to be here," said the lad, smiling.

"Nor the Countess of Ormond?"

"No; nor Murielle, either," added David, playing with the gold tassels of his mantle.

"Why?"

"I am not in her secrets."

"But Lady Murielle——"

"Came not, because there were none here whom she *cared* to meet," said the spiteful little lord, with a grimace.

The abbot of Tongland invoked a blessing; and after they had all discussed platters of good Scottish broth, which they supped with massive old spoons, that might have served at the spousal feast of King Robert and Marjorie Bruce, and very probably did so, the clatter of knives began, as the servers, pages, and pantrymen sliced down the chines of beef, the roasted pigs and brawns, or unroofed the huge pasties of pigeons and venison, and rushed here and there with trenchers of stewed hares, roasted ducks, buttered crabs, salads and salmon, manchets of flour, and confections of honey and sweetmeats, all of which were eaten pellmell, without order or course.

Meanwhile the wines of France and Spain flowed freely, and brown ale frothed up in tankards and flagons, in which the long moustaches of the guests floated, as they quaffed to each other's health, and a long continuance of this sudden good fellowship, at which, in many instances, by their eyes and whispers, they seemed to scoff in secret.

Then a band of bearded minstrels and musicians, with harp and pipe, tabor, flute, and trumpet, in the gallery, played "Pastance with Gude Companie," and other old airs, which have been long since forgotten; or, if extant, are now known under new names.

Amid all this the pale chancellor, and the grave, but soldier-like regent, were abstracted and nervous; and the emotion of the former increased as the banquet proceeded, and the *fatal moment* drew near: yet, animated by a sentiment of duty to be performed to their king and country, no thought of pity or remorse found admission in the bosoms of either.

The young king and his young noble spoke of dogs, of hawks, of horses; and archery; of hunting and tilting; but the earl seemed to disdain the puerile conversation of the yet-secluded sovereign, treating him coldly, and with an air of lofty patronage, amusing enough in one of his junior years, but sufficiently apparent to all.

Sir Patrick Gray felt that on this day the kinsmen of Murielle Douglas treated him more coldly than ever, as they deemed themselves in the zenith of their power and fantastic pride, lording it alike over the king and all his court.

"You see there my Captain of the Guard?" he heard the king say, with a kind smile, to the earl, who knit his brows, and contemptuously asked:—

"*Who* is he?"

"Sir Patrick Gray," replied the little monarch, whose eyes dilated with surprise.

"Of what—or where?"

"Of Foulis."

"Indeed!"

"A brave and noble gentleman," said James II., with an enthusiasm that made the poor soldier's heart expand with the purest joy; "lord earl, do you not know him?"

"Yes," said Douglas, frigidly; "but what of him?"

"He gave me a goshawk as a gift last New Year's-day, and I have killed with it every corbie in the woods of Bristo."

"Indeed!"

"And then at Lady-day he gave me two such noble hounds of St. Hubert's breed!"

"St. Bryde! how came such as *he* by dogs so rare?"

Sir Patrick bit his nether lip with suppressed passion at this continued insolence of tone, while the young king replied:—

"We sent him with a message to Jacqueline of Hainault—at least the Regent Livingstone did so, last year,—an errand of courtesy, for the countess was my father's friend. In passing through the forest of Ardennes, he tarried for a night at the Benedictine abbey of St. Hubert, and bought from the monks these two black hounds, the lineal descendants of those which accompanied the saint when he hunted with St. Eustace. They have silver collars, and despite my lady Glammis, sleep every night at the foot of my bed!"

"Laus Deo!" said the earl, shrugging his shoulders; "doubtless they must have somewhat of the odour of sanctity about them."

At this remark Sir Thomas MacLellan laughed, and the petulant earl turned almost fiercely to him, saying:—

"Sirrah, dare you laugh?"

"Saints and devils, my lord," retorted the Lieutenant of the Guard, "may not a man laugh?"

"No!"

"And why not, my lord earl?"

"Because to laugh is at times to assume a superiority, or a bearing of approval, which I would not permit even in our liege lord the king!"

The eyes of the chancellor met those of the regent, whose pale forehead flushed with anger at this insulting remark, though it illustrated how dangerous was the spirit they were about to crush.

"By St. Jude, Douglas, I laughed not at thee, but at thy saying," exclaimed MacLellan, breaking the momentary silence which had ensued.

"Then beware, lordling," said Douglas, who knew there was an old jealousy between the MacLellans and his people.

"I am no lord or earl either," replied MacLellan, flushing with anger in turn.

"What then?"

"One whom you know well to be a gentleman of Galloway, my lord. The king may gift coronets or titles, and *attaint* them, too; but God alone can make or unmake a loyal Scottish gentleman!"

The little king seemed almost scared by this angry outburst; but the regent and his adherents exchanged glances of approval, and they started involuntarily, for at that instant the great bell of David Tower announced the hour of three.

The fatal time had come!

Then the king's master-butcher entered, bearing aloft a vast covered platter, which, by its size, attracted the attention and excited the surprise of all; and passing deliberately round the great apartment, while many jests were made as to what new fare it contained, he placed it before the young earl of Douglas.

"Remove the cover!" said the regent, whose voice was hollow, as if it came from a coffin.

The master-butcher did so, and there was grimly revealed the old Celtic symbol of death, a black bull's head of great size, with its square nostrils, its grey polished horns, and curly forehead.

FOOTNOTES:

[2] Craigmillar.

CHAPTER XIII
THE BLOCK

I must have
A more potential draught of guilt than this,
With more of wormwood in it. — Firmilian.

A simultaneous cry burst from all on seeing this sure and terrible forerunner of a sudden death; all sprang from the table, and instinctively did so, sword in hand; for at the same moment the door of the 'tiring room was thrown violently open, and a chosen party of Crichton's vassals, led by Romanno of that ilk, constable of the castle, Andrew Gray of Balgarno, and others, rushed forward, and with levelled partisans, separated the earl of Douglas and his brother David from their more immediate friends.

"To your swords and defend yourselves, my brother and friends; we are lured — tricked to death!" cried the young earl, with prompt bravery, hewing right and left at the partisans; "A Douglas! a Douglas! cut me a passage to the king — to the throne — it is at least a *sanctuary!*"

"Hold, my lord!" exclaimed the chancellor, in a voice of thunder, as he stood with one foot on the lower step of the king's chair, and firmly interposed his drawn sword, "it is no sanctuary for thee or thine! and dare you — —"

"Slay a chancellor? Yes, if I can, and this dog regent, too, like false hounds and fell traitors as ye are!" replied the brave youth, with a scornful but heartrending smile; while, by the press of partisans levelled in a dense rank, he and his brother, with Sir Malcolm Fleming, Sir Alan Lauder, and all others disposed to resistance, were thrust close to the wall, yet they shouted resolutely, "a Douglas! a Douglas!" The chairs and banquet-tables were overthrown, and all became a scene of confusion, destruction, and dismay, from which many fled by the doors, not knowing how the brawl would end.

"Guards and gentlemen!" exclaimed the tall grim regent, as he towered above the armed throng, and roughly but firmly grasped the left arm of the bewildered king, who thought he was about to perish, like his father, by the hands of regicides, yet, like a brave boy as he was, had rushed forward to save Douglas; "guards and gentlemen, disarm this traitorous peer and all who have drawn their swords by his side in the royal presence. Put up your blade, I command you, William, earl of Douglas—the king is here, and this is his royal castle!"

"Dishonour blight it for this day's deed," exclaimed old Sir Malcolm Fleming, "and may its roof-tree be the gallows of all thy race, accursed Crichton! thou cogging villain, thou cheat and assassin! And as for *thee*, Lord regent—hah! the sword that knighted thee was never notched in battle!"

"A very carpet squire!" said Lauder, scornfully.

"Liars are both; the blade that knighted me was our Scottish sword of state; a king's hand gave me the accolade—a king murdered by traitors false as you! Now hearken to me, Douglas. Fate has this day placed the destinies of your rebellious and overweening house in the hands of a justly-offended king and his resolute ministers, so prepare for a doom upon which a short but ample career of evil actions has hurried you—that fatal doom which incensed justice is about to mete out to you and the adherents of your father. Disarm them, guards I say; by *my* voice the king commands it!"

Seeing the futility of resistance, the venerable laird of Cumbernauld tossed his sword disdainfully to the Captain of the Guard, and Sir Alan Lauder broke his blade across his knee, and flung the fragments down in sullen silence; but the earl and his brother hacked and hewed at the shafts of the partisans, inflicting many severe wounds on the hands and arms of their assailants, before they were beaten down, disarmed, when mad with fury, and secured by silken cords, torn from the curtains of the hall windows. Achanna, while pretending to save the earl, hung treacherously upon his sword arm till he was captured, and the sorrowing and bewildered Captain of the Guard had to interpose his own sword between the furious boy Lord David and Romanno, who had drawn his dagger, having been exasperated by a slash across the face. Prior to this the abbot of Tongland, the earl of Ormond, Douglas of Pompherston, and others, had all been dragged from the hall and forcibly expelled into the city, where they spread alarm and consternation through every street and alley.

The poor little king, who, with the six princesses his sisters, had been given up completely to the care of Livingstone and Crichton, since his mother Queen Jane had contracted her foolish marriage with the handsome Sir James Stewart, usually known as the Black Knight of Lorn, surveyed this terrible scene with the bewilderment of a startled boy; but, on beholding the two brothers manacled with cords, bruised, bleeding, and faint, after their brave but futile struggle, he burst into tears, and clutching the robe of the lord chancellor, besought him "to spare them."

Then, according to Balfour, in his "Annals of Scotland," and other writers, the chancellor replied sternly:—"You are but a child, and know not what you demand, for to spare them would be the ruin of you and your whole kingdom!"

"Forgive them; oh, forgive them!" continued the princely boy, wringing his hands, and appealing next to the regent; but he too replied grimly:— "Your grace knows not what you ask."

"I *do* know what I ask, and what I command. Am I not a king?" was the passionate response.

"Well, rather than obey," replied Crichton, through his clenched teeth, "I would walk barefoot over seven burning ploughshares, or over the seven times heated furnace of hell," he added, with terrible energy; "our time for vengeance has come!"

But the little monarch continued to sob and say:—"Lord regent, lord regent, I am a king."

At last he appealed to Sir Patrick Gray, commanding him to draw his dagger and cut the cords which bound the brothers and their two faithful friends; but the unfortunate captain, confounded by the suddenness of the catastrophe, impelled by his love for Murielle on one hand, his duty to the two highest officers of the crown on the other; his regard for the young king, and a remembrance of how insolently these Douglases had ever treated himself, leaned on his sword, and covered his face with his hand, to hide the emotion that warred in his breast.

Suddenly he approached Crichton, to unite his entreaties to those of his young monarch; but was roughly repelled.

"Oh, chancellor," he exclaimed, "is this my meed—this my reward for faithful service as the king's liege man?"

"If such you be, I command you, peace, Sir Patrick—guard the king, and leave the punishment of his rebels to us."

Now the voice of the regent was heard above the throng, as he shook his clenched right hand aloft.

"I arrest you, William, duke of Touraine, earl of Douglas, lord of Annandale, Longueville, and Galloway, on charges of foul treason; and you, Lord David Douglas; you, Sir Malcolm Fleming of Biggar and Cumbernauld; and you, Sir Alan Lauder of the Bass, captain of the castle of Thrave, on the same serious accusation."

"Treason?" reiterated the young earl, as he proudly raised his head; "in what have I been guilty of treason; and who dare accuse me?"

"I—the chancellor of Scotland," replied Crichton.

"Read the charges," said the regent, sternly.

"They are here," replied Crichton, unfolding a document, while all leaned on their unsheathed weapons, and listened breathlessly. "Treason, in the daily oppression of the king's subjects, at the head of two thousand horsemen, most of whom are outlawed moss-troopers and thieves of Annandale, who sorn on the king's lieges, and commit every outrage; and this ye do, though the parliament held at Perth, in 1424, ordained that *no* man should travel abroad with more followers than he could maintain. Treason in dubbing men as knights who are but sorners, limmers, and masterful rogues. Treason, in holding *cours plénières* after the fashion of parliament; and treason, in sending two gentlemen to France as your ambassadors to Charles VII."

"It is false, as all the rest!" exclaimed the earl. "I did but send them as my father desired me, when he lay dying at Restalrig, to renew his oath of fealty for the duchy of Touraine, the fief of Longueville, and other lands we hold in France; and to fix the yearly rental of the former at ten thousand crowns."

"He speaks most truly," exclaimed Sir Malcolm Fleming and Sir Alan Lauder in the same breath.

"Well, all this, though too little for a king, was too great for a subject," said the regent, haughtily.

"The extent of your power and the misuse thereof," resumed the chancellor, "with the lawless character of your followers, are pretexts enough, without others, on which to arraign you. No religion, no threats, no prayers or pretended reformation, no oaths or promises, can alter the inborn character we inherit with our blood; and what have *you*, Douglas, thus inherited? Pride, treason, contumacy, and the love of open rebellion against the crown; and these evil qualities will remain true to the fount from whence they spring; so, my lord regent, to the block, I say, with this viperous brood. If the boy is thus dangerous, what would the man be?"

"We demand to be tried by our peers," said the earl, firmly; "arraign us before the Estates."

"You have got nearly all the trial and shrift we mean to give you," said the regent, bluntly. "Romanno, away with them to the castle Butts."

The trial, if it can be called so, proceeded rapidly, for the judges had long ago resolved on the sentence, and, as one historian says, "were determined to make no allowance for the youth and inexperience of the parties—for the artifices by which they had been lured within the danger of the law, and for their being totally deprived of constitutional or legal defenders."

So, without counsel, jury, or written documents of any kind, these grim proceedings went on; but never once did the brave boys sue for pity, for mercy, or even for one hour of life.

From the hall, where the king, amid the *débris* of the banquet and combat, sank weeping on his canopied seat, the unfortunate earl and his brother were hurried down the back stair of David's Tower, and dragged to the greensward of the Butts, where the new barracks were built in 1796, and there, in the presence of the regent, the chancellor, Sir Walter Halyburton, the lord high treasurer, and other officers of state, after being barely permitted to embrace each other, they were thrown down on the block in succession, forcibly held there, and beheaded!

This terrible deed was scarcely done ere all the friends of the regent and chancellor, save their garrison, hastily quitted the castle; even as those who *now* witness an execution disperse rapidly as if it were a relief to get rid of emotions so deep as those which are excited by beholding a violent death, however judicially done.

For two days Sir Malcolm Fleming (ancestor of the earls of Wigton) was respited only because he had wedded Elizabeth Stewart, daughter of the old duke of Albany; but ultimately he too was beheaded on the same block that was yet crimsoned with the blood of those he loved so well.

Sir Alan Lauder, through the friendship of Romanno, effected his escape; while Fleming was interred in the coffin which bore the name of Murielle Douglas.

In a wild spot on the north-western slope of the castle rock, where the wall-flower and thistle flourished, and where at times the grass was spotted by the *witch-gowans*, those yellow flowers which are filled by pernicious sap, and are supposed to cause blindness, grew luxuriantly, they were all interred in one deep grave.

In 1753, when the foundations of an arsenal were being dug there, some human remains were exhumed, with several coffin-handles, and three inscription-plates of pure gold. With these relics were found the skull and horns of a bull, thereby identifying them with those victims of misrule who perished on the vigil of St. Catharine, in 1440.

CHAPTER XIV
THE TWENTY-FOURTH OF NOVEMBER

Playing at the tables, he
There was murder'd. At his shrine
Many a noble lady wept;
Many a knight of valiant line:
One mourn'd more than all the rest,
Daughter of the Genovine.
Poetry of Spain.

In the horror and bewilderment which were naturally excited by this terrible and unexpected catastrophe—this double execution which had taken place under his own eyes, and in which he felt himself thereby almost implicated, the unfortunate Captain of the King's Guard knew not what to do.

How would the powerful and hostile Douglases, and how might Murielle view him *now*?

He shrunk from the contemplation, and felt such an abhorrence of the regent and chancellor, that, although his bread and subsistence were derived from his post at court as Captain of the King's Guard, he was tempted to cast the office from him and leave the country. But to pass into exile was to lose all hope of Murielle, to relinquish her for ever; and he lived in an age when love was perhaps a more *concentrated* passion than it may be even in one of greater civilization.

To lure her with him into France,—in those old times the Scotsman's *other* home,—would be fraught with danger; for the Douglases would have interest enough with Charles VII. to procure their separation, and his commitment for life to some obscure bastille, where he would never be heard of again,—if their emissaries did not cut him off in the light of open day.

Then, on the other hand, his patron and friend, the late King James I., had made him promise to be a faithful subject and mentor to his son and heir; and, with one hand on that dead monarch's body as he lay murdered in the Black Friary at Perth, he had recorded the promise again in presence of his mourning widow.

That a terrible vengeance would be planned by the Douglases and their adherents for that *black dinner,*—as it was named,—he felt assured; for all who hated the regent or dreaded the chancellor had for years found security in the numerous strongholds of the slaughtered earl, and had there bid defiance alike to king, law, and parliament. All the lawless moss-troopers; all broken, idle, and mischievous persons, professed themselves vassals of this powerful house, which was rapidly aiming at the erection of a separate and independent principality in the southern and most fertile district of Scotland.

By the stern chancellor's wisdom, and merciless decree, the headsman's axe had struck a fatal blow at this most daring and ambitious scheme: but what might the sequel be to public as well as private interests?

And Murielle!

She knew all the perils of the age in which she lived; the daily—yea, hourly dangers to which her lover as Captain of the King's Guard was exposed; she knew, too, how many interests were hostile to their union, and that their love seemed the hopeless passion of a romance or a harper's song; yet she had still continued to love, and trust, and hope, though vaguely, for some turn of the wheel of Fortune, as loving women always do in the hours of trouble and adversity; but of what avail would all this trust and hope be *now?*

All these thoughts rushed like a flood through the mind of Gray, as he stood next morning beside the newly-heaped mound where the dead were buried.

How was he to excuse to Murielle that he was present at the butchery of her nearest kinsmen? and, *why* that he still adhered to those who so basely slew them under truce and tryst?

A shadow fell across the large earthen mound. He looked up, and his eyes met those of the inflexible chancellor.

"Good morrow, Sir Patrick!" said the latter, with a keen glance. "Art moralizing on the mutability of human things, or the vanity of human greatness?"

"Nay; my mind was full of neither."

"What then?"

"I was but thinking that it was a foul deed, my lord; this slaughter of two helpless youths, amid the festivity of a royal banquet."

"Foul!" reiterated the Chancellor, with a louring brow and flashing eyes.

"As foul as if the heart of Judas planned it; a deed at which all Scotland, if not all Europe, will cry aloud," replied Gray, stoutly.

"Then let them cry, if it pleases them to do so. By our Lady! I believe the howl you fear will not go far beyond Galloway and the Douglas lands. Of yesterday's act, I take upon myself the entire odium and responsibility, if such there be. Those who know me, and chiefly He who reads the secrets of every soul, know the great end I had in view when, in the persons of these misguided boys, I laid the heads of a viperous brood in the dust. Sir Patrick Gray!" added the chancellor, turning and stamping on the grave with his spurred heel, "better it is to have the heart of Douglas lying cold below us, than exulting that his banner could cast its shadow on the throne, and that he could rend Scotland in twain, to become the easier prey of its ancient, bitter, and grasping enemies. Nay, man, never scowl at me, but ponder well upon my words; and remember the promise you made to the king when living, and to the same king when dead, on that terrible night in the Black Friary, at Perth."

And with a significant glance, this stern statesman turned and left him, as if disdaining further defence of himself.

Gray supposed that the vast train of Douglas would assemble and depart at once, on learning the tidings of the execution: thus, if he would see Murielle, he must visit her without delay. But such a visit was fraught with danger, so great was the excitement which reigned in the city, where an assault of the castle was considered imminent.

Carefully divesting himself of everything by which he might be recognized, he put on a shirt of fine mail, which fitted him like a kid-glove. Over this he buttoned a pourpoint of plain black cloth; a steel gorget protected his neck; and a salade effectually did the same office for his head, while at the same time it completely concealed his face; and, armed with his sword and dagger, he sallied forth into the streets, where the shops and booths were closed, and at the Cross, the Butter Tron, the doors of St. Giles's Church, and other places, sullen and excited groups of citizens were mingled with the wild and unruly billmen, pikemen, and archers, who had come from the banks of the Nith and the Annan; or with armed knights, who rode hurriedly to and fro, briefly questioning each other, or gathering for angry conference. Many yet averred that the story of the execution was false, and that the earl and his brother with Sir Malcolm Fleming were merely imprisoned in the vaults of that grim fortress towards which many an angry eye was turned, and towards which many a gauntleted hand was clenched and shaken.

But James Achanna spread the truth industriously; and then a dreadful shout, or many shouts commingling into one, rang along the streets from mouth to mouth.

"Horse and spear! A Douglas! a Douglas! Fye, fye! Vengeance on the king and the pack of sworn traitors who surround him! Down with his lurdane burgesses and silken lords! Death to the regent and chancellor!"

Such were the cries heard on every hand.

"Oh, had the legate of Rome but listened to me!" exclaimed the abbot of Tongland; "oh, had his holiness but favoured me, than had Sathanas been forgiven; evil had departed from us, and we had not seen this day of woe!"

On one hand the great common-bell of the city was rung by order of Sir Thomas Cranstoun, the provost, to summon the people to arms, for their own protection and that of the king; on the other, the bells of the churches were tolling, to call them to prayer; so that as many as possible, especially "wives and bairns," might be kept from danger. The blare of trumpets, the twanging of horns were heard in wynd and alley, with the clatter of iron hoofs and clinking of steel, as Ormond, Abercorn, Pompherston, Glendoning, and other feudatories mustered their "followings;" and amid all this hubbub and dismay, this rushing to and fro of armed, pale-faced, and excited men in search of sure intelligence, our anxious lover passed through the city, and reached, unquestioned and unannounced, the outer gate of the abbot's mansion.

Just as he was about to enter, a man passed out of the archway.

This person was fully armed in a chain shirt, with a steel helmet, from the rim of which a camaile, or tippet of fine steel rings, closely interwoven, fell upon the shoulders to protect the neck. His gauntlets were of brass; he carried a dagger at his girdle, and a ghisarma in his hands. Through the open helmet, Sir Patrick Gray at once recognized the malevolent eyes of James Achanna, the follower of the Douglases, and the paid spy of Crichton, a thorough Scottish utilitarian of the fifteenth century.

"Grant me mercy, Sir Patrick," said he, with well-feigned concern, "what make you here, at such a time as this? Do you bear a charmed life?"

"You *know* me, then?" exclaimed the soldier, somewhat disconcerted.

"When you wish to be unknown, you should leave this golden chain at home," said Achanna, lifting the links of one worn by Gray above his gorget.

"How, sir,—what do you infer?" asked the latter, biting his lips with undisguised annoyance, for the chain in question was a gift from Murielle.

"I have seen it on a fairer neck, but at such a time are you safe beyond the castle gate?"

"Oh, heed me not, my good man," replied the soldier, contemptuously; "my hands could always keep my head—be sure that yours can do the same for you."

"That we shall prove," muttered the other with his malignant smile, as he passed out, and they separated.

In the adjacent wynd, or alley, he met James of Avondale and Abercorn, riding down hastily with a troop of armed followers, all excited almost to madness by the conflicting statements circulated in the city, while at the gate of the fortress, where Abercorn had gone, being anxious to learn the *truth*, the sole reply was the pointed crossbow or hand-gun, levelled at all who approached.

The subtle earl of Abercorn and Avondale knew well by the advices of his creature, Achanna, that both his nephews were effectually and for ever removed from his path, and that as next of kin, the vast possessions of the house of Douglas—their titles, lands, manors, and fortresses were his—*his beyond recall!* But as yet he found it prudent to affect to doubt the terrible story; and thus he had been swaggering over all the city in his armour, threatening with vengeance, fire and sword, the king, the regent, the chancellor, and all their adherents.

"Achanna," he exclaimed, curbing his horse, "the common rumour says my kinsmen *were slain* yesterday,—foully murdered by the chancellor and his minions under form of law."

"Alake, my lord," whined Achanna (who had detailed to him all the transaction most circumstantially, on the preceding evening), "I fear the rumour is but too true; woe worth the day! woe worth the day!"

On this the armed horsemen clenched their mailed hands, or shook their spears aloft, and muttered deep oaths in the hollow of their helmets.

"By St. Bryde of Douglas, I would give a year's rental of Touraine for the head of Livingstone, of Crichton, or even of the wretch who acted as their doomster!" exclaimed Abercorn, still acting as if inspired by grief and indignation.

"A year's rent of Touraine is a pretty sum," said Achanna, musingly.

"Ay, ten thousand crowns," added the earl, grimly.

"How freely he spends his new-won property," thought Achanna, adding aloud, "the headsman was masked, 'tis said."

"By whom?"

"The common rumour."

"Masked was he?" said the laird of Pompherston; "a wise precaution, as there is not a Douglas in the land but will be ready to whet a dagger on his breast bone!"

"Well, sirs, this perilous carle is even now within arm's length of us."

"Hah! *here*, say you, Achanna?" said Abercorn.

"Even so,—Sir Patrick Gray."

"The Captain of the Guard! Was it he?"

"None else," was the villainous response.

"And he—he," cried twenty voices.

"Is now in the Abbot's House, at the feet of Lady Murielle, or, perhaps, at the feet of the countess; I know not which he loves, for there be some in Galloway who aver he affects them both."

"In the house here—art thou sure, Achanna?" hissed the earl, through his teeth, while a livid gleam lit his dark and sinister eyes, for he bitterly hated Gray, and had *other* views for Murielle than she had yet foreseen. Moreover, a ready victim was required to appease the fury which inspired the turbulent followers of his slaughtered nephews, and none could be so fit for his purpose as the Captain of the Guard. "Art thou sure," he added, "that Gray is here?"

"Sure, as that the breath of Heaven is in my nostrils!"

"By the God of my kin, our task of vengeance is beginning!" cried Earl James, rising in his stirrups, and brandishing his sword; "a rope, a rope! A Douglas! a Douglas! Ho, Pompherston, Glendoning, Cairnglas,—let us hang this king's minion at the Market Cross! Gather a band—beset the house, and watch every avenue. Achanna, is there a secret stair?"

"Yes."

"Then beset it too," exclaimed the earl.

"Be that my task," replied Achanna, who with six armed men repaired to an angle of the abbot's garden, where, among a mass of ivy which shrouded the wall, he knew there was concealed a little arched postern, which formed the external avenue of one of those secret escapes with which all houses were furnished in those times of war and tumult.

Abercorn remained in his high-peaked, crimson velvet saddle, while posting his followers round the mansion; but Pompherston, Glendoning, and other armed gentlemen, with a tumultuous party of retainers, Lanarkshire pikemen, crossbowmen, and wild, half-naked Galwegians, who brandished axes, swords, and daggers, rushed up the stone stairs, and spread through the wainscoted apartments, in eager search of the object of their vengeance, for they were in such a mood for blood and slaughter, they would have slain the household cat had it, unluckily, fallen in their way.

But we must return to our luckless lover, who, suspecting nothing of all this, had long since passed into the house, where no one accosted or introduced him, so great was the confusion which already reigned there.

CHAPTER XV
A SECRET STAIR

Bluidie was the braid saddle lap,
And bluidie was the crupper;
Sae bluidie as my true love's hands,
When we sat down to supper.
"There's water in the siller dish,
Gae wash thy hands so bluidie;"
But my love wash'd in the water clear,
And never made it ruddie.
Cromek.

Sir Patrick Gray reached the wainscoted hall, or chamber of dais, the arched roof of which was covered, as already described, with frescoed legends of the Abbey of Tongland.

There yet stood the little Scottish harp of Murielle, and a sense of her sweet presence seemed to linger about it, with the memory of her song—"Sir Hugh le Blond." There stood the seat of her sister, the dark and beautiful Margaret, with the velvet tabourettes of her bower-maidens grouped around it. There was the chair of the young earl, with one of his leather gloves, and beside it his little Bologna spaniel asleep.

The gay groups of the other night seemed to rise before the troubled eye of Gray, as he surveyed the chamber. He sighed bitterly, and could recall with painful distinctness the faces of the unfortunate earl and the petulant boy, his brother. He forgave poor little David all his petulance now.

How difficult to realize the conviction, that within an hour he had stood by their bloody tomb—poor victims of misguided ambition, of feudal pride, and political misrule! Yet an age seemed to have elapsed since last he had seen their faces.

Suddenly he heard a light step and the rustling of a dress; a small hand drew rapidly aside the arras which covered a door, and Murielle, with bloodshot eyes and her sweet little face pale with tears and loss of sleep, rushed towards him.

"Oh, Patrick Gray, Patrick Gray!" she exclaimed, throwing herself in all the abandonment of grief into his arms, and laying her cold cheek upon his breast; "Oh my love, my heart—what new miseries, what new crimes and dangers, are these that come to cast their gloom and horror upon us?"

He endeavoured to calm and soothe her; but suddenly quitting him, she besought him to leave her, and return instantly to the castle.

"Leave you, Murielle?" he reiterated, "think of the time that has elapsed since I have seen you, conversed with you—since I have been with you alone; and think of the time that may elapse ere we meet again."

"Yet go—go," she added, clasping her hands, "if you love me, go!"

"If—ah! Murielle——"

"Leave me—shun me! this love will end in your destruction," she exclaimed with wild energy.

"I am almost inclined to stay, Murielle, and risk everything, were it but to prove how much I do love you."

"By making me miserable for ever, by seeing you perish before me—oh, even as my poor kinsmen perished!" she added in a piercing accent, while wringing her pretty hands, and half withdrawing from him.

"You are right, dear Murielle," replied the soldier gloomily: "I am in the king's service. To brave a useless danger and inevitable fate, would serve no end; yet, dearest Murielle, this interview may be our last."

"It may be—I know it in my aching heart; yet go—go, for the love of God and St. Bryde, lest some fresh crime be committed, and here. Alas! you know not Hugh of Ormond, or James of Abercorn, as I do. But why were our beloved William and David slain?" "Blame not me, dear Murielle," said Gray, kissing her pale cheek with affectionate sorrow.

"Oh, Patrick, I do not blame you," replied Murielle, in a tone of misery.

"Indeed! Yet you see him before you, and clasp him to your heart like a wanton, while he has on his hands the blood of my husband!" exclaimed a clear and ringing voice. It was that of the scornful, the lovely and revengeful, yet superb Margaret, as she burst upon them through the parted arras, her pale cheek flushing and her dark eyes sparkling, but with more of anger than grief. "Vile assassin! come you here, stained with the blood of my Douglas—my brave, young, handsome lord and kinsman—of his poor boy-brother, and that hoary-headed baron, old Malcolm Fleming, whose sword was never idle when Scotland or her king required its service! Did it require three such heads to glut the hatred ye bear to the house of Douglas and Galloway? Speak!" she added, stamping her pretty foot imperiously on the rush-covered floor; "speak, thou king's minion and Falkland-bred loon!"

"Peace, sister," moaned Murielle, "oh peace— —"

"Now, grant me patience, God!" exclaimed the furious countess, stretching her white hands upward—and supremely lovely that dark-eyed girl seemed, in her mingled grief and rage. "Go hence, I say, Murielle Douglas; let not that man contaminate you by his touch."

"Oh, sister Maggie, you know he loves me dearly, and I him."

"I know that he has been tutored well in the conventional hypocrisy of a court; and that you, Murielle, educated as you have been in our secluded castle of Thrave, are no match in art for such as he."

"Maggie," implored Murielle, beginning to writhe under her sister's severity, "he is generous as gentle, and gentle as brave!"

"But save him if you can," said Margaret, bitterly.

"There is, then, danger, madam?" said Gray, loosening his poniard in its sheath.

"Do you hear that growing clamour in the street?" exclaimed Margaret. "Sir Patrick Gray, away, I warn you. James of Abercorn, Pompherston, and others, all our most faithful followers, are around the house; if you tarry here a moment longer, they will hack you joint from joint."

"But, madame—countess—Murielle," said Gray, whose heart was swollen almost to bursting by the vituperative bitterness of Margaret, "I cannot go without a word of explanation or defence."

"We seek neither. It is enough for us to know that you stood by, in yonder royal shambles on the rock, and saw Douglas foully murdered, under tryst—*stood idly by*, with your sword in its sheath, and neither by word or blow sought to save the life of him whose cousin you profess to love. But doubtless, as captain of the king's hirelings, it was your duty to stand aloof, or guard the treble murder!"

"Sister," said Murielle imploringly, while her tears fell fast and hotly, "have we not heard the Abbot of Tongland and the Prior of St. Mary's Isle both preach, that man was born to evil, even as the sparks fly upward; but that with fortitude, patience, and resignation, we should bear our cross— the destiny assigned us; and what are we, to set ourselves in opposition to what they, the men of God, teach, preach, and practise?"

"Such cowardly precepts may suit their droning monks, but not the Douglases of Thrave," responded her fiery sister. "We have been foully wronged, and I have sworn by our Lady of Whitekirk—by her son and St. Bryde—to have a vengeance on this boy-king and his chancellor,—a vengeance so sure and deep, that every king in Christendom shall feel his heart tremble within him, if he dares to wrong a subject as they have wronged me. Ha!—hear ye *that*?" she added, as a strangely malignant gleam passed over her dark eyes.

"*Death to Gray—bring him forth—a rope! a rope!*"

"'Tis the voice of Achanna," said Sir Patrick, starting; while Murielle, on hearing the roar of men's voices and the clatter of arms without and within the house, uttered a low cry of terror, and clung to his breast.

By a hasty glance from the window, Gray saw that the court-yard was full of armed men, who, with drawn swords and bent cross bows, were crowding into the staircase. He saw James of Abercorn, who was on horseback, and who shook his gauntleted hand towards him; he saw that the garden, the gate, the wynd, and every avenue to escape were beset by glittering pikes and partisans, and a cold perspiration burst over his brow at the sudden prospect of helplessly suffering a cruel and violent death. His heart was almost too full for words; but he kissed Murielle tenderly.

"Long, long, it may be," he said, with a foreboding sigh, "ere that dear kiss can be repeated—it may be *never*; but oh, Murielle, tide what may, let no other efface it from your beloved lips!"

The voices and clatter of arms came nearer.

"Save him, sister—save him, Maggie. You may and *can* do it!" exclaimed Murielle, rushing to the door of the large chamber, which she closed, and drew across into the stone socket the massive oak bar by which it was secured. She had barely achieved this ere the din of blows from mailed hands, from sword-hilts, and the butts of crossbows and partisans, rang upon it in a shower.

Many fierce voices summoned those who were within to open; otherwise, that fire would be applied to force an entrance.

Drawing his sword and dagger, Gray was about to unclose it, and attempt to hew a passage through them—an attempt which would inevitably have ended where it began, as there were a legion of foes without, all thirsting for vengeance, eager for outrage and homicide—all men inured to daily turbulence, peril, and bloodshed.

The clatter and uproar increased rapidly, as the numbers outside seemed to multiply. The door, though of solid oak, was yielding fast, and already the blades of several swords were repeatedly passed through it, and withdrawn to give place to others.

"Save him, Maggie dear—dear sister, save him, in mercy to me, if not to himself," implored Murielle, clinging to the waist of Margaret, who stood haughtily erect, like a tragedy-queen, with a sneer upon her proud lip, while undisguised alarm was now expressed in her fine eyes, at the prospect of seeing Gray butchered in her presence, though she hated him in her heart; "save him, sister, save him!"

"Am I an armed man?" she asked coldly. "In what fashion am I to save your minion?"

"Ha!—by the stair—the secret stair. Oh God, how that door shakes—in another moment it will yield!—the secret stair—the abbot gave you the key."

"True," said Margaret, as she drew a key from her bosom, and tossed it contemptuously on the floor.

With a cry of joy Murielle picked it up, and, seizing Gray by the hand, said,

"You are saved—quick—come this way."

At the side of one of the deeply-embayed windows she withdrew the arras, and unlocked a little door which gave access to a narrow passage, formed in the thickness of the ancient wall.

"Descend here. There are twenty-one steps; the passage at the foot leads to the garden, and the wall there is low. Push open the door at the lower end among the ivy, and you are free. Heaven, in its goodness, be your guide!"

"Ah, that I had but twelve pikes of my guard to scatter this rabble like winnowed chaff! Adieu, Murielle; I shall live and escape, if I can! If not, look from your window, my love—my dear, dear love—and you shall see how toughly a brave and loyal gentleman can *die*!"

With these words, and full of desperate thoughts, Gray rushed down the secret stair, while Murielle, with a sigh almost of rapture, locked the door. Then, with a prayer of thankfulness, she thrust the key into her bosom; but, fearing it might not be quite safe even there, she cast it into the great fire of coals and oak roots which burned on the hearth.

At that moment the door was burst open, and the tall grim laird of Pompherston, with his helmet open and his sword drawn, rushed in, with a confused mob of pikemen and archers at his back.

On seeing only the countess and her sister, he and his flushed followers seemed perplexed, and turned away to prosecute their search elsewhere. But soon the clash of weapons and shouts of exultation and ferocity in the garden drew all there to join the fray.

Murielle sprang to the nearest window, and oh, what a sight she saw there!

Sir Patrick Gray issuing from the doorway of the secret passage, covered with blood and wounds; his pourpoint rent and torn; his sword and dagger bloody, after a combat maintained in the dark against Achanna and six others, who, as already related, had beset the way and attacked him, with terrible advantage, in the obscurity, which concealed alike their number and their deadly purpose.

Undismayed, with his sword in his right hand and a long Scottish dagger in his left, Gray rushed upon his assailants, and they quickly parted before him; but only to close in his rear, while fresh foes met him in front.

What a sight for Murielle to gaze upon, while, gasping and shrieking, she clung to the iron bars of the hall window, and surveyed the terrible scene below, where one poor human life was struggling so nobly and so desperately for existence against so many!

Brave heart! he will sell that life dearly, for it is doubly valuable now. Youth and love—the love of Murielle—are his, and for both he has to live and to conquer!

No slogan or shout, entreaty or threat, are uttered by him, as, with teeth clenched, brows knit, and every nerve and fibre strained, he stabs and shreds and hews about him, trampling underfoot those who fall beneath his hand.

He casts one brief and despairing glance at the window, for he knows that *she* is there; and to the horror of being thus helplessly butchered by the kinsmen of Murielle, is added the bitter consciousness that she beholds it, alike unable to assist or save him.

He is the aim of a hundred flashing weapons and infuriated men, who, in their blind eagerness to destroy him, impede and inflict severe wounds on each other.

His pourpoint hangs from his shoulders in rags, and more than one long arrow dangles by its barbed point from his shirt of mail. Now his helmet is struck from his head; an exulting cheer rises from the rabble that surge around him; but still he towers above them like a rock, and hews another, another, and another down!

Now, as he concentrates all his energies, the crowd parts before him; he has reached the outer gate, and then a cry for "rescue" rises in the street beyond.

He reels, he staggers to his knee!

Yet up he springs again. Heavens! there is a long and bloody streak across his pallid face; and now his sword-blade breaks; but he wrests another from an assailant, whom he hurls to the earth and treads under foot, lest he should rise and fight again!

On, on yet, and now he has fought his way through the gate, beyond which, on horseback, sits grim Earl James of Abercorn, like a mailed statue, surveying with fierce eyes this appalling scene; and now, faint with wounds and loss of blood, Gray staggers like a dying man towards him, and clutches his stirrup-leather.

"James of Abercorn," he cries, "by your knighthood, by God's mercy and the honour of your name, save me!"

But, with the smile of a demon, James the Gross raises his ponderous ghisarma, and strikes him twice on his bare head and upturned despairing face, which in a moment are covered with blood.

"Murielle! Murielle!" exclaims Gray, as he sinks, to all appearance, lifeless in the street; and then the wild rabble sweep over him like a human flood, to complete his destruction.

On beholding this last barbarous act, a shriek burst even from the countess, and she turned to her sister; but, alas! poor Murielle had long since sunk insensible on the cushioned window-seat.

CHAPTER XVI
THE CASTLE OF THRAVE

Sad airs like those she heard in infancy,
Fell on her soul and filled her eyes with tears;
And recollections came of happier years,
Thronging from all the cells of memory.
Barry Cornwall.

More than a year had elapsed since the terrible scene with which the preceding chapter has closed.

It was the sweet season of summer. A soft wind was passing over the pastoral uplands of Galloway, and rippling the black water of the Dee where it swept round the green islet on which stands the great feudal fortress of Thrave. It rippled, in some places, the growing cornfields, in others, the greener wild grass, bearing with it the freshness of the dew that loaded the leaves of the wayside flowers (for a shower had just fallen), with the perfume of the honeycomb, of the mountain bee that hummed over the yellow broom or purple heather-bells, on the rugged braes of Balmaghie; or over the crimson cups of the wild roses overhanging the brawling burn that rushed through bank and scaur to Woodhall Loch.

It was a summer noon; the sunny shower had passed away, and the rose-linnet, the wild mavis, and the gold-spink sang merrily on every bush and bank; and the bright sun cast the great shadow of the castle of Thrave upon the Dee, which moats it round.

There now dwelt Murielle, and others who have borne a part in our story, though a change had come over their position in life.

The Lord Chancellor Crichton had scarcely foreseen the immediate consequences of that "black dinour" in the castle of Edinburgh—a deed of detestable cruelty, though deemed politic in the spirit of the time. It naturally excited the deep-rooted hatred and fierce indignation of the numerous vassalage and powerful friends of the house of Douglas; while the youth of the noble victims on one hand, with the age and valour of Sir Malcolm Fleming on the other, together with the cold-blooded treachery which lured them all to a doom so disastrous—a mock trial and execution in the young king's presence, despite his tears and entreaties—all conduced to excite a strong sympathy among the people, who only remembered the worth and loyalty of their ancestors, and forgot those excesses, or were ignorant of that mad ambition, which had filled with jealousy the ministers of James the Second.

But while treasuring this deed of blood in their resentful hearts, and scheming for the downfall of the regent and chancellor, the Douglases were too wary now to trust themselves out of their own fastnesses, or to take immediate revenge.

The dukedom of Touraine and the county of Longueville had reverted to the crown of France; but James the Gross, earl of Abercorn and Avondale, through whose connivance the trial and execution of his kinsmen took place, succeeded quietly to all their Scottish estates. Then, to prevent the dismemberment of a territory so princely, and to preserve to the house of Douglas the Countess Margaret's portion, which comprehended Galloway, Wigton, Balvenie, Ormond, and Annandale, on the promise of obtaining a papal dispensation, through the good offices of the abbot of Tongland, she consented to espouse Earl James, that they might the better plot their vengeance and unite their power against the regent and chancellor, who, by this unexpected consolidation, saw their views baffled, and the family of Douglas, within six months, restored to its former strength and splendour.

Thus, twice before her twentieth year, had the Fair Maid of Galloway worn a wreath of roses and lucky four-leaved clover, which formed then the bridal chaplet. The young lord of her great fortress by the Dee had passed away; yet it seemed strange he had left no vacancy of heart or hearth behind him: for his place had been rapidly filled by another; and none knew Margaret's secret thoughts.

In the vast but solitary castle of Thrave, Murielle had long wept for her lover, and mourned him as one who was dead. Whether he had been slain outright, õr been simply but barbarously mutilated, she had no means of ascertaining, as the countess and her armed train had taken their departure from Edinburgh within an hour after the fatal conflict; and since then she had resided in Thrave, the most remote and strong of all her many fortresses.

Since that fatal day, Murielle had felt as if her little heart had been crushed by a hand of steel; while the society of the stern, malevolent, and gloomy Earl James, who was now lord of all their heritage, and as such assumed to be the master of *her* hand and destiny—a mastery in which he was joined by her proud, fiery, and, at times, cruel sister—made her long for a refuge among the Benedictine nuns of Lincluden; and she as often wished, in the sorrow and bitterness of her soul, that she were at rest among the graves of her forefathers, in Melrose or Dundrennan. She never saw the earl without experiencing a shudder of horror and aversion, for the memory of that terrible day in Edinburgh was ever before her; her lover's upturned face, with its despairing eyes, imploring pity from the fierce noble who smote him down with his bloody ghisarma, as he would have done a reptile.

In that age there were no newspapers; no posts or telegraphs; no books or printing, for it was twenty years before Caxton set his *first* types for Raoul le Fevre; thus the library of the great countess was limited to her missal, and a little whity-brown volume in which she engrossed recipes and so forth. Save a few games of hazard, there were no in-door amusements, or food for the mind. How wearily and drearily must the days have been passed by the dwellers in those old Scottish castles, secluded in roadless and mountain districts, when there was peace (which was seldom), and no fighting, burning, or hanging going on!

No tidings came from the court or capital to Thrave, save the strange and floating rumours brought by a passing harper on his way towards Ireland or the south; or by a cunning pardoner, travelling with his holy wares and relics to Tongland, Dundrennan, or St. Mary Isle; or by an armed mosstrooper, in his steel cap and vambraces; or a bein-bonnet laird, or gudeman (*i.e.* one who holds his land from a baron), on his Galloway cob, passing to or from the next burgh town, who, after bartering his beef, butter, and eggs, for a bilbo or suit of harness, tarried at lordly Thrave, belated or storm-stayed.

Men travelled little then by night in Scotland. Vast districts were almost roadless; and deep rivers, the fabled abode of the mischievous kelpie and dreadful water-horse, were bridgeless, and the fords were few and precarious. Lawless moss-troopers, broken men, and wandering gipsies rendered the paths insecure; nor were supernatural terrors wanting, in the shapes of bogles, spunkies, wraiths, and fairies, to render the ingle-lum of the nearest farm, the refectory of a monastery, or the hall of a baron or landholder an acceptable refuge after dark.

Of the old abbot of Tongland the inhabitants of Thrave had seen little. He had secluded himself in his abbey, which lay in a deep and woody hollow formed by the Dee, and adjoining the *clachan* which slopes down to the verge of the stream—for so they named their villages in Celtic Galloway. There he spent day after day entrenched among illuminated manuscripts and yellow parchments, searching, writing, quoting, collating, and preparing anew his application to Pope Eugene, that the Prince of Darkness might be forgiven, so that evil and discord in the world might cease for ever.

On the eccentric, but kind old abbot, Murielle rested all her hope for succour, information, advice, and assistance; but he failed to obtain authentic tidings of her lover's fate. Thus, in that great castle, which was crowded by armed men, she pined and sorrowed in secret, without a friend.

Meanwhile quantities of armour, helmets, corslets, spurs, and bridles, that came in hampers by ships from Holland, bundles of arrows and spears brought on horseback from Dumfries to the arsenal in the barbican, indicated the events that were on the tapis. Many couriers, such as Pompherston, Glendoning, Achanna, and Sir Alan Lauder, were dispatched in all directions under cloud of night, while others were arriving with secret parchments, and slips of paper concealed in the lining of their doublets, the sheaths of their daggers, and the tops of their gambadoes; missives from the turbulent John, earl of Ross, lord of the isles; from Sir Magnus Redmain, the English governor of Berwick; from Robert, the exiled and intriguing duke of Albany; from John Garm Stewart, of Athole; from Christian I., count of Oldenburg and king of Norway: and all these signs filled Murielle with anxiety and alarm, as they indicated the magnitude of the schemes and intrigues in which the fierce and subtle Earl James and her bold and ambitious sister were engaged, and the designs they were forming against the regent, the chancellor, the unfortunate people, and the young and innocent king.

CHAPTER XVII
THE BOWER CHAMBER

The summer brook flows in the bed
The winter torrent tore asunder;
The skylark's gentle wings are spread
Where walk'd the lightning and the thunder:
And thus you'll find the sternest soul,
The gayest tenderness concealing;
And minds that seem to mock control
Are order'd by some fairy feeling.
Poems by Thomas Davis.

It was, as related, a summer noon.

Earl James of Douglas, whilom of Abercorn and Avondale, still in half rebellion against a king and court from both of which he kept sullenly aloof, was hawking on the bank of the Carlinwark Loch, with Sir Alan Lauder, Achanna, and other friends, while the countess was in her bower-chamber with Murielle and other ladies of her household.

As a reward for his services, Achanna, that worthy Scottish liberal and utilitarian of the year of grace 1441, had received a purse of gold from the chancellor, and from Abercorn the office of seneschal of Thrave. Like many of his countrymen in more modern times, master James Achanna was a noisy professor of religion, and never missed a mass or service of his church; he wore an enormous rosary, and crossed himself at least a hundred times daily when any one was present. Scotland has always been peculiarly unfortunate in producing such pretenders; and doubtless, had James Achanna lived now, the same cunning and coldness of heart, the same selfishness of purpose and anti-nationality which he possessed, would have brought him fortune, place, or power, political, and assuredly provincial fame; but, under James II., he was merely a hireling swordsman, a smooth-tongued intriguer, and occasionally a "rowdy" in a suit of armour.

The windows of the bower chamber were open, and afforded an ample view of the far-stretching pastoral landscape, through which the Dee, between banks shrouded by groves of beech and willow, the fragrant hawthorn, or those old oaks which, ages ago, had echoed to the horn of the great crusader, Alan, lord of Galloway, wound to pour its waters in the Solway Firth. Through the deep and arched embayments in the old castle wall, the summer sunshine shed a flood of radiance upon the arched necks, the white hands, and glossy tresses of the group of handsome girls who drew their tabourettes around the chair of the Countess Margaret, who had just entered; for, with few exceptions, these damoiselles in silk and costly attire were the same who had attended her on that unhappy visit to Edinburgh in the November of 1440.

They were all the daughters of barons and knights—Maud Douglas of Pompherston, a lovely girl with black hair, dark hazel eyes, and a queenly bearing; Mariota Douglas of Glendoning, whose auburn hair won her the name of the *Caillean Rua* among the Galwegians; Lady Jean of the Cairnglas, and the three daughters of Sir Alan of the Bass, all lassies with "lint white locks," and others, to the number of twelve, were plying their needles busily; but Murielle sat apart, and, with her cheek resting on the palm of her hand, gazed listlessly upon the hazy landscape that spread in the summer sunshine far away from below the castle wall.

The work on which those ladies were busy was one of those huge pieces of tapestry in the manufacture of which the fair ones of those days delighted, and, when completed, it was to be a donation to the abbot of Tongland on New Year's Day, 1442, as it represented the life and miracles of St. Bryde (or Bridget), the patron of the house of Douglas; and this great web spread over all the knees and daintily-slippered feet of the fair workers, as it fell in waves along the floor of polished oak.

Therein their needles had depicted the saint in her little cell under a large oak at Kildara, in Munster, where the wild ducks that swam in the Bog of Allen and the birds that flew over the Curragh, alike obeyed her voice, and went and came at her command; and there, too, was shown how, at her desire, the milk of the cows on the Wicklow hills became butter, and how, when she prayed, it was multiplied threefold for the use of the poor; and other miracles long since forgotten.

This year had been memorable for prodigies. On the 17th of March, says Sir James Balfour, there appeared "three suns in the firmament at the noontyde of the day; and in Auguste a fearfull comett, having a crowned sword hanging from it." Where one sun is seldom seen, *three* must have produced an unusual effect; so these and similar matters formed the staple topics for discussion among the ladies of the countess, who unanimously came to the conclusion that "something terrible and startling would certainly ensue; but *what* that might be none could say—a murrain among the cattle, a famine in the Merse, a royal raid into Galloway, an invasion by the English—perhaps the death of the chancellor!"

"The last is not likely," said Maud of Pompherston, throwing back her heavy black braided hair behind the whitest and smallest of ears.

"Why?" asked all.

"I mean, if the tidings be true which my father heard yesterday at the cross of Dumfries."

"What did he hear?" asked the countess sharply, while the workers paused, and all their eyes were bent on Maud.

"That the heralds had proclaimed at the crosses of Edinburgh, Stirling, and Scone, that—that the king—"

The poor girl hesitated, for the bold flashing eye of the countess fell darkly on her, and its expression at times was rather bewildering.

"A boy of thirteen years," said Margaret bitterly. "Well, that the king——"

"Has been pleased——"

"Deluded, you mean."

"To create the chancellor Lord Crichton of Crichton in Lothian. Rumour added that his youngest son, George, would soon be made earl of Caithness, in place of the forfeited Earl Alan, who was killed ten years ago at the battle of Inverlochie."

"Anything more?" asked Margaret, beating the floor with her foot.

"The regent is to be Lord Livingstone of Callendar."

"Did the heralds not add that he granted them a coat of augmentation to their arms?" said Margaret, with hate in her eye, and the smile of a devil on her lovely lip;—"a headsman's axe and block, all bloody and proper! Well, well; so be it. We'll powder these new-fangled coronets with tears and the dust of death ere another yule be past—please Heaven, we shall!"

"'Tis said, too, that the king is about to be married to a fair lady of Flanders."

"This child!—who—who?" asked the ladies together.

"I wot not," said Maud; and the girls laughed loudly.

"Little Maggie Lauder of the Bass would suit him better, in years at least," said the countess, as she caressed the lint white locks of Sir Alan's youngest daughter, a girl of some nine years or so. "In sooth, cousin, you have a rare stock of news."

"Countess, I have more still."

"More?"

"The heritable sheriff of Perth, Sir William Ruthven of that ilk, accompanied by a party of the king's guard, have marched into Athole, and there captured John Gorm Stewart."

"A friend and ally of my husband, who had a message from him not ten days ago—he captured him, say you?"

"Ay, and slew him."

"John of Athole slain?"

"Yes, on the north Inch of Perth, with thirty of his followers; but Ruthven was also killed, and MacLellan and Gray, the commanders of the King's Guard, were wounded."

"The fools! to fight each other, when both were allies of ours; for this sheriff of Perth has a daughter wedded to George Douglas, of Leswalt, here in Galloway. So Gray was wounded—and the jesting MacLellan, too?"

On first hearing these names, the hitherto listless Murielle started, and turned to Maud Douglas; but feared to ask the question that seemed to burn her tongue.

"Is aught wrong, sister, that you start thus?" asked Margaret, half contemptuously.

"No—why do you ask?" said Murielle timidly.

"I thought a gnat had stung you."

"Oh, it was Andrew Gray, of Balgarno, who was wounded," said Maud good-naturedly, as she turned in haste to Murielle, whose anxiety she wished to relieve.

"Was your father sure of this?" asked the countess.

"The Provost of Dumfries had the surest tidings."

Margaret smiled bitterly at her pale sister.

"Alas!" thought the latter, in her heart, "*he* is not spoken of. Oh, can he be dead, that others have led where he was wont to lead?"

After a pause,

"Murielle," said the countess, with some asperity, "if you will not work with us, take your harp, and sing. Occupation will at times divert the mind, even from its most bitter thoughts. Please to give us the ballad of 'Sir Hugh le Blonde.'"

The ladies urged her to do so, but she replied briefly and wearily,—

"Under favour, I cannot sing."

"You cannot sing?" reiterated the countess, pausing in her work, and gazing at Murielle with her full black eyes, above which hung the wavy fringe of her absurdly lofty horned head-dress.

"I cannot sing that ballad—at least, just now."

"And wherefore?"

"I have forgotten it," said she, turning to the window.

"Do you remember when last you sang it?" asked Maud Douglas kindly, in a low voice.

"Oh yes, dear Maud," said Murielle, as her soft eyes filled with tears at the recollection of that night in the house of the abbot at Edinburgh, where—outwardly, at least—they all seemed so happy, and where her lover hung over her, as she played and sang *for him*, and him only.

The impetuous young countess, a little despot in her own household, grew weary of her sister's silence and reserve, for Murielle's attachment was no secret to the family; she tossed aside the tapestry, and desired Mariota, the *Caillean Rua*, to summon her pages and a musician, that they might dance and practise the *pavan*, which was a slow and stately measure then in fashion, and which took its name from the peacock, because it was danced by knights in their mantles and ladies in their trains; but Murielle said gently, but firmly, as she withdrew to a corbelled stone balcony, upon which the windows of the bower-chamber opened,—

"Excuse me, dear Maggie, I pray you; but I am not in the mood either to dance or sing."

Irritated still more by this, Margaret followed, and found her with her face bowed upon the parapet, and weeping bitterly.

CHAPTER XVIII
THE BALCONY

The nymph must lose her female friend,
If more admired than she;
But where will fierce contention end,
If flowers can disagree?—Cowper.

"Is it so with you?" said the countess, roughly grasping her arm; "is it so—still mourning for that scurvy captain of the king's morris-pikes?"

"Morris-pikes! Oh, sister, can you compare to mummers, the men who formed the van at Piperden?"

"Ay, where a Douglas routed Piercy—a service, like others, committed to oblivion now," was the bitter response.

Murielle wept in silence, while her haughty sister continued to regard her with an expression in her eyes very much akin to disdain.

The poor girl had frequently been fretted and galled by hearing a much-loved name—alas! it might only be a much-revered *memory*—reviled; yet she bore it meekly, hoping daily for a change. But weeks became months, and months became seasons, yet no change came in the bearing of her sister; which, always haughty, turned at times violent and tempestuous.

The proud Margaret felt that she had done a wrong action by her second espousal, which had raised doubts in her mind that even the papal dispensation might fail to dispel; and while she writhed under this conviction, and longed for vengeance on the slayers of that handsome lover and boy-husband—whom she secretly mourned, even when in the arms of the subtle Earl James, she felt—she knew not why—irritated, and at times exasperated, by the meek, quiet, and passive tenor of Murielle's existence.

"Tears still," she resumed, "always tears; but beware how the earl finds you thus."

"Oh, Margaret, I have studied to conceal my living sorrow from him—from you—from all."

"But in vain, for *all* have seen it. There is not a trencher-boy in the kitchen, or a groom in the stables, but knows of it as well as I do."

"Have you never considered, sister, what a terrible thing it is to have to forget—to strive at crushing all memory of the past—all hope for the future; to rend from the heart a love it has cherished for years?"

"Years!" reiterated Margaret, with an angry laugh; "you are but eighteen, Murielle."

"And you not twenty."

"Yet I have wept for a dead husband."

"And been consoled," was the unwise reply.

Margaret's cheek grew white with suppressed passion at the inference which might be drawn from this casual remark; but she said, emphatically, —

"Enough of this; my husband, to strengthen his house, has resolved that you shall become the bride of one who is second to none in Scotland; and he has sworn it on the cross of his sword, by God and St. Bryde, that it shall be so, even should he chain you to the altar-steps, in Tongland Abbey kirk."

"Oh, Maggie," said Murielle, in a piercing voice, "do not talk to me thus. I have given my heart into the keeping of Patrick Gray, and death itself cannot restore it to me, or rend it from him. Trustingly I gave it, dear sister, yonder—yonder, at the three auld thorns of the Carlinwark; so be merciful to me, for no better, fonder, or purer love than his, was ever offered up to woman."

"A king's minion!" said the countess, spitefully; "but it is the will of God you shall never be this."

"Never! Say not so; it sounds like a prophecy. Never— —"

"But as the earl, my husband, has sworn— —"

"Oh, impiety!"

"The bride of a nobler and better."

"A better, say you?" exclaimed Murielle, with an angry laugh.

"Dispute it if you can—Robert, duke of Albany."

"An outlawed traitor," said Murielle, warming in her turn; "is this your husband's scheme?"

"Yes, a scheme formed for your honour."

"It is a bold one."

"Most of his schemes are so," replied Margaret, quietly.

"Duke Robert is contracted to a daughter of Charles VII. of France," said Murielle, taking courage.

"The same power that permitted *my* second marriage, can annul his contract, and give him back his troth, from Mademoiselle Radegonde."

"Well, rather than *break* mine, and be his bride, sister, you shall see me stretched in Tongland Abbey kirk, as cold as the marble tombs that lie there!"

"We shall see," replied Margaret, biting her cherry-like nether lip, and stamping her foot in growing wrath; but Murielle threw her white arms round her neck, and said plaintively,—

"You do not, you cannot mean all you say, Maggie. Ah, do not scold, when you should guide and aid me."

"Is it not my desire to see you happy?"

"Yes," sobbed Murielle; "I know, I hope that it is."

"And my husband's?"

"My kinsman, the earl, is a fearsome man!" said Murielle, with an ill-repressed shudder.

"Have I not striven for years to be your guide, your friend, your comforter, and now——"

"You would undo all the past, by making me the wife of the exiled Albany, that your husband's terrible aims and ends may be furthered, his feudal power and splendour increased."

"By raising you, perhaps, to"—the countess paused—"to a throne, little fool!"

"A throne?" reiterated Murielle, in absolute bewilderment.

"Yes, a throne," said Margaret, in a low voice, as she bent her black flashing eyes close to her startled sister's face; "where can all this leaguing and combination with Henry of England, Christian of Oldenburg, John of the Isles, and with so many discontented barons, end, but in the destruction of Livingstone, of Crichton, and of that boy-king, in whose name they slew the earl of Douglas?"

"Saint Mary keep us, sister; but this is murder, treason, regicide!" said Murielle, in terror and incredulity.

"I am speaking in our castle of Thrave," said the countess, significantly, as she patted the strong rampart with her white jewelled hand; "but I am unwise in talking to you of schemes, the magnitude of which you cannot comprehend, and the daring of which appals you."

"Oh, Maggie, all this can end but in one way."

"How?"

"Destruction, forfeiture, and death!"

"We shall see," replied the countess, calmly smoothing back her silky hair; "but to resume about this Patrick Gray—*who* is he, that he should aspire to love my sister, the daughter of a line of powerful earls?"

"He is a gentleman of stainless reputation, the trusted subject of the late king and of his son; a loyal soldier, whom, if I choose, I might marry to-morrow, and defy you all!" said Murielle, angrily.

Margaret now laughed in good earnest at her sister.

"Defy us?" she exclaimed; "lassie, you have gone crazy! I speak not of Ormond, of Pompherston, of Glendoning; but know you not that the smallest laird who bears our name could muster lances enough to harry his father's nest at Foulis, level his tower to the ground-stone, and swing his whole generation on the nearest tree?"

Murielle knew fully the truth of this, but she felt an increasing emotion of anger at the injustice and control to which she was so bluntly subjected, and now her haughty sister spoke again.

"Bear this in mind, that thrice has Earl James sworn by his most sacred oath, God, and his father's bones 'that our heather lintie, Murielle, shall be the bride of Albany, and sib to the throne, if not one day *upon* it;' so cease to think more of this lover of yours, who, by the bye, I believe, once loved *me*."

"Loved you!" exclaimed Murielle, in a breathless voice; "*you*, Margaret?"

"Yes," continued the imperious beauty, with confidence.

"He ever admired you, and as *my* sister, felt a friendship for you; but be assured that his dear heart never wandered from me," was the equally confident reply.

"You are a child!" retorted the countess.

"Perhaps I am, to endure all this petty tyranny; but a day may come—there are times when even a poor worm may turn."

"But think no more of him, I command you, for he is better as he is, dead, than living to be the rival of Robert, duke of Albany."

"Do not tell me, sister, that he was slain," said Murielle, in an imploring voice, while, her tears again fell fast; "he is not dead. I know that he is *not* dead!"

"You *know*?" said Margaret, changing colour.

"Yes."

"Indeed—how?"

"Because I am living still!" replied Murielle, with divine confidence and hope.

CHAPTER XIX
A FEUDAL LORD

And joy is mine
When the strong castles besieged shake,
And walls uprooted, totter and quake,
And I see the foemen join,
On the moated shore all compass'd round
With palisade and guarded mound.
Lays of the Minnesingers.

The result of this conversation, the wild and daring schemes of ambition and revenge it unfolded,—schemes of which she was to be made the tool and the victim, filled Murielle with alarm, and made her more than ever resolve to seek refuge in a convent; but an escape from the guarded castle of Thrave was not a matter to be easily accomplished, as its garrison, formed of the earl's most faithful "retainers, was (as we are told in the third of volume of 'Caledonia'), never less than *one thousand armed men.*"

A recent writer says, "in Scotland, but a hundred years ago, the head of a family was paramount, and household discipline was wielded without mercy." If such was the case a hundred years ago, it was exercised with greater rigour in the days of the second James.

So poor little Murielle found Thrave with all its splendour, a veritable prison, and the earl, her brother-in-law, a haughty and exacting tyrant.

Thrave, his greatest stronghold, was built upon an island of twenty acres in extent, formed by the rough and rapid Dee, situated about ten miles above its estuary, and thirty from its source, which is among the wooded hills of Minnigaff.

There on that islet the crusader Alan IV., lord of Galloway and constable of Scotland, had a fortress, and thereon, in after times, the Black Knight of Liddesdale, the comrade of Wallace and Bruce, reared the present castle of Thrave, a vast pile, the donjon of which is yet seventy feet in height, with walls eight feet in thickness, built of common stone from the adjacent moors.

The first story of this great pile consisted of the larder, the arsenals, and the dungeon, where many a chained wretch has wept during the hours that intervened between time and eternity.

In the second story were the apartments of the men-at-arms, the warders, grooms, and pages.

The third contained the apartments of the baron, his family, their guests, and the ladies' bower-chamber, with one apartment long secluded, that in which Archibald, earl of Douglas and lord of Galloway,—he whose second son won by his valour the titles of duke of Spruce and prince of Dantzig, died on the 3rd of February, 1400. Small Gothic windows gave light to these upper chambers, and narrow slits and loopholes to the lower.

A square barbican and four round flanking towers, with a deep fosse and drawbridge, formed the external barrier. After passing these, the only entrance to the keep was by a door placed so high in the wall that it opened on the *second* floor, and this strange mode of access was farther secured by a small portcullis, grooved into the solid stone, the work of "the Brawny MacKim," the hereditary smith of the family.

To victual this stronghold each of the twenty-eight parishes which form the stewardry of Kirkcudbright had to contribute a *Lardner-mart-cow* at Martinmas, for winter provisions; and the last attempt to levy these twenty-eight cattle was made in 1747, by William Maxwell, of Nithsdale.

In the front wall of the great tower, and immediately above the gateway, which bore all the armorial achievements of the proud and lordly owners, there still projects a large granite block, named the *gallows knob*, or hanging-stone, which, in the olden time, was seldom without its *tassel*, as the moss-troopers phrased it.

"Lest this barbarous emblem of feudal power should be minus its usual decoration," says a local historian, "when putrefaction became offensive before the corpse was cut down, if a malefactor was not in custody to be tucked up, it was replenished by some unoffending vassal. The charnel into which these victims were thrown is to this day named the 'gallows slot,' and notwithstanding the time that has elapsed since the downfall of the house of Douglas in Galloway, human bones in abundance were turned up when the present highway was made through it there in the year 1800."

Such was the grim feudal dwelling where now Murielle Douglas found herself an inmate,—almost a prisoner,—foredoomed to be the tool, perhaps the victim, of the dark plots and of the ambition and pride of its lord and owner, whose general character the following anecdote will amply illustrate.

As Steward of Kirkcudbright and Lord Warden of the Western Marches, he ordered James Achanna, with a strong and well-armed band, to apprehend Sir Herbert Herries of Terregles, a gentleman of ancient family, who had large possessions in the stewardry, and bring him prisoner to

Thrave, despite the tears of his daughter, Lady Maxwell, of Carlaveroc, and the entreaties of his youngest son, who was rector of Kirkpatrick.

He was oddly charged with "daring to recover a portion of his *own* property, which had been appropriated by Achanna and other lawless followers of the house of Douglas, and further, of resisting them in arms."

Sir Herbert was a man of high courage and probity, who had given himself as a hostage to England for the ransom of James I. He had been a commissioner for the trial of Murdoch, duke of Albany, father of that Duke Robert who was now the *bête noir* of Murielle; and he had lately been one of the ambassadors who had gone to France to arrange the marriage of the gentle and unfortunate Margaret of Scotland with the Dauphin, afterwards Louis XI, the French Nero, of terrible memory.

When brought before Douglas, in the hall, he was surveyed with stern and haughty malevolence.

"Your little blockhouse of Terregles," said the earl, mockingly, as he lounged in his canopied chair, "in common with other fortlets of the petty barons of Galloway, is only occasionally decked with a dangling villain, whereas our gallows knob of Thrave has not been without *a tassel for fifty years*, and so it shall be while Dalbeattie wood grows and the Urr water runs!"

"True," replied Terregles; "and one who was my henchman, my foster-brother, and my most faithful friend, taken by your ruthless wretch Achanna, is hanging there at this moment."

"And having hung the usual time, he shall now be removed to make way for his master."

"Earl Douglas, you dare not!" exclaimed Sir Herbert, starting forward.

"Dare not! ha! ha! and why?"

"I am the king's liege man, and a baron of parliament!"

"Is that all you can urge?" asked Douglas, still mocking.

"No— —"

"What more?"

"Even now a royal herald is at the gate, with an express order for my release."

"Mahoun! its coming has sealed your doom. Achanna, tear off his ruff, and replace it with a hempen cravat," was the stern order of Douglas; so the unfortunate Sir Herbert was instantly hanged in his armour from the gallows knob, while the king's herald was ignominiously expelled.

Yet this fierce and unscrupulous lord paid large sums to the Church for masses for the souls of his ancestors, and had periodical fits of prayer and fasting, which were very troublesome, alike to his cooks and hungry retainers. At times he trembled for bad news if he saw a crow in his path, and crossed himself if he saw the new moon for the first time through a window. He smeared himself, like Achanna, with ashes on Ash Wednesday, and ate hot cross-buns with due reverence on Good Friday; and to him the abbot of Tongland, as keeper of the avenue to heaven, or the *other* place, was alternately a demigod to worship or a bugbear to avoid. Yet, withal, he had connived with Crichton and the regent in the destruction of his kinsmen, and wedded the wealthy widow of Earl William, but consoled himself with the solemn dispensation of Pope Eugene IV., who, however, was then *deposed* by the Council of Basle.

CHAPTER XX
THE MISSION

Of this great voyage which you undertake,
Much by his skill and much by my advice
Hath he foreknown, and welcome for my sake
You both shall be, the man is kind and wise.
Fairfax's Tasso.

Though left by the Douglases as dead upon the street, Sir Patrick Gray survived the horrors of the tumult at the Abbot's Gate; and though covered with severe wounds, inflicted by swords, daggers, and pikes, he grew well and hale again; but only after a year of suffering, convalescence, and confinement to a sick chamber, during which his fiery and energetic spirit writhed in inactivity—for there are some men whom it is alike difficult to subdue or kill.

Death long disputed with life and youth for the victim; but men did not die easily in these old times of brawl and battle; yet he had upon his person, as the abbot of Tongland records, "three and twentye woundis," and recovered them all.

"Men," says some one, "are unaware what toil, pain, or suffering they are capable of until they have been put to the test."

The wound inflicted by the ghisarma of Earl James was not his least annoyance, as it had laid open both cheeks; thus a cicatrized slash traversed his face, which so completely altered its expression, that after a little difference in the trimming of his hair and beard, few would have recognized him; but the lady of the chancellor, like all the thrifty dames of those turbulent and homely days, was a famous leech, and by the lotions and cosmetics she prepared for him, and applied daily with her own hands, was not without hope that within "a year and a day, or perhaps within a few months more," it would be obliterated; and all the young ladies about the young king's court, even the charming princesses his sisters, had an interest in this process, and the progress of his recovery, for the Captain of the Guard was one of the handsomest men of the time, and a favourite with them all.

He had been conveyed to the chancellor's apartments in St. Margaret's Tower, within the castle of Edinburgh, and there for many months he had been tended with every care, till the period at which we now return to him.

The wily chancellor was not unjust. He felt that Sir Patrick Gray had suffered much in the king's service; loss of health, almost of life, and the loss perhaps of a beautiful mistress, were hard things to encounter, for he knew that the bloody events of the 23rd and 24th of November had opened up an impassable chasm between Gray and the family of Douglas.

Crichton loved all who loved the king, and this was the great tie between him and Gray, whose friendship he strove sedulously to cultivate and preserve, though the more open soldier detested the mode by which the regent and chancellor had striven, so futilely, to crush the mighty house of Douglas.

Gray's weak state after his many wounds, combined with his grief, at what he deemed the loss for ever of Murielle, affected him so much, that during the severe winter of 1440 he nearly sank under his sufferings. He rallied, however, by youth and inborn strength, though good St. Giles, of Edinburgh, to whose altar, in the spirit of the times, he devoted several pounds of wax and silver, got the whole credit of the change.

Lady Agnes of Crichton and the courtiers said he was "dying of love." The chancellor could believe in a stout man-at-arms dying of a slash from Earl James's battle-axe, but *not* of love for Murielle, his kinswoman, however beautiful and gentle she might be; so he only smiled at their surmises, and when Gray was able to ride a little every day on a quiet horse led by his page, Crichton resolved to find him some active employment so soon as he was stronger.

So Gray, as we have said, writhed in inactivity when his friends and kinsmen, MacLellan and Andrew Gray, of Balgarno, had marched from Stirling to Athole to capture the great freebooter, John Gorm Stewart. He had heard from Andrew Gray of the conflict on the north Inch of Perth, where the sheriff had been cloven down by the two-handed sword of Stewart, who, in turn, had been slain by MacLellan, but not until he had so severely wounded the latter, that he had been compelled to return for a time to his castle of Raeberry, on the shore of the Solway Firth.

And during this long period of seclusion and inactivity Gray had longed with all a lover's restless longing for some tidings of Murielle; but those about the chancellor were either unwilling or unable to afford him any.

So the time rolled wearily on.

One afternoon he was sitting dreamily in the recess of a window of St. Margaret's Tower, which stood upon the western verge of the castle rock, but was demolished during the long siege of 1573.

It was a somewhat gloomy apartment (it was *then* three hundred and eighty years old), built in the Saxon style, with grotesquely-carved heads and zig-zag mouldings round the arches, and hung with long russet-coloured tapestry, which had been worked by the hands of Annabella, the queen of Robert III., to hide the bare, rough walls. This tapestry was old now; its tenter-hooks were rusty, and it swayed in the currents of wind, which passed through the fireplace, on the shelf of which, in memory of the good queen who once dwelt there, was inscribed the pious request, —

Sancta Margarita, ora pro nobis.

Beneath the windows was the verdant slope whereon three mounds, of solemn aspect, were traceable. The coarse dog-grass, the white gowan, and pink witch-thimbles (or foxglove), grew there in rank luxuriance now, and as they swayed in the evening wind, were all that marked where lay the three victims of that terrible vigil of St. Catharine.

The autumnal sun was sinking. The vast and fertile plain of wood and wold which stretches from the foot of the castle rock for fifty miles to the westward, was steeped in warm light; and the sun's diverging rays of ruddy gold, as he sank behind the rugged ridges of Corstorphine, filled all the western sky with a shining glory, which threw forward, in strong, black outline, the intervening woods and rocks, hills and knolls.

Gray's eyes were apparently fixed upon the dark mountains and the beautiful plain, all brightness and fertility; but they dwelt on vacancy, for he saw, instead, a graceful head, with a mass of wavy hair, long-lashed, gentle eyes, of a violet blue, a soft face, with a brilliant complexion, and a slightly rose-tinted cheek.

There was a sound in his ear too.

It was the voice of Murielle, conjured up with all a lover's memory in an age of poetry, romance, and enthusiasm, when knightly faith and purity, and even somewhat of fading chivalry, were lingering in the northern land.

A hand was laid on his shoulder; he started, and on turning met the keen eyes, the thoughtful face, and tall thin figure of the chancellor, who was clad in his fur-trimmed gown, which was girt at the waist by an embroidered girdle, whereat hung, as usual, his tablets, pouch, and dagger.

"You did not hear the servitor announce me, Sir Patrick," said he; "were you dreaming of Elf-land, or some far-off day of happiness?"

"Your pardon!—though not much given to flights of fancy," replied Sir Patrick, starting, "I *was* in a dreamy mood."

"Nay, do not rise, but rest—and say how fare you,"

"Ill enough, my lord," replied the captain, passing a thin wan hand across his pale brow with a troubled air; "ill enough, and weary too."

"In body?"

"Yes—and in spirit."

"That is a matter beyond the skill of such a leech even as my good wife Agnes."

"Her kindness and care are only equalled by my gratitude; and see," added Sir Patrick, smiling, "she has hung at my neck her own miraculous pomander-ball, lest the plague that rages now in Fife might here infect me. But I am weary of resting and of idleness; yet alas! and alake! Sir William, I fear me this arm will never curb a horse's head again; and as for handling my sword, a child might twitch it from me at the third pass! Here an arrow-head was wedged between the bones of the right forearm; but I gave the archer a notch on the knuckles that will mar his shooting for life."

"Well, there is some comfort in that," replied the chancellor, "and greater had there been, could you have notched the head of Abercorn, or Douglas as he is entitled now."

A hectic flush crossed the face of Sir Patrick, who replied, huskily: "After what had taken place on the preceding day, I would not have struck a blow at *her* kinsman, even to save my life!"

"After *what* had taken place?" reiterated the chancellor, gloomily.

"Ay, on the vigil of St. Catharine," continued Gray with firmness, and something of reproach in his tone.

"Enough of that," said the other, hastily, as he passed his handkerchief over his brow, and replaced it in his embroidered pouch; "I have other things to speak of than those which are past and beyond all human remedy. But was it not a cruel act and merciless deed in Earl James to smite down a poor gentleman, who clung to him, bleeding, faint, and despairing——"

"It matters not, Sir William—it matters not; I have made up my mind to leave Scotland."

"Indeed!" exclaimed Crichton, with astonishment.

"For some—it may be for many, many years,—perchance I may return no more."

"How—what mean you?"

"That Charles VII. of France wants soldiers to aid him in his wars against the English and Burgundians, and I shall seek his camp for knight-service; or it may be, that I shall go further off, to the distant East, where the Greek empire, under the Emperor Constantine, is now threatened by the accursed pagans of the Sultan Mahomet, and where brave hearts and sharp swords are wanted to defend Christian women and the altars of God from desecration; and so there are times, chancellor, when I think I shall even find a stranger's grave on the banks of the Bosphorus."

The chancellor, who had no wish that the king should lose so faithful and valiant a soldier as Sir Patrick Gray, whom he knew to be resolute, and somewhat obstinate in purpose, listened to this bitter outburst with some concern; but, patting him on the shoulder as he might have done a restive horse, he replied, smiling, "Leave Greek and Turk to fight their own battles; abide you by your king; and when the time comes, as come it must, let your grave be dug, not in the land of the sun-burned and God-abandoned pagans, but in the old kirk of Foulis, where your Scottish forefathers lie. Moreover, can it be, that you have forgotten your promise to King James—that you would be a faithful friend and mentor to his son?"

"True—true—I have," replied Gray, biting his nether lip till the wound in his face made him wince; "but you know, chancellor, that I am pledged to Murielle Douglas, and that I cannot bide in Scotland without her."

"I may find a way to let you leave it, and yet preserve your promise to King James,—a way that shall suit your restless humour; but speak no more to me of Murielle Douglas," said the chancellor, as his brows knit and his eyes loured. "Listen: I have other views for you; it may be a royal alliance itself."

"Royal?" was the perplexed reiteration.

"Yes."

Here Sir Patrick Gray, who knew that he was really loved by this unscrupulous statesman, gazed at him with a curiously-mingled expression of surprise, amusement, and grim disdain; but being a poor soldier and loyal gentleman, with no heritage but his sword and spurs, he felt himself compelled to listen, though almost degraded by having to do so.

"You are aware, Sir Patrick, that the king has several fair sisters?" began the chancellor.

Sir Patrick bowed.

"Each is lovely, though still in girlhood—and, under favour, lovelier, it may be, than the little lady who dwells among the king's rebels in Thrave—for rebels are they to the heart's-core, though not yet in arms."

Gray's pale face flushed, and for a moment the scar upon his face grew nearly black; but he merely said, "Well;" and the chancellor, while playing with his pouch and dagger, resumed, in an easy conversational tone.

"All the crown-lands, the king's rents, castles, baronies, mills, mails, and fishings, cannot find dowers royal enough of these six dames, his sisters, at present. Do you understand me?"

"Not exactly. You must be more plain, my lord chancellor."

"'Tis not the first time that a king's daughter has wedded a simple knight."

"In old ballads, Sir William; and I would be a *simple* knight indeed to cast my eyes so high."

"The queen-mother is now the wife of the Black Knight of Lorn," said Crichton, with the air of one who finds a convincing argument.

"But he is a different man from the poor captain of the king's paid pikemen! St. Mary! a sorry figure would I cut, riding up to my father's tower-gate, with my princess behind me on a pillion, and settling there to become a scrape-trencher, while she assisted my mother in brewhouse and bakery! Take heed, chancellor; I need not be dazzled thus, to keep me faithful to my king. So, enough of this! I am not ignorant that all these princesses are promised, not to simple knights, but to foreign princes."

"Not *all*," said the chancellor, with an air of annoyance; "the Princess Margaret is, I know, contracted to Louis, the dauphin of France."

"A troublesome brother-in-law he might prove to the younger son of the laird of Foulis," replied Gray, laughing outright.

"The Lady Elizabeth——"

"Is contracted to the duke of Brittany; and in a month Eleonora will be the bride of Sigismund le Debonnair, archduke of Austria, and duke of all the dukes in Almaynie; while the Lady Mary will be wedded to the lord of Campvere."

"I knew not that you were so well versed in state secrets," said the chancellor coldly, with an affected smile.

"You forget, my dear Sir William, that your good lady has been my nurse."

"There is the Lady Annabelle."

"A child," said Sir Patrick, laughing louder to conceal the annoyance that rankled in his heart; "oh! oh! Sir William, I should have to wait ten years at least till my wife grew up. Dost take me for a fool, a very mooncalf, though I have listened to you? But to the point: say what service you seek of me, as I have made up my mind to leave Scotland in a month. Believe me, I need no bribe for faith and service to my king; and, as to Murielle Douglas, the wealth of Prester John of the Indies, if such a man there be, with the love of an empress, would not win me from her, though it may be that, with this gash on my face, she—she might shrink from me now."

"Did I not say that I might suit your humour and also serve the king?" asked the chancellor.

"How?"

"Hearken," said Crichton, placing a hand on the arm of Gray.

"Say on," said the latter impatiently.

"In two years from this, the king will take upon himself the government of the nation, and I shall retire me to my old castle of Crichton, in the Glen of Tync, beyond the Esk, and spend there my latter days in peace."

"The government—in 1444—this boy?"

"The boy will then be fifteen, and he is a manly boy withal. The time is coming when he must be contracted to a foreign princess, and, through the lord of Campvere, Duke Arnold of Gueldreland has made overtures on the part of his daughter Mary, now in her ninth year. To these overtures the regent and myself, with the consent of the lords of council, have thought it meet to respond, and you shall bear our missives to the duke, who is now either in Gueldreland, in Brabant, or Burgundy, I know not which; and in due time I, with a fitting train, will set out for his capital. But promise me to be secret as you are faithful in this matter, and remember it is in the service of *the king.*"

"In this embassy I promise to do all that may become a loyal man—save wed the Lady Mary of Gueldres herself; for, after all you have proposed, by the mass! I knew not where your generosity might end."

"Good!" replied Crichton. "To-night I ride for Stirling, to see the regent and Queen Jane; when I return, you shall have your sealed letters of credence, and Dirltoun the treasurer shall pave the way with gold."

The chancellor shook his hand with kindness, and retired, leaving the frank and single-hearted soldier to consider the journey before him; the yet greater separation by land, water, and time, it would make between himself and Murielle, and also to surmise whether the proposal merely veiled some deeper and more distant object; for, since that fatal 24th of November, Gray had ever a doubt of the regent, the chancellor, and their projects.

"He overshot the butt—his cunning hath outdone itself," muttered Gray. "Did he not think a ward of the crown would content the king's poor soldier for a bride? but a princess—ha! ha!" And he uttered a merry but scornful laugh.

As the twilight deepened, and the shores of the Forth blended in the distance with its darkening waters, he thought over all that had passed; but was not left long to his own reflections, for a grey-bearded pikeman of his guard drew back the moth-eaten arras, and announced his kinsman, Sir Thomas MacLellan, of Bombie.

CHAPTER XXI
GRAY'S DEPARTURE

Awake, awake! lover, I bring, I bring
Most gladsome news, that blissful are and sure
Of thy comfort; now laugh, and play, and sing.
Full soon thou shalt achieve thine adventure,
For in the heaven decretit is thy cure.
Remains of James I. of Scotland.

"Welcome, my good and merry friend!" exclaimed Gray, starting forward to greet him;—"lights, wine, and a jolly greybeard of usquebaugh," he added to his servant;—"and you have returned."

"'Tis but an hour since I alighted at an hostelry, with two hackneys, a sumpter-nag, and my best suit of armour, packed on the saddle of my black horse—you remember it—with the curtal tail."

"Your wounds——"

"Are well and whole, though, sooth to say, the two-handed whinger of John Gorm was somewhat heavy for one's patience, and cut through my chain-shirt and jack-wambeson, as if they had been pie-crust. But I am recovered now. The pure breeze that comes over the broad Solway and whistles round the turrets of old Raeberry has made me a hale man again."

"Would that I could say the same," sighed Gray.

"That slash on the face——"

"Won't please a woman's eye now, I fear me."

"But to wed one who objected thereto would be to throw one's ace in the game of matrimony," replied MacLellan, tossing upon a settle his sword, jewelled dagger, and laced mantle; "yes—even were she a princess."

"Soho, man! talk not of princesses—I have just had my choice of six."

"Six!—daughters of the queen of Elphen?"

"Nay, six of flesh and blood, and declined them all," said Gray, laughing.

"What riddle is this?—or has a fairy indeed been with you?"

"You shall hear."

Lights had now been brought, and the candles, in the brass sconces which hung on the tapestried wall, cast lines of steady radiance across the otherwise gloomy old chamber. The arras was drawn across the windows, in the gratings of which, as well as through the battlement of the tower overhead, the wind was whistling. Red and white wine, in flasks of Venetian silver, glittered on the table; and to these was added usquebaugh, in one of those stone jars which came from Flanders, and had in front a bearded mask; whence the Scottish name of "greybeard" for a whisky-jar to this day.

The friends drew their seats close to the table.

MacLellan carefully wiped the dew from his sword, a short weapon, the steel of which was embrowned—a fancy of the time (whence, perhaps, the "berry-brown blades" of old songs)—and in it were little flutes, to permit the blood to run off when used in mortal strife; for our Scottish sires studied all these little matters to a nicety. MacLellan's handsome and athletic figure was displayed to advantage in his steel cuirass and gorget, his hanging sleeves, and long black riding-boots, the tops of which were strapped to his girdle. His face was ruddy and sunburnt; his black curly hair was closely cropped, in the fashion of the time; he had a moustache, though then military men wore it seldom, and none but the old indulged in beards.

With considerable animation, he related his adventures among the hills and forests of Athole,—the capture of the great freebooter,—the sudden resistance offered by him and his followers at Perth,—and the conflict on the north Inch, without the city wall. To all this Gray listened with some impatience, nor did he begin to evince any interest until the lieutenant, at the conclusion of his narrative, detailed his sojourn at his castle of Raeberry, in Galloway.

"What news bring you from that part of the country?" he asked.

"The burden of the old song—rief and stouthrief, oppression, hamesücken, and outrage, on the part of the Douglases, who make all bow to their rule; so that no man, of whatsoever rank he be, or however strong his dwelling, can lie down to sleep with the certainty of being a live man at the dawn of day."

"And what of dame Margaret?"

"Well," replied MacLellan, holding a glass of red wine between him and the light, to watch the gossamer beeswing as it floated to and fro, "you have heard, of course, how loosely the wedding-ring hung on her fair finger?"

"How—how?" asked Gray, impetuously.

"Is it possible that you do not know?" asked MacLellan, with surprise.

"What? I have heard nothing here."

"That she is wedded to James, earl of Abercorn, who is also now of Douglas."

"Wedded!" reiterated Gray, with unfeigned astonishment in his eyes and voice, as he now heard of this strange and formidable alliance for the first time; "wedded to the widow of his nephew?"

"Exactly—the poor boy who lies below the castle wall without; and a strong alliance our regent and chancellor may find it prove."

"But what says the church to this?" asked Gray, after a pause.

"The Countess Margaret is heiress of Galloway, Wigton, Balvenie, Ormond, and Annandale—a good slice of braid Scotland," replied MacLellan, in a bantering tone, as he hated the Douglases; "James, umquhile only of Abercorn and Avondale, is a mighty lord; so the most reverend father in God, Alexander—by divine permission bishop of *Candida Casa* (so run the pastorals to his pretty flock, the moss-troopers)—put a good round sum in gold nobles in his pouch, dozes away in his episcopal chair, and troubles not his mitred head about the matter; for is not Abbot John of Tongland, the keeper of the earl's conscience, a Douglas? By St. Paul, it is hardly wise or pleasant to call oneself by a different surname on the other side of the Nith, and I have some thoughts of getting permission from the king-of-arms, to call myself Archibald or Sholto Douglas—they are all one or other—as a surer warrant for a whole skin."

"Truly, we live in strange times!" pondered Gray; "and Murielle—Lady Murielle—you have not spoken of her?"

"Men say she is the same little moping, mooning nun, as ever."

"Beloved Murielle!" thought Gray in his heart, "And say, kinsman, how does she look?"

"Lovelier than her wont. She improves as she grows older, like this wine of Alicant; but there is a pensiveness about her——"

"A pensiveness?"

"That must be very flattering to you."

"Jesting again," said Gray, with annoyance.

"Under favour, not in the least."

"Then you really saw her, MacLellan?"

"How could I have judged of her beauty or pensiveness else?"

"Often?"

"Once only, my friend."

"At Thrave?"

"No, faith!" replied Sir Thomas, laughing and shrugging his shoulders; "I have a wholesome dread of that ugly gallows knob above the castle gate. But I did see her, however, and so closely, that her cramasie skirts rustled against my leather gambadoes, as she passed me."

"Where—where?"

"In the Lady Chapel of Tongland. I would have helped her to holy water from the font, but it was frozen hard and fast; for it was Candlemas day, and the Dee below the abbey wall was a sheet of ice, from rock to rock."

"You saw her," said Gray musingly, with a soft smile, as if he conjured up her face and form; "you saw, and yet did not speak with her?"

"By St. Cuthbert, 'twere as much as my life is worth to have done so, begirt as she was by Earl James's surly swashbucklers and rusty helmetted moss-troopers; but, from all I can learn in Galloway, she believes you dead."

"Oh—impossible!"

"Why so? Did she not see you stricken to the earth by the swords and mauls of more than a hundred wild Galwegians, Douglases, and devils?"

"True, she must have seen it—if, indeed, she could have looked upon it."

"Be assured that curiosity will conquer alarm—even love, at times," responded the sceptical MacLellan.

"A fatal mistake may result from all this."

"What mean you by a fatal mistake—a marriage?"

"Yes," said Gray, with a bitter sigh.

"It is not unlikely," replied the lieutenant, carelessly, while polishing his cuirass with a leather glove.

"How—why do you say so?"

"Nay; I did but echo your own thoughts."

"I have none; I am full of sorrow and bewilderment."

"Earl James and his countess are leaving nothing undone to strengthen their hands for some great enterprise. All men in Galloway say so, from the Brig of Dumfries to the Point of Kirkcolm; for the *black dinner* is yet fresh in their minds, and the marriage of Lady Murielle to a powerful lord might— might——"

"Say on."

"Add a few thousand men to their strength, should the Douglases make a Raid out of Galloway."

"Oh, how many secret tears must all this have cost her! She believes me dead: dear Murielle! I could joyously die for her—"

"Joyously to *live* for her, would be to act the wiser part," said the other, with a loud laugh.

"Ever mocking, MacLellan. It is enough to madden me, this doubt and fear; these bold schemes on one hand, her gentleness and ignorance of my fate on the other; while I am under pledge to leave Scotland for Flanders on the king's service, and may not—nay, I cannot return sooner than half a year hence, having a voyage to Sluys by sea, and a journey to Gueldres on horseback before me. I would give this gold chain for a trusty messenger to Galloway."

"You should add for a *bold* one; as some courage is required to convey *billets-doux* under the gallows knob of Thrave."

"Jesting again, kinsman," said Gray, reproachfully.

"Nay, I do not jest," said MacLellan, suddenly becoming serious. "Within a month from this, I return to my house at Raeberry, which I am strengthening by new walls and towers, as I know not what mischief James the Gross may be hatching; and I give you my faith as an honourable man, that I will see Murielle Douglas, and bear to her your farewell messages. This I will do, if the act should cost me liberty and life. I have often, ere this, perilled both for a less matter."

Little did the brave Lieutenant of the King's Guard foresee that these were no idle words, and that this rash promise to his friend would cost the exact penalty he so heedlessly named, and would send down his story among the many dark episodes of the Scottish annals; but of this, more anon.

Gray's heart was filled with gratitude by the offer, and after MacLellan retired, he began to look forward with more confidence, and even pleasure, to his projected mission into Flanders, as a scene of new adventures, and an agreeable change after the sufferings and monotony of the past year.

Within a month after the conversation just detailed, Sir Patrick Gray had embarked at the old Timber Holfe of Leith, and sailed from Scotland on board the *St. Regulus*, a caravel belonging to the monks of St. Mary, at Pittenweem, who were great traders and shipowners in those days.

At the same time MacLellan, faithful to his promise, contrived to convey a letter from him to Murielle, who was so worn out by the daily persecution she experienced, and being assured of her lover's death (indeed, Achanna swore to have seen his tomb in the church of St. Giles), that she was on the point of consenting in the desperate longing for peace, to receive the addresses of the duke of Albany, who was then in exile on the Continent. But now, suddenly hope revived in her heart; the bloom came back to her cheek, and the light to her eye; strength of purpose returned to her, and she resisted so strenuously, that the subtle earl and his imperious countess found their schemes completely marred for the time.

As a proof that he still lived, she displayed Sir Patrick's treasured letter, which had fallen at her feet attached to an arrow, shot, she knew not by whom, as she walked one day by the margin of the isle on which the castle stands; but her sister tore the missive from her hands, stigmatized it as a vile forgery, and rent it to fragments, which she trampled under foot in presence of her bower maidens.

Then the sombre earl swore his deepest oath that, if the bearer could be discovered, he would soon be dangling from the gallows knob above the gate.

So Murielle, in new happiness, prayed for the safety of her lover, while his ship bore merrily across the summer sea towards the coast of Flanders.

Meantime the earl, to perfect his political intrigues with Albany, to make his sure peace with Pope Eugene IV., who had privately disapproved of his marriage while publicly dispensing him, resolved to visit Rome. He was not without hope, by change of scene and distance from home, to divert the mind of Murielle, and bend her to his purpose.

He prepared a brilliant train of knights and followers, and took with him the abbot of Tongland, who volunteered to smooth over all difficult matters at the Vatican, and who hoped, moreover, as he displayed a mighty parchment, that, "before he returned to the wilds of Galloway, the master of lies and iniquity, the father of all evil and evil devices, should once more have become a pure spirit, clad in a shining raiment."

CHAPTER XXII
THE LOWLANDS OF HOLLAND

To Norroway, to Norroway,
Out owre the saut seas' foam;
The King o' Norroway's daughter,
'Tis thou maun bring her home!
Old Ballad.

Though the season was summer, the *St. Regulus* of Pittenweem did not cross the German Ocean without peril; for one night, and during the following day, there blew a tempest from the south-east, which drove her so far from her course, that the tacking to and fro of a whole week were required ere she could regain the lost distance; for the reader must bear in mind that the high-pooped, high-prowed, and low-waisted craft of those days, were very different from the screw-propellers and iron clippers of the present age; and heavily they lumbered along, with Dutch lee-boards, basketed tops, their spritsail-yards, jack-staffs, and other ponderous hamper.

So, when the gale abated, the *St. Regulus* was off the coast of England, and the tall, surf-beaten cliff, with the old castle of Scarborough, were seen in the distance, as the red rays of the morning sun fell on them from the eastern sky.

And now, as the *St. Regulus* squared her yards to bear up for Sluys, a new danger presented itself.

A great ship of England, which had hitherto been concealed by a bank of mist, was seen bearing down towards her, with St. George's ensign flying, and a large white rod or pole lashed to her bowsprit. This was the sign of *amity* on the seas in those days, and it was by this token that Sir Andrew Barton, in after years, was lured by Lord Howard to destruction in the Downs; but, as all shipmen were generally addicted to a little piracy, the captain of the *St. Regulus*, who was a douce native of the East Neuk, and a lay brother of St. Mary, of Pittenmeen, having a valuable cargo consigned to the famous merchant John Vanderberg of Bruges (who two years before had discovered the Azores), deemed discretion the better part of valour; so, hoisting all the canvas he could spread aloft, he squared his yards and bore right away before the wind.

Immediately on this, the crew of the English ship blew their trumpets, and fired several stone shot from their culverins; thus plainly indicating that though both countries were at peace, they did not deem that the treaty extended into blue water, and that they would make a prize of the Scotsman if they could.

Sir Patrick, who had donned his armour, and appeared on deck with his two-handed sword, was not without fear that the ship might have been dispatched to intercept *him,* and spoil his embassy by the influence the earl of Douglas possessed in England—a country which in all ages left nothing undone to break the political ties, which then existed between Scotland and the continent.

But the *St. Regulus* sailed like an arrow before the wind; and thus, long ere mid-day, her pursuer was far distanced and hull-down in the ocean.

With this single incident she had a prosperous voyage, and on Lammas-day in August made the low flat coast of Flanders, and came to anchor in the then fine harbour of Sluys, close to the strong old castle, where the Duc de Bouillon was kept after his capture at Hesdin; but since those days the sea, which has gradually been washing away the isle of Cadsand, has almost filled up the basin of Sluys.

Sir Patrick Gray landed with his horse, armour, and cloakbags, and presented his credentials to Hervé de Meriadet, the burg graf, who commanded a body of Walloons, in the castle, "where," says the abbot of Tongland, "he was honourably entertained for three days, after which he set out for the court of the duke of Gueldres," which lay about one hundred and fifty miles distant, in the land beyond the Maese.

Though Flanders had been the scene of many bloody battles, and disastrous wars, the people were industrious and peaceful; and then it was not necessary, as in turbulent and warlike Scotland, to travel armed to the teeth; yet, to be provided for any emergency, Sir Patrick Gray wore an open helmet, a gorget, a chain shirt, and gloves of fine mail, with his sword and dagger.

In his cloakbag was a round sum in the current coin of the day, such as Henry nobles valued at twenty-two shillings; salutis, riders, and dauphines, at eleven shillings; and Rhenish guilders at eight, issued to him, in goodly canvas bags, by the treasurer depute, from the rents of the king's lands in Ettrick forest and Gosford in Lothian, which had then been due. Moreover, he had ample letters of credit upon John Vanderberg of Bruges, and two Scottish merchants in Campvere.

Though far from Murielle Douglas, he felt his heart grow light as he surveyed the flat green fields where the sleek cattle browsed, the sandy isles of the Scheldt, where the brown windmills tossed their arms in the breeze; the dull sedgy streams, where great lubberly barges were dragged to and fro by horses of equally lubberly aspect; the taper church spires seen at a vast distance across the far stretching heaths; or the old castles amid the thick primeval woods of Flanders. Health and strength had returned to him amid the bracing air of the German Sea. His purse was well lined; he had a good horse under him; a sharp sword by his side; an honourable commission to execute; and so he rode cheerfully on, with an almost boyish emotion of novelty and longing for adventure, making his heart expand and its pulses quicken, he knew not why.

He was now in Flanders—"the lawlands o'Holland," so famed in many a Scottish song—and whose name is so interwoven with the annals of our exiles and soldiers of fortune.

On the first day of his solitary journey he passed through Ardenburg, which is a league from Sluys, and was *then* the capital of maritime Flanders; and from thence proceeding along the left bank of the Scheldt he reached Hulst, a small but very ancient town in Dutch Brabant, where he took up his quarters at a Benedictine monastery, whose superior was brother of the burg graf of Sluys, by name Benoit de Meriadet of Burgundy.

When he set forth next morning he saw plainly in the distance the magnificent spire of the great cathedral in the marquisate of Antwerp, reddened by the dun morning sun, standing like a slender pillar of flame, above the vast extent of level pastures which border the Scheldt, and rising far above the dense white motionless mist which the heat of the August morning was exhaling, from the fens and marshes, through which the river flowed so turgidly and slowly towards Zealand and the German Sea.

After a twenty miles' ride through a green and fertile but most monotonous country, he found himself in busy Antwerp, and under the shadow of that colossal spire, which was then one of the wonders of the world, and which was visible alike from the laceworks of Mechlin, the ramparts of Ghent; the plains of Louvain; and the sandy shores of the distant Zealand isles.

CHAPTER XXIII
OUR LADY OF ANTWERP

In her did beauty, youth, and bounty dwell,
A virgin port and features feminine;
Far better than my feeble tongue can tell,
Did meek-eyed wisdom in her features shine;
She seemed perfay, a thing almost divine.
James I. of Scotland.

Antwerp was then in the zenith of its commercial glory, and to a traveller like Sir Patrick Gray, who had never seen a larger city than the little Edinburgh of James II. clustering on its rocky ridge, surrounded by forests of oak and pathless hills, the great Flemish town, in the splendour of its mercantile prosperity, with a population of more than two hundred thousand souls, presented a scene of varying wonders, amid which he was almost disposed to forget his embassy, and to linger for a time.

Nor was this desire lessened, when Maître Baudoin, a garrulous little Frenchman, who was keeper of the hostelry at which he lodged—the "Grille of St. Laurence"—informed him that, "by recent rains, all the roads between the Scheldt and Maese were impassable; that the sluices of several of the barrier fortresses had given way; that the rivers had overflowed their banks; and that the Peel Morass, which lies between Brabant and Gueldreland, was, for the time, an actual sea. Moreover," he added, "it is but a few days until the 15th of the month, when the Feast of the Assumption will be held in the cathedral of our Lady of Antwerp, with a splendour never before witnessed in the city; people are arriving from all quarters, and Monseigneur l'Evêque de Mechlin has found a young lady of great beauty and high rank, to appear as our patroness in the procession."

"Though this may be no inducement to a lover, it may be one to a storm-stayed traveller," replied Gray; "but who is this lady, Maître Baudoin?"

"Ah—who indeed, messire!" replied the hosteller shrugging his shoulders; "who indeed!"

"What—is she the Princess Mary of Gueldres?"

"Pardieu! no one can tell who the lady may be, save herself and Monseigneur l'Evêque; it is always kept secret."

"Why—how?"

"You see, messire, secrecy and mystery enhance the charm of her appearance. It is very droll."

"And she is sure to be beautiful?"

"Superbe, messire!"

While the master of the hostel ran on thus, and then proceeded to enumerate all the great personages, such as Monseigneur the prince of Ravenstein, MM. the marquises of Berg and Anvers, the count of Nassau, and others who were sure to be present with their ladies, esquires, and men-at-arms, Gray mentally resolved to tarry for a day or two and witness the spectacle, prior to which he could see all the marvels of this great Flemish capital.

A vast city it was, with its long and quaint streets of old and steep-roofed houses, built of painted brick and carved wood, with a stork's nest on every chimney; the pavement full of life and bustle, and swarming with ruddy-cheeked young fraus, each having a dozen petticoats; and bulbous-shaped Flemings wearing the old proverbial big red or brown trunk-hose, bombasted with sawdust or tow, and bedecked with rows of shiny buttons at the side; its booths, its shops and stores, crammed with treasures and merchandise from all parts of Christendom and the East—the mysterious realms of Prester John; while boats and barges, all glittering with brown varnish paint and gilding, plied to and fro under the bridges of the Scheldt or its canals, laden with boxes, barrels, and bales, or with ruddy fruit, green vegetables, or ponderous cattle, or with men, women, and children, long-robed priests, and mail-clad soldiers, all gabbling and laughing in the guttural *patois* of the old Lotheringian kingdom. Then there were the long and stately rows of linden trees and the ramparts of the citadel; while, with scores of little shops nestling between its countless buttresses, high over all towered the mighty cathedral, the glory of Antwerp, with its sixty-six chapels, its roof that springs from one hundred and twenty-five pillars—its altars, statues, and pictures, with that gorgeous steeple which seems to pierce the sky, and the carvings of which are so exquisite that Charles V. said, "it should be put into a case and shown only on holidays."

On its summit, four hundred and fifty feet above the busy streets, there hung, in those days, four great copper pans, in which the burghers were wont to kindle fires on the approach of an enemy; for the Gueldrians, Lorainers, Burgundians, and even the Frieslanders from beyond Utrecht and the waveless Zuider Zee, worked the wealthy Antwerpers sore mischief in time of war and tumult.

In this vast city Gray resided unnoticed and unknown, and spent several days pleasantly enough; so the great festival came to pass before the waters subsided on the frontiers.

On the night of the 15th August, after vespers, when the brilliant procession was to issue from the cathedral, Gray armed himself, and, guided by Maître Baudoin, of the *Grille de Ste. Laurence*, obtained a good place near the porch of the cathedral; within, without, and all around which were assembled the thousands of Antwerp to witness the procession, in which so much of a religious pageant with civic mummery were to mingle. The excitement was increased by the wide-spread rumour that a young foreign girl of high rank—a princess at least—had been chosen on this occasion to represent our Lady of Antwerp; thus all the city were on tiptoe in honour of the occasion, the patroness of their cathedral, of the city, and of all Christian women.

The armed vassals of the powerful and wealthy bishop of Mechlin formed a lane, with their partisans parting the crowd before the cathedral gate. Each soldier bore a torch, and the lurid glow of these fell fitfully on their bearded visages, their steel caps and breastplates, or tipped with seeming fire the points of their partisans. Beyond, the wavering gleam lighted partially the sombre and dusky masses of the people, who crowded all the thoroughfares like a human sea.

The thirty-three bells of the cathedral were tolling, and from the depths of its long-drawn aisles and echoing arches strains of the sacred music within came forth and floated over the bowed heads of the hushed and expectant multitude.

At last the bells rang out a merrier peal; the gilded gates revolved, and, when more torches were lighted, a glow of sudden splendour seemed to fill the great portico of the church, and all the white marble statues of saints, kings, and warriors seemed to start from their canopied niches into life.

There was a palpable vibration among the people—a heaving to and fro of the human tide—as the glitter of the coming pageant appeared in the arched depths of the church; but the heaving was steadily repressed by the steel points of the levelled partisans, while here and there a half-stifled shriek from a woman, or a gruff Flemish oath from a man, announced that the pressure was greater than their patience could endure. But now the procession was seen slowly descending the steps of the portico, and exclamations of pleasure and astonishment burst from time to time in front of the masses; and these, as usual, served but to excite the curiosity and irritate the temper of the less fortunate who were too far off in the rear, or were hopelessly crushed against the adjacent houses.

First came the twenty-eight corporations of the city, clad in gowns of fine cloth, with their banners and insignia; the nine nobles, with their swords and coronets borne by pages; the nine masters of the streets, with their swords and keys; the two burgomasters, and a giant eight feet high (on heels of cork), bearing the banner of Antwerp, heraldically charged with two human hands.

Maître Baudoin informed Gray, in a hasty whisper, that, in ancient times, a giant named Antwerpen had lived there amid the swamps, and was wont to cast into the Scheldt all who displeased him, having previously cut off their hands; and this was the legend of the city's coat armorial.

"And see, messire," added the little Frenchman, "by St. Louis here comes one of his teeth!"

As he spoke, an *echevin* passed, bearing on a silver platter this palladium of Antwerp—a gigantic *human* tooth, said to be "a handbreadth long and sixteen ounces in weight."

The shouts of wonder and laughter excited by the giant, with his shaggy black hair and beard, his red, pimpled nose and mighty scimitar, were hushed when, preceded by choristers and boys swinging silver censers of incense, the dean of the cathedral, with his twenty-four canons and the confraternity of the Holy Circumcision, in all the splendour of their full canonicals, were seen descending into the street and passing on amid the flare of a thousand uplifted torches, a mass of muslin, lace, and embroidery.

Next came the twelve apostles, with their respective badges, each represented by a handsome young man, and all clad in flowing robes of brilliant red, blue, or yellow serge: St. Peter, with his keys, and St. Paul, with a sword; St. Andrew, with a cross-saltire; St. James Minor, with a fuller's pole; St. John, with a cup, out of which an ingeniously-contrived winged serpent strove to fly; St. Bartholomew, with a knife; St. Philip, with a cross-staff; St. Thomas, with a goodly Flemish partisan; St. Mathias, with a battle-axe; St. James Major, with a pilgrim's staff and gourd; St. Simeon, with a saw; and St. Jude, with a club.

Then came an effigy of Judas, with a red beard, dragged by the headsman of the city, and surrounded by a score of merry imps, with horns and tails, all whooping and dancing, as if eager to convey his soul to the shades below; and their tricks and gambols filled the crowd with laughter.

The princess of Ravenstein, robed in pure white, with a diadem sparkling on her brow, a palm-branch in one hand and a flaming sword in the other, was borne past as St. Catherine upon a car, the wheels of which were concealed by flowing drapery.

Preceded by his banner, next came the abbot of St. Michael, an edifice founded by a son of the Palatine, Count Herbert of Picardie; and then, under a canopy borne by the marquises of Antwerp and Berg, the counts of Bommel and Nassau, came the bishop of Mechlin, with his crozier and mitre, his vestments glittering with precious stones and massive embroidery, and all the clergy of the diocese following, with their hands crossed on their breasts, and their eyes lowered on the earth, in token of Christian piety and humility.

But now the excitement reached its height, while something of awe was mingled with the hushed curiosity of the people, and every mailed soldier held his streaming torch aloft, when twelve stout monks of St. Michael's Abbey, all marching slowly in their black cassocks, approached, with a species of throne upon their shoulders, and on that throne sat a female, who represented our Lady of Antwerp.

This chair seemed a veritable blaze of precious stones, as the ladies of the city yearly contributed their jewels to decorate it. Little children, dressed as seraphs, with snow-white wings, nestled at its base, and over it there seemed to float a curiously-contrived silver cloud, amid which shone thirteen stars, that sparkled in the light of the torches.

The lady who personated the Virgin in this strange procession was said to be very beautiful, so Gray pressed vigorously forward to obtain a glimpse of her; and his resolute aspect, his scarred face and athletic form, his long sword and shirt of mail, repressed even the officious petulance of the men-at-arms, who would have thrust him back as a stranger, or one who was unknown to them; and little Maître Baudoin profited by this influence to secure a good place, and rubbed his hands with nervous ecstasy.

On came the marching monks with the glittering throne, and Sir Patrick Gray could see that they bore up a beautiful female figure, clad in robes of the greatest value—for gold, silver, and precious stones were lavished in their adornment, while a glory, composed of diamonds, sparkled and blazed around her sweet young face, which expressed, alternately, alarm, awe, and pleasure at the scene below, and the part she felt so honoured by enacting before so vast a multitude.

Maître Baudoin, who clung to the skirt of Gray's pourpoint, uttered loud exclamations of rapture; but the Captain of the Guard was voiceless as one whom Heaven had stricken dumb; for how great was his bewilderment, how deep were his emotions, how profound his surprise, on recognizing in the damsel who was borne past on that brilliant throne, as our Lady of Antwerp, the features of Murielle Douglas—his own Murielle—whom he fondly believed to be far away in the wilds of Galloway!

CHAPTER XXIV
MAÎTRE BAUDOIN

Thou seest we are not all alone unhappy;
This wide and universal theatre
Presents more woeful pageants than the scene
Wherein we play in. — As You Like It.

Sir Patrick Gray so entirely lost his self-possession, that he was rapidly swept away, jostled, tossed and pushed here and there, by a rush of the crowd, who were making off to another part of the city where the procession would again be seen as it passed; so, after futilely struggling, and even fighting in some instances, he found himself in a dark street near one of the many bridges of the Scheldt, which flows through Antwerp by no less than eight channels, and there he paused, alone and breathless, with one hand pressed on his brow and the other on his sword.

Was it a dream, or a phantom raised by his nerves or organs of vision being disturbed by the terrible wounds he had received, and by the long and feverish hours of illness and agony he had endured in the castle of Edinburgh?

Again and again he asked this question of himself, without being able to resolve the matter satisfactorily.

He heard the bells of the cathedral still tolling; he saw the variegated lamps that glittered on its glorious spire; he heard even the hum of the distant multitude; but he dared not return and trust himself to look again, lest he might become mad, for already his brain felt weak and giddy, and he cast a haggard glance at the dark, still water that flowed with mud and slime under the quaint old bridge of the Scheldt, as strange wild thoughts occurred to him, but he thrust them aside with shame.

He looked back to the cathedral, and again he seemed to see that fair young face with its diamond tiara, and the almost ethereal form, with the finest and snowiest of Mechlin lace floating like a cloud of frostwork, cold and pure, about it. In a foreign city, amid more than two hundred thousand inhabitants, his chances of discovering *who* this lady was, and how she bore a resemblance so marvellous, became very slender, if she were known alone to the bishop, who made it part of his sacred drama or mystery to preserve her incognito from all—even from his clergy.

Had he been less a lover—had he waited, he might have seen *other* faces nearly as familiar as that of Murielle, though less startling and bewildering; but, swept away as he had been by the crowd, and having neither power nor presence of mind to regain his place, he saw no more of the procession; and, after long wandering, he thought of returning home.

The night was now considerably advanced; the cathedral bells had ceased to toll; the lights had disappeared amid the delicate traceries of its spire; there were neither moon nor stars, and there came not a breath of wind to disperse the frowsy vapour that overhung the city, and which rose from the many branches of the Scheldt. Sir Patrick had lost his way; his ignorance of the language and of the vast old city forced him to wander to and fro, vainly searching for his hostelry, "the Grille of St. Laurence;" but day dawned before he discovered it and presented himself, to the joy of Maître Baudoin, who feared that he had become embroiled with some of the bishop's men-at-arms, or the Marquises Brabanciones, in the citadel—a surmise which naturally led the maître to ponder upon the value of Sir Patrick's horse and its housings, and also of his cloakbag, which might thereby fall into *his* possession.

"How came you to leave me, messire, in such a hurry and at such a time?" asked the little Frenchman.

Gray frankly told him that he thought—indeed that he was almost certain—he had recognized a dear friend in the damsel who appeared as our Lady of Antwerp.

"*Ah, Mère de Dieu!* do you say so?" exclaimed Maître Baudoin, with sudden interest, "then *who* is she?"

"That is exactly what I wish to know; and shall know, too, ere noon be past."

"*Ay, ay, pardieu!* but no one can tell you."

"None!"

"Save Monseigneur l'Evêque himself."

"The bishop of Mechlin?"

"Yes, messire."

"I will fly to him!"

"But he left the city after the show was over. I saw him myself, as with all his knights and men-at-arms, and with several ladies— —"

"Ladies, say you?"

"Yes, in horse-litters; he passed out by the gate of St. James."

"For where?" asked Gray, starting up.

"I know not."

"Do none in Antwerp know?" asked Gray, impatiently.

"Some say for Mechlin—others for Breda."

"Get me a fleet horse, Maître Baudoin—I can pay you well—I must see this bishop—"

"Horses?—do you mean to ride to *both* places at once?"

"No—to the nearest first."

"Vain, vain, messire," said the hosteller, shrugging his shoulders, "be assured that he will not tell you."

"Not if I implore him to do so?"

"Not if you dashed out your brains—*morbleu!*"

"Where did the lady go after the procession dispersed?"

"Back to the cathedral—it is the custom."

"Oh! she may be there yet."

"*Ouf*, messire! would you have a pretty girl to sleep all night among these cold marble knights and dead bishops? She has left it, of course; but amid the thousands who have left or are leaving the city, and the great trains of the prince of Ravenstein, the counts of Nassau, Bommel, and others, now departing by all our gates and bridges, the task of tracing and discovering her would be no sinecure."

Sir Patrick stamped his right foot with vexation.

"If I had your devil of a bishop on Scottish ground, I would soon wrench the secret out of him."

"Perhaps so, messire; but he has at Mechlin an ugly wheel whereon folks are sometimes broken alive; and that is not pleasant. Is messire *sure* that he recognized the lady?"

"Sure, Maître Baudoin, as that I now speak to you. Oh! I would know that sweet face among ten thousand."

"Sweet—hum;" the little Frenchman began to get quite interested; "is she a countrywoman of messire?"

"Yes."

"A sister?" persisted the hosteller, who burned with curiosity.

"No—no."

"Perhaps she is the mother of messire?"

"Prater, how thou talkest! she is my best beloved—my betrothed wife!" said Gray, with enthusiasm.

"*Diable! Bon Dieu!*" exclaimed Baudoin, making a pirouette. "Messire must not despair."

"I do not despair, Maître Baudoin; but I am sorely bewildered," said poor Gray, passing a hand across his scarred forehead.

"Messire, with your permission, I shall tell you a little story."

"Say on, my friend."

"Have you perceived near the church of Jesus—just about thirty paces from it—a well, covered with curious ironwork?"

"Yes; what about it?"

"The branches from which the pulley hangs are rich with foliaged work of iron, and are deemed a miracle of skill. They were the *chef d'œuvre* of a famous young smith of Antwerp who dearly loved the daughter of a great painter, and desired greatly to win his esteem; so he lavished all the energies of his soul, and all the cunning of his hands, all his skill and experience, upon that piece of ironwork; but when it was finished, monsieur the painter viewed it coldly, and said, crustily,

"'I cannot agree to have you for a son-in-law.'"

"'I am rich, young, and skilful,' urged the unfortunate lover. 'I am a smith.'

"'For *that* very reason you shall not have my daughter; for she shall wed a painter, and a painter only!'

"Our smith did not lose heart, but he threw his beloved hammer into the well, where it lies to this day; he assumed the pencil and palette, and after working assiduously, he rapidly became a master in the art; he excelled even the surly old painter who had disdained him; he won for himself a high position in our city, and with it his beautiful young mistress; and all this you may see graven on the brass plate of their tomb, near the gate of the cathedral. But does messire hear me?"

"Yes; but, prythee, Maître Baudoin, what the devil has all this story about painters and smiths, palettes and draw-wells, to do with me?"

"Everything."

"How? I am not in a humour for jesting."

"It is a homily," said the Frenchman, with a low bow.

"Leave homilies to monks and friars; but for what is yours meant?"

"To teach you to hope much and to persevere long; even as that poor lover persevered and hoped."

Three days longer Gray lingered in Antwerp, searching and inquiring everywhere in vain, till at last, in despair of unravelling the mystery, on the subsidence of the waters of the Maese, he ordered his horse, bade adieu to the gossiping Maître Baudoin, and set out for the court of the duke of Gueldres; having at last all but convinced himself that the face which he had recognized in our Lady of Antwerp was the creation of his own imagination, or at most some very remarkable resemblance.

Yet it was *no* vision he had seen during the night of that festival—but Murielle Douglas herself—the veritable object of all his hope and love.

We have already stated that the earl of Douglas had left Scotland ostensibly to visit Pope Eugene IV., taking with him the countess, Murielle, and a brilliant train.

The latter, says Tytler (in his "History of Scotland"), consisted of six knights, with their own suites and attendants, and fourteen gentlemen of the best families in the realm, with a retinue of eighty men-at-arms on horseback. Among these were Sir John Forrester, of Corstorphine; Sir Alan Lauder, of the Bass; William Campbell, thane of Cawdor and constable of the castle of Nairne—"all knights," adds Lindesay, of Pitscottie, "whose convoy maid the earle so proud and insolent, that he represented a kingis magnificence wherever he went. Out of Flanderis he passed to France, and out of France to Italie, and so forwardis to Rome, where the Romanes having knowledge of his cuming, mett him with an honourable companie, and veri princelie received him within the toun."

In this quotation, however, we are somewhat anticipating the course of events, for Gray and Murielle were yet to meet before the earl and his retinue left Flanders to visit the court of Charles VII. of France.

CHAPTER XXV
SNICK AND SNEE

Murder, madam! 'Tis self-defence. Besides, in these skirmishes there are never more than two or three killed; for, supposing they bring the whole body of militia upon us, down with a brace of them and away fly the rest of the covey!—The Lying Valet.

Gray had been repeatedly warned by the friendly hosteller, Maître Baudoin, to beware of travelling in the dusk after passing the boundary of the marquisate of Antwerp, as hordes of disbanded Brabanters and Walloons, the refuse of the wars between Charles of France and the duke of Burgundy, were lurking among the thick woods that lay about Endhoven, and in the then great swampy wilderness, known as the Peel Morass; and these outlaws were led by a kind of leader whom they all tacitly acknowledged, Count Ludwig of Endhoven, who had been expelled from the Burgundian army for his barbarous and outrageous conduct, after having his spurs hacked from his heels, and his coat of arms publicly riven and defaced, by order of Philip the Good.

Gray thanked Maître Baudoin for his friendly warning, and rode on his way, like a soldier and a careless fellow as he was, thinking no more about it.

Refreshed by the halt at Antwerp, his horse carried him with great speed next day. He passed Nonne Kloster, and towards evening, found himself approaching Endhoven, in Brabant, after a fifty-miles' ride.

At the verge of the flat horizon, the sun was setting, but through the evening haze, its light shed a golden lustre upon everything,—the quaint farmhouses, the summer woods, the sluggish canals and browsing cattle,—casting far across the fields the shadow of every village spire and poplar tree; but now here and there rose little hills or swelling eminences to relieve the tedium of the scenery, for tedious it was to a Scottish eye, though the fruitful soil was cultivated like a garden, for he was in the land of cheese, milk, and butter.

Two miles from the town of Endhoven, stood a wayside hostelry, of quaint aspect, overshadowed by a gigantic oak-tree, on one of the lower branches of which swung its signboard, and under which were placed a rough table and benches for the accommodation of those who choose to loiter there, and refresh them in the open air.

Weary and athirst, Gray alighted from his horse, and knocking with his dagger hilt on the table, brought forth the tapster, who had been observing his approach, from the ivy-covered porch of the hostelry, which seemed to be literally a mass of green leaves, with quaint gablets, and chimneys sticking up in all directions, and curious little windows, peeping out, without order, regularity, or architectural design.

In a jargon, half Flemish and partly French, "eked" out with a word or two of Scottish, Gray ordered a flask of wine for himself, and a feed of corn for his horse, which was led into the stables.

While drinking his wine, and pondering whether he should halt there for the night, or push on to Endhoven, the evening bells of which were ringing in the distance, the sound of voices at an open window made him aware that several fellows of a very rough aspect were observing him from a room, where they seemed to be drinking and playing with dice, and, doubtless, they would have been smoking too, had that useful mode of spending time and money been discovered.

On turning from them, his attention was next arrested by perceiving a knife, formed somewhat like a dagger, dangling at the end of a string, from the lower branch of the tree under which he sat, and there it swung to and fro in the wind.

Each time he raised his eyes to this knife, he heard loud laughter, and a clapping of hands among those who were evidently observing him; and though resolving, if possible, to avoid all brawls, his brow flushed, and his heart beat quicker, on finding himself, as he conceived, insulted by a rabble of Flemish boors.

But in his ignorance of the customs of the country, he knew not that the knife was hung thus as a challenge to snick and snee, as it was named, a combat then common among the lower classes in Flanders, as it was in Holland, in later years.

The bravest or most rash bully of a village or district, usually hung up his knife thus, in some conspicuous place, as the knights of chivalric days were wont, in a warlike fit, to obstruct the high roads, by hanging their shields on a bridge, or by the wayside, to invite all comers, and whoever touched or took the weapon down was compelled to fight the proprietor, or be branded as a coward.

Before engaging, the combatants sometimes tested their strength of arm, by driving their knives into a deal board, and then they were only permitted to use so much of the blade as had penetrated; others broke off the points. On closing, each used his cap or hat as a shield, to protect his face; but such encounters seldom ended until one, sometimes both duellists, had their cheeks, noses, and foreheads slashed and disfigured.

The knife in question, a long, sharp, and assassin-like weapon, continued to swing to and fro within arm's-length of Gray, who, on perceiving something engraved on the buckhorn haft of it, took it in his hand for examination; on this a shout of exultation, too boisterous to pass unnoticed, came from the topers in the hostelry.

Sir Patrick had only time to perceive that a coronet and the letter E were engraven on the handle, when he tore it down, and dashed it right through the latticed window where it fell among those whose mirth seemed so easily excited.

After the silence of a moment, a storm of oaths and threats, mingled with shouts and drunken laughter, greeted this act of hostility, and from the door of the tavern there issued six men, all tattered in dress, bloated by drinking, ruffianly in aspect, and all variously armed with swords, daggers, and mauls. Three of them had rusty helmets and breastplates, which had evidently seen much service.

On the approach of this unexpected rabble, Gray quietly drained the last of his wine, threw down the price thereof, and then starting up, laid his hand on his sword, as one who seemed to be the leader, came boldly and brusquely up to him.

Tall, strongly made, and athletic in form, this personage presented a curious combination of character in his features, which were naturally noble and handsome, but disguised by the masses of his uncombed hair, distorted by ferocity, and bloated by drunkenness. He wore a pair of enormous moustaches, which were twisted up almost to his ears; his attire, which had once been richly laced, was full of rents and holes. He wore a cuirass and back-plate, on each of which a coat of arms was engraved; his neck being destitute of gorget, revealed by its bareness that he was not proprietor of a shirt; a battered helmet, from which the barred vizor had been struck in some battle or brawl, covered his head; his gauntlets and boots were of different fashions; he carried a short battle-axe in his right hand, and in his left the knife which Gray had just tossed through the window.

"Sangdieu!" he exclaimed, in French; "do you know the penalty incurred by what you have done, messire?"

"I neither know nor care," replied Gray, coolly; and then turning to the hosteller—a fat old Flemish boor, who had also come forth, and was trembling at the prospect of a fray upon his premises—he added, "Maître, please you to bring my horse—and do so instantly, as I have no desire to cross my sword with this fellow and his *coquinaille*."

At this epithet, which signifies "a pack of rascals," they uttered a simultaneous shout, and raised their weapons, but Gray confronted them resolutely with his drawn sword.

"My horse, I tell you, fellow, lest I cut you in two!" he reiterated to the loitering hosteller. On this, his roan, the same horse ridden by him when Earl William entered Edinburgh, was brought at once towards the tree, but the armed rabble placed themselves between it and the proprietor.

"Does messire mean to fight me, whom he has insulted and challenged by touching *this* knife," demanded the leader; "or der Teufel, does he mean to— —"

"What!" said Gray, "be wary of your words, sir."

"To fly like a coward?" said the other, with a German oath.

"I do not fight with every ignoble ruffian I may meet; there are some whom I would disdain to chastise, and thou, fellow, art one! Yet, if the hosteller would but bring me a good heavy whip, I would make you dance to a tune of your own."

"Sangdieu! do you know to whom you are speaking?" cried the other, whose rage completely sobered him.

"Some robbers or outlaws, I suppose."

"A robber—yes, for misfortune has made me so; an outlaw—yes, for tyrants made me so; but I am *your* equal, and perhaps superior, for all that!"

"Indeed! Then who the devil are you, that thus molest peaceful people on the open highway?"

"I am Ludwig, count of Endhoven!"

Gray started on hearing the name of the very personage against whom Maître Baudoin had so solemnly warned him; but, inspired with an emotion of pity for nobility fallen so low, he took his purse from his girdle, and said, "Rumour says you have been a soldier: I am one, and will share what I have with you; but first you must stand aside from between me and my horse, as I can brook no intimidation."

The other laughed scornfully, and said, "In the first place, messire, it was from being a soldier that Philip of Burgundy made me a thief, and changed my cote d'armes into a beggar's gabardine. In the second, I do not ask for that which I can take by force; in the third, I obey no man's orders—yours least of all, when horse and purse, and all you possess, are my lawful spoil."

As he spoke, he made a sudden rush forward, with the intention of tearing away the purse from Sir Patrick, who, quick as thought, sprang back, and received him right upon the point of his sword, with a force which made the iron corslet ring, and stretched its wearer on the earth.

With a shout of rage, he sprang to his feet, swinging his axe in both hands, and, with his five companions, surrounded Gray. Sharp was the conflict that ensued, and most likely it would have terminated fatally for him; for although he dealt many a severe wound, it was long since he had thus used his sword; and since that fatal day, after "the Black Dinner," his wrists had been weak and stiff: but now the distant tramp of horses was heard, and the hosteller, to scare the combatants from his premises, exclaimed, "Gott in Himmel! Herr Count, here comes the burg graf of Gueldres, with his banner and escort!"

On hearing this, Count Ludwig, whose face was streaming with blood from a slash Gray had given him, accompanied by his five companions, sprang over a hedge close by, and, taking to flight, sought refuge where horsemen dared not follow them, among the recesses of a swampy forest.

They had scarcely been gone three minutes, and Sir Patrick had just recovered his breath and equanimity, when a grey-bearded cavalier, all armed save the head (for his helmet hung at his saddle-bow), rode up, attended by three knights, who each wore the jewel and mantle of the Golden Fleece of Burgundy, and by twenty men-at-arms on horseback, one of whom, an esquire, carried a long lance with a square banner, charged with the lion of Gueldres.

CHAPTER XXVI
THE ROYAL LETTER

O mony a mile Sir Patrick rode
Throughout the border land;
To gie that letter braw and braid,
Into the earlis hand.—Old Ballad.

Reining in his horse, while all his party did the same, the elder gentleman, who was without the helmet, but wore a plumed cap, and who appeared to be the leader, hastily addressed Gray in German, but finding that he did not reply, repeated his question in French.

"There has been fighting here, messire?"

"As you may plainly see," replied Gray quietly, while carefully wiping his sword-blade, for the lofty bearing of the speaker displeased him.

"About what did you quarrel?"

"Faith, I can scarcely tell you."

"Speak, messire!" said the other, authoritatively.

"A knife that hung from the branch of a tree, it would seem. You have strange fashions among you here in Gueldres," said Gray, with returning anger.

"You are not yet in old Gueldreland, but in Brabant," replied the other; "you appear to be a stranger?"

"Yes, messire, I am a stranger," replied Sir Patrick, who had now mounted, gathered up his reins, and had his horse fully in hand, ready for any emergency, and resolved to admit of no molestation.

"May I ask what object takes you towards Gueldreland?"

"You may, messire, but what if I decline to reply?"

"I can prove that I have the right to ask such questions, and to enforce answers."

"I am come from the court of Scotland to visit old Duke Arnold—is he in Gueldres?"

"No; in Brabant."

"That is unfortunate."

"Not so much so as you suppose. But with whom were you fighting?"

"Those who fought with me: some outlaws, to all appearance, but they got more than they gave."

"Outlaws!" reiterated the armed horseman with displeasure.

"A rabble led by one who called himself Count Ludwig of Endhoven."

"Ha!" exclaimed the other, while all his followers uttered exclamations expressive of surprise and interest.

"Is it thus," said Gray, "your lords of Gueldres amuse themselves upon the highway?"

"I tell you, messire, that you are in Brabant. So these were Ludwig and his Brabanciones? I would give a thousand guilders for his head! But there was blood upon your sword?"

"I laid Count Ludwig's cheek open from eye to chin."

"Then beware you, messire: he is cruel as a pagan, and revengeful as an Italian; and he will track you and seek you day and night while you are among us, to work you mischief, unless, in the interim, he is broken alive upon the wheel by some burg graf or burgomaster. You are going, you say, to the court of the duke of Gueldres?"

"Where I am not likely to arrive soon if I remain chattering here," replied Gray coldly, as he disliked the inquisitorial manner of his questioner, who laughed and said,—

"Are you seeking knight-service? If so, you had better turn your horse's head towards Burgundy, where Duke Philip III. is putting his sword to the grindstone."

"Nay, messire," replied Gray, with increasing displeasure; "I have come on a mission from the court of Scotland, where I have the honour to be Captain of the King's Guard."

"Your name?"

"Sir Patrick Gray, younger of that ilk."

"And this mission?" said the other hastily.

"Concerns not you, messire, but the marriage of the Princess Mary d'Egmont," replied Gray, moving his horse away.

"To your young king?—good. You have, then, a letter for—for the duke?" said the other, following him.

"Yes."

"Permit me to see it. Excuse me, messire, but I have both reason and authority for my request."

Gray, who thought he had been rather unwise in stating the object of his mission to a total stranger, reluctantly opened a pocket in his saddlelap, and drew forth a large square letter, which was covered with a silken wrapper, tied with white ribbon crosswise, and sealed with yellow wax, the colour used by the kings of Scotland and France.

"Messire, you will perceive that it is correctly addressed," said Sir Patrick; "and it is my best credential for being reserved."

"Exactly; I thank you," replied the other, taking the letter in his gauntletted hand, and deliberately tearing it open.

"Messire!" exclaimed Gray, furiously, as he drew his sword; "are you mad, or weary of life, that you dare to open a letter— —"

"For Arnold d'Egmont, count of Zutphen, and duke of Gueldres, you would say?"

"Yes, surrender it, messire, or by every saint in heaven, I shall kill you where you stand!"

"Beware—beware!" exclaimed some of the attendants, lowering their lances.

"And why beware?" demanded the sturdy Scot.

"Because I am Arnold himself," replied the old duke, with a hearty laugh, in which the three knights of the Golden Fleece joined.

"You, monseigneur?" said Gray, sinking the point of his sword, and reining back his horse.

"Behold my banner and escort, with Ravenstein, Berg, and Nassau, my three most faithful friends."

"Pardon me," said Gray, sheathing his sword, and reining back his horse.

"I have nothing to pardon, Sir Patrick Gray," replied the duke; "we shall all ride forward together, but this letter, which you have travelled so far to lay before me, is written in the young king's name, and announces, that so soon as affairs are peaceful in his kingdom, his lord chancellor, accompanied by John, bishop of Dunkeld, and Messire Nicholas Otterbourne, official of Lothian, with a suitable train, will visit our court at Gueldres, to receive the Princess Mary, and conduct her to her new home. Poor child! she is very young and tender, to be trusted among your unruly mountaineers.

The letter shall be laid before the duchess and council. Meantime, messire, I thank you for the care with which you have brought hither the missive of your king, and the valour with which you were ready to defend it, at all hazards, even against four-and-twenty mounted men."

Sir Patrick bowed low, and kissed the hand which the duke extended towards him.

"You will ride on with us, Sir Patrick," he resumed. "I have a hunting-lodge near Vlierden, on this side of Peel Morass, seventeen miles distant. There we shall halt for to-night, and to-morrow depart for the capital."

CHAPTER XXVII
THE CASTLE OF ENDHOVEN

I behold the pageants splendid
That adorned those days of old;
Stately dames like queens attended,
Knights who wore the Fleece of Gold.
Longfellow.

The three knights who wore the Golden Fleece of Burgundy, proved to be the prince of Ravenstein, the marquis of Berg, and Englebert, count of Nassau, who was hereditary burg graf, or governor of Antwerp, and who, when a mere boy, in 1404, had espoused the heiress of Loeke and Breda. The prince of Ravenstein's territory lay between Gueldres and Brabant; it is now merged in the duchy of Cleves, but his castle still stands near the Maese.

Gueldres was an ancient and then very powerful dukedom, though it shrank to a petty state after the declaration of independence by the maritime provinces of the Netherlands in 1579, when it lost Nimeguen, the county of Zutphen, and Arnheim, and afterwards Ruremond, which was made over to Prussia; and since then, these portions have frequently changed their masters and form of government.

In the days of Arnold d'Egmont the duchy contained sixteen cities, two hundred and thirty villages, five great fortresses, and a vast number of castles.

The old duke treated Gray with great condescension, and conversed freely with him as they rode on together.

He inquired in what battle Gray received the severe wound the mark of which yet remained upon his face; and for the first time since he had left Scotland, our hero felt his heart glow with petty anger, in having to acknowledge that he had gained it in a mere street brawl with the enemies of the king,—the adherents of the turbulent and unruly house of Douglas.

"Tête Dieu!" said the duke; "that is the family which gives the king, your master, so much trouble. By Saint Louis, *I* would make quick work in disposing of them."

"They can bring twenty thousand men into the field," urged Sir Patrick.

"The great lord of Douglas is now in Flanders."

"Here—here in Flanders!" exclaimed Gray.

"Not in my territories; but on the other side of Brabant, and when last heard of he was travelling with a brilliant train of knights towards Breda, for the purpose of visiting that city, after which he passes forward to France. He was at the Feast of the Assumption in Antwerp, but proudly and haughtily kept aloof from all."

This unexpected intelligence filled Gray with emotions of a varied character, and solved a great mystery, the recollection of which had greatly troubled him.

It was, then, really Murielle Douglas whom he had seen, and no visionary or fancied resemblance; and he felt a glow of pleasure at the conviction that he had looked upon her face so recently, that he had breathed the same air with her; and that even now she was separated from him, not by the stormy German Ocean, and many a league of hill and glen; but only by a few miles of level land, and he mentally resolved, at every hazard and danger, that on leaving the duke of Gueldres, he would follow the Douglases to Breda, and that if they had departed, he would track them elsewhere; so powerful a noble, with so brilliant a retinue, would be easily traced in Flanders.

Pleasure, anticipation, and excitement, made him alternately gay and abstracted; thus he could barely attend with becoming reverence to the kind old prince who, being anxious to make a favourable impression on one who seemed the trusted subject of his intended son-in-law, drew his attention to the various castles, spires, and other features of the country, beguiling the way by many a story and legend, as they rode towards his hunting-lodge, at which they were to pass the night.

It stood upon the Gueldrian side of the Peel Morass. The latter included great tracts of land now dry and fertile, which were then deep swamps; and strange old stories lingered there, of broken dykes and bursting sluices—of overflowings from the Waal and Maese, with inundations from the Zuider Zee, by which whole farms were swept away, strong castles overthrown, and villages submerged; and of mermaids and mermen being swept by the retiring waters to flounder in the slough until they were captured; and the duke averred that in the days of his ancestor, Reinold II., duke of Gueldres, two had been instructed in Christianity and taught to make reverence to a crucifix,—a story corroborated in later times.

The "History of the Seven United Provinces," published at London in 1705, tells us, that "one day, when the sea had broken the banks and overflowed one part of the country, some young damsels of Ednam, going in a boat to milk their cows, found a nymph, or sea-woman, who lay half-covered in the mud, after the waters had been drained off. They drew her out and carried her to Ednam, where they taught her to spin and dress herself like other women; but they could not teach her to speak, nor lose the inclination which she had to return to her former element. There is an author who pretends that they imprinted in her some knowledge of a God, and that she made her reverence as she passed a crucifix. But it was not in Holland only," adds the historian, "that they found mermen in those days. There were some taken on the coast of Norway, which had on them the cross, the mitre, and all the pontifical habits of a bishop; but they only sighed after they were taken, and died very quickly."

Night had closed when the party reached the hunting-lodge, which was an old castle of some extent and considerable antiquity.

"This," said the duke, "is the hereditary mansion of the counts of Endhoven; and under its roof Count Ludwig, the last of that line, was born."

"Where he is not likely to die," added the count of Nassau.

"Since his attainder it has been mine."

"There is a strange story connected with it—or rather with the parents of Ludwig," said the count of Nassau, a noble with a long grave and pleasing countenance.

"His father was a cruel passionate and vindictive man, who used his countess so barbarously that she was wont to carry a dagger in her boddice, for her protection. Six months after Ludwig was born, she died of a broken heart, and the dagger, as she requested with her last breath, was buried with her. For a few weeks the count drank deeply, gamed and hunted, it seemed to all, as if to drown thought; but after a time he recovered, and to lighten the old castle, which seemed so grim and gloomy now, he carried off a beautiful peasant girl from the neighbourhood of Endhoven. Long and bitterly did the girl weep, on finding herself in his power, and earnestly she prayed to be permitted to return to her parents and to her lover, with whom she had been on the point of marriage; but the wild count only laughed, and forced her to drink cup after cup of Rhenish wine, and to sing and play on her ghittern.

"One day, when he was caressing and endeavouring to console her in his own rough way, he swore a terrible oath that he would love her till death, and no one else!

"Believe him not!" exclaimed a hollow voice behind—a voice like that of the dead countess. At the same moment a lean and wasted arm and hand, grasping a dagger, came out of the stone wall, and the count fell dead, stabbed to the heart!

"In his breast was found the countess's dagger—the same weapon that had been buried with her!"

As the count of Nassau concluded this strange story, they rode through the dark archway into the barbican of the castle, which seemed old and gloomy, even to Gray, who had come from a land of grim and guarded fortresses.

CHAPTER XXVIII
THE COURT OF GUELDRES

Here he saw the king approaching,
And he ended gallantly;
Left the crowd of knights about him,
Bending to the king his knee.
Poetry of Spain.

As we have much to narrate, we must hasten over the mere diplomacy in which the captain of the guard was concerned.

Next day the duke's party traversed the marshes of Peeland, and reached the city of Gueldres. A fleet horseman having been sent on before, Gray was received with considerable state at the ducal castle, in honour of the king, his master.

The capital city of Gueldres was then surrounded by marshes which added materially to its security, by making all approaches to it difficult and dangerous to invaders or strangers. It was girt by ramparts and deep trenches, through which flowed the river Niers, and thus it was deemed the strongest place in Flanders.

It was a curious little town of narrow streets, overshadowed by galleried houses of quaint aspect, with projecting eaves and steep roofs; old churches, grim and mysterious in architecture; and convents with high and sombre walls. The mass of the population seemed to be industrious Flemish artisans, mingled with the usual number of peasants, who brought their wares to market; cowled monks, dozing at the gates in the sunshine; and helmeted men-at-arms dicing and drinking in the hostelries.

Twenty great bombards were fired from the ramparts of the ducal castle, as a salute in honour of Sir Patrick's arrival, and the great banner of the duchy, *azure* a lion *or* crowned, for Gueldres; with a lion *gules* for Zutphen, was displayed on the keep, while a body of knights, archers, and well-mounted men-at-arms stood in military array within the gates. Gueldres was then famous for its cavalry, and for the spirit of its people, who were deemed so warlike, that to lessen their military genius and secure the possession of that province in his family, Charles V., in after times, excluded its natives from his armies.

The great ducal fortress, a portion of which was built in 878 by Wichardus a Ponte, the first lord of Gueldres, on his marriage with a daughter of the count of Zutphen, was deemed the strongest castle in the Netherlands, till its demolition by the Prussians in 1764.

There, in that old castle, situated amid the thick woods and rushlands, through which the Niers flows towards the Maese, Gray was presented to the duchess, Katherine of Cleves; to her daughter, the future queen of Scotland; the little princess Mary, then in her ninth year; and to her brother, prince Adolphus, by whose wickedness in after years the house of Gueldres was ruined, and its possessions merged into the line of Burgundy.

For when Adolphus rebelled against his father, old Arnold d'Egmont, and shut him up in a close prison, he was disinherited, and his title and patrimony sold in 1473 to Charles the Terrible, Duke of Burgundy, for a yearly pension of fourscore and ten thousand golden crowns of the Rhine; but no thought or anticipation had they then of those dark days that were coming, when civil war and misrule would rend the land asunder; and so old Duke Arnold feasted royally the knight who had come from the Scottish court, in presence of all his peers, the knights of the duchy, the governors of the country districts, and the deputies of Nimeguen, Arnheim, Ruremond, and Zutphen, his four great counties or provinces.

He presented him with a cassock, embroidered with gold and precious stones, worth a thousand ducats. The Duchess Katherine in the name of the princess, her daughter, entrusted him with a valuable ring for the young king, her future son-in-law, to whose ministers letters were prepared, expressive of the pleasure with which the coming ambassadors would be received.

Four days Sir Patrick remained at the castle of Gueldres, and then, leaving with impatience to overtake the Douglases about Breda, he bade adieu to the ducal court, and was convoyed, as the abbot of Tongland relates, twelve miles on his way, as far as Wees, by Prince Adolphus, the counts of Bommel and Nassau, with forty gentlemen on horseback "in cassocks of brocade, each with a gold chain at his neck."

Sir Patrick rejoiced when all this ceremony and state were over; when he was once more alone, and at liberty to pursue his own way towards Breda, which, however, he was fated never to reach.

CHAPTER XXIX
A STRANGE RENCONTRE

"I wake to sad reality, the days of youth have fled—
The flower, the shrub, the velvet turf have long ere now
been dead; The brook that ran so merrily has ceased to
bubble by, The pebble bed whereon it flowed is broken up
and dry."

As Sir Patrick Gray had no desire to traverse again the swampy wastes
of the Peel Morass, with the chance of perhaps encountering, when alone,
Ludwig of Endhoven, and his ruffianly Brabanciones, he took the way which
led towards the principality of Ravenstein, intending to cross the Maese and
travel to Breda through Dutch Brabant.

Eagerness to see, to meet, to rejoin Murielle, or to make his presence
there known to her, made him travel without delay; but in his ignorance of
the route, through a flat country, destitute of those strong natural features,
to which his eyes were accustomed at home, caused him frequently to make
mistakes and detours; thus the evening of the first day found him only at the
town of Grave, which had a fortress, situated by the margin of the Maese,
and of such strength that it was deemed the Key of Gueldreland, and had
thus been the object of many a bloody contest between the dukes of Brabant
and the earls of Holland.

As the town was small, he soon found an hostelry, and delivered his
horse to the groom and his sword to the tapster, according to what was then,
and for long after, the custom in all places of entertainment; but retained his
chain shirt and dagger while he sat at supper in the large public room, or
chamber-of-dais, in which were two gentlemen, apparently travellers like
himself, and similarly employed, in deciding upon the merits of broiled
fowls and a stoup of Burgundy.

Full of his own thoughts and of Murielle, reckoning the miles of flat
and monotonous Flemish scenery that lay between them, the hours that
must intervene ere he could see her; the mode in which he should discover
himself, the promises he would exact, and the vows he would repeat,
Gray took no notice of the strangers, who conversed freely, and somewhat
noisily, over their wine, their brusquerie of manner appearing to increase as

the twilight deepened with their potations; so that when Gray was at last roused from his reveries and looked towards them, the dusk was so great that he could scarcely discern their features.

They were talking of the proceedings of the great ecclesiastical council, which was then sitting in the Swiss archbishopric of Basle, and of the laws it was framing for the extirpation of heresy—topics upon which all men were beginning to question, or rather to *sound* each other, as such questions, in those days of the stake and faggot, were fraught with danger. They conversed in French; but finding that Gray sat resolutely silent, one turned and said to him abruptly, "Pray, sir, what think you of Procopius?"

"Of—who?" said Gray, with hesitation.

"Procopius, the Shaved."

"The leader of the Hussites?"

"Yes—the protesting heretics."

"I think him a bold Bohemian captain," was the cautious reply.

"What think you of his disputation at the holy council of Basle?" continued the other.

"I am not capable of judging."

"Peste! Did he not bear hard on the monks?" persisted the querist.

"I am not aware," replied Gray, with increasing reserve, "as I have not heard; but what said he?"

"At the head of two hundred gentlemen of his party, the valiant Procopius came before the council, and stoutly maintained that monkery was an invention of the devil.

"'Can you prove this?' asked Cardinal St. Julien, while his face flushed red as his stockings.

"'Yes!' replied the Bohemian, stoutly.

"'How?' thundered the cardinal, knitting his brows.

"'Thus; will you deny that the Saviour did *not* institute it?'

"'We do not.'

"'Then,' quoth Procopius, ''tis plainly an invention of the devil,' whereat Ænies Sylvius Piccolomini——"

"He who was in Scotland?"

"Yes; burst into a fit of laughter, which however did not prevent him from committing several poor devils to the flames in the course of the evening, where they spluttered and burned bravely for the amusement of all good Catholics."

"We have had some such work at home, where John Resby and Paul Crawar have perished at the stake, for preaching doctrines which some term false and others simply new."

"How do *you* term them?" asked the second traveller.

"Sir," replied Gray, "I am a soldier, and, being neither priest nor clerk may not know the difference."

"So you are of Scotland?" said the first stranger, suddenly relinquishing his French for the old dialect then spoken by the upper classes of the northern kingdom; "we bid you welcome, as countrymen. Pray join us—and harkee, tapster, let us have lights and more wine—we too, sir, are of Scotland."

More Burgundy was promptly brought, and on four torch-like candles of yellow wax being lighted in four great brass sconces, Gray was enabled to observe the aspect and bearing of his fellow travellers, or rather sojourners at the hostelry.

Both had their hair cut closely round above their ears, in the unbecoming fashion of twenty years before. They were moustached, but had their beards and whiskers shaved off in what was then the Scottish mode; they wore armour, with skirts composed of horizontal steel bands, called taces, with circular epaulets, to protect the armpits from sword thrusts, with spikes on the oriellets of their helmets.

The tallest and most handsome forcibly recalled to Gray's memory the late King James I.; he seemed to have something of that unhappy monarch's voice too, but his air and manner, though soldierly and stately, were reckless and blasé, and at times even abrupt and rough, yet not altogether unpleasing.

The other had pale grey cunning eyes, which were either bloodshot by dissipation, or reddened by the fire of innate cruelty, and they twinkled so far apart from his nose that it appeared almost impossible for him to see an object with *both* at once, for each seemed to be looking at the ear which adjoined it, and his hair and beard were a fiery red. But what were the emotions of Gray, and how firmly did he grasp his dagger, while a gust of fury filled his heart—a fury which he had great difficulty in repressing—when, in this person we have just described, he recognized that venal wretch, James Achanna!

By the light of the sconces the latter and his companion had a full view of Gray, but they seemed not to recognize him, for, as already stated, the ghisarma of Earl James had laid both cheeks open, thus a hideous wound traversed his whole face like a livid bar sinister. It was slowly passing away, however, for the old duchess of Gueldres had given him a rare balsam, which she said would effectually efface the scars; but as yet they, and a new curl which Gray had fancifully given his moustache, had so effectually altered his appearance, as to conceal his identity from this ruffianly swashbuckler of the earl of Douglas.

"So you are of Scotland, sir?" resumed the other traveller.

"I am come from thence but lately," replied Gray; "and may I ask your names?"

"Certainly," replied our old acquaintance, with perfect confidence; "I am James Achanna, a gentleman of the Lord Douglas, a name at which men prick their ears in Nithsdale, whatever they may do in foggy Flanders."

"And I," said the other, "am the Lord Rosse."

"Rosse!" reiterated Gray; "pardon me, sir, but, under favour, we have no such lord in Scotland."

"Not when I am *out* of it," said he, laughing.

"I know not the title," added Gray, coldly.

"Indeed! one seems to be soon forgotten then. Shall I state to you more fully that I am Robert Stewart, duke of Albany and earl of Rosse."

"The son of Duke Murdoch!" exclaimed Gray, starting from his seat with mingled surprise and respect.

"Yes; son of that Duke Murdoch, who, with his second son, and Duncan, earl of Lennox, was foully butchered at the Lady's Rock, before the castle gates of Stirling. Vengeance has a long and bitter memory! and by that extrajudicial murder, for such I will maintain it to be in the face of Europe, I have been since boyhood an exile, a wanderer, and now, when little more than thirty years of age, my hair is greyer than my poor old father's was, when his venerable head rolled in the sand beneath the doomster's axe."

Gray bowed low, for respect to the royal blood was strongly graven then in the hearts of the Scots, in none more than his, and Albany, though exiled and outlawed, in consequence of the malpractices of his father (who had been regent during the detention of James I. in England), was the cousin of King James II.

"And *you*, sir?" asked Albany, loftily.

"I am your grace's most humble servant," replied Gray pausing, as he dreaded to tell his name before Achanna, lest it might reveal to the Douglases his royal mission, and blight his hope of meeting Murielle.

"But your name, sir," said the duke, with growing displeasure; "your name?"

"Yes," added Achanna, imitating him, "we must have your name."

"I am the laird of Luaig," replied Gray, with ready wit, taking the name of a little obscure loch, which lies in a narrow glen near his father's castle of Foulis.

CHAPTER XXX
BOLD SCHEMES

Many have ruined their fortunes; many have escaped ruin
by want of fortune. To obtain it the great have become little,
and the little great.—Zimmerman.

"Luaig, laird of Luaig," said Albany, ponderingly; "I do not recognize the name."

"Lairds are plenty as heather hills in the far north country," said Achanna, sneeringly.

"And I have been long enough in France and elsewhere to forget even my mother tongue, as well as my dear mother's face; yet she was Isabel of Lennox," said Albany, sadly; "but lairds in the north are plenty, I know."

"And poor as plenty," added Achanna.

"True, sir," said Gray, "and hence my mission here in Flanders."

"How; I was just about to inquire," observed the duke; "seek you knight's service?"

"Yes; fortune has made me a free lance."

"And ready to follow any banner?"

"Yes; provided it find me in food, horse, and armour."

"Then follow *me*," said Albany, "and ere long, my friend, I may find work for your sword at home."

"At *home*; do you mean in Scotland?"

"Aye, in Scotland; how now, Achanna, why the devil dost twitch my sleeve?"

"As a warning that your grace should be wary."

"Here thought and speech are free. True, we have not eaten a peck of salt with our new friend, the laird of Luaig, but at this distance from that bloody rock which lies before Stirling gate, we may trust him nevertheless," said the reckless Albany, draining his wine cup at a draught; "wilt follow me, Luaig—is it a bargain?" he added, holding out his hand.

"But whither goes your grace?"

"To tread the same path my hapless father trod," replied the duke, with something of dignity and pathos in his manner.

"It may lead, alas!—--"

"To the same bloody doom, you would say?"

"Yes; I would pray your grace to be wary."

"I care not; I shall live and die, Robert Stewart, duke of Albany and earl of Rosse, if I die not something better."

A cunning smile twinkled in the hawk-like eyes of the unfathomable Achanna.

"Sit with us, Luaig," said Albany; "my heart ever warms to my countrymen, though cold as ice to my little cousin their king; and there are times when I hope to close my eyes peacefully in the same place where they first saw the light, the old castle of Rothesay by the sea—the waves that flow through the bonnie kyles of Bute, and past the hills of Cowal; but of all that more anon. Sit with us, sir, the more the merrier."

"With this poor stoup of wine?" said the prosaic Achanna, peering into the tankard with one of his cunning eyes.

"True, the old saw did not add that," said Albany, rattling the purse at his girdle; "but gibe me not about it. What can be worse than having too much liquor?"

"Having none at all," returned the thirsty parasite.

"*Laus Deo!* you are right, Achanna. Hallo, tapster! more wine, and quickly too. Think of Robert of Albany having for a server that slipshod varlet, who is all breeches and horn buttons! But you seem to have been severely wounded, laird of Luaig?"

"Almost to death," said Gray, and while Achanna, as if inspired by some undefinable suspicion, surveyed him keenly, he writhed at having to falsify so much, and trembled for the next question; but, on the wine being placed on the table, the careless Albany filled their cups to the brim, saying, "Drink, my friend, drink of this, it comes from the land of old Duke Philip the Good, and you will find it better than arquebusade," he added, referring to a medicinal lotion then famous for gun-shot wounds.

"May I ask in what direction your grace is travelling?" inquired Gray, who had some anxiety in the matter.

"The direction that suits our fancy," replied Achanna.

"I spoke to the duke of Albany," said Gray, with a flash in his eye, and a gush of fury through his heart.

"True, and Albany can answer for himself," said the duke; "we are travelling with all speed to overtake the earl of Douglas and his friends."

"Who are now at Breda?" said Gray, eagerly.

"No; they are at—how name you the place, Achanna?"

"Where?" asked Gray, as the latter hesitated.

"At Bommel."

"Is it distant?"

"Nay, 'tis thirty miles nearer than Breda, and we shall reach it to-morrow."

"And to-morrow, perhaps, I may see *her*," thought the lover in his heart.

"To the great Earl James of Douglas, Abercorn, and Avondale, and to our happy meeting," exclaimed Albany, draining another large cup of wine.

Rendered reckless by years of disappointment, by dissipation, and the mortifications incident to exile and dependence, the unfortunate young duke, the victim of circumstances and the treasons of his father, drank, as seemed to be his wont, deeply; and, as he did so, unfolded unwittingly no doubt to Gray (and to the great discomposure of Achanna), the extent and daring of the designs entertained by the Douglases; and he continued to do so, regardless of their more wary and more subtle follower, who, with one eye glistening apparently on each, listened impatiently, and seemed to scrutinize Gray as if he would have read his soul.

That Albany should be plotting with Douglas to subvert the king's power, or to usurp his crown, did not excite Gray's wonder; but his heart almost died within him, when the duke, in a half-serious and half-bantering way, mentioned incidentally, the proposed firmer and more lasting alliance between the great earl and himself, by marriage with Murielle Douglas; and had it not happened that the worthy master James Achanna's dagger fell from its sheath upon the floor, and that he had to stoop beneath the table to pick it up, keen and sharp as he was, he could not have failed to remark the pallor which overspread the lover's face, and the wild light that flashed in his eyes, at this crushing information. However, rallying all his energies to seem collected and cool, after a pause, Gray said,

"But, under favour, is not your grace contracted to a daughter of Charles VII. of France."

"Yes; I believe my father, poor duke Murdoch, made some such arrangement ere his head was cut off—when I was a child, and his captive nephew, James I., was twangling on his ghittern to Jane Beaufort in the gardens of Windsor."

"Believe! are you not certain?" said Gray earnestly.

"Since I have been among Hussites, Parisians, Bohemians, and Germans, I have been certain of nothing my friend—not even of my own existence— for this is a land of fog and philosophy; but I would have been much more certain of that spousal contract, had Monseigneur Charles the Victorious been a little more liberal with his French crowns, and a little less so with his French compliments, as I could live on the first, but not on the second. Moreover, I think my little princess Radegonde is not quite pleased with me, since my affair with Madame d'Armagnac."

"Who is she?"

"A woman more beautiful than Agnes Sorel—the lady of beauty. I have seen them both together. And then, as the devil would have it, I got embroiled with Madame la Marchale de Loheac, while her patriotic husband was fighting those insolent English last year in Bretagne and Anjou."

"But—but, your grace," stammered Gray, who felt as if he was on the eve of losing his Murielle for ever, "you are solemnly betrothed to Mademoiselle of France."

"I am—and what then?"

"Such a contract cannot be broken."

"Save by the pope, so the earl of Douglas is now on his way to Rome with Dame Murielle; I mean to accompany them, and so may you, if you care for attaching yourself to my fortunes, or misfortunes rather. That contract, moreover, was made when my father was regent of Scotland, and the king was a prisoner of war in England—and Mademoiselle of France considers me but as an outlaw now." Then after humming a lively French air, Albany said, "'tis said Murielle Douglas sings like a throstle, when winging its way aloft on a beltane morning. The throstle!" he added, letting his chin drop on his breast with an air of tipsy sadness, "Ah! that makes me think of poor old Scotland, which, despite these desperate plots, I may never see again, and my heart is wrung within me, when I think of the bonnie birken woods that shed their autumn leaves upon my mother's grave."

After a pause Albany suddenly raised his head, and Gray was moved to perceive that his fine dark eyes were full of tears; but he again filled and drained his cup of wine, and it had the effect of completely intoxicating him.

"It has been arranged that your grace was to meet the earl on his travel?" asked Gray.

"Yes; and he sent our good friend Achanna, with a message inviting me to join him and my intended little duchess at Bommel," replied Albany, laughing; "and so I have been travelling so fast, that my horses must have discovered an impatient lover was in the saddle; but what the devil dost think was master Achanna's first information for me?"

"I cannot guess," said Gray, not much interested in the matter.

"That she has a lover already."

"A lover!" exclaimed Gray, in a very different tone.

"Aye, a lover here in Flanders," hiccuped Albany, while Gray sat breathless, and toyed with his dagger in the shade.

"His name?" said he.

"Sir Patrick Gray, captain of my dear cousin's royal guard. *Laus Deo!* if I discover him, he is extremely likely to rot in Flemish earth, while his papers may be of service to us."

"How so?"

"Because he is on a mission from the earl's three enemies—my cousin, his regent Livingstone, and the chancellor Crichton—aid me to discover—to kill him, and in Lennox, I will more than double your lands of Luaig."

"And object of this mission—"

"Ah! that is just what we want to know, though many say, 'tis but to Arnold d'Egmont of Gueldres, anent a royal marriage. But I'll brook no lovers, no rivals, near my throne—*Laus Deo*, no! and I would give all I have—not much certainly—to be as near this Sir Patrick Gray as I am to *you* at this moment. But a friend of mine is on his track already, I believe—one whom he cannot hope to escape."

"A friend?" said Gray.

"An unfortunate and valiant Count of Flanders."

"Who?"

"Ludwig of Endhoven, a captain of Brabanciones; by St. Christopher our lover is not likely to escape *him*—eh, Achanna! but now let us to bed—to bed; for we must be in our saddles by cockcrow to-morrow. Achanna, your arm," said the poor young duke, staggering up; "Lua-Luaig—fare, sir—fare you well."

"Good night to your grace, and God be wi' you!" said Gray, opening and closing the door as they separated.

After the duke and Achanna were gone, he sat long and late, full of anxious and bitter thoughts that came thick and fast upon him. He felt agony at the idea of Murielle being about to be sacrificed to the wild, ambitious, and revengeful schemes of the earl of Douglas and the duke of Albany; and he actually trembled lest her heart might have changed or her fancy have been dazzled, for he now remembered with pain the banter of his comrade and kinsman, MacLellan. He pitied and despised the outlawed duke, yet he trembled for the trouble, which he, with the earl, when combined, might give the young king James, their master. He was filled with wrath at the resolution, so fully expressed, to destroy himself, and starting to his feet, he was about to get his sword from the tapster, and summon Achanna forth into the moonlight, which shone brightly, to upbraid him with his villany, and then kill him on the spot; and in doing so, he would not have committed a crime, but have acted simply in the spirit of the age. However, cooler reflection showed that he might serve Murielle, the king, and himself better, by preserving his incognito. So master Achanna, that utilitarian Scot, who would have sold his own father and his mother to boot, without compunction, slept that night without a yard of cold iron in his body.

Yet, as it was impossible for Gray to travel with Duke Robert and this scurvy companion to Bommel, he resolved to set forward alone. Thus, after a restless night, he was up and mounted an hour before sunrise, and while the frowsy haze hung thick and yellow over the pale-green willow-copse of the Maese, veiling all Grave and the quaint old castle of Otho, lord of Cuick and Haverale, he was far on his journey to Bommel.

CHAPTER XXXI
BOMMEL

What mad jest is this, my masters?
I know not where the damsel lives, not I;
But see to it, that ye molest her not!—Old Play.

After passing Alphen, Sir Patrick crossed an old stone bridge, and found himself in the Bommelerwaard, a fertile island, formed by the Waal and the Maese; and about noon, he reached the object of his destination, the quaint and ancient town of Zalt-Bommel, which stands upon the left bank of the former river.

The ducal banner of Arnold d'Egmont was waving on the castle built by Otho III. of Nassau, count of Gueldres, who walled the city in 1299, and therein dwelt Jacques de Lalain, the governor, then named the Dyck Graf, who kept the town in awe with his cannon, but more by his sluices, by opening which, he could lay the whole district under water, and drown every citizen in five minutes.

While riding forward, Gray had revolved in his mind, a hundred plans for making himself known to Murielle, but none seemed practicable; and then, with no other conviction, than the double necessity for being wary, and procuring a disguise, with a heart that beat lightly though anxiously, he passed through the wide and busy streets of Bommel, along the quays of its now choked-up harbour, and found quarters at an hostelry, that stood near the gardens of the ancient college of Canons, which was founded in 1303, by Reinold the warlike count of Gueldres.

Here he sent for the keeper of a frippery, as a clothing establishment was then named, and obtained the dress of a Muscovite merchant, a long gown of brown cloth trimmed with red braid and sables, a cap of black wolf's skin, and a short crooked sword, which he slung in front by a brass chain, in the oriental fashion. He laid aside all his military trappings, save his chain shirt, which the disguise he had adopted completely concealed, and after dinner he sallied forth into the city in quest of adventure and of Murielle.

It was fortunate that he had obtained so complete a disguise and so readily, for at the corner of a street he was overtaken by three reckless horsemen, who passed at a hard gallop, and so closely, that he was nearly ridden down.

They were the very persons he wished to avoid—the duke of Albany, count Ludwig of Endhoven, and James Achanna. He endeavoured to follow, and see whither they went; but they rode rapidly, and were soon out of sight.

The masses of the population, their bustle, and the business they seemed to transact, with the wealth and luxury he saw on every hand, excited the astonishment of Gray, who had come from a land that was simply warlike and pastoral; for in that age Flanders was the central point of European commerce—the market of all the products of the south, the north, and the Levant.

"As in the course of human affairs," says Schiller, "here a licentious luxury followed prosperity. The seductive example of Philip the Good could not but accelerate its approach. The court of the Burgundian dukes was the most voluptuous and magnificent in Europe, Italy itself not accepted. The costly dress of the higher classes, which afterwards served as patterns to the Spaniards, and eventually with the Burgundian customs, passed over to the court of Austria, soon descended to the lower orders, and the humblest citizen nursed his person in velvet and silk. The pomp and vanity of dress were carried by both sexes to extravagance. The luxury of the table had never reached so great a height among any other people. The immoral assemblage of both sexes at bathing-places, and others of reunion for pleasure and enjoyment, had banished all shame."

This state of society was new and bewildering to the plain soldier, who had come from the hardy and frugal land of the "rough-footed Scots," as he strolled along the thoroughfares of Bommel, disguised as a merchant from Muscovy, without a word of the Muscovite language, and as ignorant of whether he should pretend to import tallow, tar, hogsbristles, iron and flax, or the preserved fruits and luscious wines of the sunny Levant. Thus fearing that his disguise might lead him into a scrape or predicament, he avoided the harbour and mercantile portions of the city, and sought those in which he was most likely to meet some of the earl's train, or discover his locality.

After two days of hopeless inquiry, as the most prudent people are at times the most rash, he conceived the idea of relinquishing his disguise, of resuming his former attire, and applying to the Dyck Graf, who was a Gueldrian noble, and by birth a Burgundian of high rank, when luckily chance threw in his way the most fortunate person he could have met.

He had visited all the churches in time of mass and vespers, hoping to see the earl, or some of his numerous retinue, and on the third day, just as he was leaving, with a heavy heart, the gorgeously-carved porch of St. Genevieve, he heard a familiar voice say —

"Yes, yes, it is all very bad and wicked of the Burgundians no doubt; but are not all the world so? When, through my humble efforts and the agency of our Holy Father, the great master of evil is purified and restored to the place he fell from, such things shall be no more. *Veritas mea et misericordia mea cum ipso; et in nomine meo exaltabitur cornuejus!*"

"Oh, by good St. Genevieve, this can be no other than my worthy friend and kinsman, the abbot of Tongland!" said Gray, joyously, as he pressed through a crowd of bubous-shaped Flemings, towards where the old abbot, who wore a travelling cassock and calotte cap, with long flaps, stood near a pillar conversing with one whom he knew to be the chaunter of the abbey, an official who conducted the choir and had charge of the library, to increase the MS. stores of which, he had accompanied the earl to the Continent.

"Oh that I were now at Rome, instead of loitering here in Flanders," resumed the abbot; "how many souls might yet be saved!"

"The devil hath been long at his work, father abbot, since that tempting day in the Garden of Eden," said Gray, laughing, as he took the abbot's hand in his.

"Good morrow, sir," said the churchman, coldly, as he scrutinized the strange costume and scarred face of the speaker.

"You do not know me?" exclaimed Sir Patrick.

"Nay, sir, not I."

"'Tis well," said Gray, with a bitter smile, as he remembered his wound, "I seem a Muscovite, but the cowl does not make the monk. I crave a word apart, lord abbot—I have that to say, which you must hear alone."

When they withdrew a pace or two back, Sir Patrick lifted his fur cap, and displayed his features more fully.

"Heaven grant us its peace," exclaimed the abbot, with astonishment; "'tis my kinsman, Gray of Foulis!"

"Hush," said Gray, placing a hand upon his mouth.

"Rash boy, and bold as rash, what seek you here in Flanders?" asked the abbot, with gloom, alarm, and almost anger expressed in his face.

"I came on the king's service; but now I seek Murielle Douglas—and Murielle I shall see, father!"

"Beware, lest you find death instead."

"I know the penalty, if discovered," said Gray carelessly; "but in this disguise, and with a face so altered, I may escape, as I have already eluded, the penetrating eyes of the villain Achanna."

"But the earl—he whose projects are so high—so deep—so terrible!" urged the priest in a whispered voice of agony.

"He will not dare to touch me here in a fortified town—"

"What! You expect Earl James to be a saint in Gueldreland, though he is a devil in Galloway? What saith Horace—that those who cross the seas change their climate but *not* their mind."

"I know with what intention *he* has crossed the seas, and for what object he will return."

"You do!" said the abbot, in a husky whisper.

"Aye, as well as you, father abbot, who are the keeper of that pretty burden, his conscience. I have seen, yea, and supped with, Robert, duke of Albany."

"Hush!" said the abbot, glancing at his chaunter.

"Ah—'tis your turn to say *hush* now."

"You have seen him—this poor outlawed prince?"

"Yes, and spent an evening with him—an interesting, if not a jovial one, certainly; and in his cups, he unfolded some very pretty schemes, concerning which, I shall be silent, until I tread again the streets of Edinburgh."

"Oh, be wary, kinsman—be wary!" said the abbot, in a voice that betrayed increasing alarm.

"The duke modestly asked me to aid in a little plot against my *own* life, and made me several fair offers to lure me to his service against the king."

"Offers, of what?"

"Lands and titles."

"He is liberal, as that Fell Spirit, who took our Lord unto the mountain top, and offered Him cities and empires, when he had not an inch of land to give—not even the mud that adhered to his cloven hoof. Oh, that I were now at Rome!"

"But Murielle is to be made the tool—the victim of these desperate plotters—and you know it, father, you know it!"

"Ah," said the abbot, with a groan, "there you sting my inmost heart."

"Then how must *mine* be stung? but you will enable me to meet—to console her?"

"I—impossible!"

"There is nothing impossible in it," continued Gray, with earnestness; "you must—you shall! Ah, I do not threaten you—I implore. Think of all we have suffered for each other; think of what we may yet be condemned to suffer, by those, whom Evil Fortune seems to have made the arbiters of our destiny."

"'Tis very sad, and very true," replied the abbot, slowly, "but I *dare* not."

"You are a priest, and may dare anything," exclaimed

Gray, passionately, "and here I swear, that if you do not take me to Murielle, or bring her to me—in short, if you do not enable us to meet, by all that we revere in heaven and on earth, and by the bones of St. Genevieve, I will cast myself in the earl's path, and brave him and his followers to the last; and you know what is sure to ensue *then*."

"Your instant destruction."

"Promise me—promise," urged Gray, in whose eyes the tears were starting as he pressed the hands of the old abbot.

The latter was kind and gentle hearted, and loved his young kinsman too well to withstand his entreaties long; he felt his resolution waver, and strangely enough became a little irritated.

"By St. Bryde, of Douglas, I would we had never met," he exclaimed; "although Sir Patrick, the sequel might have been the worse for you."

"Where does she reside?"

"With the earl and countess," replied the abbot, briefly.

"Of course," said Gray, impatiently, "but, where are they?"

"In a house belonging to the Dyck Graf, and adjoining the great church and the college of canons. I am to-night to bring her—"

"Where, father—where?"

"To this church of St. Genevieve."

"Oh, how happy was the chance that brought me hither! You will allow me to go with you?"

"Impossible—never; by my habit, my order—"

"Why—why?"

"Your relations with her, and my office—"

"Your office will protect us; it is ordained that you should succour those in distress, and Murielle and I are both in need of succour. Father Abbot—dear kind friend, you agree."

"Be then silent and wary, and meet me at the porch here, at the hour of seven this evening," replied the abbot, suddenly giving way.

"God will reward you—I never can—adieu, adieu!" said Gray, in the fulness of his heart, and in a voice which became husky with emotion, as he hastened into the street, with a giddy head and a light heart, muttering: "I shall see her—to-night I shall see her! but ah, by the dial, it lacks five hours of the time!"

CHAPTER XXXII
THE CHURCH OF ST. GENEVIEVE

When stars are in the quiet skies,
Then most I pine for thee;
Bend on me then thy tender eyes,
As stars look on the sea!
For thoughts, like waves that glide by night,
Are stillest when they shine;
Mine earthly love lies hush'd in light,
Beneath the heaven of thine.—Bulwer.

To Gray it appeared as if the day would never pass, and he spent the hours of it in thinking over all he would say to Murielle, and all she might probably reply. He glanced at his mirror—would the scar on his face shock her? Doubtless, but she would love him the more for it, and then it would wear away in time. Then he consulted the gnomons of the sun-dials at the street corners, and the clocks of the numerous churches, and to the eyes of an impatient lover, the shadows of the former, and the hands of the latter, seemed alike to stand still.

Yet inevitable Time, which may neither be anticipated or withheld, passed slowly, and surely on. The shadows of the quaint streets, of the carved and traceried steeples, and of the battlemented castle, with its grey old walls and muddy sluices, fell far to the eastward, along the grassy meadows of the Bommelerwaard; the storks were already in their nests on the steep old gables, and long before the appointed hour, Gray was at the porch of St. Genevieve, where, with anxious eyes, he scanned the passengers, and the thoroughfares in every direction.

At last *seven* tolled from the spire, and every stroke reverberated in his heart. They had not yet come, and just as a sigh of impatience escaped him, a hand was laid upon his shoulder; he turned, and beheld the abbot of Tongland, and standing behind him, on the upper step of the porch, a pace or two within the church, was a lady, wearing a Flemish hood and veil. Gray's heart rose to his lips, as he sprang towards her, and pressed in his the hands of Murielle.

"Beware, Sir Patrick," said the abbot, "we cannot permit such transports here, and in view of the passers, too! Retire into the north aisle, while I betake me to the south, for I have still some leaves of my daily office to read; and when that is over, I shall rejoin you. Be secret—be wary!"

With this advice, the politic old Churchman left Gray and Murielle to themselves, being perfectly well aware that his presence, could in no way enhance the joy of this sudden interview.

The quiet tenderness of Murielle moderated the ardor of Gray; both trembled with the depth of their emotions, and the girl's eyes were full of tears of affection and fear, for she felt as if Gray had been restored to her from the tomb, and sometime passed before she could speak with coherence.

"Ah, that I should miss your presence here for a moment," said Gray, "but I was watching the passers in the streets."

"While I watched *you* from the church!"

"And how did you enter it—I have been an hour at the porch."

"We came by the postern, which adjoins the great garden of the Dyck Graf's mansion."

"Where you reside?"

"Yes."

"And the earl, too?"

"Yes—but he is hunting with the Dyck Graf. Oh, these wounds on your face," said Murielle, stroking his cheek with her pretty hands, and kissing it; "oh, mother of God, what must you have suffered?"

"More than tongue can say, Murielle, and more in mind than in body; but these scars are the relict of that dreadful day, when Earl James so mercilessly struck me down,—as I besought mercy or quarter—not for my own sake, but for *yours*."

"And when I thought to have died—great is my wonder that I did not, for strenuously the earl, the countess, and all in Thrave strove to convince me of your death."

"But you received my letter, by Sir Thomas—my good and brave MacLellan?"

"Yes—and it restored me to hope, to life as it were, by the assurance that you lived—you, whom all about me wished should die."

Gray drew her close to his heart, and a soft sweet smile overspread the childlike face, while he pressed to his again and again the little rosebud mouth. At that moment he heard something like a cough or snort; Gray looked round, but saw only the shadows of the pillars that lay in long lines across the tessalated floor of the church.

"I thought, Murielle, I should have gone mad with perplexity when I saw you at Antwerp," said Gray.

"At Antwerp—you saw me there?" replied Murielle, a little beam of gratified vanity lighting up her eyes.

"In the procession of the assumption; but the strange part you bore—how came that about?"

"Through the desire of the earl and the bishop of Mechlin (or as some name him, Malines), whom he knew in Scotland as secretary to the Legate Æneas Sylvius Piccolomini; but, believe me, I had no desire to appear as I did."

"And how long do you remain in Bommel?"

"A week."

"Thank heaven! then we shall meet often. Have—have you yet seen the outlawed duke of Albany?" asked Gray; hesitating with the question, while burning with impatience for the answer.

"No," said Murielle, blushing in spite of herself; "I have declined."

Gray pressed her to his breast.

"You know then, dearest, of what the earl is capable," said he; "of forcing you to become the bride of another, who will further his designs and strengthen his power at home and abroad."

"Yes—yes," replied Murielle, weeping; "I knew it—already has he broadly hinted as much."

"Already!"

"And commanded me to obey; ah, pardon me for making this admission!" said she imploringly.

"Pardon you?" reiterated Gray.

"Yes; but the earl rarely condescends to hint."

"Oh my beloved heart!"

"I meant not to add to your griefs, dearest, by naming a rival whose rank renders him so formidable,—but—but—" tears choked her utterance.

"And this rival is the duke of Albany—a French minion—an outlaw; the son of a traitor who plotted for the lawless detention of James I., in

England; a roué and swashbuckler, who consorts with the robber, Ludwig of Endhoven!"

"'Tis indeed he, to whom they would sacrifice me," said Murielle, clasping her poor little tremulous hands, and weeping bitterly. Gray remained silent for some moments, while love, pity, and alarm wrung his heart by turns.

"I know it—I know it," said he gloomily, "for Albany's own lips informed me."

"You see, dear Gray, to what lengths Douglas and my sister will go in their thirst for vengeance. The young king dethroned or slain; his banished cousin crowned by English aid as Robert IV., the house of Douglas would become more powerful than ever, and thus attain in the land a strength which none could crush, and before which Livingstone and Crichton assuredly must fall."

The vista these projects opened up, when thus plainly stated, startled even the gallant heart of Gray!

"But Albany dare not," said he huskily, while grasping his dagger; "*this* should end his treason long ere it reached the mature length his father's did."

"Douglas and Albany will dare anything," sobbed Murielle; "alas, poor me! I am, my sister says, but a child, and a very weak one in their iron hands."

"Then be a woman—let us escape and seek safety by flight together. We are but thirty miles from the sea, where we can soon find a ship for Scotland, and ere the earl's return we may be ready to defy him."

"Oh to what would you tempt me?"

"To save yourself and me. Once wedded, once again in Scotland, under the protection of the king, a boy though he be, we might defy your kinsman and all his followers."

"Oh no—no!" said Murielle, shaking her head mournfully.

"To Gueldres then. Duke Arnold will succour and protect us," urged Gray vehemently.

"Worse still!"

"Oh Murielle, in pity to yourself and me——"

"Nay, nay, this must not be," said the abbot of Tongland angrily, as he came suddenly forward; "Sir Patrick Gray, this is a breach of faith with me. In friendship to her, and you my kinsman—for I dearly love you both—I permitted this meeting; but have no intention that it shall take a turn so startling—so dangerous for the honour of Lady Murielle, and for the lives of us all perhaps! Come—come with me lady, we must return at once."

"But we shall meet again,—good Father Abbot, say we shall meet again?" urged Gray.

"Once, I promise you, once ere we leave Bommel, on the *third* evening from this, at the *same* hour," said the abbot, hurrying Murielle away, for at that moment several Flemish ecclesiastics entered the church.

As Gray wished to avoid every one, he withdrew; but resolved that, come what might of it, in his next interview with Murielle, to save her from the perils that were impending. She still loved him truly, and there was every consolation in the knowledge that she did so; yet her love would not save her from Albany when Douglas chose to play the tyrant.

But the abbot's *protégé*, the serpent, was abroad, and there were many mischiefs to be plotted and many to be worked ere Murielle could be saved from her persecutors.

As she and the abbot passed through the postern door which opened from one of the aisles into the garden of the Dyck Graf—a door over which there may be seen to this day, a strange sculpture of a mitred cat preaching to twelve little mice—a man who had evidently been listening shrunk back into the shade. This person was the somewhat ubiquitous James Achanna, who, inspired alike by impatience and malevolence, repaired immediately to his lord and chief the earl.

CHAPTER XXXIII
HOUSE OF THE DYCK GRAF

With every exertion, the best of men can do but a moderate amount of good; but it seems in the power of the most contemptible individual to do indescribable mischief.— Washington Irving.

While the lonely Sir Patrick Gray, full of sombre and exciting thoughts, retired to his hostelry to consider and to plan the deliverance of Murielle from her own family, the house of Messire Jacques de Lalain, the Dyck Graf or hereditary governor of Bommel, which had been assigned as a temporary residence to the powerful Scottish noble and his retinue, became brilliantly lighted up.

In the principal chamber were grouped together many of the personages whom we last saw together, at the abbot's house in Edinburgh, on that eventful evening of November, 1440. It was noble in aspect, loftily ceiled, and floridly decorated in the Flemish fashion of that age of profusion, the walls and roof being covered with quaint devices and heraldic blazons, by Jan Van Eyck, a native of Maeseyk, who, in 1410, attained great perfection in the mixing of oil colours. Within a fireplace, lined with Dutch tiles, blazed a pile of logs across the massive bar of the and-irons. On an oaken buffet stood a gigantic lion, formed entirely of Delft ware, the crest of Gueldres, as it sprang from a ducal crown. From the ceiling hung a gilded chandelier, a veritable pyramid of candles, which shed a flood of light upon the guests below.

And striking groups they formed, the ladies having long veils of the richest white lace, falling from the summits of their lofty horned head-dresses; while their other garments, cote-hardies and skirts, were of the finest silk, taffeta, and gauze, covered with pearls, jewels, and embroidery; the hues and fashion of the attire of all these noble demoiselles making them resemble the queens of clubs and spades, just as we may see them on a pack of cards.

The apparel of the gentlemen was much of the same material—gay in colour, and gorgeous as embroidery and jewels could make it, with here and there a richly engraved cuirass of Milan plate, a gorget of burnished steel, or a diamond studded dagger-hilt, to impart a military character to the wearer.

An old cavalier, with a high bald forehead, a beard so long that Ferdinand of Toledo might have envied it, and who wore the mantle and jewel of the Golden Fleece of Burgundy, was conversing in French with the earl of Douglas. He was Jacques de Lalain, a noble Burgundian knight, hereditary Burg Graf of the town and castle of Bommel. While seeming to converse with the earl, who was speaking of King Charles VII. and Duke Philip the Good, and what might result from a war between France and Burgundy, with the adverse parts which Scotland and England were certain to take therein, he was gazing with pleasure on a group of Scottish girls, who by the fine carriage of their heads, their general bearing, and more than all by the whiteness of their hands, evinced that they inherited the best blood and highest breeding in the land.

They were, in fact, the Countess Margaret and Murielle, her sister; the countess of Ormond; dark-eyed Maud Douglas, of Pompherston; Mariota, of Glendoning; the golden-haired Caillean Rua; Lady Jean, of Cairnglas; and the three daughters of Sir Alan Lauder. The gentlemen who conversed with them, and played at chess with some, at tables (an old name for backgammon) with others, were the knights and esquires of the earl's retinue.

Amid these were two persons already introduced to the reader— Robert, duke of Albany, and Ludwig, count of Endhoven, whom as a simple Burgundian knight, he had, with his usual recklessness, dared to introduce to this high circle.

It was not without secret emotions of pleasure and satisfaction, that the *blasé* royal outlaw beheld the girlish beauty of Murielle. Though in no mood for marrying, and long since used to consider women only as tools or playthings, to be cast aside when no longer needed, he conceived that he might find such a wife, for a time, the reverse of a tedium or an encumbrance; and, that on the simple condition of wedding her, he could enter with ardour into those daring schemes which promised vengeance to Douglas and a throne to himself.

Gay, handsome, and richly dressed, he leaned upon the high back of her chair, and insisted on conversing with her, flattering himself that he was making considerable progress, though the memory of Gray's sad loving eyes, and of his lover's kiss, yet lingered in her mind; but she was too well bred to treat the duke as he deserved; too gentle and too timid to repel him; and, moreover, too proud to acknowledge the footing upon which he affected to place himself with her—a position on which she was daily rallied by the countess and her ladies of the tabourette, until her little heart waxed wroth.

There were times also, when Albany, piqued by a coldness and reserve that were new to him, actually nursed himself into the conviction that he was desperately in love with this little beauty—if love in a heart so *roué* were a possibility.

Near them sat Count Ludwig, affecting to be entirely occupied with a bloodhound, which the Dyck Graf had presented to the countess. It was a spotless dog, of "Black St. Hubert's breed," but *white* as snow, and was named Souyllard, after that famous hound of the prince of Lorraine, which is thus extolled in the "Noble Art of Venerie:"

> "My name first came from holy Hubert's race;
> Souyllard my sire, a hound of singular grace."

The reckless Ludwig, as he gazed on the beauty of Murielle, began to conceive some very daring schemes on his own account, as his armed Brabanciones, to the number of some hundreds, lurked in the Peel morass and woods on the other side of the Waal. He allowed his imagination to run riot, and while affecting to caress the powerful hound on the one hand, and converse with the abbot of Tongland on the other, he saw before him only the sweet girl's gentle eyes, which drooped, and her little coral mouth, which paled, whenever his bold glance fell on her.

The abbot and she exchanged smiles from time to time. He was full of commiseration and alarm for Sir Patrick Gray, whose preceptor he had been, and he was thinking of that peaceful and pleasant time in Tongland Abbey, when he was wont to take him once daily to read the works of St. Augustine, or a page of the Gospels in old monkish Latin. Each of these stood under an iron grating in the church, where a leaf of them was turned daily for the behoof of the learned or the pious; but Gray and MacLellan, like wayward boys, to get rid of the task which bored them, stole the key of the grille, and threw it into the Dee.

The poor old abbot had very little idea of the real character of the personage with whom he was conversing; and the reader may imagine the astonishment with which the robber count listened to him, and the undisguised merriment with which he treated his great project regarding the restoration of the Man of Sin. In short, Count Ludwig deemed our worthy abbot neither a well-deserving divine nor eccentric pedant, but a veritable madman, and so often muttering several times, "Der Teufel hole dich!" or "Sangdieu!" and so forth, he ceased to listen, and continued to gaze covertly at Murielle.

The recent interview with her lover gave a brilliance to her beauty, and a radiance to her expression; her slight but finely rounded form, being clad in cloth of silver under a robe of white gauze, seemed to stand forth in brilliant relief from the dark tapestry of the room. A silver caul confined her hair; her ornaments were all Scottish pearls, and everything about her appeared pure, girlish, and angelic—and so thought both the *roué* duke and the ruffian count.

Her eyes wandered frequently to the latter, though he terrified her, and she knew not why; but she pitied him for having such a terrible scar on his face, and it made her think of Patrick Gray. Little dreaming that *his* sword had inflicted it, she timidly inquired of the duke where that wound was received.

"In a battle with the Burgundians," replied the others readily, "a desperate one, when he slew all their men-at-arms."

"But is not he of Burgundy?" said Murielle with surprise.

"Ah, true; I meant to say with the French—but they fight so many," added the unabashed duke.

After this Murielle relapsed into silence, for she listened to Albany rather than conversed with him. Hitherto she had steadily refused to meet him; but she was too little in stature and too gentle in spirit to be a *heroine* either in romance or history; and perceived now the futility of resisting further to receive him, as it had been arranged that the duke was to accompany the earl to Rome, to the end that during the journey he might ingratiate himself with her, and that *there* the marriage would be performed, after his betrothal to Mademoiselle of France had been cancelled by the Vatican—a measure which the French king, since Albany's change of fortune and position, most earnestly desired.

And now James Achanna entered, with a smile spreading over his cat-like visage, when he saw how this goodly company were grouped.

He wished to gain the ear of the earl, but that formidable personage was conversing with the Dyck Graf.

When approaching he passed close to Murielle, who, while seeming to listen to Albany, was lost in reverie, and was unconsciously drawing from her pretty finger a pearl ring which Gray in happier times had given her. At that moment it suddenly slipped from her hand, and rolled among the rushes of the floor.

Quick as his wicked thought, Achanna let his handkerchief drop in the same place, and adroitly picked them up together.

"Good," he muttered, "this may prove useful."

We shall soon see what use he made of this ring.

Cautious in action, stealthy in step and eye, sharp in question but vague in answer—his eyes and ears ever open, and his tongue always prepared to speak in an age when men were slower in word than deed,—James Achanna was indeed a fitting tool for an unscrupulous feudal lord. Taking the opportunity of the Dyck Graf addressing a few words to the countesses of Douglas and Ormond, he said to the earl in a whisper,—"Would it please you, my lord, to play a game with me at tables?"

Then perceiving that the earl glanced at him with some disdain in his eye and hauteur in his manner, the politic Achanna added in a low voice,—"I have that to say which must be said instantly, and which none must overhear."

"Oh, we are to play a double game!" replied the earl with a sudden glance of intelligence; "bring hither the tables, the men, and the dice."

Achanna and he withdrew into the recess of a window. The tables were speedily opened, the men were marshalled, and the game began; but Achanna waited until his lord should make the first move.

"Proceed," said the latter impatiently.

"I am, then, to make the first move?"

"If it please you—begin."

They bent their heads near, as if interested in the game, and proceeded to push their men about vaguely, but vigorously.

"I told you, my lord, that I had met a certain Laird of Luaig," commenced Achanna.

"Yes, yes, at Grave."

"Well, I had my suspicions that the pretended laird of Luaig was no other than he we all wot of."

"Whom mean you—Gray?"

"Sir Patrick Gray of Foulis, captain of the king's guard; and now my suspicions are confirmed."

The earl started, and his eyes flashed with dusky fire, but controlling his emotion he simply asked,—"How?"

"I discovered him by watching the Lady Murielle. Cogsbones! I knew that the cock bird would soon find the hen."

"Sirrah," said the earl frowning, "you speak of a sister of the countess of Douglas—quick to the point, lest I hang you from that window by one of the curtain ropes!"

"Your pardon, Lord Earl; my speech is ruder than my thoughts," cringed the other.

"Quick!" continued the earl, almost grinding his teeth.

In a few words Achanna rapidly related the interview, which, *by chance*, he had overheard, in the church of St. Genevieve, and the earl was filled by such a tempest of anger that he became all but speechless; yet by a great effort of self-control, an effort the more painful that such exertion was quite unusual—he contented himself by glaring from under his black bushy eyebrows at poor unconscious Murielle with an expression as if he would have annihilated her.

"Think you the abbot took her there to meet him?" he asked in a hoarse whisper.

"Where?"

"Thou ass! to the church of St. Genevieve?"

"Heaven forfend! no; 'twas he who saved her from Gray," whined the sycophant vassal.

"It is well," said the earl in a quiet voice, but with fury still kindling in his eye and quivering on his lip; "were it otherwise, by St. Bryde, I'd unfrock and scourge him through these streets of Bommel with a horse halter, a mitred abbot and my confessor though he be!"

"Who, think you, my lord, brought to Lady Murielle at Thrave, the tidings that Gray still lived?"

"I would give this golden chain to know."

"I overheard — —"

"His name—his name?"

"Sir Thomas MacLellan, of Bombie."

"Gray's kinsman, the lieutenant of the guard?"

"Yes, my lord," said Achanna, sweeping into his girdle pouch the gold chain which the earl quietly passed to him; "and long ago I had further proof that it was he."

"But for the assurance she received, by letter, of Gray's existence, she would now, I doubt not, have been duchess of Albany, and might have spared us this journey to Rome."

"You remember, my lord, that the letter was tied to an arrow, which struck the turf at her feet as she walked by the side of the Dee?"

"Yes, I remember to have heard so."

"I found that arrow, and a week after, Malise MacKim, the smith, found a quiver full lying among the rushes. The two chevrons *sable* of MacLellan were painted on it, and the letter which bore the arrow was one of the same sheaf, the same shaft, notch, and feather; for, but a week before, Sir Thomas had bought them in the Friars Wynd, at Dumfries, as he passed south from Edinburgh."

"So, so!" said the earl, grinding his teeth; "if God and St. Bryde of Douglas permit me once again to cross the bridge of Dumfries I shall have a vengeance on MacLellan, so sure and deadly, that all Scotland shall ring with it from sea to sea."

And terribly the earl kept his vow.

"But where," he added, "is our lover at present?"

"That I have yet to discover."

"The Dyck Graf," began the earl, starting up; but Achanna caught his sleeve, saying, "Nay, nay, my lord, he will be certain to protect him. We cannot make a raid in Flanders as we might in Nithsdale."

"True, we must be secret. Oh, that I had them both, this Gray and MacLellan within ten Scottish miles of our gallows knob at Thrave, I would soon mar the interference of the one and the wooing of the other. I would summon all the Corbies in Deeside to his spousals."

"Leave the sequel to me, lord earl," said Achanna, in a low impressive whisper, "and Sir Patrick shall be punished even to *your* heart's content."

"Assure me but of that, Achanna, and thou shalt pocket a thousand silver crowns," said Douglas, pressing the hand of his trusty vagabond.

With his natural ferocity of disposition, and being usually in the habit of giving full vent to every gust of fury, the earl found great difficulty in preserving an aspect of external composure during the remainder of the evening; but immediately on the Dyck Graf's departure for the castle of Bommel, the company broke up, and Douglas prepared to retire, with a scowl on his brow, and bitterness in his heart.

"God—den to you, father abbot; art still labouring hard to ruin the empire of the prince of darkness? Oh, if ever thou shouldst fall into *his* hand!" said he with a mocking laugh, as he passed the worthy churchman, who started at the sound, for Douglas seldom laughed, and *never* in merriment.

Achanna and Count Ludwig, who had been extremely ill at ease in the vicinity of the Dyck Graf, now withdrew together to plot mischief and to discover Gray.

"James Achanna," said Albany, as they were bowing themselves out, "remember that I am to see you to-morrow."

"At Carl Langfanger's auberge, *The Forester*."

"Yes, at noon."

"I am at the disposal of your *highness*," said Achanna, using the title by which kings were then addressed in Scotland and England.

Albany started, and the colour mounted to his usually pale temples as he said, "Sir, I desire that you will not address me thus."

"Why!" asked the earl with surprise as he paused in the doorway.

"Because I consider it premature, and as such unlucky."

"Your grace, perhaps, is right," replied the earl, gloomily, and somewhat contemptuously; "however, time will show."

CHAPTER XXXIV
NOON—THE PLOT

'Twas thus these cozening villains laid their scheme
Against his life, his youth, and comeliness:
Woe worth the end!—Old Play.

Three miles from the southern gate of Bommel, on the road which led to Ameldroyen, there stood a solitary auberge, or wayside tavern. It was named *The Forester*, from the circumstance that on a signboard it had a hideous representation of a hunter sounding a horn, and this passed for a likeness of Liderick du Bucq, the first forester of Flanders.

The signboard, moreover, informed the passers, in tolerably-spelt Flemish, that there was entertainment for man and horse, with good German beer within; while a green *bush*, which hung over the door in the more ancient fashion, announced that there also could be had the good wines of Alicant and Burgundy, with perhaps the strong waters of Anjou and Languedoc, *i.e.*, brandy.

The country in its vicinity was lonely, and thinly populated. Save a wind-mill or two, and a gibbet on an eminence, with a man hanging thereon between the spectator and the sky, there was little to be seen but the dense forest, which then spread for miles along the banks of the river Waal, and away towards Bois-le-duc and Ravenstein.

This auberge, a rickety old house, the roof and walls of which some masses of ivy and woodbine alone seemed to hold together, was kept by Carl Langfanger, an old Brabancione, or disbanded soldier; and it was, in fact, one of the many secret rendezvous of Count Ludwig's military outlaws.

On the day after the night just described, three horsemen arrived at the auberge about noon, and within ten minutes of each other. They placed their horses in a shed behind the edifice, where a Brabancione, named Gustaf Vlierbeke, a very "ragged robin" indeed, acted as groom. They then met in an upper room, on the bare and dirty table of which wine, unasked for and unordered, was placed; and, we may mention, that their swords and daggers were *not* required by the slipshod tapster, though such was the custom in those days in all well-ordered taverns throughout Christendom.

These three personages were the exiled duke of Albany, the outlawed count of Endhoven, and that "Scottish worthy," Master James Achanna.

Their greetings were more brief than courteous, and after imbibing each a long horn of wine, they drew their chairs close to the table, as if to confer confidentially.

"More wine now, that we may not be interrupted hereafter," said Albany, as a preliminary.

"Have we not had enough?" asked Achanna, warily.

"Bah! I am not a hermit, and have no need of endeavouring to resemble old Anthony of Padua."

"Der teufel! our fair ones would not esteem you the more for seeking to do so," said Ludwig.

The duke smiled complacently, caressed his well-pointed moustache, and played with the tassels of his velvet cloak.

"Duke," said Ludwig, "you have sworn to love this lady?"

"Love her?" reiterated Albany, ponderingly.

"Yes; whether she will or not."

"Whom do you mean?"

"Teufel! who but Murielle Douglas!" said Ludwig, with surprise.

"Oh, of course, I swore it," said Albany, suddenly seeming to remember.

"Ah, there are moments in life when a man swears anything to a woman so pretty," replied Ludwig, burying his red nose in his wine-pot.

To elude discovery, as he knew well that the soldiers of the Dyck Graf and the halberdiers of the burgomaster were somewhat solicitous about his movements, Count Ludwig had adopted a new disguise. He was dressed like an Italian fantasin, in a jacket and pantaloons formed of long stripes of cloth of the Douglas colours, and wore on his breast a scutcheon, charged with those three stars which formed the paternal coat of the earl, for one of whose followers he wished *pro temp.* to pass. For this purpose he had smoothed over his usual ruffianly exterior, cut off his long bravo *lock* of hair, and, to enhance the respectability of his appearance, wore a large rosary.

"We have met, duke," said he; "so to the point. What have you to propose?"

"Simply, that we must get rid of our troublesome lover," replied Duke Robert, mixing two kinds of wine, Burgundy and Alicant, and draining them at a draught.

"But first, we must discover his residence," suggested Achanna.

"Carl Langfanger, our worthy tavernier, will soon do that for us," said Ludwig.

"I am not unskilful in the use of my sword," said the misguided duke of Albany; "I have already been victor in four duels, three in Paris and one in Flanders, and might be victorious in a fifth. Why should I not challenge and fight him? Count Ludwig, wouldst bear my glove to this man?"

"What, your highness—grace, I mean!" stammered Achanna, with one of his hateful smiles, "would you commit *all* that is at issue to the chance of an unlucky sword-thrust? Nay, nay, I'll to the earl—this must not be."

"So say I, sangdieu! Der teufel hole dich!" growled Count Ludwig, whose oaths were alternately French and Flemish; "I have a bone to pick with our traveller, and, by Gott in himmel! I will have satisfaction for the slash he gave me on the face."

"Please yourselves," said Albany, with a bored air, applying again to the wine, as if he was in haste to intoxicate himself; "only rid the earl, Lady Murielle, and me of him."

"We will arrange a most lover-like rendezvous, and as sure as the devil hath horns, we shall catch our amorous traveller," said Ludwig; "what say you, Messire Achanna, and you, Monseigneur, Mein Herr, or how der teufel am I to address you?"

"A rendezvous," repeated Achanna, "where?"

"Here."

"At this solitary auberge?"

"Der teufels braden! what would the man have? The more solitary the better, and where can a fitter place be found? My trusty Brabanciones all within call, and close by the wood with its wolves, ha! ha!" and Ludwig burst into a loud laugh, which expressed cruelty and ferocity, but *not* merriment.

"As for the snare, it is easy when we have this to bait our trap with," said Achanna, displaying the pearl ring, for the loss of which poor Murielle was then breaking her little heart. He then related how he became possessed of it, and with what intention.

"Good, good! ter teufel! it is admirable," shouted Ludwig, striking the rickety table with his clenched hand. "But after luring him here with this, what do you propose to do?"

Achanna glanced at the duke of Albany, who was already dozing off to sleep, with his flushed forehead resting on his hands, and said, "What do *you* propose—a combat at snick and snee?"

Ludwig ground his teeth with rage, at the recollection of that affair at Endhoven, and said, with a strange smile, "Listen: my Brabanciones are all very good fellows, but are very irritable and very excitable; and so, in a moment of their excitement and irritability, they may burn out our prisoner's eyes with *this iron*, when red hot," said the bantering ruffian, suddenly displaying a curious steel instrument, fashioned apparently for the express purpose of blinding, as it had the form of a spur, or the letter U with a handle, the points for entering the eyes being about two inches apart.

"He will die, and in torment!" exclaimed Albany, with an expression of disgust on his handsome, but tipsy face; "and if I engage in aught so rascally, may the Devil twist my neck!"

"I fear that is a task reserved for one of less rank," muttered the rash count of Endhoven, in a low voice.

"Say you, sir!" thundered Albany, starting to the full height of his tall figure, and turning the buckle of his belt *behind* him. As this was a challenge in those days, Ludwig changed colour.

"I pray your grace," urged Achanna, starting forward.

"Dost think I will permit this Flemish flouting-jack to make a jest of me?" said the duke furiously.

"Nay, mein Herr—Gott in himmel! I made no jest of you," said Ludwig, unwilling by a brawl to frustrate his own private objects, and future profit.

"Very well—very well—carbonado him if you please, but trouble me not on the subject," replied Albany, with an air of *ennui*, as he drained his cup again.

"This process of yours will certainly kill our man," said Achanna, in a low voice, as Albany sank his head on the table, already overcome with wine.

"Not immediately," replied the count, with a diabolical grimace. "My Brabanciones will tie him naked on an old bare-backed horse—place a blazing brand under its tail, and then set it loose, mad with pain and fear in the forest among wolves. Der Teufel! a rare thought! but not a word of all this to your soft-hearted duke of Albany," whispered Ludwig; "I do not think he would admire my rough mode for disposing of a rival. He would be for measuring swords with him quietly, and getting run through the body. But I—der Teufels braden! I have this slash on the face to avenge, and with the assistance of my friends, the wolves of the Waal, I shall do it amply! When Ludwig of Endhoven shows his teeth the wolves laugh!"

The singular cruelty of this proposal almost exceeded the malevolence of Achanna, who had no other idea than having Gray cut off by violent means; but as the victim stood in the path of his lord the earl, and a thousand crowns were the price of his removal, Achanna considered it a somewhat secondary matter *how* it was effected.

Carl Langfanger was despatched into the city of Bommel, with an accurate description of Gray, and of his Muscovite disguise, and with instructions to inquire at all the hostelries, to discover his present quarters. He was also entrusted with the ring of Murielle, which he was to deliver as his credential, and armed therewith, to request Sir Patrick to meet her near the auberge, named *The Forester of Flanders*, on the Ameldroyen road; and old Carl, a practised plotter, and most careful rascal, departed with confidence to discover their victim, and arrange the rendezvous.

"Are we safe in trusting this man, Carl?" asked Achanna.

"He is sure as he is secret," replied Ludwig; "I would have gone on this mission myself, but I must beware of that old devil the Dyck Graf; for Duke Arnold of Gueldres has sworn to punish me in the same fashion that Count Peter of Orscamp was punished by Baldwin With-the-Hatchet."

"How was that?"

"The poor count was frequently put to his shifts, as I am, and having fancied two bullocks, which belonged to a widow at Vandal, Baldwin ordered him to be cast in his armour into a cauldron of boiling oil, in the market-place of Bruges, where he perished miserably, before a mighty multitude."

"And Duke Arnold has set a price upon you?"

"A thousand guilders. So you see, my friend, I am of some value to the state."

So Achanna thought, and he began to conceive, that these guilders, if he could earn them, would form a very seasonable addition to the thousand crowns from the earl.

Meanwhile, he had no suspicion that the subtle outlaw with whom he plotted had conceived the idea of luring Murielle to a rendezvous there or elsewhere, by means of the same ring, after her lover had been disposed of; and thus, if the snare proved successful, he resolved to delude alike the duke and the earl, and bear her off for his own purposes to one of those wild forests with which that part of Flanders then abounded; and with all the secret paths, strengths, ruined castles, and lurking-places of which, his predatory life had long rendered him familiar.

Drowsily and tipsily the unfortunate duke of Albany slept, half reclined upon the table. While he was in this position, and during the absence of Achanna for more wine, Ludwig took care of his purse, and some other little matters of value, which he might otherwise have lost; and so night closed in upon the solitary auberge, while Langfanger, its proprietor, was pursuing his inquiries amid the busy streets of Bommel.

CHAPTER XXXV
NIGHT—THE SNARE

'Tis not so. Slowly, slowly dies the night,
And with it sinks my soul down from the point
Where late it stood a-tiptoe.—All the Year Round.

Longing for the next evening—the *third* appointed by the abbot, as the time when he was to meet Murielle again, Sir Patrick Gray sat at the latticed window of his room, gazing listlessly down one of the long and picturesque streets of Bommel, then darkening in the twilight and haze, amid which the lamps were beginning to twinkle in the shops and booths. Seven was tolled from the college bell of the Canonry close by. He started at the sound, and with a glow of pleasure, reflected, that at the same hour to-morrow, he should see and be with her he loved.

While this idea occupied him, the tapster announced a visitor, and Carl Langfanger was introduced. On perceiving a stranger, Sir Patrick experienced some uneasiness, as he believed that his presence in Bommel was unknown to all, save Murielle Douglas and the abbot of Tongland.

In addition to the profits of his wine and beer house, and the little pickings which his secret relations with Count Ludwig enabled him to have, our worthy Carl Langfanger, was ostensibly a farrier and horse doctor, who, by painting and patching up old nags, made them—though the veriest Rosinantes—pass for chargers of spirit and mettle; thus he was so well known at all the hostelries in Bommel, that a short time enabled him to discover the temporary residence of Sir Patrick Gray.

This cunning boor had attired himself in a dark suit of respectable broad-cloth, with a clean white ruff round his neck, and a wooden rosary of portentous size at his right wrist; thus he had all the air of a worthy citizen, though his scrubby black hair was brushed straight down to his small stealthy eyes, and cut off squarely above his long and pendant ears.

"You wish to speak with me?" said Gray, in French.

Langfanger, who had served in several countries, replied readily in the same language: "I have a message to monsieur!"

"From whom?"

"A fair demoiselle," replied Carl, in his most insinuating voice, and a glitter in his cunning eyes.

"Indeed—then carry your message elsewhere—you have come to the wrong quarter, my friend," replied Gray, curtly, as he detected something of the bravo in the air of his visitor.

"But the demoiselle is in distress," urged Carl, with some alarm lest his errand might fail.

"I am not the burgomaster, and knights errant are out of fashion, my friend; but *who* is she?"

"I know not her name, messire," stammered Carl, who had omitted to inform himself of this rather important particular.

"By whom—and in what manner is she wronged?"

"Mademoiselle said that this ring, which I have the honour to present, would inform monsieur of everything," said Carl, stepping forward.

"This ring," reiterated Gray, becoming suddenly interested and perplexed, on recognizing the trinket he had given to Murielle in other days, at the Three Thorns of the Carlinwark, near Thrave; and he kissed and placed it on his finger, for it was a signal with which he could neither delay nor trifle.

What might this summons portend?

Carl Langfanger, who was smoothing down his obstinate forelock, while estimating the value of the victim's habiliments, replied, that by the safety of his sinful soul, he knew not.

Was she in immediate danger?

He did not know that either; but she seemed in great tribulation.

"You have seen her, then?"

"Within an hour, messire."

"Where—and where does she now await me?"

"Near an auberge—*The Forester of Flanders*—three miles from Bommel; an auberge of the best character, messire."

"In what direction, my good friend?"

"Ah—I am messire's good friend now!—the way to Ameldroyen."

"Among the forests?" said Gray, with increasing alarm.

"Exactly, messire."

It seemed most unaccountable that Murielle should anticipate the evening fixed by the abbot, and appoint a wayside auberge as a place of meeting; but the presence of her betrothal ring could not be doubted; and she was in danger, or tribulation, as this apparently suave and honest fellow admitted. What lover could linger or doubt?

"You will come, messire?" entreated Carl.

"Come—instantly! my sword and cloak——"

"Nay, messire, I have the honour to mention," said the sleek Carl, "that mademoiselle does not expect you until the cathedral bells have rung the hour of nine, and when the lamps are hung in the spire."

To Gray this information was more perplexing than ever.

"Near the auberge," continued Carl, "is a stone cross, one hundred paces to the right of the road, where a votive lamp burns—there she will meet you."

"Grace guide me!" exclaimed Gray, "what mystery is this? Is not that district a perilous one after nightfall?"

"There are certainly some clerks of St. Nicholas in the woods at times," said Carl, with pretended hesitation.

"What manner of clerks are they?"

"Disbanded Brabanters, who are their own paymasters."

"Robbers, in fact," said Gray, sharply.

"Ay, robbers, and all kinds of wild fellows."

"Come! this is pleasant for one who will be alone."

"Messire shall not be alone," said Carl, "for I shall be there as a guide."

"Thanks and largesse to you, most worthy varlet," said Gray, gratefully, though feeling more and more bewildered. He then put some money into the hands of Carl, who, glad that his mission was over, hurriedly withdrew, and within an hour duly reported his progress to the count of Endhoven, who still remained at the auberge, though Albany and Achanna had returned to the house of the Dyck Graf, to wait the event of the night.

Gray sat in a turmoil of thought after Carl had retired. The idea of a snare never occurred to him. The presence of Murielle's ring lulled every suspicion, if he had one; and he kissed it again and again, for it had been on her finger since that night when first she admitted that he might love her, when the summer moon was wading the fleecy clouds above the Galloway hills that slept in her silver sunshine, which cast the towers of Thrave in sombre shadow on the black waters of the Dee.

As it did not suit the purpose of master Carl Langfanger to have any outrage committed *in* his auberge—a place on which the officials of the Dyck Graf had more than once cast eyes of suspicion—it had been arranged that Gray should be waylaid at the solitary cross, and there disarmed, mutilated in the horrible manner suggested by the barbarous count of Endhoven, who is recorded to have treated more than one of his prisoners thus, especially, a poor pilgrim from Antwerp and a merchant of Bruges.

This votive wayside cross had been erected by the eldest son of Reinald, the warlike duke of Gueldres, as a propitiation for his unnatural conduct, in making a captive of his father, who died in 1325.

It stood in a wild and solitary place, among heath and gorse, midway between the highroad which led to the auberge, and the forest that spread along the banks of the Waal. After the gates of Bommel were shut for the night, the vicinity of this cross was a place avoided by all belated people, in consequence of the lawless nature of the district, and of those terrible wolves, whose lair was also the forest.

As the night drew on, Count Ludwig, Carl Langfanger, Gustaf Vlierbeke, and some ten or twelve other outlaws all Brabanciones, and well, but variously armed, issued from the auberge, and repaired to the vicinity of Duke Reinald's Cross, where they concealed themselves in a hollow, close to the path, among some thick willows and alder trees.

"Der Teufel!" grumbled the count, "I hope our lover won't keep us long waiting, for the night breeze that comes from the Waal is cold enough already; so what will it be an hour hence!"

"For that reason I have brought with me, herr count, a jar of Languedoc brandy," said Carl Langfanger.

"Thou art a priceless fellow!" exclaimed the count, with unfeigned ardour, as he took a long draught from the stone bottle, and then passed it round; "and now, Carl, light the brazier—hast got any charcoal?"

"A little sack full; and we have plenty of dead branches hereabout."

"Right! Place it under the bank, where the glow will be hidden by the willows. Set it a-light, I say; 'twill serve to keep us warm, and to heat our branding iron at the same time. Who watches on the roadway?"

"Gustaf Vlierbeke," replied two or three at once.

"Bon! he has the eyes of a mole."

The charcoal, with the addition of some dried branches, was soon glowing in the iron brazier, and it shed an uncertain glow on the patched and parti-coloured garments, the rusty weapons, the pieces of battered armour, the squalid and dirty visages of the ruffians who crouched together, waiting for the coming prey, with watchful ears and stealthy eyes, that had became bloodshot, haggard, and wild in expression, with years of cruelty, lust, debauchery, and rapine; and which brightened only as Carl's long jar of French brandy came round to each in turn.

"Herr Count, there are the lights now, in the cathedral spire," exclaimed Carl, who descended from the top of the grassy bank, whither he had crawled to listen.

"Then the gates of Bommel are being closed; der Teufels braden! where tarries our lover? he should be here by this time!" muttered Ludwig, thrusting the fatal iron deeper in the charcoal, and playing nervously with the haft of his dagger; "is the old mare from the tan-yard ready?"

"All ready for her rider," replied Carl, with a cruel grin; "Gustaf Vlierbeke," he added in a husky whisper, "hear you aught on the roadway?"

"Nothing, but the wind and the tossing leaves."

Mutterings of impatience followed this reply.

"Gustaf has only one eye," said a Brabancione.

"The other was knocked out by the boll of a crossbow at Briel."

"Then, why the devil make him scout?" said a third lurker, in a growling tone.

"Because he has the eye and the quickness of a bloodhound," said the count; "ay, of Souyllard himself. It begins to seem that we shall have a great deal of trouble with this teufel of a Schottlander! Carl could easily have disposed of him at the hostelry, as I did yesterday with the rich pilgrim who was on his way to Strasbourg, and who died, unfortunately, just after sharing with me the contents of his bottle and wallet."

"Died! how?"

"By the severing of the thyroid cartilage."

"What the henckers is that, herr count?"

"The hump in the wind-pipe, where the apple stuck."

"In plain words — —"

"Exactly," said the count, passing a finger round his throat, a piece of pantomime which excited the ferocious laughter of his followers; yet they waited with great impatience, and the time seemed to pass the more slowly, that they were without watches or other means of marking it. Gustaf Vlierbeke was withdrawn from the post of scout, and replaced by Carl Langfanger when the lights in the cathedral spire were reduced to two.

"Two lights, der teufel!" exclaimed the count; "they indicate the hour of ten: He must have been warned of our snare, and—hark! what is that?"

"The bay of a wolf, herr count."

"Yes, the moon is rising now, and our charcoal is smouldering fast."

Time passed on slowly; the slower that they waited with fierce impatience, and the night became colder as the stars increased in number and brilliance overhead. Some of the Brabanciones sat idly gnawing their shaggy moustachios; others whiled away the lagging minutes by putting an edge on their swords and daggers, with some of the stones which lay near. It seemed weary work for them at best, for the stone jar was empty now.

At last only *one* light remained in the great spire of Bommel, and it twinkled like a planet in the distance.

"Eleven!" exclaimed the count, starting to his feet, and, amid muttered oaths of rage and disappointment, they were rising to disperse, when Carl Langfanger crawled back, with tidings that a horseman was coming rapidly along the highway. Again the charcoal was blown up by Gustaf Vlierbeke, who made a bellows of his lungs; again the spur-shaped iron was inserted deeper, teeth were set, fierce eyes sparkled, and weapons were grasped and drawn.

On came the solitary rider—on and on. His horse's hoofs rang louder with every bound as he drew nearer, and all held their breath when he suddenly reined up abreast of the cross, in a little niche of which an oil lamp was flickering in the gusty wind.

"Der teufel—'tis he at last!" said the count, as the rider turned his horse to the right and cautiously approached the cross. Then springing from their ambush, with loud yells of exultation and ferocity, the Brabanciones rushed upon him! His horse's bridle and his stirrups were grasped on both sides; and before a cry could escape his lips, the victim was dragged from his saddle, struck to the earth under a shower of blows, and manacled by a strong cord.

"Light a torch, and drag him into the hollow," cried Count Ludwig, whose order was roughly and promptly obeyed.

CHAPTER XXXVI
DUKE REINALD'S CROSS

He wrapp'd his cloak upon his arm, he smote away their
swords, Striking hard and sturdy buffets on the mouths of
those proud lords; Snapping blades and tearing mouths,
like a lion at his meal, Laughing at the stab of dagger, and
the flashing of their steel. All the Year Round.

Great was the impatience of the earl and of his satellite, James Achanna,
to learn the result of the snare they had laid for Sir Patrick Gray. If successful
in its cruelty, the first felt assured that a formidable obstruction to his plans
would be removed for ever; and the latter flattered himself that he would
be a richer man by a thousand silver crowns of the Rhine. Then he had his
plans to mature for turning Count Ludwig into as much ready money as the
Dyck Graf would pay for him. Our utilitarian felt that he was on the eve of
making his fortune!

That the ill-fated Sir Patrick Gray had left his hostelry punctually,
Achanna had already ascertained, and duly reported to the earl.

"It is easier," says Goldsmith, "to conceive than to describe the
complicated sensations which are felt from the pain of a recent injury and
the pleasure of approaching vengeance," but in the present instance, it was
the mere delight of cruel and wicked hearts in a lawless revenge (without
the sense of real injury) that fired the hearts of the earl and Achanna.

They had not an atom of compunction!

Albany was aware, by the recent interview at the auberge, that his more
favoured rival was to be removed; how, he scarcely knew (he had been so
tipsy), and *how*, he little cared; but he pitied—for this exiled and outlawed
prince was not quite destitute of generosity—Murielle, as the poor girl, in
joyous anticipation of the morrow's meeting with her lover, had assumed
her cithern, and all unconscious of the horrors impending, sang one or two
sweet old Galloway songs; but they failed to soothe either the savage earl,
or his more unscrupulous follower, who, from the recess of a window,
surveyed her with gloomy malignity in his cat-like eyes, which, as already
described, were situated singularly far apart in his head, from the conical
top of which his red hair hung in tufts.

When the hour of ten was tolled from the spire of the cathedral (where time was regulated then by great hour-glasses), the curiosity of Douglas and Achanna could no longer be repressed.

"You have an order from the Dyck Graf to pass the gates," whispered the earl.

"Yes; at any hour."

"Then set forth; seek that fellow whom you name: what is it they call him?"

"Count Ludwig of Endhoven."

"A rare noble, by the Mass! Seek him and bring me sure tidings of what has transpired."

Within twenty minutes after this, Achanna had mounted and left Bommel, after duly presenting to the captain of the watch his pass, signed by Jacques de Lalain. Taking the road to Ameldroyan, he rode slowly — very slowly at first, listening to every sound; but all seemed still by the wayside, and coldly and palely the waning moon shone on the waters of the Waal, and of the sluices and marshes which there intersected the level country. The windmills — unusual features to a Scotsman's eye — stood motionless and silent, like giants with outstretched arms.

Now a sound came upon the wind at times, and he reined up his horse to listen. Anon he rode forward again, for that sound made him shudder. It was the wild weird cry of a wolf in the forest, baying to the moon.

Feeling alternately for his sword and his crucifix (just as a Spaniard of the present day would do), he neared the appointed spot, and his keen eyes detected a lurking figure which withdrew at his approach. This was Carl Langfanger the scout.

A cruel joy filled Achanna's heart with a strange glow, and his large coarse ears quivered like those of a sleuth-bratch in his eagerness to catch a passing sound.

Was it all over — were the thousand crowns his? Had Gray been blinded by the burning iron, manacled, stripped and bound to the goaded horse which was to bear him to the wild forest, and to the wolves' jaws? Did the baying he had heard in the distance announce that the chase was over, and their repast begun — that horse and rider had been torn limb from limb?

He asked these questions of himself as he rode on. Soon he saw the votive lamp that flickered before Duke Reinald's cross. Then he detected a red gleam that wavered under some willow trees. It came from the brazier in which Ludwig had heated the blinding iron. He spurred impatiently forward. There was a shout, and amid cries of, "Der Schottlander, donner and blitzen, der Schottlander!" he was struck from his horse and pinioned in a moment, before he could utter a cry for mercy or for explanation.

The wretch had fallen into his own trap.

His clothes were roughly rent from his body, and if he opened his mouth the point of a sword menaced his throat. Covered with blood and bruises, and screaming like a terrified woman for mercy, he was dragged into the hollow where Count Ludwig was seated before the brazier, with the brandy-jar by his side.

Amid shouts of ferocious laughter and imprecations his head was grasped by several of the ruffians, while Carl Langfanger drew forth the gleaming iron from the brazier. Achanna uttered a last scream of terror and agony on beholding it, and then his voice seemed to leave him. The cold bead-drops burst upon his throbbing temples; his eyes started from their sockets as if to anticipate their doom, and the pulses of his heart seemed to stand still—he could only sigh and gasp.

He felt the hot glow upon his cheek—already it seemed to burn into his brain, and he gave himself over for lost, when there was a sudden shout and a rush of horses' hoofs; he saw the flashing of swords above his head, and heard the rasp of steel on steel as the blades emitted red sparks. There was a sudden shock, and a conflict seemed to close over him as he fell to the earth on his face fainting, and some time elapsed before he became sufficiently conscious to understand that he was free, and rescued by the valour of a single horseman, who was clad in a helmet and chain shirt, and whose sword was dripping with the red evidence of how skilfully he had used it in the recent fray.

But what were the emotions of James Achanna when by a sudden gleam from the expiring contents of the brazier, as the night wind swept through the hollow, he recognized in his preserver, Sir Patrick Gray of Foulis!

Astonishment with craven fear prevailed; but not the slightest emotion of gratitude. He felt rather a glow of rage and bitterness that Gray, by a mistake, or by loitering so long, had been too late for his own destruction!

Sir Patrick, as Achanna learned, had left his hostelry in sufficient time to be at the false rendezvous; but being without an order from the Dyck Graf to pass the gates, (a document with which he had not provided himself, lest a knowledge of the application for it might lead to his discovery by the Douglases) he had been refused egress by the guards; and after spending an hour in attempting every gate of Bommel—an hour of impatience and fury—during which he strove in vain to corrupt by gold the trusty Walloons who watched them, he swam his horse at last through the Waal, and having thus to make a great detour, arrived at a most critical time for the fate of Achanna, who gazed at him, speechlessly and helplessly, afraid to utter a word lest Gray might recognise his voice, and pass through his body the sword which had just saved him.

Sir Patrick, however, *did* recognise him as he cut his cords, but not immediately; though there was no mistaking his hideous visage and green cat-like eyes, or the red hair and beard that mingled together.

"So it is thee, James Achanna," said he; "dog and son of a dog, had I met you mounted and armed as I now am I would have slain you without remorse or mercy. As it is, go, and remember that you receive your miserable life at the hand of one who spares it rather from profound disdain, than that you may have time for repentance—a time that may never come to you!"

With these words Gray smote him on the cheek, sheathed his sword, remounted his horse, and, bewildered by the whole affair, rode rapidly off, leaving Achanna to find his way back to Bommel as he best could.

Sir Patrick was filled with rage, but he knew not against whom to direct it. He half suspected that a snare had been laid for him, and then dismissed the idea, believing that the circumstance of his being in Bommel, or even in Flanders, was unknown to all save the abbot and Murielle, the mission on which Crichton had sent him being almost a secret one: for these reasons he did not make himself known to Achanna *by name*.

It was not until dawn, when the gates were open to admit the boors and peasantry to the markets, that the rescuer and the rescued made their way, but by different routes, into Bommel; and a scurvy figure the latter made when he presented himself at the residence of the Douglases, minus horse, arms, and clothing, with an ill-devised tale of his having been assaulted by Brabanciones, while the fierce jibes of the earl, and the narrow escape from a dreadful death, inspired him with more hatred than ever against Gray and Murielle, for he had learned to combine them in one idea.

CHAPTER XXXVII
THE THIRD EVENING

Good fortune and the favour of the king
Smile upon this contract; whose ceremony
Shall seem expedient on the new-born brief,
And be performed to-night.
All's Well that Ends Well.

After what had occurred at Duke Reinald's cross, and being bewildered by the whole affair of the ring—an affair which seemed so inexplicable, Gray armed himself with more than usual care, and covering his fine, flexible chain shirt, gorget and sleeves of tempered Milan plate, by the ample brown and red-braided Muscovite gown, he repaired punctually at seven o'clock to the church of St. Genevieve. He entered with an anxious heart, and kept a hand on his sword, as he knew not by whom, or in what fashion he might be greeted; but, to his joy found Murielle and the abbot awaiting him in the appointed place.

Murielle was smiling and happy; but the abbot was sombre, gloomy, and abstracted.

A recent conversation which had passed between him and the earl of Douglas had revealed more of the latter's terrible political, or rather insurrectionary projects, than the abbot conceived to be possible. The poor old man was dismayed; his very soul shrank within him at the contemplation of his lawful and anointed king dethroned, and his native country plunged in civil strife, to gratify the proud ambition and guilty vengeance of a turbulent and predatory noble. A wholesome fear of that ugly architectural feature, the gallows knob of Thrave, might have prevented him from daring to think of circumventing the plans of the earl had he been in Galloway; for Douglas, though slavish in superstition and in ritual observances, was sternly severe to all who marred his purposes, or crossed the path of his ambition, or even of his most simple wish: thus he who hanged the good lord of Teregles in his armour, might not hesitate to hang an abbot in his cassock. But here in Flanders, far from local feudal influences, the superior of Tongland felt himself more free to act, and he had been all day revolving in his mind the means of putting the lord chancellor and other ministers of James II. in possession of facts which would enable them to guard the interests of the throne and of the people from confusion, from invasion, and an anarchy like that which followed the demise of the good king Alexander III., and in the person of Gray he had the means of immediate communication.

Anxious to solve a mystery, Gray said hurriedly, "You have lost a ring Murielle?"

"My ring—ah, yes, and an omen of evil I deemed that loss to be; for it was the betrothal ring you gave me at the Thorns of the Carlinwark. It was lost two nights ago—or abstracted from me——"

"The latter most likely—but permit me to restore it," said he, tenderly kissing her pretty hand; "it nearly lured me to my death, for now I verily believe that a deadly snare was set for me."

"Oh, what is this you tell me?" she asked with alarm.

"Sad, sad truth, my own love."

"A snare? Oh, it is impossible, since none know that you are here, but our lord the abbot and I."

"But others, Murielle, do know," replied Gray, and he briefly related the affair of the preceding evening; the visit of Carl Langfanger with the ring and the message as from herself; the delays which had happily occurred, and how he had reached the Wayside Cross too late for the purpose of his secret enemies, but strangely enough in time to save Achanna from a mutilation and death, which were no doubt intended for another. Murielle was stupefied.

"Achanna—say you this man was James Achanna?" sobbed Murielle, becoming very pale and trembling.

"Certainly 'twas he; oh, there is no mistaking that hateful visage of his."

"Then you are indeed lost!" said she, clasping her hands; but the abbot who had hitherto remained silent and gloomy, patted her head kindly, and said—"My own good daughter, hearken to me; trust in Heaven and hope—hope, the friend of happiness."

"But hope, Father Abbot, will desert us, unless——" said Gray, hesitating, as he turned imploringly to Murielle.

"Unless what?" said the abbot.

"Murielle becomes my bride—my wife!"

"Sir Patrick Gray——"

"Her ring is here; a betrothal ring it is, and a wedding-ring it shall be," continued Gray with increasing vehemence, as his voice with his emotion became deeper. "Good father abbot, my kinsman and my friend, you who knew and loved my father and mother well, you who were the guide and mentor of both, even as you are of me, will not hear me now in vain! The dangerous schemes of this ambitious earl——"

"Enough, enough," interrupted the abbot gloomily, as he waved his hand; "to my sorrow and fear I know them all, and own they terrify me."

"Then, to save our young king from many deadly perils, and our country from civil war—to save this miserable Duke Robert from the block on which his father perished—to save the house of Douglas from destruction, and, more than all, to save herself from misery, Murielle must wed me!"

Murielle opened her tremulous lips to speak, but Gray added impetuously,—"To-day—to-night—now, instantly!"

"Now?" reiterated the abbot.

"Now, or it may be never!"

"Oh, what is this you say?" said Murielle, shrinking closer to the abbot.

"The solemn, the sad, the earnest, but the loving truth, dear Murielle," urged Gray, his eyes and heart filling as he spoke with passion and tenderness.

Much more followed, but they spoke rapidly and briefly, for time was precious.

"You will end all this by wedding me, my beloved," said Gray in her ear, as he pressed her to his breast, and stifled her reply by kisses. "Then at midnight we shall leave Bommel together for the sea-coast, from thence to Scotland and the king! Say that you will become my wife—here are the altar, the church, the priest, and his missal—here even the ring. Oh, say that you will, for with life I cannot separate from you again!"

"My love for you," sobbed Murielle, "is stronger than my destiny——"

"Nay, 'tis destiny that makes you love me."

Her tears fell fast, but her silence gave consent.

The abbot felt all the force of his kinsman's arguments, and the more so that they were added to his own previous fears and convictions. He wisely conceived that the marriage of Murielle to Gray would prove the most irremovable barrier to the proposed matrimonial alliance between Douglas and the duke of Albany. He was aware that by the performance of such a ceremony, he would open an impassable gulf between himself and his lord and chief; but he felt that he owed a duty to the king, James II., in saving him from a coalition so formidable as a union between the adherents of the outlawed prince and rebellious peer; a duty to Murielle, in saving her from becoming the hapless tool of a conspiracy, the victim of a *roué* husband and a ruinous plot; and a duty to his kinsman and friend, whom he had every desire to protect and serve.

Thus he suddenly consented, and summoning his chanter, and a curé of the church, whom in his writings he names "Father Gustaf Dennecker, of the order of St. Benedict," he drew a missal from the embroidered pouch which hung at his girdle, and before our poor bewildered Murielle knew distinctly what was about to ensue she found herself a bride—on her knees before the altar, and the marriage service being read over her.

It proceeded rapidly. Murielle felt as one in a dream. She saw the open missal, from the parchment leaves of which some little golden crosses dangled; she saw the abbot in his purple stole, and heard his distinct but subdued Latinity, as he addressed them over the silver altar rail. She was aware of the presence of Gray, and her little heart beat tumultuously with awe and love and terror, while reassured from time to time by the gentle pressure of his hand—that strong and manly hand which had grown hard by the use of his sword-hilt. She heard the ring blessed, and felt it placed upon her marriage finger!

She heard the muttered responses of Father Gustaf and of the old chanter of Tongland Abbey, who, in his terror of the earl, was almost scared out of his senses; and then came the sonorous voice of the abbot, as he waved his hand above her, and concluded with these words:—"Deus Israel conjugat vos; et ipse sit vobiscum, qui misertus duobus unicis: et nunc Domine, fac eos plenius benedicere te."

She arose lady of Foulis, and the wedded wife of Sir Patrick Gray, from whom death only could separate her; but she reclined her head upon his breast, and sobbed with excitement, with joy, and alarm.

After a pause the abbot closed his missal, and as he descended from the altar his eye caught a pale grim face behind the shadow of a column. It vanished, but as the blood rushed back upon the heart of the startled abbot, he thought the features of that face were those of James Achanna, and *he was right!*

"You must now separate; the future depends upon your secrecy and discretion, as a discovery will ruin all, and we have not a moment to lose," said the abbot, who felt more dismay in his heart than at that moment he cared to communicate.

"What a time to separate!" exclaimed Gray almost with anger.

"You separate but to meet again," said the abbot imperatively, but in a low voice, lest there might be other eavesdroppers; "away to your hostelry, Sir Patrick, get horses, and make every arrangement for immediate flight. If you leave Bommel at midnight, by riding fast you may both reach the coast of Altena long before day-break, and there find a ship for Scotland."

"Let us escape now; why delay a single hour?"

"That may not be; your flight would be discovered, and the followers of the earl would be aided in a pursuit by those of De Lalain the Dyck Graf. The time to choose is when all are abed and asleep, or ought to be, and I will provide the order to pass you through the gates of the city. The doors of our residence are secured every night by Sir Alan Lauder, who keeps the keys with care, as if he were still in Thrave, and feared the thieves of Annandale. You know the window of Murielle's sleeping apartment?"

"It overlooks the garden above an arbour."

"Be within the arbour when this church bell strikes twelve; keep your horses in the street, and I myself, as far as an old man may, will aid your flight together. You will pass through the church by the postern, and then God speed ye to the sea! Till then, farewell, and my blessing on ye! Ah, well-a-day! all this toil, all this trouble, all this peril had been saved us, if—if——"

"What, my Lord?"

"The master of evil and of mischief had been but forgiven and restored to his place—but the time shall come," said the abbot, remembering his pet crotchet, as they hastily separated; "that blessed time shall come!"

CHAPTER XXXVIII
A WEDDING NIGHT

> "Their swords smote blunt upon our steel,
> And keen upon our buff;
> The coldest blooded man of us
> Had battering enough;
> 'Twas butt to butt, and point to point,
> And eager pike to pike;
> 'Twas foin and parry, give and take,
> As long as we could strike."

Gray seemed to tread on air—he felt as one in a dream—but a dream to be realized—as he hurried through the streets of Bommel to his hostelry, to pack his mail (a portmanteau), to order his horse to be in readiness, and to procure one for Murielle; while his emotions of love for her, and gratitude to the abbot, left no room in his honest heart for exultation that he was about to outwit his enemies, and by bearing her away avenge the wrongs they had done him.

While he is busy with the hosteller, his grooms, horses, and arrangements, let us return to one who was quite as busily taking measures to circumvent them—the inevitable Achanna.

In less than half an hour after his disappearance from the church, he was closeted with the earl, who had just risen from his knees, having been on a *prie-dieu* at prayer before a crucifix and case containing some crumbs of the bones of St. Bryde—the chief palladium of the house of Douglas.

"What tidings now," said he, "for thou art always abroad in the night, like an owl or a rascally kirkyard bat? *Miserere mei Deus!*" he added, concluding his orisons.

The earl was in a good humour; the formula of his prayers and his adoration of the relics had partially soothed his ferocious spirit; but on hearing what had occurred his fury was on the verge of taking a very dangerous turn, for, snatching a dagger from his girdle, he seized Achanna by the throat, and tearing open his collar and pourpoint, threatened to stab him for not having prevented this secret and—so far as some of his plans were concerned—most fatal marriage from taking place by killing Gray on the spot.

"At the steps of the altar?" gasped Achanna, struggling to free himself.

"Anywhere; what mattered it, wretch, where you slew my enemy?" thundered Douglas, hurling him in a heap against the wainscot.

"But—but, my lord—bethink you—'twere a sacrilege, and the Dyck Graf would have broken me alive on the wheel, even were I, like yourself, a belted earl."

"True; we are not now within a day's ride of Thrave," said the earl almost with a groan, as he sank into a chair, and, overwhelmed by what seemed a sudden and irremediable catastrophe, gave way to undignified fury and abuse. He dared not trust himself in the presence of Murielle, lest he should commit some fatal violence, or in that of Albany, lest he might betray the source of that unbecoming discomposure, which filled his proud heart with shame at himself; and a rage at Gray, which words cannot describe. Thus a long time elapsed before he could arrange his thoughts after hearing Achanna repeat at least twice all he had seen and overheard in the church of St. Genevieve.

Desiring his pages to admit none (even the countess), he turned to Achanna with his usually swarthy visage turned white and livid by the fierce emotions that filled his heart.

"We must dissemble, Achanna," said he in a husky voice; "we must conceal this from Albany—from all; but we must nevertheless destroy Sir Patrick Gray—yea, this night, within a few brief hours, shall Murielle Douglas be maid, wife, and widow! and as for my lord the abbot, may the curse of the souls of my kindred and of St. Bryde be on him, for a meddling mock friar! If I had him as near the Nith as we are near the Waal, I would set him a-swimming with a millstone at his neck for his handiwork to-night! Yet, *laus Deo!* I dare hardly address him, for, as it is, he withholds absolution from me for many, many sins already committed. Torture! men call me a tyrant, yet I am the slave of a tyrant—of a priest;—and Lady Murielle, she means to escape to-night?"

"By the window which overlooks the arbour in the garden; oh, I heard all planned very distinctly."

"I shall be there with my sword; then woe to our new-made husband," said Douglas, with a cruel smile.

"Nay, my lord, I can propose a better plan than having recourse to steel," said Achanna, with one of his wicked leers, as his plotting brain was again at work; "Gray's bones seem made of malleable iron, but fire will conquer even that."

"Your last scheme," said the earl, with a withering glance, "did not prove very successful; but what is your new one?"

"Bethink you, Douglas, of the old story of the castle of Kirkclauch."

"At Girthavon, in Galloway, or Girthon, as folk name it now?"

"Yes, Douglas," replied Achanna, who, in the old Scottish fashion, called his leader by his name as frequently as by his title.

"What of it? Speak quickly, for time is precious."

"It belonged to a desperate mosstrooper, named Græme," said Achanna, in his most insinuating voice (while adjusting his habiliments which the earl had torn in his wrath), and speaking in his native Gaëlic, which was the language of Galloway till after the reign of Mary, and, while he spoke, he seemed to purr like a pleased cat, and pleased he certainly was, when any wickedness was to be done. "This Græme had plundered, in open raid, the lands of the laird of Muirfad, who, in revenge, drew him into an ambush and slew all his men. Full of rage and shame at his defeat, Græme fled to his old tower at Kirkclauch and vowed to have a terrible vengeance; but lo, ye! Gordon of Muirfad appeared suddenly before the closed gates with his exulting followers, and summoned the almost lonely man to surrender. They had a long parley, in which Græme, while piling oiled faggots, straw, and other combustibles against the wooden barrier, offered Gordon a sum in gold as black mail. The offer was accepted, and the money was to be handed through an eyelet-hole in the top of the gate, where the warder was wont to sit watching the roadway with his arblast. Standing upon his horse's saddle to reach this shot-hole, Gordon passed through his right hand, over which Græme, with a laugh of derision, threw an iron chain, and thus noosed him hard and fast to the stone arch above. He then fired the pile below, and retired, saying, 'You're welcome to your black mail, Muirfad, but by my soul you will find it rather hot!' The flames rose fast, and the fettered man shrieked in vain, for even his own kinsmen failed to rescue him, while Græme escaped by a secret postern, leaving the tower of Kirkclauch and all who were in it a prey to destruction. Muirfad was roasted in his armour like a buttered crab, and sorely would the Gordons have revenged this, had they dared; but Græme fled to Girthavon, 'the sanctuary by the river,' and became a monk."

"Thou chattering dunce, what have I to do with all this?" asked the earl, who had listened to the story with an impatient and sombre countenance.

"Does it not give you an idea, my lord?"

"No; but what is yours?"

"That we burn Sir Patrick Gray in his boots, and in the same fashion."

"At Kirkclauch?"

"No; here in Bommel, and this very night too."

"How? Speak quickly, for I am not in a mood for trifling," said Douglas, examining the point and edge of a beautiful Parmese poniard which dangled at his girdle, as if it were the readier means of ridding him of his enemy.

"Be pleased to listen to me with a little patience, lord earl," whined Achanna, "and I shall yet win those thousand crowns of the Rhine. My plan is very simple. Lady Murielle proposes to escape at midnight from the window above the arbour in the garden, which lies between this house and the church of St. Genevieve. Instead of the bride, I shall be at the window — —"

"To stab this new and most precious brother-in-law of mine?"

"No; to secure him, as Græme secured Gordon, by an iron chain, and then fire the faggots with which the arbour below shall be previously filled. By St. Bryde! he will roast in his armour like a nut in its shell."

"A rare vengeance!" said the earl, rubbing his hands, and almost laughing at the prospect of a punishment so signal and so terrible. "He will be deemed a Brabancione or housebreaker; at all events, we shall leave Bommel by day-break on our way towards Paris. Tell our master of the horse and the duke of Albany to prepare. Send hither Sir Alan Lauder, and to you, Achanna, I commit the care of this matter. You failed me once — —"

"If I fail again, trust me no more," replied Achanna, as he retired to put his plans in operation, and felt with regret that by this suddenly projected departure from Bommel, he would lose the thousand guilders he had hoped to obtain by the capture of Count Ludwig.

The earl concealed his recently acquired information from all, even from the countess, as he mistrusted her discretion. He contrived to meet even his father confessor with a bland smile at supper, though he trembled with suppressed passion on perceiving the timid, constrained, preoccupied manner of Murielle; and then he laughed inwardly as he thought of the grim tragedy about to ensue.

After supper, he suddenly and emphatically desired the countess to remove Murielle from her present sleeping chamber, to one in a more distant part of the mansion, and there to lock her in for the night.

His will, immutable as the laws of Draco, was immediately obeyed, and thus, at the time when Murielle expected to join her lover, she found herself terrified, bewildered, and weeping in a solitary room, the grated windows of which faced the high black wall of the old Canonry.

Achanna meanwhile had filled the arbour with wooden faggots, dry branches, straw, and other fuel, on which he poured more than one jar of oil. He procured a strong chain bridle, and stationed himself at the window of the apartment, which Murielle had hitherto occupied, and there awaited his prey.

"What do these changes mean?" asked the countess.

"To-morrow you shall know all," replied the earl, with one of his crafty smiles, as he turned and left her.

Slowly passed the hours, and they were hours of agony to Murielle. She knew not how much, or how little, was known to her family of late events, but that they suspected something her sudden seclusion fully evinced. What would be the sequel?

The hours were tolled in succession from the spire of the church of St. Genevieve—ten, eleven, and at last twelve—*midnight*. So certainly as these hours struck, Gray would come and find himself deluded. He would *now* be in the garden—now at the arbour—with his eyes anxiously fixed on her window, and she—a sudden emotion of rage filled her heart—rage that they should arrogate such power over her, and dare to treat her like a child; but this gust did not last long, and was followed by a shower of tears.

She rushed to the iron gratings of her windows, and strove to shake them with her tender little hands. There was no escape, no hope, no succour, and as the last stroke of twelve reverberated in her heart and died away, life seemed to die with it.

Then came a sound upon the night wind. It was the clamour of voices, mingled with the clash of weapons; and next there spread upon the darkness a red and lurid light, that wavered on the gloomy walls of the Canonry, that lit up the buttresses of the Church of St. Genevieve, and the wainscoting of her room. What did all this portend? Where was Patrick Gray, her world, her all, now more than ever her Alpha and Omega? Was he beset by the Douglases? Oh, if so, she would soon learn to abhor her own name.

She muffled her face and ears in her skirt, to shut out sight and sound, for both seemed to portend but death and woe.

When she looked up again the light had disappeared, all was dark, and all was still, save the beating of her heart, and the throbbing of her temples.

Let us return to Sir Patrick Gray.

He made all his arrangements with the prudence and rapidity of a soldier. He had his horse (his favourite roan) prepared, and carefully saddled; he had procured a stout nag, with a lady's pad, for Murielle, and he acquainted himself thoroughly with the route to be pursued by Op Andel and Alm Kerque to Altena. Then he waited with impatience for midnight, the time that would give him freely and for ever his bride, his wife, his long-loved Murielle, despite the wiles, the overweening power, and the unrelenting treachery of Douglas and his adherents.

Brightly shone the moon in the clear blue sky; the church spires, snowy white, with all their carvings and tracery, their painted windows, and glittering crosses, stood sharply up from the sea of pointed roofs which covered the city of Bommel, but Gray wished for darkness and obscurity. A small cloud came from the flat horizon, and anxiously he watched its progress; but it was of fleecy whiteness, and passed over the moon's yellow disc like a gauze veil. He prayed that she would go down before the appointed time, and being on the wane, she luckily did so—at least, ere half-past eleven, fair Luna was hidden by the thick woods that grew near Ameldroyen, and by the yellow haze exhaled from the sedgy banks of the Waal.

The time was near! He could count the minutes now; before he had reckoned by hours.

His heart beat quicker; he felt athirst, and drank a last cup of wine, as he bade adieu to his hostelry for ever, and mounting his roan, took the palfrey by the bridle, and forgetting all about the closed gates of Bommel, and that he was without an order from Jacques de Lalain (unless the abbot had procured it), turned his steps towards the church of St. Genevieve.

The padlocked chains which closed the ends of the streets were a serious obstruction in the dark, but he made his horses clear them by a bound, and each time they did so, he dreaded that the patrols of the Burgher Guard, or night watch, might hurry after him, to discover what horseman was abroad so late, and on what errand. But unseen he reached the church, and securing the horses in a dark recess, between two deep buttresses, by fastening their bridles to the carving of a niche, he hastened through the north aisle, and issued by the postern into the garden of the Dyck Graf's house. Then he saw the trellised arbour, and above it the window of Murielle's apartments.

A light was burning there; a shadow crossed it—it was she, and his heart leaped! All around was still and dark and sombre as he could have wished.

As he approached the window, a female figure in a hood and veil appeared. Gray hurriedly clambered to the roof of the arbour, the trellis-work of which formed a most efficient scaling-ladder, and reached the window, which was about twelve feet from the ground.

"Murielle—your hand—we have not a moment to lose!" he whispered, and held up his arms to receive and assist her.

At that moment he felt his right hand strongly grasped and seemingly fettered, as a chain was thrown round his wrist. He attempted to withdraw, but was firmly held.

"Murielle!" he exclaimed, in astonishment. There was a mocking laugh, and as the hood fell off, his eyes met those of James Achanna, glittering far apart like those of a huge bird.

"Pray to St. Simon that he may lend you his saw, or to St. Jude for his club, to break this fetter," said Achanna, as he secured the chain to an iron staple in the window-sill; "but the flames will be here, hot and red, before either of them," he added, suddenly brandishing a lighted torch, in the bright glare of which his flushed face and protruding green eyes now resembled those of a devil. Astonishment and rage trebled the great natural strength of Gray. He grasped Achanna by the throat with his left hand, and though the would-be assassin strove to free himself, by savagely thrusting the blazing torch in the face of his victim, the latter dragged him over the window: down they came, battling together—the chain and staple parted, and the two enemies fell crash through the frail arbour, upon the heap of combustibles below. These, by their previous preparation, the torch ignited in a moment. A fiery blaze at once lit all the garden, while Sir Patrick Gray and Achanna rolled over each over, struggling to get at their daggers, each to despatch his antagonist.

Achanna was below and Gray above, and as the dagger was worn far back on the right side in those days, the first could by no means get at his weapon, as it was completely under him. Gray's strong left hand clutched his throat with deadly tenacity, and his chest was also crushed; but Gray searched in vain for his dagger. It had dropped from his belt in their fall, and his sword was broken in three places by the same circumstance, but with the heavy hilt and a fragment of the blade which adhered to it, he rained a torrent of blows upon the head and face of his adversary, whom he resolved to despatch as he would have done a snake, or a viper, for it was now a combat to the death between them.

All this terrible episode occurred in a few moments, and Gray in his fury, would inevitably have destroyed Achanna, had there not rushed from the house, the earl of Douglas, the lairds of Pompherston, Glendoning, and Cairnglas, with Sir Alan Lauder, and several other persons, some of whom were in their breeches and shirts, others in helmets and cuirasses; but all with torches or candles, and drawn swords.

Fortunately for Gray, twelve soldiers of the burgher guard, whom the uproar had alarmed, came up at the same moment, with their ponderous Flemish partizans, or our story and his life had ended there together, for the Douglases would infallibly have cut him to pieces.

Intent now on escaping, and preserving both his life and his *incognito*, Gray fought with the vigour of despair. Wrenching a partizan from a Waloon soldier, he struck right and left to hew a passage through his assailants. He knocked down Douglas of Pompherston, and severely wounded two of the night watch, by piercing their cuirasses of boiled bull-hide; but being pressed furiously by their comrades, he was soon beaten to the ground, disarmed, dragged away through the streets, and carried to the castle of Bommel, where he was thrust into a common dungeon and left to his own reflections, which were neither very lucid nor lively.

His horses, his leathern mail or portmanteau, and papers became the spoil of the Douglases; his rich cassock coat, the gift of Duke Arnold, and the ring which he was commissioned by Katharine, the duchess of Gueldres, to convey to the young king, her future son-in-law, became the prey of James Achanna, who openly appropriated and wore both, and whom the earl sent to Messire Jacques de Lalain, the Dyck Graf, to request that Gray, "as a notorious outlaw and consorter with Ludwig of Endhoven, should be broken alive upon the wheel, by noon next day."

All his papers were gone; thus he could afford no written or satisfactory account of himself, and obstinately refused to say what object brought him into conflict with Achanna, as he was determined that the name of Murielle—his wife—should not be compromised, even in a foreign country.

It was soon known and proved by the evidence of the officious and now terrified keeper of the hostelry, at which he lately lodged, that he had assumed at times, if not constantly, the dress and character of a Muscovite merchant.

"For what reason?" asked De Lalain; but Gray declined to answer.

Was he a spy of Philip of Burgundy, or of Charles of France? was the next surmise. But the latter at that time had no thought of war or politics, and was forgetting everything in the arms of Agnes Soreau (commonly called Sorel), a beautiful demoiselle of Touraine. The fact of disguise looked very suspicious, but none knew exactly of what.

Again Douglas urged that he should be executed without delay; but grief and despair threw Gray into a burning fever, "ane het sicknesse," the abbot, his kinsman terms it; so the Dyck Graf declined to be precipitate, but kept him a close prisoner, and on the day after this affair, the earl of Douglas, with all his retinue, accompanied by the duke of Albany, left Bommel, and took the road by Ameldroyen, towards the frontier of France.

CHAPTER XXXIX
A GLANCE AT HISTORY

Visions of the days departed,
Shadowy phantoms fill my brain;
They who live in history only,
Seem to walk the earth again.
Longfellow.

The spring of 1443 was ripening into summer around the Scottish capital. The green corn was sprouting in the fields; the April gowans and the budding whins made gay the upland slopes and braes.

Many months had elapsed since Sir Patrick Gray should have returned to court with an account of his mission. The Regent Livingstone and the chancellor became impatient, and despatched Patrick Lord Glammis, Master of the Household, to the court of Gueldres, from whence he soon returned, with a duplicate of the letters entrusted to Gray, of whom no trace had been discovered, since Prince Adolphus and his retinue had separated from him at Wees, when on his way to the coast, and at the distance of twenty miles from the castle of Gueldres.

This was somewhat perplexing; the old chancellor, who had a strong friendship for Gray, now really mourned for him as one who was no more, believing that he had been slain in some mysterious manner, and the young king wept before the Lords of the Secret Council, to whom Glammis made his report. Crichton knew that the earl of Douglas had been in Flanders, with all his chosen followers, and their unscrupulous character made the friends of Sir Patrick fear the worst.

In those days, posts there were none, letters were few, travellers fewer, and one half of Europe knew nothing of the other; but, nevertheless, distant rumours informed the regent and chancellor of Scotland that Douglas and his train, with the forfeited duke of Albany, after a brief sojourn at the court of Charles the Seventh, had passed on towards Rome.

In his rage at the abbot John, the earl vowed "to raze Tongland Abbey to its ground-stone," and to do many other absurd and impossible things; but one threatening wave of the abbot's hand, and a denunciation from his otherwise good-natured lips, brought the superstitious noble on his knees, grovelling, and in prayer, which was invariably replaced by fury and maledictions as soon as his mentor retired. He promised to forgive Gray, and within the hour despatched Achanna with one of his many letters to the Dyck Graf of Bommel, urging his secret execution. He then ordered the abbot to return to Scotland, and in the same breath begged he would accompany him to Rome; and the abbot, being most anxious for a personal interview with the sovereign pontiff, silently consented to do so, though despising in his heart the titled penitent he followed.

John Douglas, abbot of the Premonstratensian monks of Tongland, held for the haughty earl, the keys of heaven and of hell, and made him writhe in his superstitious soul at the terrible conviction.

In 1444, as Crichton had arranged, the king took into his own hands the government of the nation, in a convention of the Three Estates, which met within the castle of Stirling, and at the same time, the papal legate came from beyond the sea, in great pomp and bravery, to exact a solemn oath of fealty to Rome from all the Scottish Bishops. Such oaths were beginning to be requisite now, for already had the smoke of those funeral fires, to which they had consigned Resby the Englishman, and Crawar the Bohemian, "infected all on whom it was blown."

The poor chancellor had his hands full of troublesome business, for the Scottish lords were again at their old hereditary occupations, rapine and slaughter.

Patrick Galbraith, a follower of the earl of Douglas, quarrelled with Robert Semple, of Fulwood, about who should command in the royal fortress of Dunbarton, where one was governor of the upper, and the other of the lower castle. The sword was speedily resorted to; Semple was slain, and a strong garrison of Douglas-men occupied the place. The Lindesays and Ogilvies fought the disastrous feudal battle of Arbroath to decide whose chief should be bailie of that regality; and there fell on that bloody field, Alexander, earl of Crawford, six knights, and six hundred men-at-arms.

Then Robert Boyd, of Doughal, ran his sword through Sir James Stewart, of Auchminto, at a lonely place near Kirkpatrick, where the summer woods grew thick and green, and carried off his wife to the castle of Dunbarton, where she brought forth a child prematurely, and died of grief and terror in two days after. Archibald Dunbar stormed the great castle of the earl of Hailes, slew the inmates, and gave it up to the Douglases, while the moss-troopers of Annandale, lest their weapons should rust, kept all the western marches in hot water by their raids and devastations, which were seldom confined to their own border.

The sisters of the king were actually considered in danger, so daring or so enterprising were the younger knights of the Douglas faction; thus the princesses Jane and Eleonora departed to visit their sister, the unhappy dauphiness of France, but arrived too late to see her. She had died of a broken heart, having sunk under the cruelty of her husband (afterwards Louis XI., of infamous memory) and shame at the false charges of Jamet de Tilloy. Eleonora became the wife of Sigismund, archduke of Austria; but the princess Jane returned to her first love, who was the Scottish earl of Angus.

"All the mischiefs at home," says Buchanan, "were imputed to the earl of Douglas, who did all he could to conceal the misdemeanour of his followers, while he studied to afflict the men of different parties; in consequence of the vastness of his power, it was almost a capital offence to call aught he did in question. His influence compelled Sir James Stuart, of Lorn, the king's uncle, to fly the realm, because he spoke freely of the desperate state of the people; and his ship was taken at sea by Flemish pirates, among whom he ended his life in misery."

Such was the hard fate of the Black Knight of Lorn, the husband of the Queen Dowager of Scotland—Jane Beaufort, the fair flower of Windsor.

The English, as usual, took advantage of these turmoils to enter Scotland and burn the tower of Dumfries; so in return for this piece of attention, the Scots, under Lord Balvenie, burned Alnwick, and laid waste to Northumberland, reducing it almost to a desert; and soon after fifteen thousand English, under the Lord Piercy, were cut to pieces on the frontier, as they were about to cross a second time.

The Cheviots, said by a modern writer, to be "a clasp riveting Scotland and England together," were then deemed, like the Tweed and Solway elsewhere, but a natural barrier placed by the hand of God between two rival kingdoms. War brought famine and disease in her ghastly train, and so closed the year 1448.

Previous to this, the chancellor taking advantage of the lull caused by the defeat of the English and the capture of their leaders, the earls of Northumberland and Huntingdon, assembled a suitable train and sailed for Flanders, to bring home the young king's betrothed bride, for whose reception, great preparations were made at court.

Crichton was long absent, as he went by the way of Tours, to renew the ancient league with France, which was again ratified by him and other Scottish ambassadors for James II.; and by Thibaud, bishop of Maillerais, the Sieur de Pretigni and Messire Guillaume Cousinat, on the part of Charles VII.

After this the lord chancellor rode towards Gueldres.

CHAPTER XL
THE PRISONER

It might be months, or years, or days,
I kept no count—I took no note;
I had no hope my eyes to raise,
And clear them of their dreary mote.—Byron.

Meanwhile, during the occurrence of all these stirring events where was Sir Patrick Gray?

A prisoner of state in the castle of Bommel, detained there, to all appearance, hopelessly, by order of Jacques de Lalain, the Dyck Graf.

This official knew not whether to believe the information and reiterated statements of Sir Patrick, or those of the vindictive earl of Douglas. The secret manner in which Gray had resided in Bommel, and the disguise he had assumed, were denounced by the burgomaster, as unworthy the character of an envoy and the captain of a royal guard; they were declared suspicious, though no one could exactly say of what bad errand or object. Then, in that unexplained midnight brawl, concerning the origin of which Sir Patrick maintained an obstinate silence, he had wounded almost to death two citizens of good repute; and he was totally without papers or property to verify the account he gave of himself, as all he possessed had fallen into the hands of the Douglases, who had destroyed the former and appropriated the latter.

The hatred displayed by a noble so powerful as the earl and by his brilliant train of followers towards him, and their urgent demands for his execution, with or without a trial, convinced Jacques de Lalain that some great mystery was involved; that his prisoner was a man of considerable importance; and that it would be alike impolitic to hang or to release him. Hence he ordered, that he should be well attended, and comfortably lodged in the fortress of Bommel, but closely guarded and confined to the tower of Otho III.

Arnold d'Egmont, duke of Gueldres, had already begun to be embroiled by his unnatural son, Prince Adolphus, and was absent at the ducal court of Burgundy; thus to numerous letters on the subject of his unfortunate prisoner, the Dyck Graf received no explicit answer, so time rolled wearily and drearily on.

And what of Murielle? was the constant thought of Gray.

She was now his, irrevocably his, and while aware of his existence could not, either by force or fraud, become the wife of another. Amid all the misery of a protracted captivity, there was comfort in his conviction, till after-thoughts suggested how heartless was the existence to which their precipitate marriage had perhaps condemned her!

But might not their enemies, by forgeries and false statements, delude her into an idea of *his* death, as they had attempted to do before? Douglas dared not trifle with the power and terror of the Church; so Gray drew consolation from his memory of the earl's superstition, if not of his religion.

Yet there were times when his mental agony became great; for no news from Scotland or of the external world ever reached his prison.

Was Murielle still living? Had the wild schemes of Douglas and Albany prospered? Was the latter on the throne as Robert IV., with the terrible earl for his lieutenant-general, his ally in council and his right arm in war—crowned like Baliol of old, by domestic treason and foreign treachery? Was the young king dead, a prisoner, or an exile in France or England? Was Albany's betrothal to Mademoiselle Radegonde, the eldest daughter of Charles VII., annulled? What changes were taking place in his secluded mountain home? Who were dead—who living, and who wedded? Was he quite forgotten there?

Such were the questions ever in his heart and on his tongue.

Slowly passed the weary days till they became months, and then season succeeded to season. Five times had Gray, from his barred window in that old tower of Otho count of Gueldres, seen the golden grain gathered on the flat and distant fields; five times had he seen the land ploughed, and sown, and reaped; and five times covered with the white mantle of winter, when frost locked the waters of the Waal, and moored, harder than ever hempen cable and iron anchor did, the great brown-varnished barges in the sedge-bordered canals, when the storks forsook their nests on the snow-covered gables, when the holy water froze in the stone fonts of the churches, and when the bulbous-shaped Flemings put on at least six pairs of additional breeches. At such a season as this, the poor prisoner pictured in fancy the crackling yule-log that blazed in his father's hall at home—the old kirk of Foulis all bedecked with green bays and greener holly—his mother mourning by the winter hearth for the loss of her absent son; and then his heart grew sick as he thought of his blighted love, his wasted life, and all the thousand memories of his native land.

He thought, too, of what he had seen in more than one Flemish market-place, in Antwerp, at Gueldres, Endhoven, Bommel, and elsewhere; the cruel and periodical exhibition of a long-secluded prisoner, in whose heart hope, and even the memory of the outer world, were long since dead; "for there on particular days," says a certain writer, "these victims are presented to the public eye, upon a stage erected in the open market, apparently to prevent their guilt and punishment from being forgotten. It is scarcely possible to witness a sight more degrading to humanity than this exhibition:—with matted hair, wild looks, and haggard features, with eyes dazzled by the unwonted glare of the sun, and ears deafened and astounded by the sudden exchange of the silence of a dungeon for the busy hum of men, the wretches sit like rude images fashioned to a fantastic imitation of humanity rather than like living and reflecting beings. In the course of time we are assured they generally become either madmen or idiots, as mind or matter happens to predominate, when the mysterious balance between them is destroyed."

Gray remembered to have seen these miserable captives thus exhibited, and his heart died within him with terror, lest such might be the fate reserved for himself.

So the year 1448 was in its spring when he reckoned that Murielle was no longer a girl—that in fact she would be about her four-and-twentieth year. He strove to picture what the girl would be now, when expanded into a woman! Would he ever see her more, or be free to tread his native soil again? Alas! there were times when he feared his brain would turn.

Count Ludwig had long since been taken in the adjacent forest, after a hard conflict between the soldiers of De Lalain and his Brabanciones, many of whom, including Gustaf Vlierbeke, and the industrious Carl Langfanger, were slain, and gibbeted on the trees. The wretched count was broken alive on the wheel, before the Church of St. Genevieve. He survived the torture for three days, before the public executioner gave him the final *coup* with an iron bar, and his head on a spike now rendered the market-place of Bommel horrible to its frequenters.

Gray heard of this barbarous execution in his prison, and he almost envied the reckless robber, for death seemed a triumphant release from tyranny, misery, and mental suffering.

In February, 1448, on a dull morning, when the yellow winter fog hung like a pall over the level scenery of the Bommelerwaard, Gray was roused from sleep by the roar of twenty great bombards, the concussion of which shook the old castle of Count Otho to its foundations as they exploded in a salvo.

Had an enemy, the French or Burgundians, attacked it suddenly? His heart leaped with joy at the desperate hope. He rushed to the grated window of his room, and saw in the court-yard beneath, the Dyck Graf, with his sword and mantle, his knightly girdle and collar, mustering and arraying his garrison in their armour, pikemen, crossbowmen, arquebusiers, all steady Walloons and German lanzknechts. Then came the clangour of the church bells, and cheers of a multitude without, who seemed to be rushing through the streets towards the gate of the fortress, while still the great brazen bombards continued to belch forth flame and thunder from the battlements.

"What has happened?" asked Gray, as he rushed half dressed from his room to the court-yard. "Oh, Messire," he added to the Dyck Graf, "in pity tell me?"

"Only a salute, messire," replied the governor curtly, in French; but as Gray observed, with more politeness than usually was accorded to him.

"To whom?"

"A demoiselle of the highest-rank."

"But her name, Messire?" urged Gray.

"The young queen of Scotland, who comes this way with her train," replied the Dyck Graf.

Gray almost gasped with joy.

"The daughter of duke Arnold?" he inquired.

"Yes; of Monseigneur the duke of Gueldres; she has been married to your king at Brussels, and is now on her way to Scotland."

"I am saved—saved at last!" exclaimed Gray, in a burst of happiness, so genuine that even the grim De Lalain was impressed by it. "Oh, my God, I thank thee! (oh, my Murielle!)—and—and, messire, is the king here?"

"Tonnere de ciel! how inquisitive you have become."

"Messire, after all I have endured you may excuse me, for many a sun has risen and set—many a tide has ebbed and flowed since I became a prisoner here, spending years, whose agony is known to Heaven and to myself only!"

"Well—the king is not here; the princess was married to him by proxy—the chancellor of Scotland being his representative, before the altar of St. Gudule."

"Sir William Crichton?"

"I think that is his name, messire; and by St. Genevieve!" he added as the clanking iron gates were rolled back by the warders, "she hath a brave retinue of lords and knights, and, as many of them are your countrymen, we shall *now* be able to verify the truth of your statements."

Within an hour after this, Sir Patrick Gray found himself a free man, and surrounded by his countrymen and friends, all loyal gentlemen of the court, who knew him well. He was cordially embraced by the old chancellor, who presented him to the young Queen Mary, and placed him by her side, as the captain of her husband's Royal Guard.

Messire Jacques de Lalain, on perceiving the turn matters took with his prisoner, began to fear that in the zealous execution of his office he had made a mistake. He offered innumerable apologies to Gray, and as he was not ungenerous, he presented him with a rich suit of Flemish armour, a fine Toledo, a Spanish gennet, and a catella or chain, having fifty links of fine gold, as an *amende* for all he had endured.

Of all who accompanied the chancellor, he inquired about the Douglases; but could only learn that they were at Rome, and probably would not return until after the great jubilee, which took place then every fiftieth year, in honour of the foundation of Christianity.

The young queen's train embarked at Sluys, in Scottish ships, and crossed the German sea in safety.

On the 1st of April, 1448, she landed at Leith, and as an illustration of "how dull and common-place fiction is when compared with truth," the Dyck Graf of Bommel, and Sir Patrick Gray, who had been so long and so hopelessly his prisoner, rode side by side, as she proceeded towards Edinburgh, and they bore over her head a canopy of cloth of gold upon the points of their lances.

Gray's noble horse and gorgeous armour were now as conspicuous as his soldierly bearing and manly beauty; for both had now returned, and in his five years of captivity the scars inflicted by the ghisarma of Douglas had disappeared, or nearly so.

Patrick Cockburn, of Newbigging, now provost of Edinburgh and governor of the castle, received the queen at the head of the magistrates and all the men of the city, in armour—"boden in effeir of weir," as it was then termed.

Mary was accompanied by the lord chancellor Crichton, John Raulston, bishop of Dunkeld, who was lord privy seal, and Nicholas Otterburn, a canon of Glasgow. The prince of Ravenstein, the marquis of Berg, and Englebert, count of Nassau, hereditary Burg Graf of Antwerp, who were each followed by a brilliant train of attendants, wore the collars and mantles of the Golden Fleece. The prince bore the banner of the bride's uncle, Philip III., surnamed the Good, duke of Burgundy.

Then came the bishops of Liege and Cambrai, riding upon white mules, with long footcloths.

The king's two brothers-in-law came next, Francis, duke of Brittany (a prince who slew his brother Giles), and the Archduke Sigismund of Austria, each attended by knights, banners, squires, and pages, in glittering costumes. With them came Louis II., duke of Savoy, prince of Piedmont, and husband of the princess royal of Cyprus, with his banner borne by the duke of Montferrat, who wore a scarlet tabard, with the silver cross of Savoy.

The lord of Campvere, a handsome and black-bearded man, the husband of Mary of Scotland (fifth sister of James), came next in a suit of armour glittering with gold carvings and precious stones. He bore a great banner—*azure*, with the lion *or*, crowned for Gueldreland, and *azure* a lion *gules* for Zutphen, impaled, with the lion of Scotland, within its double tressure of *fleur-de-lis*.

Herré de Meriadet, hereditary Burg Graf of the castle of Sluys, bore the banner of the count of Nassau, *azure* sprinkled with crosses *argent*. Meriadet, a tall and stately man, was then famous as one of the best knights in Europe, and the people received him with acclamation. He wore a silver helmet of great beauty and remarkable form, which he had struck in battle from the head of an emir of Granada, when he served the king of Castile in his wars against the Moors, and its snow-white plumes drooped upon his shoulders, and were reflected on the dazzling surface of his armour, which literally blazed in the noonday sunshine.

Bombards were fired, and bells were loudly rung in many a sacred edifice now numbered with the things that were; and so "with a grate traine of knights and ladeys" (as Balfour has it), the queen was conducted to the church of Holyrood, and there solemnly married to the young king, then in about the nineteenth year of his age, and in the bloom of youthful strength and comeliness; and Mary his bride charmed the people by her girlish loveliness. They were never tired of extolling her fair hair, which fell in golden masses on her snowy neck and shoulders; her violet-coloured eyes, and her full yet curved lip, which expressed the softness of love, with that firmness of character so needed in a queen of the turbulent Scots.

This was the second time that the houses of Scotland and the then powerful and independent dukedom of Gueldres had been connected by marriage.

Alexander, son of Alexander III., espoused Margaret, daughter of Guy de Dampierre, earl of Flanders; and had he lived, and she been queen of Scotland, the disastrous wars of the Edwards and the victories of Wallace and Bruce had never been heard of; but he died at Roxburgh, in 1283, when in his twentieth year. Margaret interred him at Lindores, in the old abbey church of St. Mary, and soon after became the wife of Reinald, the warlike duke and count of Gueldres.

CHAPTER XLI
CRICHTON

> The towers in different ages rose,
> Their various architecture shows
> The builders' various hands;
> A mighty mass, that could oppose
> When deadliest hatred fired its foes,
> The vengeful Douglas bands. — Marmion.

Amid all the rejoicings on the occasion of this royal marriage the heart of Gray was sad.

Time had not lessened his love for Murielle Douglas, and he grew sick at heart when contemplating the apparent hopelessness of his separation from her: yet she was his wife, whom no man could take from him, while life remained; but so broken did he become in spirit, that notwithstanding all the barbarity and wrong he had endured from the Douglases and their chief, there were times when he resolved to seek the presence of the latter, and, divested of sword, dagger, and armour, make the desperate attempt of offering his ungloved hand, "which," as the chancellor told him with a grimace, "he might as safely thrust into the mouth of a hungry tiger."

The young monarch, who loved Gray and pitied him for his story, heaped favours upon him, such as fine horses, rich armour, purses, and swords, enabling him to appear to the best advantage among the brilliant foreign chivalry by whom the Scottish court was then crowded — knights who were the flower of France, Bretagne, Gueldres, and Burgundy — men whose sons were to win the great battles of Charles the Bold, and to die by his side on the field of Campo Basso.

To all whom he trusted the manner of James II. was most winning; it was the old hereditary charm of his family, who seemed never to forget the maxim, — the higher the head the humbler the heart.

For his diplomatic services in this marriage and other matters, Crichton, as already mentioned, had been created a peer of the realm; and when the beauty of the young queen and the dowry she brought are considered, he had some reason to congratulate himself on a result so successful.

Philip of Burgundy bound himself to pay his niece, the bride, sixty thousand pounds in gold, as a portion merely of her dower, while James settled upon her ten thousand crowns, secured on land in Atholl, Methven, Stratharn, and Linlithgow; and he relinquished all claim to the duchy of Gueldres, after which a league offensive and defensive was concluded between that province, the kingdoms of Scotland, France, and the dukedom of Burgundy.

A series of brilliant tournaments were held in honour of these events; and the Dyck Graf of Bommel, with his brother, Messire Simon de Lalain, with Messire Herré de Meriadet, Burg Graf of Sluys, three Burgundian lords of high descent and esteemed valour, challenged "an equal number of Scottish chivalry to joust with lance and sword, battle-axe and dagger."

This defiance was promptly responded to by a knight named Sir James Douglas, James Douglas, Lord of Lochlevin, and Sir John Ross of Halkhead, constable of Renfrew. The latter was attended by Sir Patrick Gray, while Sir Thomas MacLellan and Romanno of that Ilk attended the other two, ready to take part in the *mêlée* if the strife became a bloody one. A space near the castle rock of Stirling was selected for the lists, and gaily-decorated galleries were erected for the king, the queen, and court, the lords and barons of parliament.

On the appointed day, the six champions, after hearing mass, presented themselves, clad in velvet and cloth of gold, before the king, and after each had made a low reverence, they retired to six painted pavilions to arm; after which, lanced, horsed, and in full and splendid armour, with closed helmets, they entered the lists at opposite extremities; and when twelve brass trumpets made the summer sky and castle rock re-echo to their united blast, the knights rushed on each other, three against three.

"For Scotland!" shouted Ross and the Douglases.

"Vivat Burgundie!" replied Meriadet and the De Lalains.

Such were the war-cries on each side.

Their tough ash spears were splintered in an instant, the fragments springing high in air from the ringing coats of tempered steel. Panting and quivering, with flashing eyes and snorting nostrils, the gaily-trapped horses recoiled upon their straining haunches, till wheeled round, and urged forward again, by spur and knee, by voice and bridle, and fiercely the combat was renewed, as the six knights closed up, hand to hand, with flashing swords and swaying battle-axes.

Sir James Douglas and Sir John Ross, and the Dyck Graf and Simon de Lalain, were so equally matched that not one of them could obtain the least advantage over the other, though they fought till all their armour was defaced, and, save Douglas's dagger, all their weapons were broken; but Herré de Meriadet, by one blow of his battle-axe, unhorsed the lord of Lochlevin, as he had formerly done the emir of Granada, and hurled him to the ground.

On seeing this, and fearing the conflict might have a disastrous termination, the king, at Crichton's request, threw down his truncheon, and the jousts were ended, just as Gray, MacLellan, and Romanno were about to join in the *mêlée* with the three Burgundian squires.

So passed this year, and then came the next, in which rumour reached the Scottish court of how the turbulent earl of Douglas and his warlike followers comported themselves in the Eternal City, during the festivities which opened with the year of the Jubilee, 1450; for there the Scottish knights, who wore the red heart on their helmets and surcoats, became involved in a brawl with the Roman populace on the crowded bridge of St. Angelo, and betook them to their lances, swords, and mauls as freely as if they had been in the High Street of Edinburgh, or the Broad Wynd of Stirling, and played the devil in the capital of his holiness, spearing and trampling the people under foot; and they it was who caused that tremendous pressure by which, as history records, ninety-seven persons were killed at the end of the bridge, by being simply crushed to death.

Pope Nicholas V., who had lately succeeded the unfortunate Eugene, was so inspired by indignation, that all hope of a fuller dispensation for the earl and his countess was at an end. There too were dissipated all the poor abbot of Tongland's expectations of having the prince of darkness restored to favour, for, as he records in his papers, the very name of "Douglace gart ye paip to scunner;" so, in despair, he committed to the flames the memorial he had prepared on behalf of his ubiquitous protégé, and abandoned his pet project for the time.

Then, to the infinite satisfaction of Murielle, the earl, separated from the duke of Albany, and hearing how high his rival Crichton stood in favour at the Scottish court, and that, under Romanno, troops had been sent into Galloway to ravage the Douglas lands, and punish their disorderly occupants, he returned secretly and with all speed homeward, for the express purpose of cutting off the chancellor by the strong hand, and more than ever determined on carrying out his old schemes of vengeance.

Passing through England in the spring of the year, after some treasonable correspondence with Henry VI., he arrived in Scotland, and, unknown to Crichton, secretly ensconced himself at Dalkeith, the castle of his kinsman, James, third lord of Dalkeith, while Achanna and another follower, bribed by the proffer of a gauntlet filled with silver crowns, watched the movements of the chancellor, who was then suffering from ill health, his advanced years, and the cares of the state, and who resided in the castle of Edinburgh. An opportunity for mischief soon presented itself.

It chanced that on Lady Day, in March, the chancellor left his residence to visit his own house of Crichton, which stands about twelve miles south from the city. He was accompanied by Sir Patrick Gray, Sir Thomas MacLellan, Romanno, constable of Edinburgh Castle and master of the king's ordnance, Patrick Lord Glammis, and about twenty gentlemen, all well mounted and armed.

The day was fine and clear, the sharp March winds blustered through the hollows and swept the last year's leaves before it over the uplands, where the fresh soil glittered in the sunshine, and where the hoodie-crow searched in the furrows for worms; the birds were singing in the hedgerows, where the buds were springing into greenness; the air was mild and cool, the fields were assuming a verdant hue, though the brown spoil of the departed year lay damp and rotting in the mountain runnels, and along the sedgy banks of loch and stream. The rich aroma of the land came on the passing breeze, that shook the old woods of Drumshelch and Dalrigh.

Over miles of land now covered by the "modern Athens," for ages into times unknown and far beyond the knowledge or record of man, the oaks of these old woods shook down their autumn leaves upon the lair of the elk, the snow-white mountain bull, and of those ferocious Scottish bears, which in after-days, as Martial tells us, were used by the pagan Romans to increase the torture of those Christians who perished on the cross. Drumshelch was one of those old primeval forests, from which the first dwellers in the land named themselves Coille-dhoinean—Caledonians, or the men of the woods.

Though the month was March, the season having been moist, the peasantry were consigning the whins to the flames, though such was contrary to the law of James I., and the white smoke of the muir-burn, as it was named, rolled along the hills of Braid and the more distant slopes of the Pentlands like a mimic conflagration.

It was spring, and one of the most delightful days of the season, when men's hearts grow buoyant, they scarcely know why. Even Gray felt its influence, for it gave him new emotions of pleasure and of hope. It was little more than the commencement of a new year; but it was one the end of which none could foresee. He had heard that the Douglases were returning. How little could he imagine that Murielle was then only six miles distant from him, where the strong old castle of Dalkeith, from its wooded slope, overlooked the lovely Esks.

He conversed gaily with the knights and gentlemen of the chancellor's train, as they rode down the steep winding street, named the Bow, and passed to the eastward along a narrow way between hedgerows, which bordered the city on the south in the long deep hollow, on the opposite bank of which then stood only one edifice—the solitary church of St. Mary-in-the-Field, surrounded by its burying-ground. It was a lonely bridle-road this path through the hollow—a place where the birds carolled by day, the glow-worms glittered by night, and the brown rabbits started from side to side at all times.

Three crow-stepped and gable-ended edifices, then standing far apart, were there. One belonged to Richard Lundy, then a monk, and afterwards abbot of Melrose; another was a little chapel of Holyrood which stood at the foot of St. Giles's churchyard; the third was an old farmhouse.

This narrow and solitary hedgerow was then the southgate and the future Cowgate of Edinburgh.

As the chancellor and his train issued from it into the more open country, they took no heed of two armed horsemen—for all men in Scotland went armed—who left the city before them, and who, after frequently looking back, as if reckoning their number and watching their route, disappeared at full speed to the southward.

At a rapid pace our friends crossed the ridge of Kirk-Liberton, passing between the fortlet of the Winrams and the holy well of St. Catherine. They crossed both the wooded Esks, and ascended the long line of cultivated hill, then an open waste, known as the Roman camp of Agricola, where the mounds and trenches which his warriors dug in the year 80 may still be distinctly traced; and then southward in the distance, the chancellor's retinue could see his castle of Crichton on the western slope of a green eminence, where its walls and towers, a glorious relic of Scotland's stormy days, all built of red coloured freestone, glowed ruddily in the light of the evening sun. And this feudal fortress appeared to rise higher on its steep as the proprietor's train descended into the deep and marshy valley which it overhangs.

Crichton is a vast quadrangular fortress, exhibiting in its stone staircases and arcaded court, wonderful architectural beauty and great strength, as it adjoined that part of the wild and lawless border-land which lay nearest to the Scottish capital. Toned down by time, its corroded carvings, so rich and so florid in their details, impress with astonishment the wanderer who comes suddenly in view of its mouldering remains, as they stand in a lonely glen, remote and secluded alike from road and railway, from tourist and traveller. A fallen tower has now choked up the terrible *massy-more* or secret dungeon, and the chambers where Mary Stuart and Bothwell held high revelry—where the lady of Hailes wept for the slaughter of her lord and all his kindred at Flodden, and where the wily old chancellor wove his plans for the downfall of the Douglases, are now roofless and windowless—the abode of the fox and the fuimart—the ravenous gled and the hoodie-crow.

As the chancellor's train, all of whom being men of rank were in bright armour, rode by the narrow bridle-path, between the green pastoral hills, and entered Crichtondean, through which flows a sluggish streamlet, known as the Scottish Tyne, but which becomes a rushing river when it reaches the ocean at Dunbar, they were soon visible to the inmates of the castle, several of whom waved their handkerchiefs from the keep, where the great bell was rung and a banner displayed, while the Milan plate and steel of the visitors were seen to glitter in the sunlight, between the masses of alder tree which *then* clothed the now bare and desolate sides of the narrow valley.

Those white handkerchiefs were waved by the chancellor's lady, who had so kindly nursed Sir Patrick Gray, his daughters, Agnes, wife of Alexander, master of Glammis, and Elizabeth, afterwards Countess of Huntly, two of the most beautiful women of the time, who were on the bartizan with several of their friends and attendants. But as their father, with his retinue, banner, and horsemen, disappeared where the alder-woods grew thickest, they heard a tumultuous shout, the sound of a trumpet, and the clamour of many voices, ascending to their ears on the breeze of the valley.

Conversing merrily with Sir Patrick Gray, the old chancellor rode his ambling nag at an easy pace, with a favourite hawk, the gift of his neighbour, the Knight of Locharwart, perched on his bridle hand. Trusting in the strength and character of his retinue, in his diplomatic rank, to his many ripe years, and the supposed absence of his enemies, he was without armour, and wore a long black velvet cassock-coat, which was sufficiently open to show an undershirt of white satin slashed with red, and secured at the waist by an embroidered baldrick, at which hung a heavy sword and Parmese dagger, the hilt of which was composed of a single crystal. His long white hair escaped from under his Scottish bonnet of black velvet, and floated on the tippet of miniver which covered his shoulders and was clasped at the throat by a jewel.

He pointed to the great column of smoke which ascended from the chimney of the kitchen-tower, and laughed while reminding his friends of the good cheer which awaited after their ride over the hills on a clear March day; but something less easy of digestion in the shape of cold iron awaited them; for at the narrow part of the road, where it took an abrupt turn, and where, as already stated, the alderwood grew thickest, there arose a sudden shout, in front and on both flanks, while a band of men-at-arms, lanced, horsed, and with closed helmets, rushed upon them from an ambush.

"Jamais arrière! a Douglas! a Douglas! Revenge for the Black Dinner!"

These shouts made all acquainted with whom they had to deal. Gray, MacLellan, Romanno, and others, shut down their helmets, and betook them to sword, axe, and "morning star," as those ponderous maces borne by knights at their saddle-bows were named.

Two of their unexpected assailants had coronets of jewels upon their helmets, and all had their coats-of-arms, but chiefly the terrible *Red Heart and three stars*, painted on their breastplates. All knew their foes in an instant, as heraldry was a science in which every gentleman was then well versed.

"To your swords, gentlemen; forward, and break through this pack of knaves!" exclaimed the old chancellor, tossing his hawk into the air, as he knew it would wing its way straight home. Then drawing his sword, he added, "Help yourselves, sirs, and Heaven will help you!"

There was a tremendous shock in the rough and narrow pathway, a clashing of swords, and the dull, dinting crash of iron maces and mauls on steel casques and shoulder-plates; several men fell to rise no more, and many were severely wounded. The chancellor was the aim of all the Douglases. Gray and MacLellan stood nobly by his side, yet he received many severe wounds, till he became almost maddened by pain and the prospect of a cruel death at the hands of his bitterest enemies.

"Then," says Buchanan, "the Lord Crichton, though an aged peer, slew the first man who assaulted him, passed his sword through a second, and leading a charge of his retinue, broke right through the Douglases;" but just as he was sinking with fatigue and loss of blood, Sir Patrick Gray, by his battle-axe, broke the arm of one assailant, clove the helmet of another, and drew the chancellor across the saddle of his own charger, a powerful Clydesdale war-horse, presented to him by the king, and calling to MacLellan, Lord Glammis, and Romanno, to "cover his retreat, and keep the foe in check," he galloped up the steep and winding path which led to the castle, and deposited his now senseless friend in the arms of his terrified daughters. Pell-mell up the grassy slope, fighting every foot of the way, but in full flight, their friends were now driven by the victorious Douglases, who were more than a hundred strong, till they reached the chancellor's fortress, when its gates received them, and then a shot or two skilfully discharged from a culverin by Gray and Romanno drove them off, brandishing their weapons and shaking their mailed hands in token of future vengeance. Ere they went one opened his helmet and displaying the dark and swarthy face of the great earl, exclaimed hoarsely, "Hark ye, my lord chancellor: I have drawn once more my father's sword, and by St. Mary, and St. Bryde of Douglas, I will not leave James Stuart one foot of Scottish ground—nay, not even the moat-hill of Scone. By our blessed Lord, before whom this relic of St. Bryde is holy, I swear it! so judge what shall become of *thee!*"

And with these terrible words, after kissing an amulet which hung at his neck, he galloped away, and with his followers disappeared down Crichtondean.

In this rough mode did Gray, for the first time, learn that the Douglases were again in Scotland, and that Murielle must now have returned.

He had now ample scope for thought, reflection, and for daring schemes, which he knew not how to put in operation.

After this rash escapade, the Earl of Douglas retired to Thrave, in Galloway, and for some time the chancellor remained in his stronghold, until his wounds were healed and he could return to court.

By this epoch the reader must have begun to perceive what a pleasant time a Scottish statesman must have had of it in those old feudal days.

CHAPTER XLII
KING JAMES II

Oh, men of Scotland, though you cannot raise
Your long past monarchs from the silent bier;
Their deeds are worthy of your highest praise,
And simple gratitude demands a tear.
Let no base slander on their memory fall,
Nor malice of their little faults complain;
They were such men as, take them all and all,
We ne'er shall look upon their like again!
Written in 1771.

James II. was one of that old race of kings whom the now forgotten bard, above quoted, called upon posterity to remember. At this period of our story he had reached his twenty-first year, but experience had already made him older. The sole blemish to his very handsome countenance was that small red spot which won him the sobriquet of James with the fiery face. He was considerably above the middle height, and was firmly knit in form; his eyebrows were strongly marked, and a dark glossy moustache, curling round his finely cut mouth, mingled with a short peaked beard. His rich brown hair hung, in the profusion of the time, over his ears, in thick masses called "side locks." He was rapid in thought, bold in speech, and prompt in action, fiery and impetuous in temper; resolute and even desperate in avenging a wrong; and of his wild impulsive nature, his most unruly subject, the Earl of Douglas, was, ere long, to have a terrible proof; but yet, like the Moorish knight of Granada, James was said to be,

Like steel amid the din of arms,
Like wax when with the fair.

Some weeks after the outrage which closes the last chapter, on a day when the sun of June, by its golden light and genial heat, was ripening the young corn in many a fertile haugh, and on many a swelling eminence where now the modern city spreads its streets and squares, James was seated in one of the upper chambers of David's Tower, in the Castle of Edinburgh. It was the same in which King David died on the 7th May, eighty years before, and in memory of him there still hung above the fireplace the mail shirt and barrel-shaped helmet which he had worn at the battle of Durham.

The vaulted apartment was gloomy, and through the basket-shaped gratings of the windows which faced the east the rays of the summer sun came slanting in, filling one portion with strong light, and leaving the other involved in dusky shadow.

Clad in a long scarlet dressing-gown, trimmed with miniver, the king was reclining in an armed chair, with his feet on a velvet tabourette. In his hand, bound in painted vellum, and elaborately clasped with silver, was one of those old French metrical romances which had been translated into Scottish for him by Sir Gilbert the Haye, who was chamberlain to Charles VII. of France; but his thoughts ran not upon its lines, nor the fighting giants, cunning dwarfs, wandering knights, and castles of burnished steel which filled its pages; neither was he attending to the mass of yellow parchments and papers which the high treasurer, and Lord Glammis, the master of the household, were arranging for his inspection; nor was he heeding the occasional remarks of his favourite, the Captain of the Guard, who, clad in half armour, lounged in the recess of a window; but the king's face confessed, by the sadness of its expression, that his thoughts were at Stirling, where his beautiful young queen—his golden-haired Mary d'Egmont, of Gueldres—was confined to her chamber, sick and ill and weary, after the premature birth of her first baby, which died two hours after it came into the world, to the great disappointment of the king and nation.

The great battle of Sark had been recently fought on the borders, and there fifty thousand English, led by "the stoute Earl of Northumberland," had been routed by less than thirty thousand Scots, with the loss of Sir John Pennington and Sir Magnus Red Main, two of the most celebrated soldiers of Henry VI.; and now, from the window at which Gray stood in David's Tower, he could see far down below, where several thousand labourers were daily and nightly at work, enclosing the capital by its *first* walls, with embattled gates upon the south, east, and west; and, for defence on the north, others were converting the old royal gardens in the valley into a sheet of water—the Nor'loch of future times; these protections for the city being among the earliest measures of the young and politic monarch, "in dread of the evil and skaith of oure ennemies of England," as he states in his charter to the citizens, who loved him for his valiant conduct and fatherly care of them.

"I am well nigh sick of hearing so many petty items," said the king, wearily, interrupting Andrew, abbot of Melrose, the lord high treasurer, a tall, pale-visaged, and sharp-eyed man (on whose white head time had long since marked a permanent *tonsure*), who had been reading over several papers for his information; "yet I suppose I must hear them: say, lord abbot, how stands our privy purse?"

"I have disbursed to-day to foreign heralds one hundred and fifty pounds," replied the treasurer.

"Heralds! On what errand?"

"They came on the part of Henry of England, to ransom Lord Northumberland's son, who was wounded and taken prisoner at Sark by Sir Thomas MacLellan; who had already ransomed him for the value of his horse and armour," replied the abbot. "Shall I read on?" The king nodded, and the abbot proceeded in this manner, jumbling all kinds of items strangely together. "'Item: for your highness's new suit of Milan harness 20*lb.*' 'For eight score and eighteen runlets of wine from a Fleming of the Dam, to wit, Master Baudoin of Antwerp, 500*lb.*' For silken stuffs, furs, minivers, spices, and sweetmeats, for the queen's household, paid to John Vanderberg of Bruges at the fair of Dundee, 800*lb.*'"

"Good, my lord — and the total?" said the king.

"Maketh 1480*lb.*," replied the treasurer after a pause.

"By St. Andrew! we shall have but little left to keep those Douglases in check on the one hand, and those pestilent English on the other, if our household accounts go thus," said James, with a dubious smile.

"'To your highness's chamberlain in Mar, for driving all your brood mares from Strathavon to Strathdon, 5*sh.*'" resumed the treasurer, reading very fast to avoid interruption; and then followed innumerable other items, all written in obsolete Scottish (which, like our dialogues, we translate), such as twenty-nine weeks' pay to the king's falconer; to the master gunner of Lochmaben, for stone and iron cannon balls, and for repairs; to Sir John Romanno for a thousand bowstaves; to Henry, the smith, for dies for the new coinage; to the keepers of the balefires along the borders; for garrisons there, and for the hanging of those who supplied the English with horses or cattle; to the driver of the oxen when the ten bombardes of the wine of Gascony came from Perth for the court's summer drink——

"And were intercepted by the earl of Douglas, or some of his reivers, and drunk in Thrave," commented the king.

"To the hunter of wolves in Stirling Park, for three wolves' heads laid at the outer gate, 18 pennies, according to the act of parliament. This closes the record; but the monks of Holyrood have sent your majesty a thousand silver crowns."

"That is well," said the king, who had long since relinquished his romance in despair; "but the lord abbot hath twenty-seven parish churches, and might, at this emergency, have lent me a trifle more."

"Perhaps; but even with all the altar-offerings, lesser tithes, pasque presents, and dues for baptism, marriage, and funerals, there is but little left to give after the yearly expenses of so great a monastery are paid."

"There spoke a brother abbot, and *not* a treasurer," said the king laughing, while the churchman coloured as he tied up his rolls with a ribbon. "Laus Deo! I am thankful we have come to an end; but we shall need all the money we can collect, my lord."

"True; for evil tidings are on the wind," said Lord Glammis, approaching a single pace and pausing.

"Of what—or whom?" asked James, with a louring eye.

"The Douglases again."

Sir Patrick Gray started from his reverie to listen.

"What of them now?" asked the king impatiently.

"Sir Alan Lauder and a man named James Achanna, both followers of the earl, have slain a king's vassal within the Holy Gyrth of Lesmahago."

"Treason! But that is a mere nothing now," said James bitterly.

"And worse than treason, for it is sacrilege!" added the abbot of Melrose, with gathering wrath. "When your highness's sainted ancestor, King David I., in the pious times of old, granted that cell unto the monks of Kelso, he wrote, that 'whoso escaping peril of life and limb flies to the said cell, or cometh within the four crosses around it, in reverence to God and St. Machute, *I grant him my firm peace.'*"

"And so they violated this holy sanctuary?" said James.

"Yes; and hewed the poor man to pieces with their Jethart axes."

"His offence?"

"Was wearing the royal livery,—being the gudeman of your majesty's mills at Carluke."

The king started up, and was about to utter some hasty speech, when a smart little page, clad in a violet-coloured doublet, with long hose of white silk, drew back the tapestry which overhung the arched door, and announced that the lord chancellor craved an audience in haste.

"Admit him," said James, advancing a step, as the old statesman, pale and thin from the effect of his recent wounds and by the advance of years, entered, propped upon a long silver-headed staff. "You look grave, my lord," added the king; "but I pray you to be seated."

"I have evil tidings," began the chancellor, hobbling forward and coughing violently.

"The very words of my Lord Glammis," said the king; "can aught else come to the ear of him who wears a Scottish crown?" he added, biting his nether lip.

"Say not so, after our late glorious victory at Sark!" exclaimed the chancellor; "but, nevertheless, I *have* evil news," he added, taking from the velvet pouch which hung at his embroidered girdle several letters, folded square, and tied with ribbons, in the fashion of the time. "I have two grave matters to lay before your majesty. We are more than ever humbled and insulted by this overweening earl of Douglas, and, through you, the entire nation! The king of Scotland," continued the chancellor, warming and striking the floor with his cane, "is the fountain of Scottish honour, and thus I maintain, that if the king is insulted so are *we*; for if a stream be polluted at its source, every rill that flows from it becomes so too; but we must end these matters by the sword—we must wipe out our wrongs in blood, and regild our tarnished blazons in the reddest that flows in the veins of our enemies, the men of Douglas-dale and Galloway!"

"These wild men are yet untamed," said the tall thin treasurer, shaking his bald head.

"But *not* untameable," responded the fiery old chancellor, with a spark of rage in his hollow eyes.

"To the point, my lords, under favour of the king," said Sir Patrick Gray, gnawing his moustache in his impatience.

CHAPTER XLIII
A LADLEFUL OF GOLD

Thou shalt not yield to lord nor loon,
Nor shalt thou yield to me;
But yield thee to the braken bush
That grows on yon lilye lee.—Old Ballad.

"What more have I to hear of this false noble and his followers?" said the king, after briefly, and to Gray's great annoyance, rehearsing the whole story of the murder of his vassal, the miller of Carluke, in the sanctuary of Lesmahago.

"The earl has lawlessly seized, and ignominiously imprisoned, in his hold of Thrave, a good and loyal servant of your majesty."

"That is nothing new; but what is his name?" asked James, grasping the arms of the chair, and thrusting aside the tabourette with his foot, while his hazel eyes flashed fire with anger, and his dark brows were knit.

"Sir Thomas MacLellan, of Bombie," replied the chancellor, with grave energy.

"My friend—the Lieutenant of my Guard!"

"My brave kinsman!"

Such were the exclamations of the king and of Sir Patrick Gray, who had come from the sunny recess of the window, and in deep anxiety stood near the chancellor's chair to listen. In his anger, James snatched from the table his amber rosary and dagger of mercy, as if about to utter some vague threat or malediction, and then cast them from him, though the latter was the gift of his brother-in-law, Sigismund of Austria, and was hilted by a single agate.

"Sir Thomas MacLellan, of Bombie," resumed the chancellor, gravely and earnestly, "your majesty's steward of Kirkcudbright, is now a prisoner in the castle of Thrave manacled with the heaviest chains MacKim, the earl's smith, can forge, and hourly is menaced with death."

"And wherefore has this been done?"

"The whole of this new outrage is detailed to me in a letter from the abbot of Tongland, who has at *last*—the pedantic fool! the very dunce!—(excuse me, my lord abbot of Melrose)—abandoned the earl, his chief, and has secluded himself in his abbey, despairing, I presume, of the reformation of Douglas, as of that of the devil himself, concerning whom he so lately visited Rome."

From the letters of the abbot, the lord chancellor then proceeded to relate that there were three reasons for this capture and imprisonment of the Steward of Kirkcudbright. The *first* was, that Sir Thomas, who was chief of a powerful Celtic tribe, possessing all the peninsula between the Dee and the Solway, had taken part with the late Sir Herbert Herries, of Terregles, his kinsman, against the Douglases, and had thereby excited the ready wrath of the earl. The *second* cause of hatred was, that he had borne a letter from the Captain of the King's Guard to the Lady Murielle Douglas, and had shot it to her feet by an arrow, as she was walking near the castle wall of Thrave. The *third*, that he had refused to join a league, and sign a bond for levying war against the king. For these three causes the earl, taking advantage of MacLellan being at his own castle of Raeberry, whither he had retired in consequence of a sword-wound received from Lord Piercy at the battle of Sark, despatched three hundred men-at-arms under James Achanna to bring him dead or alive to Thrave, after sacking and demolishing his residence.

Achanna marched on this lawless mission; but true to his infamous nature, he preferred fraud to force. Raeberry, of which there now remains but a deep fosse, overhung a dreadful precipice, on the bluffs of which the united waves of the Solway Frith and the Atlantic pour their fury. It was deemed impregnable, and was protected on the north by a strong rampart, a drawbridge, and a deep trench. Achanna, aware of these difficulties on one side, and perils on all the rest, seduced one of the warders—a man in whom MacLellan trusted most—by promising, that if he would leave the secret postern open, "for a single hour, upon a certain night, he should have a ladleful of gold."

The wretch agreed. The wicket was left unbarred, Achanna and his band rushed in, overpowered the inmates of Raeberry, and dragged Sir Thomas from bed, severely wounding his nephew, William MacLellan, a brave boy, who fought to save him. On finding that he had been betrayed by his most trusted servant, and to the Douglases, Sir Thomas exclaimed in the bitterness of his heart,—

"Wretch—oh, wretch! mayest thou live to feel the despair that wrung the heart of Judas when he flung to the accursed Jews their thirty pieces of silver."

At these words, the abashed warder shrunk back, but the hireling Achanna laughed loudly, and ordering his prisoner to be bound with cords, conveyed him on horseback to Thrave, where the imperious Douglas, after loading him with fetters, insults, and opprobrium, thrust him into the dungeon.

"All these outrages, to a steward of our stewardry—a loyal knight and baron—the Lieutenant of our Guard!" exclaimed the king, in mingled tones of regret and rage; "verily the time has come for me to exchange my crown either for a helmet, or for the tonsure of a shaven friar. And this dog of a warder——"

"Met with the stipulated reward of his treachery, and in a manner little to his liking, on presenting himself next evening at Thrave to receive the promised bribe."

"'Thou shalt have it, false limmer,—every farthing,—yea, godspenny and principal,' said Douglas, sternly; 'though in a way, I trow, but little to your advantage.'"

"'How, my lord?'" asked the trembling wretch.

"'Molten hot, and poured down your dog's-throat, to warn my warders of Thrave what they may expect if they so betrayed *me*, and not to sleep with their doors unlatched. Away with him to the kitchen, and let this be his doom!'"

"In vain did the wretch shriek for mercy on his bended knees; he was dragged to the kitchen of the castle, and there the commands of the earl were literally and awfully obeyed. The skimming-ladle of the great pot was filled with new gold *lions* (each of which had the image of St. Andrew on one side, and a lion rampant on the other); after being molten to a seething mass, they were poured down the throat of the warder, and in ten minutes after, his mutilated corpse was flung into the gallows slot." [3]

FOOTNOTES:

[3] The metal was molten by the command of Douglas, and poured down his throat; and thus he received both his reward and punishment at the same time.—"History of Galloway," 1841, vol. i.

CHAPTER XLIV
THE BOND

Let never man be bold enough to say—
Thus, and no further, shall my passion stray;
The first crime past compels us into more,
And guilt grows *fate*, that was but *choice* before.
Aaron Hill.

The silence of a minute was, perhaps, the most severe comment which followed this story of more than Oriental barbarity. Indignation made the fiery young king almost speechless. He snatched from the table one of those Beauvais goblets, which were then greatly esteemed and were mounted with silver-gilt. It was full of water, and he drank it thirstily.

"My brave kinsman—so young, so faithful, and so merry!" exclaimed Sir Patrick Gray, with more of grief than anger in his tone; "I would give my life to save his; for it must be in imminent peril."

"No such sacrifice will be necessary," said the king; "we shall write to this daring lord, commanding him at once, on peril of his allegiance, to yield up Sir Thomas MacLellan of Bombie to our messenger, and set him forth of Thrave."

"But who," asked the chancellor, "will be daring enough to bear such a message into the wilds of Galloway, beyond the land of the Annandale thieves?"

"That will I, and blithely, too: MacLellan would do as much for me," replied Sir Patrick, with energy.

"Reflect, my friend; a royal herald were safer," said the king. "You are the enemy of Douglas in more ways than one."

"How, your highness? I am not wont to reflect much in time of peril."

"True, Sir Patrick; but this mission becomes doubly one of life and death, and of many perils to you; for loyalty to me is, perhaps, your smallest crime in the eyes of Douglas," said the king.

"Then I have reflected. Douglas shall release my father's sister's son, or I shall cleave him to the beard in his own hall!" exclaimed Gray, with a sudden burst of passion.

"That would not mend the matter much; and I should only be in thee but one faithful subject the less, and faithful subjects are rather scarce at present. Alas! my valiant friend, this strong traitor is likely to hang thee like a faulty hound—even as he hanged the gentle and noble Herries of Terregles."

"I have given my word to ride on this perilous errand, and, with your majesty's permission, go I shall," said Gray, resolutely.

"Good," said the chancellor, striking his long cane on the oak floor; "a soldier's word is his bond for weal or woe."

"In the cause of our king and kindred, I will do all that MacLellan would, were he free. Oh! your highness, write at once; furnish me with due credentials; time in this is precious, and the waste of it perilous!"

"When shall you depart on this mission?"

"So soon as I can get my horse and armour; within an hour, I shall have left these new walls of Edinburgh many a mile behind me."

"'Tis well—good service is ever promptly done."

"I am the subject and soldier of your majesty," replied Gray, bowing with modest confidence.

"And a faithful one!" added the king, giving his hand to his favourite, who was now in his thirty-fifth year, with a fine martial face, a clear bright eye, and a heart that was brave as it was tender and true. "But know you the language of these wild men among whom you are venturing— the *fremit* Scots of Galloway?"

"I know but little more than our Lowland tongue, with a smattering of Flemish and French, picked up when I had more leisure than desire to learn them—the castle of Bommel; yet I can make a shift to use others, too, that are more universally known."

"How?"

"I can make love to the women and show my purse to the men," said Gray, with a gaiety that was half assumed; "I'll warrant they will both understand me."

"I fear me, Sir Patrick, you may have to show your sword more frequently, on a king's errand though you be; but within an hour a letter shall be prepared."

"And within that time, with the permission of your highness, I shall be armed and mounted," said Gray, bowing low again and retiring in haste.

There was a momentary silence after this, for the mission on which Gray was departing was one of great peril to himself. Indeed, as Lord Glammis observed, "he was the last man in Scotland who should have undertaken it."

"Chancellor," said the king suddenly, "you spoke of a bond, or league, as a *third* cause for the hatred of Douglas against Sir Thomas MacLellan. What is this document?"

"A matter so formidable, so seriously affecting the welfare of the realm, and the honour of your crown, that I know not in what language to approach it; but the abbot of Tongland has sent me a copy of the actual deed."

The manner of Crichton became so grave and earnest that the king changed colour, and the master of the household and the abbot of Melrose, who remained silent and somewhat apart, exchanged glances expressive of interest and alarm.

"Say on," said James briefly, and striking the floor with his heel.

"The earl of Douglas, for the aggrandisement of his power and family, has formed a league offensive and defensive with the earls of Crawford and Rosse—a league by which he hopes to bid complete defiance to your royal authority, and to bring *forty thousand men at a day's notice* into the field against it; and to this compact they have bound themselves by rebellious and sacrilegious but solemn and terrible oaths, that each shall aid and assist the others and their friends against the *whole world*."

The chancellor then handed to James a duplicate of this remarkable bond, which was signed and sealed by Douglas; by Alexander (with the long beard), earl of Crawford, who was surnamed the Tiger, and was sheriff of Aberdeen, and bailiff of Scone; Donald, earl of Rosse and lord of the Isles; Hugh Douglas, earl of Ormond; James Dunbar, earl of Murray; Douglas, Lord Balvenie; James Hamilton, lord of Cadzow, and many others of the highest rank.

On beholding this terrible bond, James felt for a moment as if the crown which had come to him from a long line of monarchs was about to be torn from his head. He grew very pale, then perceiving that the keen and deeply-set eyes of his stern, faithful, and uncompromising chancellor were fixed upon him, he rallied his spirits and said, "This must be crushed in the bud, lest in its bloom it crush us."

"And to crush it we must first dissemble, and take these rebels in detail—break the rods separately which while in a bundle might defy our efforts."

"I must have a *personal* interview with this daring earl of Douglas," said the king, "even if I condescend to ride to Thrave for it. But meanwhile Gray shall bear to him three documents— —"

"Three?" reiterated Crichton, looking up.

"He shall be written to intreating, rather than demanding, the release of Sir Thomas MacLellan, who refused to join this infamous league. I shall entrust Gray with a second missive containing a summons to a conference, and assuring Douglas of a restoration to favour, and forgiveness for the past, provided he break this bond, and as a guarantee— —"

"Yes—yes," interrupted the old chancellor, grinding his almost toothless gums; "he will require something of that kind, while the memory of that 23rd of November, 1440, is fresh in Galloway."

"Then as a security the earl shall have a letter of safe conduct, to and from the castle of Stirling, signed by our own hand. Let this be seen to at once," and the king, as if weary of the morning, but in reality crushed and overwhelmed by its terrible revelations, retired to another room, muttering as he did so, "Oh, my poor father, who perished by the swords of regicides! how happier would I be if seated with you at the feet of God, than on this throne of Scotland?"

So thought James II. in 1450; how many of his descendants had better reason to utter the same bitter prayer, ere throne, and crown, and sceptre passed away from them.

Exactly one hour after the king retired, Sir Patrick Gray, carefully armed and splendidly mounted, departed on perilous, and—considering the state of the country, the lack of fords, roads, bridges, and hostelries— distant journey of ninety old Scottish miles. Over his suit of mail he wore a surcoat, on which the royal arms were embroidered to show that he rode on the special service of the king, and that to molest him involved the penalties of treason.

His departure was viewed with deep interest by the court and his soldiers. All expressed doubt and pity, for the unscrupulous character of Douglas inspired all men with terror, and as he rode off, the old warder at the castle gate shook his silvery head while saying, "By my faith, Foulis, ye'll come back faster than ye gang, gif ye e'er come back ava—but God speed ye the gate, man!"

CHAPTER XLV
SIR PATRICK GRAY'S JOURNEY

Oh, name the mighty ransom; task my power;
Let there be danger, difficulty, death,
To enhance the price.—Tamerlane.

It may easily be supposed that, with all his anxiety for the fate of his
kinsman, Sir Patrick's desire to see, or be near Murielle, was also near his
heart; and inspired by this double object, he rode rapidly, and tasking the
speed of his horse, passed through districts the features of which have long
since been changed by time and cultivation: for rivers that were then broad
and deep have shrunk to mere rills, and rills have disappeared; stone bridges
have superseded dangerous and subtle fords, where the luring kelpie lurked
for the drowning wayfarer; lochs and morasses have become fertile fields;
dense forests, where the wild bull bellowed, and the savage boar whetted
his tusks on the gnarled oak, have been cleared away; populous towns have
sprung into existence, where whilom the thatched hamlet stood; churches,
wherein generations had worshipped God in fervour and holiness, and
where Scotland's best and bravest men were laid under tombs of marble
and brass, have been ruined and desecrated, as if by the hands of sikhs or
sepoys; but hills whereon the mosstrooper drove herd and hirsel, and where
the wild furze and whin grew in luxuriance, have been rendered arable to
their steepest summits, and fertile, even, as the most fertile parts of Lothian.

By many an old Roman road formed by the warriors of the adventurous
Agricola, and those of the discomfited emperor Severus—old ways, where
the rank grass grew among the causeway stones, he travelled, and soon
reached the wild heathy uplands of Stobo that look down on the green vale
of the Tweed, and then the steeps of Hells Cleuch, which are furrowed by a
mountain torrent that rushes red and foaming to join the broader waters of
the Forth. On by the wild morasses of Tweedsmuir, where an ancient Celtic
cross that stood amid the rough obelisks of a Druid Temple of the Sun, was
the only landmark for that savage and solitary pass, which was overlooked
by the barred and battlemented tower of many a rude mosstrooping laird.

On—on yet past Moffat, secluded in its lovely vale amid its almost
inaccessible hills, above the dim summits of which the pale blue mist
was floating, and the black eagles were soaring, past its naked or heathy

mountain gorges, through which the yellow rays of the setting sun were falling on the moss-covered shealing, and the browsing herd and hirsel; and on the old square castles of red sandstone, built with seashell mortar, the abode of many a turbulent baron.

He was now amid the tremendous scenery of the Southern Highlands; and there, after a ride of fifty miles from Edinburgh, he tarried for the night with the priest of the village church, as he wanted rest, seclusion, and secrecy. There, as at one or two other places, he arranged for a relay of horses, as he knew not what might be the issue of his expedition; and ere it was over, he had reason to thank Heaven for his foresight.

Refreshed and newly horsed, he departed next day with the rising sun, and soon saw the moors of Kirkmichael and the mossy monolith of the six corpses, where Wallace slew Sir Hugh of Moreland and five other Englishmen; and ere long Dumfries, so red and sombre, with its spires of St. Michael and of many a convent and friary, rose before him, and with its long bridge of the thirteenth century—then considered the rival of that of London—spanning by thirteen carved Gothic arches the broad blue waters of the lovely Nith, where, between green and undulating shores, they rolled, glittering in the sunshine, towards the Solway Firth.

The ruined castle of the false Comyns yet overlooked the river; and the jangle of the convent-bell at Nunholm came and went on the noonday wind.

He advanced along the bridge, the passage of which was barred by an iron gate and portal of old red sandstone. It was quaint and time-worn, having been built by the Lady Devorgilla, of Galloway, the mother of the mock-king, John Baliol. Above it were the arms of the burgh—a chevron with three *fleurs-de-lys*; St. Michael winged and trampling on a serpent, with the motto, "a' at the Lower Burn," the slogan and the muster-place of the inhabitants. At this gate a toll on corn, merchandise, and passengers was collected for the benefit of the Franciscan monastery, which the pious Lady Devorgilla had founded for the salvation of her soul, and of the souls of her ancestors and posterity, in the full-flowing Christian charity of an age which is branded as the dark and superstitious simply because we know little or nothing about it. After this gate was passed, and its iron grille had clanked behind him, the heart of Gray beat faster, for he was now completely in Galloway—the land of his love and of his enemies.

The warder or loiterer, who looked across the Nith from the old castle of Dumfries, saw the flashing of armour in the noonday sunshine, as our solitary horseman rode furiously on, and, from his speed, supposed that some warden-raid or invasion was at hand; and the old Franciscan who dosed on a seat by the friary wall woke up from his dreams, and, in dread of either, muttered an *Ave Maria gratia plena*, &c., and dosed off to sleep again.

The peasant on the rigs of Teregles saw him passing like a whirlwind, and thought, with an angry sigh, that he might soon have to exchange his blue bonnet and grey maud for a breastplate and bourgoinette; for such speed never betokened an errand of peace, but of tumult and war.

Evening saw the messenger traversing the uplands of Tracquair, where the heaths are dark, the rocks are bleak, and where the black cattle browse in the grassy haughs; and past "the Bush" so famed in song; it was then a thicket of birchen-trees, through which a mounted trooper could ride unseen, even with his Scottish lance, six ells long, uplifted at arm's length.

Here, by the side of a lonely bridle-path which crossed a waste moorland, he found a man lying dead. His breast was exposed and exhibited a deep spear-wound, in which a sprig of thorn was inserted, and around which the last drops of blood had grown black and coagulated. A grey-robed priest was near the body on his knees, engaged in prayer. Gray reined in his horse, and, waiting until the churchman had ended, said,

"What does this slaughter mean, father?"

"It is the thorn-twig," said the monk, with a bewildered air.

"Explain?" said Gray, impatiently; "I have no time to read riddles."

"It is the cognisance of the Laird of Pompherston."

"And what does it mean, now?"

"Art so dull, or come from such a distance, as not to know?" asked the monk, throwing back his cowl and looking up with surprise in his grim and bearded visage.

"I confess that I am."

"Well, it signifies that this unfortunate, Donacha MacKim, the gudeman of Bourick, has been slain by the Douglases, for having been in arms against them at Raeberry; so Pompherston took a twig from his helmet and placed it where you see—in that bloody lance-wound. And now, sir, for our Blessed Lady's sake, aid me to convey him to Tracquair, that he may have the rites of a Christian burial."

"Under favour, good father, that I cannot do, as I ride for life and death on the king's service," replied Gray, in a tone of regret.

"A perilous errand here, while the Douglases are all abroad," replied the monk, shaking his shaven head.

"In arms?" said Gray, starting.

"No—hunting, and they have ridden over all the countryside, from the Bush aboon Tracquair to the Carlinwark at Thrave."

The setting of the sun found Gray beyond the waters of Urr, which he crossed near that mysterious mound known as the Moat of Urr, and on his left saw the Dub o' Hass, where many a foreign galliot and Scottish caravel were at anchor, and the banks of which were then and for long after, according to local tradition, the haunt of the Mermaid of Galloway, whose wondrous beauty was such that no man could behold her without a love that became madness, and whose hair was like shining gold, through the links of which her white shoulders and bosom shone, as she floated on the crystal water, inspiring men with passion that ended in death.

> Her comb was o' the whitely pearl,
> Her hand like new-won milk;
> Her breasts were like the snowy curd
> In a net o' seagreen silk.

But, thinking more of armed men than of alluring mermaids, Gray rode to where stood a little hostelry, kept apparently by a vassal of the kirk, as the signboard bore the papal crown and cross-keys; so he tarried there to refresh himself and horse again. He was received with profound respect, but with a curiosity the suppression of which seemed difficult, as the royal blazon which he wore upon his surcoat was seldom seen on *that* side of the Nith, though the hostelry was established as a halting-place for the wealthy abbots of Tongland, Newabbey, and the priors of St. Mary and Lincluden, when passing that way with their retinues.

The edifice was simply a large thatched cottage, divided in two by a partition named the *hallan*; beyond it was the principal fireplace, the lintel of which projected far over the hearth, and was wide enough to show the row of hams hung there to be smoked, and the iron bar whereon the kail-pot swung. Within this apartment—for the fireplace was really one—lay a whinstone seat, called the *cat-hud*, and a stone bench, the place of honour for strangers, and thereon Sir Patrick seated himself, by the gudeman's request.

Above the mantelpiece hung the black iron morion and two-handed whinger of the latter—with kirn-cuts of corn gaily ornamented with ribbons—the trophies of the last year's harvest home. The floor was of sanded clay; the ceiling showed the open cabers of the roof; while a long dresser laden with shining utensils, a few wooden creepies or stools and meal-arks, formed the furniture of this Scottish hotel of the fifteenth century.

The adjacent Moat of Urr was alleged to be full of fairies who danced in the moonlight round its strange concentric circles; and they were further said to be great bibbers of the good wine kept for the use of the before-mentioned abbots and priors; thus "mine host" of the papal tiara and keys had always a fair red cross painted on the ends of his runlets when they were landed at the Dub o' Hass; but the green imps nevertheless found a key to his cellars, and used gimlets of mortal mould to draw off the Canary and Alicant.

The gudewife of the house had just increased the number of King James's subjects and Earl Douglas's vassals by a male child, when Gray arrived; and near him, in the ingle, the nurse was administering to it the *ash-sap*, with due solemnity, by putting an ash-stick in the fire of peats and bog-pine that blazed on the hearth, and receiving in a horn spoon the juice which oozed from the other end. This was the *first* food of the newly-born children of the Gael, and when older they received their first flesh on the point of their father's sword or dagger.

With half his armour off, listless and weary, Sir Patrick Gray sat by the rustic fire on the ingle-seat, and some time elapsed before he became aware that the eyes of a stranger, who reclined on an oak settee in a shaded corner, were fixed with calm but firm scrutiny upon him.

This personage wore a scarlet cloth hood, which was buttoned from his chin to his breast, having a cape that covered his back and shoulders. His massive frame, which was of herculean proportions, was cased in a doublet of black bull's hide, having the hair smoothly dressed, and it was tied with a succession of thongs and little iron skewers. A kilt of coarse tartan, with hose of untanned deerskin, revealed his sturdy knees, which seemed strong as oak knots, and hairy as those of a gorilla. Secured by a square steel buckle, a broad buff belt encircled his waist, at which hung a double-handed sword and poniard of mercy. His great brawny hands were crossed upon the shaft of a ponderous iron mace, having a chain and "morning star," and as he rested his chin thereon, his vast black beard hung over them, while he surveyed the Captain of the Guard with his wild, keen, and fierce dark eyes, the natural expression of which, under their black and shaggy brows, seemed a scowl.

Everything about this man seemed expressive of colossal proportions and brutal strength. As if danger might not be distant, with an air that in another would have seemed bravado, but in him was quite natural, he drew his mighty sword, examined the point, tested the spring of the blade, and smiled with a grim satisfied air, as he sheathed it again.

In most of the incidents of our story we have been compelled to follow and to portray the course of events with the care of an historian rather than of a romancer; and thus must we detail, or rather *translate*, the conversation which ensued between Sir Patrick Gray and this burly Celtic giant, as it was maintained in a strange mixture of old Doric Scottish and the Celtic language then spoken by the inhabitants of Galloway.

"What may the last news be among you here?" asked Sir Patrick.

"What could they be but of sorrow?" growled the other.

"I doubt it not where Earl James abides."

"You are a bold man to say so," replied the Galwegian.

"I am in the king's service, my friend, and a good cause gives courage; but, beside the storming of Raeberry, and the lawless capture of Sir Thomas MacLellan, what is there new in Galloway?"

"The foul slaughter of the laird of Sandwick, whom the Douglas troopers fell upon in Kirkandrews, and killed when at his prayers,—and this was yesternight."

"Another act of sacrilege?"

"Air mhuire! so my lord the abbot of Tongland terms it; but they were dainty gentlemen who followed the laird of Glendoning," said the other, with bitter irony; "they cared not to stain the floor or altar of God's consecrated church with blood; so they dragged old Sandwick forth, though he clung to the iron altar-rail, and drew him to the louping-on-stane at the grave-yard gate, and there hacked him to pieces."

"It was like these men of Thrave," said Sir Patrick; "but a day of vengeance for these continued atrocities must come, and speedily too."

As he said this the host, who was making a posset of Alicant on the hearth, looked up with terror; but the strong man with the mace laughed bitterly, and added, as he struck the floor with his mace,

"Dioul! the sooner the better for me."

"And who are you?" asked Sir Patrick.

"Would you be a wiser man for knowing?" was the cautious and not over-courteous response; "yet I care not if I tell: I am Malise MacKim,—"

"What—Malise, the hereditary smith of Thrave—MacKim the Brawny?" exclaimed Gray, with something of alarm in his tone.

"Yes," said the other through his clenched teeth.

Gray, by a twitch of his belt, brought his dagger conveniently to his hand; MacKim saw the movement, and smiled disdainfully.

"Has the earl wronged you?" asked Sir Patrick.

"To the heart's core," was the emphatic reply. "Oh, mhuire as truidh! mhuire as truidh! that I should ever have it to say—I, whose fathers have eaten the bread of his race for generations—ay, since the *first* handful of earth was laid there to form the Moat of Urr—yea, yea, since first the Urr waters ran, and leaves grew in the wood of Dalbeattie!"

"What has happened?"

"His people have this day slain my brother Donacha MacKim, near the Bush aboon Tracquair, and have carried off his daughter, who was the love of my youngest son; but I have seven—SEVEN sons, each taller and stronger than myself, and I will have sure vengeance on Douglas, if he grants it not to me; and this I have sworn by the cross of St. Cuthbert, and by the soul of her I love best on earth, my wife Meg."

The black eyes of the gigantic smith glared with genuine Celtic fury and hate as he said this; he beat the floor with his roughly-shod feet, and his strong fingers played nervously with the shaft of his mace, the chain and morning-star of which (a ball a pound in weight, furnished with four sharp iron spikes) lay on the floor. Gray, as he surveyed him, reflected that it was extremely fortunate that the smith's fealty to Douglas had been broken, otherwise he might have proved a very unpleasant companion for the night in that small and solitary hostelry, situated, as it was, in a hostile and lawless district. This meeting, however, taught Gray to be wary, and thus, though knowing the country well, he affected to be a stranger.

"Is the abbot of Tongland at Thrave?" he asked.

"No; the earl, in sport, poured a ladleful of gold down the throat of the Raeberry warder; so his father confessor pronounced a malediction upon him, and retired to the abbey at Tongland, in disgust and despair at his cruelty."

"How far is it from hence to the clachan?"

"About ten miles."

"And to the abbey?"

"It is beside the clachan."——"Good."

During that night Gray slept with his door and window well secured, with his sword drawn under his head, and his armour on a chair by his bedside, to be ready for any emergency. The lassitude incident to his long journey on horseback by such rough roads—for then they went straight over hill and down valley, through forest, swamp, and river—made him sleep long and late on his bed of freshly-pulled heather; thus the noon of the next was far advanced before he set out once more.

Malise MacKim, his sullen acquaintance of the preceding evening, conducted him for some distance beyond the Urr, and told him, what Gray already knew well, that if he wished to reach the clachan of Tongland, he must pass the Loch of Carlinwark on his right, and pursue the road that lay through the wood on the left bank of the Dee.

"And whither go you, my friend?" he asked, as the gigantic smith was about to leave him.

"To join my seven sons, and scheme our vengeance; yet what can mortal vengeance avail against the earl of Douglas?" — —"How?" said Gray; "in what manner?"

"Know you not that he wears a warlock jacket, against which the sharpest swords are pointless?"

"What do you mean?" asked the soldier, keeping his horse in check.

"I mean a doublet made for him by a warlock in Glenkens, woven of the skins of water-snakes caught in a south-running burn where three lairds' lands met, and woven for him under the beams of a March moon, on the haunted Moat of Urr."

Gray laughed and said, "I should like to test this dagger, my poor MacLellan's gift, upon that same doublet."

"Moreover," said the smith, lowering his voice, while a deeper scowl impressed his grisly visage, "it is said in Galloway here, that when Earl James, a child, was held by his godmother at the font in Tongland Abbey Kirk, the blessed water, as it fell from the hand of Abbot John, hissed upon his little face as upon iron in a white heat."

"Peace, carle! can a stout fellow like thee be moonling enough to give such stories credence?"

"'Tis folly, perhaps, to think of them, betouch us, too! so near the Moat of Urr," said the smith, with a perceptible shudder, as he glanced covertly over his shoulder.

"And why here more than elsewhere?"

"Know ye not?" asked the smith, in a whisper.

"You forget that I am a stranger."

"True. Then it was on *this* spot that James Achanna, the earl's sooth fast-friend and henchman, sold himself to Satan, after conjuring him up by performing some nameless rites of hell."

"Adieu, and God be wi' you," said Gray, laughing, yet nevertheless making the sign of the cross, for the place was savage and solitary, and he was not without a due share of the superstition incident to his age and country. Turning his horse, he rode rapidly off.

As he did so, a cunning smile passed over the swarthy face of Malise MacKim, who swung his mace round his head as if he were about to brain an enemy.

The day was far advanced, when, at Kelton, Gray crossed the Dee by a flat-bottomed boat, near a place where a group of peasants were assembled under a gallows-tree. Thereon hung a man, and there, by paying a fee to the doomster of Thrave, persons afflicted by wens, or similar excrescences, came to obtain the benefit of the *deid-strake*—a touch of the dead hand being deemed a certain cure.

When Gray saw the poor corse swinging in the wind, he remembered the fate of Sir Herbert Maxwell, and reflected how easily Douglas might release Murielle from her marriage-ties by putting him to death, as he had done that powerful baron; yet his heart never trembled, nor did he swerve from his resolution of attempting to save MacLellan, in spite of every danger.

CHAPTER XLVI
AN UNEXPECTED GUIDE

And a good evening to my friend Don Carlos.
Some lucky star has led my steps this way:
I was in search of you. — The Spanish Student.

Before Gray crossed the Dee at Kelton, there came over the scenery a dense white mist, which rolled like smoke along the hills, and hung in dewdrops on his horse's mane and bridle, dimming the brightness of his armour and the embroidery of his surcoat. In this obscurity he lost his way amid the waste muirlands which the road, a mere bridle-path destitute of wall or fence, traversed. Then a sharp shower of hail fell, the stones rattling on his steel trappings as on a latticed window; and through the openings in the haze, the far-stretching dells and pastoral hills of Galloway seemed wet and grey and dreary.

The country was singularly desolate; he met no person to direct him; thus, amid the obscurity of the mist and the approaching evening, he knew not where he was, but continued to ride slowly and vaguely on.

Anon a breeze came, and the grey clouds began to disperse; the hail ceased, and the haze rolled away like finely-carded wool along the sides of the hills. The setting sun of August beamed forth in his farewell splendour, the mavis and merle chorused merrily in the sauch and hawthorn trees; for a time the hill-tops became green, and the high corn that waved on the upland slopes seemed to brighten with the partial heat and moisture. After a time, Sir Patrick found that he had penetrated to the border of Glenkens, then the wildest and most savage part of Galloway. Wheeling round his horse, he rode fast in the direction from whence he had come, and just as the sun's broad disc began to dip behind the grassy hills, and to shed its warm light upon the windings of the Dee, from an eminence he could see afar off the vast square keep of Thrave looming black and sombre, with the dusky smoke ascending from its great chimney-stalks into the calm sky in steady columns, unbroken by the breeze.

Soft was the evening light, and softer now the air, and no sound but the occasional lowing of the black cattle, or those nameless country noises which seem to come from afar, broke the stillness of the vast pastoral landscape.

The Dee has all the characteristics of a Scottish stream: now gliding stealthily and sullenly through deep pools and dark rocky chasms, where the wiry pine, the crisp-leaved oak, and the feathery silver birch cast their shadows on the darting trout or the lurking salmon; now chafing and brawling in white foam over a precipitous ledge of red sandstone, then gurgling down a bed of "unnumbered pebbles;" and now sweeping broad and stilly past a thatched clachan, a baron's moated tower, a ruined chapel, where bells were rung and masses said when Alan was lord of Galloway and constable of Scotland; then round some statelier fane like Tongland, or a vast feudal strength like Thrave of the Douglases.

After seeing the latter, Gray rode slowly and thoughtfully, for it brought the face, the form, the voice, the smile, and all the image of Murielle more vividly before him. The scenery, the place, the very air, seemed full of the presence of her, his loved and lost one.

And now the moon arose, but not brilliantly; it shot fitful gleams between weird masses of flying cloud, with a pale and ghastly effect which made the gnarled trunks of the old trees seem like spectres or fantastic figures. Erelong, Gray entered a long and narrow glen, clothed on each side by a thick fir forest, where the density of the wiry foliage was such that the darkness became quite opaque.

Here he suddenly found himself joined by a horseman, who came either from the wayside thicket or out of the ground—it might have been either, so unexpected was his appearance. A gleam of the moon, as it came down a ravine, showed that this man and his horse were of great strength and stature. He wore a hunting suit, with a sword, bugle, and small steel cap which glittered in the moonlight.

"Under favour, I presume, we may travel together?" said he, bluntly.

"Provided the road be broad enough," replied Gray in the same manner, for there was something in this man's voice which strangely affected him, causing his hair to bristle up, his pulses to quicken, and the almost obliterated wounds on his face to smart.

Whence was this emotion? Where had he heard that voice before? Where seen that grim and sturdy figure? Each looked from time to time at the other, and seemed anxious to make out *who* or what he was.

"Go you far this way?" asked the stranger.

"No," replied Gray, curtly.

"May I ask how far?"——"I am bound for Thrave."

"Indeed," said the other, looking fixedly at Gray, as they walked their horses side by side; "have you made a long journey?"——"From Edinburgh," replied Gray, briefly.

"You are a bold man to pass through the Johnstones of Annandale and the Borderland at this time."

"How bolder at this time than at any other?"

"That you may soon learn," replied the stranger, laughing at Gray's tone of displeasure.

"I am Sir Patrick Gray of Foulis, captain of the king's guard, and am bound to ride wherever he may order, and woe to those who dare obstruct me," said Gray, peering forward to discern the speaker, who started visibly at this reply, and after the silence of a moment said, "I too am bound for Thrave. For two days past I have been abroad hunting, but have missed or outridden my friends. Well, what may the news be from the good town of Edinburgh? and how fare the king, his carpet knights, and cock-sparrow courtiers, eh?"

"Were I not riding on the king's errand, which makes my life more precious than if I were riding on my own, I would find you a more fitting reply than words," said Gray, who could scarcely repress his rising wrath, for the tone of the other chafed him.

"You have chosen a perilous time, assuredly, to enter Galloway on the king's service," observed the stranger, loftily; "and if my words displease, I can give full reparation when your errand is sped."

"'Tis enough, sir," said Gray, hoarsely; "on the morrow I *shall* have sure vengeance. No man shall slight the king in my presence, and live."

"By my sooth, his last messenger—the Rothsay herald, who came hither anent the laird of Teregles—left Galloway faster than he entered it. We are about to teach this James Stuart, that the realm of Scotland was not made for *his* especial use. What? after fighting for centuries, and defeating Romans, Saxons, Danes, and Normans—in short, all the invaders of England—we are now to tremble before this boy-king and his little Gueldrian wife? Has he forgotten how his father died?"

"How—what mean you?" asked Gray, making a vigorous effort to control his passion.

"In the Black Friary at Perth," said the other, grinding his teeth, "with the swords of Grahame and Athole clashing in his heart."

"Be assured our king has *not* forgotten it—but hush—be wary."

"And wherefore hush?" was the fierce response.

"Because they who did that deed, the most foul murder of God's anointed king, perished miserably on the scaffold more than twenty years ago. Their ashes have long since mingled with the earth, for fire consumed and the wind of heaven scattered them; but their names exist in the execration of all good men and true."

"Hard words," said the other, scoffingly; "hard words, sir, for us, who are on the eve, perhaps, of a most just rebellion against his son, if he and his Flemish princess, with that old fox, Crichton, push us too severely; and then I think his dainty Falkland knights, and well-fed Lothian infantry, may find it perilous work to march through Nithsdale and penetrate among the wild hills of Galloway."

Gray did not answer; they had now emerged from the wood, and the Loch of Carlinwark was shining like a mirror in the full splendour of the moonlight. At some distance he could discern the three old thorn-trees, where, on a similarly calm and lovely moonlit night, he had first plighted love, life, and hope, to Murielle; and now, as then, he could see Thrave, her home and her prison, casting its long black shadows on the Dee.

"Here is Thrave," said the stranger, reining up his powerful horse beside the barbican-gate.

"And you, sir?——"

"I am James, earl of Douglas," replied the other, sternly and loftily; "you are on the king's errand, Sir Patrick Gray—'tis well; I bid you welcome; but remember, save for that tabard which you wear, by the bones of St. Bryde, I would hang you by the neck from that stone knob above the gate!"

Gray bowed and smiled bitterly, as they rode into the court-yard, and he found himself inclosed by the gates and surrounded by the followers of his mortal enemy.

He had shuddered on passing under the barbican-gate, for a man was hanging at the gallows-knob above it. Gray knew the dread custom there—that each culprit or victim was replaced by another, and he knew not *who* the next "tassel" might be.

The night-wind lifted the dead man's hair at times as the body swung mournfully to and fro. Beneath this ghastly object, in the blaze of the torches which were upheld by a crowd of liveried serving-men and savage-looking kilted Galwegians, there shone a great shield of carved and painted stone. It bore the arms of the ancient lords of Galloway—azure a lion rampant, *argent* crowned with an imperial diadem, impaled with the countless quarterings of the Douglases.

The moon was waning now; but the number of torches, as they flared on the walls and grated windows of the vast keep, made the court-yard seem light as if the night was noon.

As Gray dismounted, a familiar voice reached his ear, saying, "Thanks, brave friend and kinsman—you have perilled much to save me!"

"Thou art right, MacLellan—I come by the king's orders, so take courage!" replied Gray, looking about him; but from *which* of the black gratings of that lofty edifice the voice came his eye failed to discover.

A cruel smile passed over the grim face of the earl, as he said, "Sir Patrick Gray, it is ill speaking between a full man and a fasting; so get you to bed for to-night; after breakfast to-morrow, we will consider your errand from the king; and you have my knightly word for your safety while within the walls of Thrave."

"And how, when I leave them, my lord?"

"That is as may be," said the other, turning on his heel.

With these dubious, or rather ominous words, the earl retired, and within an hour, Gray, after partaking of some refreshment alone, found himself lying on a couch with his armour on and his drawn sword by his side, endeavouring to court sleep, with his mind full of the terrible novelty of his situation; and not without a sense of charm, for he knew that Murielle was near him, and that the same roof covered them both.

On a tabourette by the bedside were placed a night-lamp, a cup of sack posset, and the earl of Douglas's dagger as a symbol of peace and protection—that he had armed his unwelcome guest against even his *own* household; for such was the custom of the age and country.

CHAPTER XLVII
HUSBAND AND WIFE

First rose a star out owre the hill,
And next the lovelier moon;
While the bonnie bride o' Galloway
Looked for her blythe bridegroom;
Lythlie she sang as the new moon rose,
Blythe as a young bride may,
When the new moon lights her lamp o' love,
And blinks the bride away.—Cromek.

Sir Patrick Gray sprang from a couch, where dreams, rather than sleep, had pressed thick and fast upon him. He rose while yet the summer sun was below the green Galloway hills, and while the dark waters of the Dee were veiled by the white mists of the early morning.

His mind was full of Murielle, and he was not without hope, that while all the numerous household and powerful feudal garrison were yet abed, he might find some means to communicate with her—to see, to speak to one so beloved—one from whom he had been so long, so wickedly separated—his seven years' wedded wife!

It seemed to Gray, while thinking of this, that some one had been softly and timidly tapping at his door.

Gently drawing back the numerous bars of wood and iron, with which the doors of all bed-chambers in old Scottish mansions were furnished in those days and for long after, he stepped into an arched corridor; then, on looking along its dusky vista, he saw a female figure approach, and what were his emotions on beholding the sudden realization of his dearest wish—Murielle, who had left the room thus early on the same errand and with the same desperate yet tenderly loving hope, had been watching the door of *his* chamber.

She seemed pale and wan, as one who had been sleepless; but though more womanly and more full in figure, she was otherwise unchanged as when he had seen her last, on that happy and yet unfortunate night, in the church of St. Genevieve, in Flanders.

"At last, my Murielle!"

"At *last* we meet—but oh! for a moment only."

They clasped each other in a tender embrace—heart to heart, and lip to lip. His face was bent on hers, and her tears of joy and fear fell fast.

"You love me still, Murielle?"

"*Still!*" she reiterated reproachfully—"oh, with all my life and strength."

"But to what a hopeless love and aimless life have my passion and its selfish ties consigned you!" said he; "we are the slaves of others and of destiny."

"Such have we ever been, since that fatal day on which my cousins, William and David, were slain. That was in 1440, *ten* long, long years ago; but—"

"A crisis in our fate is coming now, dear Murielle."

"But say why—oh, why are you here—here in Thrave, here, where your life is in peril so deadly?"

"I am come, in our good king's name, to demand MacLellan's release, and to invite the earl, under cartel, to meet the council at Stirling, that all these evils may be peacefully ended."

"I pray to the kind Father of all, and to his Blessed Mother, who is in heaven, that it may be so," sighed poor Murielle. "But oh, I am so weary, weary—so sad and weary here! They keep me quite a prisoner, though not so cruelly as they keep Sir Thomas MacLellan; for I am told by Marion Douglas that he is confined in the pit."

"Mahoun! say you so, dearest—in that horrid vault?"

"Yes; but hush—we may be overheard."

"Ah! my brave and noble kinsman—such a doom! Was it not in that dungeon that Earl Archibald, the first duke of Touraine, kept MacLellan, the laird of Borgue, chained, like a wild beast, till he became a jabbering idiot, and when found by the prior of St. Mary's Isle, he was laughing as he strove to catch the single sunbeam that fell through the grated slit into his prison— yea, striving fatuously to catch it with his thin, wan, fettered hand—the same hand that carried the king's banner at the battle of Homildon!"

"Do not frown thus, my dearest heart," said Murielle, weeping; "I have little need to add to the hatred that grows apace in every breast against the name of Douglas."

"Do not say in *every* breast, sweet Murielle—sweet wife," he added, pressing her close and closer still in his embrace; "for my heart is wrung with anguish and with love for you, and of this love God alone knoweth the depth and the strength!"

Murielle continued to weep in silence.

"My love for you," resumed Gray, "and my duty to the king, whom my father, old Sir Andrew Gray, taught me to love, respect, and almost worship, are impulses that rend my heart between them. At the risk of my life I have ridden here on the king's service, alone, with no protection but my sword, my hand, and, it may be, this royal tabard—a badge but little respected on this side of the Nith or Annan."

"And you came——"

"To see you, and to save MacLellan from the fate of Sir Herbert Herries. God wot, though, I would give the last drop of my blood to serve my kinsman. A king's herald might have borne the mandate as well as I; but the hope of seeing you—of hearing your dear voice, of concerting some plan for your escape and future freedom from a tyranny that is maddening,— chiefly, if not alone, brought me into the wilds of Galloway—the very land and stronghold of the enemies of the throne."

"Say not the enemies," said Murielle mournfully. "I hope that men misjudge us sorely."

"I hope they do; yet there are strange whispers abroad of a rebel league with the earls of Ross and Crawford, with Henry of England, and the lord of the Isles—a league to dethrone the king and plunge the land in ruin. But let us speak at present of escape—of flight——"

"My disappearance would be your destruction; all Galloway, with hound and horn, would be upon your track."

"True—Douglas gave me his word for safety only while *within* the walls of Thrave," said Gray, bitterly.

"The most sunny summer-day may have its clouds, dear Patrick; but here, in this dull residence, with me it is ever cloud, and never sunshine—I mean the sunshine of the heart. My time is passed, as it were, in perpetual winter. I have no solace—no friend—no amusement, but my cithern and the songs you loved so well——"

"And love *still*, Murielle, for the sake of you!"

"So cheerlessly I live on without hope or aim, a wedded nun, amid councils of fierce and stern men, whose meetings, debates, and thoughts are all for opposition, and revenge for the terrible deed of 1440."

"In other words, Murielle, men who are ripe for treason and rebellion."

"Why *will* you speak or think so harshly of us?" she asked so imploringly that Gray kissed her tenderly as his only or best reply.

"And that spiteful beauty your sister—what says she of me now?"——"That you are the king's liege man," was the cautious answer.

"She is right, my beloved one—I am his till death——"

"And our enemy!" said a sharp voice close by them, like the hiss of a snake.

They turned and saw Margaret, the countess of Douglas, standing at the entrance of her bower-chamber, the tapestry covering the door of which she held back with one hand. She was clad entirely in black, with a long veil of fine lace depending from the apex of her lofty head-dress, enveloping her haughty head and handsome white shoulders. She was somewhat changed since Gray had seen her last, for angry passions were lining her young face prematurely; her marvellous beauty remained in all its striking power; but it was the beauty of a devil—*diavolessa*, an Italian would term it. Ten years of feud and anxious hostility to the crown and its adherents had imparted a sternness to her fine brow, a keen boldness to her black eyes, and a sneering scorn to her lovely lip that made her seem a tragedy queen.

"And so another errand than the king's message, anent his minion's life or death, has brought you hither, scurvy patch!" said she scornfully; "but by St. Bryde I shall rid our house and my sister of such intrusive visitors!"

"Madame," Gray began, with anger.

"Varlet—would you dare to threaten me?" she exclaimed, holding up a clenched hand, which was white, small, and singularly beautiful; "but, my gay moth, you will flutter about that poor candle until your wings are burnt. I have but to say one word to Douglas of this clandestine meeting and he will hang you in your boots and tabard above our gate, where Herbert of Teregles and many a better man has hung."

"Oh, sister Margaret," urged Murielle, trembling like an aspen-leaf.

"Ha—to speak that word would remove the only barrier to your being duchess of Albany—and why should I *not* speak it?" she continued fiercely and with flashing eyes; "Why should I not speak it?"

"Because, dear Maggie, you have still some gentle mercy left, and Heaven forbids you," said Murielle, clinging to her pitiless sister.

"Begone, madam," said the latter imperiously; "your instant obedience alone purchases my silence. But here comes Sir Alan Lauder."

So ended abruptly, as at the abbot's house in Edinburgh, this unexpected meeting. Terror for her lover-husband's life made Murielle withdraw instantly with her sister, just as Sir Alan Lauder of the Bass, who was still captain and governor of Thrave, approached with an undisguised sneer on his lips to say that the earl would receive Sir Patrick Gray at brekfaast, in his own chamber, and there give his answer to the king's message.

CHAPTER XLVIII
DOUGLAS AND GRAY

And darest thou, then,
To beard the lion in his den,
The Douglas in his hall?—Scott.

Clad in a robe of fine scarlet cloth, which was lined with white fur, and fastened by a brooch or jewel at the neck, and which was open just enough to show an undershirt and long hose of buff-coloured silk, the earl of Douglas was seated in a high-backed easy-chair, which was covered with crimson taffety. His feet were placed on a tabourette, and close by, with his long sharp nose resting on his outstretched paws, crouched Souyllard, the snow-white bloodhound, uttering deep growls from time to time.

Breakfast, which consisted of cold beef, partridge-pie, flour cakes, wheaten bread, honey, ale, and wine, was spread upon the table, which, like the rest of the carved oak furniture, and like the castle itself, seemed strong enough to last twenty generations of Douglases. The equipage was entirely composed of the beautiful pottery of Avignon, which was all of a dark-brown metallic tint, like tortoise-shell, but perforated and in relief.

At the earl's hand, in the old Scottish fashion, stood a flat-shaped pilgrim-bottle of usquebaugh. It was from Beauvais, and bore a Scots lion, with the three *fleurs-de-lys*, and the name of *Charle Roy VII.*, for it was a personal gift from the then reigning monarch of France to Douglas, when last at his hunting-castle in the wood of Vincennes.

A painted casement, one half of which stood open, admitted the warm rays of the summer sun through the deep embrasure of the enormously thick castle-wall, and afforded a glimpse without of the far-stretching landscape and the windings of the Dee, and, nearer still, the green islet it formed around Thrave, on the grassy sward of which some noisy urchins and pages belonging to the feudal garrison were gambolling, playing at leapfrog, and launching stones and mimic spears at an old battered quintain, or carved figure of an armed man, which stood there for the use of those who practised tilting.

As Gray entered in his armour, with his surcoat on and his helmet open, readier for departure than a repast, the earl, without rising or offering his hand, bowed with cold courtesy, with a sardonic smile on his white lip and hatred in his deep-set eyes. He made a signal to a page who was in attendance to withdraw, and they were immediately left together. "I said last night that it was ill speaking between a full man and a fasting," said he; "we are both fasting this morning, so, Sir Patrick, let us eat, drink, and then to business."

As they were both anxious to come to the point at issue, after a few morsels of food and a draught of spiced ale, the grim earl spoke again:—

"I have read the king's letters—that anent the laird of Bombie, and that which invites me to a conference at Stirling, with a safe conduct to me and all my followers. By my faith, Sir Patrick, I think their number, in horse, foot, and archers, will be their best safe conduct. The first letter demands— —"

"The release, the instant release of my kinsman, Sir Thomas MacLellan, of Bombie, and of that ilk, steward of Kirkcudbright, whom you unlawfully and most unworthily detain here a prisoner," said Gray, whom the cool and insolent bearing of Douglas exasperated beyond the point of prudence. "What if I refuse," asked the latter with an icy smile.

"That the king and council will consider."

"What if he be dead?"

"He is *not* dead," exclaimed Gray with growing excitement; "last night I heard his voice, for he addressed me as we entered the barbican."

"Ha!" said Douglas sharply, with a furious glance.

"But dead or alive, lord earl, in the king's name I demand his body!"

"That shall I grant you readily," replied Douglas grimly, as he blew on a silver whistle which lay on the table. The arras of the doorway was raised, and there reappeared the page, to whom the earl gave a ring, which he drew from his finger, and said, "Tell James Achanna to lead forth the laird of Bombie from the vault, and to obey my orders."

The page bowed and retired; and he observed, if Gray did not, the terribly sinister expression which at that moment filled the earl's eyes.

"You said *lead forth*, my lord; hence my kinsman lives, and I thank you," said Gray with more composure.

"Some men die between the night and morning, others between the morning and the night;—but now about this conference at Stirling: what boon does the king hold out as an inducement for a Douglas to risk so much as an acceptance of royal hospitality?"

"Boon, my lord?"

"By St. Bryde, I spoke plainly enough!"

"'Twas said the restoration to you of the office of Warden of the Marches towards England, the seat at the Privy Council, and the commission of Lieutenant-General of the Kingdom."

"In short, all of which I was unjustly deprived, by Crichton's influence, during my absence in France and Italy," said the earl, removing the breast from a partridge.

Gray did not reply, for at that moment the castle bell was tolled slowly, and a strange foreboding seized him. "With the recollection of the Black Dinner of 1440 before me, by the Devil's mass! I would require some great boon to tempt me, assuredly," said the earl, with a laugh which had something diabolical in its sound.

"My lord, there will be the king's safe conduct."

"King's memories are precarious. Since the day of the bloody banquet at which my kinsman perished, I have been, as it were, a man of granite in a shirt of steel—immoveable, implacable—and feeling no sentiment but the longing for revenge!"

The earl, with a sparkling eye and a flushing cheek, spoke as feelingly as if he had *not* had a secret hand in the execution of his nephews, nor won anything by it.

"King James," he added, "has yet to learn what a ten years' hatred is!"

"Ten years?" reiterated Gray, as he thought of Murielle.

"Ten years—we are in the year 1450, and for the ten which have preceded it, my armour has scarcely ever been off," said the earl; "and even in my own hall the sword and dagger have never been from my side."

"For the same reason, my lord, you have kept other men's armour on, and others' weapons on the grindstone," replied Gray; "but endeavour to be as good and loyal as your fathers were, earl of Douglas—renounce your evil leagues, and bonds for rebellion, else you may find the king alike more wise and powerful than you imagine."

"I seek not advice from you, laird of Foulis," said Douglas, with proud disdain. "Within sound of the bells of Holyrood, or those of St. Giles, your king may be both powerful and wise; but on this side the Moat of Urr, I have my doubts of his power or wisdom."

"How, my lord?"

"He would scarcely be wise to venture into the wilds of Galloway, even with all the forces he and that fangless wolf, his chancellor, may collect; and never powerful enough to do so, with the hope of success." — —"Daring words, when said of one who is king of all Scotland."

"But I am lord of all Galloway, and I shall uphold its ancient rights and laws in battle, as stoutly as Earl Archibald did in Parliament."

"An old story, my lord," said Gray, rising.

"True; in the days of Robert II.," added Douglas, rising also.

"In 1385," observed Gray, with a scarcely perceptible smile.

"I forget." — —"Though you forget many things, my lord," said Gray, rashly and impetuously, "do not imagine that you or they are forgotten."

"Does this imply a threat, my cock-laird of the north country?" asked Douglas, with profound disdain.

"As you please—I am a plain soldier."

A ferocious expression darkened the earl's face; but Gray drew back a pace, and laid a hand significantly on his tabard.

"Sir Patrick Gray, I advise you to get your horse and begone!" thundered Douglas, starting to his feet. "Without there! Order Sir Patrick's horse to the barbican-gate!"

"But your answer to the king?" said Gray, tightening his waistbelt, and preparing for a sudden start.

"That I shall convey in person to Stirling."

"And my kinsman — —"

"Dead or alive?" said Douglas, with a sullen glare in his eye. Alarmed by the expression of the earl's face, Gray said earnestly: —

"Lest you might not obey the king's commands, proud lord, or might scoff at my humble request, I bring you a mother's prayer for her son."

"A mother's?" said Douglas, pausing as they descended the staircase together.

"The prayer of my father's sister, Marion Gray, for her son's release." — —"It comes too late," muttered the earl under his black moustache, as they issued into the sunny court-yard of Thrave.

CHAPTER XLIX
THE FATE OF MACLELLAN

Lift not the shroud! a speaking stain
Of blood upon its sable seen,
Tells how the spirit fled from plain,
For there the headsman's axe hath been.
Ballad.

"The king's demand shall be granted, but rather for *your* sake—come hither," said the earl.

There was a cruel banter in his manner, a bitter smile on his face, and Gray grew pale, and felt the blood rush back upon his heart with a terrible foreboding as they crossed the court-yard.

Then his eye at once detected something like a human form stretched at full length upon the ground, and covered by a sheet. About it there could be no doubt—it was so cold, white, angular, and fearfully rigid. Upon the breast was placed a platter filled with salt—a Scottish superstition as old as the days of Turpin—and close by lay an axe and bloodstained billet, about which the brown sparrows were hopping and twittering in the warm morning sunshine. With a choking sensation in his throat, Gray stepped resolutely forward.

"Remove this cloth," said the earl to some of his people who were near; and on their doing so, there was seen the body of a headless man—a body which Gray knew too well to be that of his friend and kinsman, for on the breast of the soiled and faded pourpoint was embroidered a gold scutcheon, with the three black chevrons of MacLellan.

"Sir Patrick, you have come a little too late," said the sneering earl; "here lies your father's sister's son; but, unfortunately, he wants the head, and a head is an awkward loss. The body, however, is completely at your service."

Grief and indignation almost choked Gray's utterance. He knelt down and kissed the cold right hand, which yet bore the mark of an iron fetter, and then turning to the earl, said, "My lord, you may now dispose of the body as you please; but the head——"

"Behold it on the battlement above you!" [4]

Gray mounted his horse, which was at that moment led to the outer gate by the earl's grooms; and mistrusting them, though feeling as one in a terrible dream, before putting his foot in the stirrup he carefully examined his bridle, girths, and crupper. Then, says Sir Walter Scott in his history, "his resentment broke forth in spite of the dangerous situation in which he was placed":—

"My lord," said he, shaking his gauntleted hand close to the earl's beard, "if I live you shall bitterly pay for this day's work; and I—Patrick Gray of Foulis—tell thee, that thou art a bloodthirsty coward—a disgrace to knighthood and nobility!"

He then wheeled round his horse, pressed the sharp Rippon spurs into its flanks, and galloped off.

"To horse and chase him!" cried the earl, furiously. "I will ride to Stirling, false minion, with *your* head at my saddle-bow! To horse and follow him—this venturesome knight must sleep beside his kinsman!"

"But he came on the king's service," urged Sir Alan Lauder, as he put his foot in the stirrup of his horse, when some twenty or thirty mounted moss-troopers came hurriedly from the stable court.

"Bah! love-lured and destiny dragged him hither. Let slip Souyllard the sleuth-bratch. Horse and spear, I say, Lauder and Achanna—a hundred crowns for the head of yonder minion! I swear by St. Bryde of Douglas and Kildara, by the Blessed Virgin and her son, never to eat at a table, sleep in a bed, to rest under a Christian roof, or to lay aside sword and armour, till I have passed my dagger through the heart of Patrick Gray, dead or alive!" —
—"If you break this terrible vow," said Sir Alan, aghast at the earl's fury, and the form it took in words.

"Then I pray Heaven, at the judgment day, to show such mercy to me as I shall show my enemies," was the fierce response.

It was fortunate for the earl that he soon found a friar to release him from a vow, the fulfilment of which must have entailed a vast deal of trouble, fuss, and discomfort upon him and his followers.

"A hundred crowns and St. Bryde for Douglas!" was the shout of the moss-troopers, as they dashed through the outer gate, and with their light active horses, their steel caps, jacks, and spears, they clattered over the drawbridge; but Gray, after escaping six or eight crossbow bolts, was already three miles before them, and spurring in hot haste along the road towards Dumfries.

It was a fortunate circumstance for him that he was well mounted on a fleet, strong, and active horse; for he was a muscular man, and heavily mailed, while his pursuers, being Border Prickers, wore but little armour, and their wiry nags were used to scamper on forays in all weathers and seasons by day and night, over moor, and moss, and mountain sides.

Gray knew well that if taken his death was certain; for Douglas, reckless, ruthless, and bloodthirsty, by nature, was certain now to give full scope to his long-treasured hatred.

He no longer heard the whooping of his pursuers; he had either distanced them, or they were husbanding their energies for a long chase; but there came after him at times, upon the hollow wind, the grunting bark of the sleuth-bratch, by which he was surely and savagely tracked, Souyllard, the earl's favourite white bloodhound, and the heart of the fugitive swelled anew, with grief and rage, and hatred of his unrelenting tormentor.

He was far from shelter or succour, for until he reached the Lothians, all the land belonged to his enemies, or to those who dared not protect him. For miles and miles before him stretched flattened hills and open plains covered with waving heather, the purple tints of which were glowing in the noonday sun, and these tints deepened into blue or black on the shaded sides of the glens. The whirr of the blackcock was heard at times, as it rose from the pale green or withered yellow leaves of the ferns that grew among the rushes, where the trouting burn brawled, or by the lonely ravine, the red-scaured bank, or stony gulley, which Gray made his foam-covered horse clear by a flying leap.

Louder and nearer came the savage bay of the sleuth-bratch, and Gray, as he looked back, could see it tracking him closely and surely; while about three miles distant the border spears of his pursuers glittered on the summit of a hill.

He had swam his horse through the Urr and spurred on for miles, and now before him lay Lochrutton, with its old peel-house, named, from its loneliness, the castle-of-the-hills; then, as he was about to cross a foaming tributary of the loch—a stream that tore, all red and muddy, through a stony ravine—the bounding sleuth-bratch came upon him, and sprang at his horse's flanks, just as the terrified animal rose into the air to cross by a flying leap.

Clenching his gauntleted hand, Gray struck the fierce brute on the head, and it fell into the rushing torrent; but gained the other side as soon as he, and sent its deep, hoarse bay into the air, as if to summon the pursuers. Now, the terrible sleuth-bratch was running parallel with his horse's flanks, and vainly he strove to strike at it with his sword. His temples throbbed as if with fever, and now, for air, for coolness, and relief, he drew off his barred helmet; then he tossed it into a bush, for the double purpose of staying the hound and concealing it as a trace of his flight. Spurring on—he redoubled his efforts to escape; he called to his horse—he cheered and caressed it, while the perspiration of toil oozed through the joints of his armour, from his gorget to his spurs.

The terrible white hound was preparing for a final, and, doubtless, a fatal spring, when a man, whose head and shoulders were enveloped in a scarlet hood, suddenly rose from the whin bushes amid which Gray was galloping, and, by a single blow from his ponderous mace, dashed out the brains of the dog, killing it on the spot.

Gray had just time to perceive that his preserver was Malise MacKim, the smith of Thrave, when he passed on like a whirlwind; and now he saw before him, in the distance, the lovely and far-stretching valley of the Nith, the long bridge, the red-walled town, the spires, and the old castle of Dumfries. He dashed through the portal of the bridge, and pushed on by the way for Edinburgh; but, owing to the rough and devious nature of the roads, night overtook him among the wilds of Tweedmuir. If he drew bridle for a moment, he still heard the tramp of hoofs in his rear, for now fresh horsemen had joined in the pursuit; and, but for the relays he had so wisely provided, and of which he only once availed himself, he had assuredly been taken and slain.

At Moffat, he obtained his own favourite horse from the priest of the village church.

"Will you not, for safety, have your charger's shoes reversed?" said the churchman, as Gray mounted.

"Like King Robert of old; but there is no snow to reveal the track."

"But there is mud, and the ways are deep and soft."

"True; but who is here to do it for me?"

"The smith at the forge."

"Nay, nay, good father," said Gray, shortening his reins; "hear you that!" a whoop and a bugle blast, came together on the night breeze; "I must even trust me to my good Brechin blade and Clydesdale nag; for both are our good king's gift," and he set forth with renewed speed.

He had good reason for declining to loiter, for just as he rode off, the mountain pass, which opens into the valley, rang with shouts and the rush of many iron hoofs, as the laird of Hawkshaw and the Hunters of Palmood, with Sir Alan Lauder and a band of Douglas moss-troopers, came galloping down.

On, on, rushed the fleet horse, with its small head outstretched, and cutting the night air, as the prow of a ship cleaves the water. The taper ears lay flat on its neck, the mane streamed behind like smoke from a funnel, and the quivering nostrils shot forth white puffs of steamy breath at every bound; while foam and blood mingled together on its flanks, as the sharp Rippon spurs of the daring rider urged it fast and furiously on.

This flight of Sir Patrick Gray from Thrave suggested to Scott the escape of Marmion from the future chief of the Douglases—the earl of Angus, at Tantallan.

FOOTNOTES:

[4] One account states that the body of MacLellan was interred in the church of Kirkconnel, and some old inscription is quoted in proof; another, that he was conveyed to the abbey church of Dundrennan, where a monument was erected to his memory; but it is much more probable that he would be interred in the church of Kirkcudbright.

CHAPTER L
WILL HE ESCAPE?

Black is my steed as a cloud of rain,
There's a star of white on his brow;
The free gales play with his feathery mane,
And lightnings gleam round his feet of snow.
Polish Poetry.

Dark foliaged glens and heathy hills, furrowed fields and wayside cottages, with the pale smoke curling through their roofs of yellow thatch and emerald moss; rock-perched towers, with corbelled battlements and grated windows; deep fordless rivers, pathless woods, and uncultivated wolds, seemed to fly past, and still the steed with its bare-headed rider rushed on at a frightful pace, as if it was enchanted, or bestrode by an evil spirit, like that of Lenore in the ballad of Burger.

The moon was shining brightly now.

Near Stobo the pursuers came so close upon Gray that he began to fear escape was impossible—the more so, as fresh blood-hounds were baying on his track. On reaching the Tweed, instead of crossing it by a ford—the river was deeper everywhere then than now—he waded or swam his horse up the current for about a hundred yards, and *backed* it into a low-browed fissure or cavern which he discovered amid the rocks.

Dismounting, he drew his sword and dagger, threw the bridle over his left arm, and stood at the cavern mouth to confront all or any who might come near, and resolved if they discovered his lurking place to sell his life dearly; but he felt how much the long ride in heavy armour over rough ground had impaired his natural strength. His sinews were stiffened, his overtasked muscles were swollen with pain, and his mind was as weary as his body.

On the silver current of the Tweed, as it brawled over its broad bed of pebbles, the moon shone bright and clearly; close by, a tributary from the hills rushed over a brow of rock, and formed a feathery cascade, which plunged into a deep pool. There the peasantry affirmed that a kind fairy was wont to appear at times, and to bend over the cascade, mingling her white arms and floating drapery with the foam, as she sought to save those wayfarers whom the evil kelpie in the darksome linn below sought to drown and devour.

Nor hideous kelpie, nor lovely fairy were visible to-night; but now came the hoarse grunting bark of four large sleuth-bratches, as they leaped with heavy plunges to the margin of the stream: there the scent was lost, and they were once more, as at every running water, at fault, so they ran snorting and sniffing to and fro among the leaves, reeds, and water-docks, with the breath curling up from their fierce red nostrils like white steam in the clear moonlight.

Then came furious surmises and angry oaths as a dozen or more moss-troopers galloped down to the bank of the stream, and rode in an excited manner hither and thither, seeking to put the dogs upon a track or trail. Through the leafy screen of his hiding-place, Gray could see their fierce and sun-burned faces, their rusty helmets and battered trappings, their long reed-like lances that glittered in the moonshine; for those moss-troopers, in their well-worn and half-barbaric accoutrements, were the very Cossacks of the Scottish borders.

James Achanna now came up and spurred his horse across to examine the ford, and uttered a shout of exultation on discovering the trace of horses' hoofs recently impressed in the soft mud.

Gray drew a long breath, and felt the edge of his sword, for he thought the critical moment was at hand! But now a trooper, with an oath expressive of disappointment, drew the attention of all to the circumstance that the marks were those of a horse which had gone *towards* the ford and must have crossed it for the south, and that, if they were made by the hoofs of the fugitive's nag, he must have doubled like a hare. On hearing this, Gray blessed his own foresight in having backed his horse upward from the stream.

The moment this hint was given to the rest, who had no particular views of their own on the subject, they put spur to their horses and galloped away, almost in the direction from whence they had come. As soon as they were gone, Gray came forth from his lurking-place, mounted, and rode off towards the north leisurely and at an easy pace.

He was soon on the border of the fertile Lothians; the far-stretching range of the Pentlands rose upon his left, with their heathy summits tipped by the rising sun; the long ridge where the trenches of Agricola's camp overlooked the woods of Dalhousie, the Dalkeith of the Douglases, and the vale of the two Esks, was soon surmounted, and afar off, "piled deep and massy, close and high," he could see old grey Edinburgh rising in the distance.

Haggard, wan, and wild in aspect, weary and torn,—minus a helmet and with his dark hair streaming behind him; his armour rusted with perspiration, and by frequent immersion in the rivers he had forded or swam; his spurs dripping with blood, and his sinking horse covered with foam and quivering in every fibre; his embroidered surcoat frittered by brambles and thorns—the Captain of the King's Guard passed through the streets of Edinburgh, and reached the castle, thus actually returning, as the old gate-ward had shrewdly predicted, "faster than he gaed awa."

The Master of Crichton (the chancellor's eldest son), the favourite page of James, conducted him at once to the latter, who was in the same apartment of David's Tower, and occupied with the same translated romance of Sir Gilbert the Haye.

"What of MacLellan?" said he, starting up.

"MacLellan is dead, sire," replied Gray in a scarcely audible voice, and in a burst of grief and excitement "My kinsman—my friend—he has gone to heaven; but he was foully murdered, and in cold blood, by the base Lord Douglas, and I shall avenge him—yea, fearfully, I swear it by Him at whose throne he is now perhaps kneeling!"

"And I will aid your vengeance, Gray," added the king, pressing his hand.

Then, when Sir Patrick had related his story, James vowed deeply in his heart, if he could not conciliate Douglas, to CRUSH him and break his terrible bond, or let himself be crushed in the contest.

CHAPTER LI
STIRLING

Ye towers within whose circuit dread,
A Douglas by his sovereign bled;
And thou, oh sad and fatal mound,
That oft has heard the death-axe sound.—Scott.

To Gray it seemed as if Heaven or fate had conspired with Douglas to keep him and Murielle separate for the period of their natural lives; though King James assured him that his day of retribution, if not of happiness, must soon come now.

The king of Scotland was most anxious to avoid the horrors of a civil war with those obnoxious peers, who openly boasted, that on a day's notice, by the Fiery Cross, they could array forty thousand men against his throne and authority. He was really, and naturally so, alarmed by the bond or league of the Douglases and their confederates; but the summer passed, and the spring of the next year drew on, before the haughty earl would agree to meet his sovereign in solemn conference at Stirling. Then James promised Gray that all disputes would be ended, and that the wish which lay nearest his heart—the surrender of his wife to him—would be granted.

How vain were the hopes of the good young king; and how little could he or any one foresee the terrible sequel to that long-wished-for interview!

An ample letter of safe conduct was sent to the earl of Douglas, in custody of Sir William Lauder of Hatton, a knight of Lothian, one of his chief friends and followers; and thus armed and, as he deemed, protected, he entered the quaint and beautiful old town of Stirling, where James was then residing; for then, and for five generations after, Stirling was the Aranjuez, or Versailles of the Scottish kings, and on its decorations they were unsparing of treasure and of care.

It was on the morning of Shrove Tuesday, the 20th of February, 1451, that the earl arrived, accompanied by Hugh Douglas, earl of Ormond; Dunbar, earl of Murray; James, Lord Hamilton of Cadzow; Sir Alan Lauder; the lairds of Pompherston, Glendoning, Cairnglas, and, of course, James Achanna,—in all they were many hundred horsemen. They made no parade or show, save of war; for all these nobles, knights, and their followers, were mounted, mailed, and armed to perfection, so as to be in readiness for any emergency; and they were all men of approved and even reckless valour.

The early winter was past; the vast valley or plain, through which the wondrous links of Forth wind like a silver snake towards the German Sea, was assuming that brilliance of green which is the first indication of reviving nature.

The notes of the woodlark and throstle-cock were heard in the woods of Craigforth; the moles were busy on the fallow uplands, and the gnats swarmed in the sunshine about the budding hedgerows; in the park below the castle walls of Stirling, the bare-legged urchins of the town were busy "throwing at cocks" tied to stakes—a barbarous custom by which Shrovetide was always celebrated in Scotland, as well as in south Britain; others were playing at foot-ball, or shooting at the butts with little arblasts; and the shouts of their merriment rang upward in the clear and almost frosty air, to where Mary of Gueldres and her ladies were seated at the windows of the royal dwelling, many hundred feet above the grassy glen. But all left their sports, and hastened to the gate which opened towards the old Druid oaks of the Torwood, when the brass bombardes of the fortress rolled their thunder on the still atmosphere, and made the Ochil mountains echo in salute to the doughty earl of Douglas, while the clarions and trumpets of his train rang before the barrier-porte of the ancient burgh.

His family banner, twelve trumpets, with a royal herald and pursuivant, preceded him; and as he passed up the quaint streets, where the burghers at their windows, galleries, turrets, and forestairs, hung out pennons, tapestry, and garlands, and received him with acclamations, he deemed it all a tribute to his rank, and to his mighty feudal and mightier political power; although this display was merely the joyous outpouring of their hearts at the prospect of an amicable end being put to the jealousy and hate which had separated the chief of the Douglases—that line of glorious old historic memory—from a brave and high-spirited monarch whom they loved. It was all in the spirit of the old ballad—

> God save the king, and bless the land
> In plenty, joy, and peace;
> And grant henceforth that foul debate
> 'Twixt noblemen may cease.

The earl's cuirass was of Milan steel, magnificently damascened, studded with gilt nails, and furnished at the armpits with little espalettes of gold. From under his open helmet, which was surrounded by a coronet, he looked around him with a smile of surly satisfaction; but his most powerful friend, Sir James, the lord Hamilton of Cadzow, said, solemnly and sternly,

"Let not all this delude you, Douglas, to forget on this day the wrongs of your race."

"Forget?" reiterated the other, grimly; "forget, said ye, Cadzow? If I forget my father and my kinsmen, so may God, his blessed Mother, and St. Bryde of Douglas, forget me! No, Hamilton, never shall I forget the good and doughty Douglases who have gone before me, for their lives were lives of danger, and their mail-clad breasts were Scotland's best bulwarks in the stormy days of old."

"I know all that; but our bond—and the king"—said Hamilton, hesitatingly.

"Well, he is neither priest, philosopher, nor exorcist, like that old knave of Tongland, who has left me to my own sins and devices; so what can he make of the matter?"

"When we are within yonder castle on the rock, he may perhaps term it treason."

"He dare not!" was the bold reply.

"I beseech you to beware, my lord earl," said Lord Hamilton; "I have a strange foreboding in my heart, and I warn you now—even as the good Sir Malcolm Fleming warned Earl William—to remember that before the gate of Stirling lies a mound, on which have rolled the heads of Murdoch of Albany, of his two sons, of Duncan, earl of Lennox, and many others."

"What of that?" asked the earl impatiently, as if he disliked the subject.

"In one minute more, you will be at the mercy of the king," said Hamilton, who was alike bold and wary.

But the earl laughed scornfully and rode on, while the majority of his vast retinue separated to seek quarters in the town, as the castle could not have held them.

"There is yet time to pause—even to return," resumed Hamilton, as he all but seized the earl's rein.

"I know not what you mean, Cadzow; but I care not, and *he dare not*," said Douglas, as he reined up his horse and dismounted at the gate of the castle.

Before it was a strong palisade, within which the soldiers of the king's guard were under arms, with their helmets, corslets, plate sleeves, and partisans glittering in the sun. At their head were Sir Patrick Gray, and his kinsman, Gray of Balgarno, clad, not in state dresses, but complete armour, as if for battle.

Sir Patrick and the earl exchanged angry and hostile glances as they passed each other. There was a considerable pressure about the gate, as the chief followers of Douglas crushed after him through the narrow outer wicket; and there a strange fracas took place between Cadzow and the grim old Sir Alexander Livingstone of Callender, who, after he had relinquished the regency, had been appointed justice-general of Scotland, with a peerage in perspective.

Sir Alexander snatched a partisan from the hands of his son, Sir James Livingstone, who was captain of the castle of Stirling, and when Hamilton (his own kinsman and friend) attempted to enter, he placed the shaft across the wicket, and roughly thrust him back.

Inspired by a sudden fury, Hamilton shut down the visor of his helmet, and, sword in hand, was rushing upon Livingstone; but the strong and determined old knight resolutely held him back till the gates were shut, and thus he, with many more of the earl's train who might have proved troublesome from their number and disposition, were excluded.

"Sir James Hamilton," says history, "was very angry at this usage at the time; but afterwards learned that Livingstone acted a friendly part in excluding him from the probable danger into which Douglas was throwing himself." It was a conference the end of which none could foresee.

It is somewhat remarkable that, after a brawl which seemed so significant of perils yet to come, Douglas (unless he was ignorant of its occurrence) should have passed through the embattled porch of the fortress; but now all the barriers were closed, and no course was open but to *dree his weird*—to follow his destiny!

CHAPTER LII
HOW THE KING BROKE THE BOND

Little honour it won thee
For smooth was thy greeting;
Thou wast bid to the feast,
In the hall was your meeting.
In the hall was your meeting,
But thou stained it with slaughter;
When there's blood on the hearth,
Who can wash it with water?
From the Gaelic.

Veiling his just indignation under a bland exterior, King James II. received the turbulent earl kindly and with condescension; and after some amicable expostulations on the subject of the men he had so lawlessly put to death in Thrave and elsewhere—the ravages he had committed upon the lands of his enemies—the towns he had burned and the castles he had stormed, all seemed to become cordiality between him and his much-too-powerful subject.

Of these startling acts they conversed as quietly and easily as modern men may do of an election, a bill before parliament, or any ordinary and everyday affair; yet they were dangerous topics to comment upon at such a time, for by the king's side were still the Lord Chancellor Crichton, Sir Alexander Livingstone of Callender, the Lord Glammis, Sir Patrick Gray, and others; while near Douglas were the Earls of Crawford, Murray, and Ormond, with Pompherston, Glendoning, and others, all, more or less, involved personally; but now, on looking round, the earl missed the powerful chief of the house of Hamilton.

"Is not Cadzow here?" he asked, changing colour.

"He remains in the town," said Sir Alexander Livingstone with a smile which there was no analyzing; "but if it please you, lord earl, I shall send him a message."

"Do so, Laird of Callender," replied the earl, "and for the first time in my life I shall thank you."

"We shall see," replied Livingstone as he withdrew to an antechamber, where he disengaged the gold spur from his right heel, and giving it to James's page, the Master of Crichton bade him "see the Lord Hamilton, of Cadzow, and give him this spur, with a kinsman's best wishes for its speedy use."

The spur was duly delivered—the hint was accepted, and the brawl at the gate seemed explained; for within an hour, Hamilton and *his* followers were far on the road to Clydesdale and the castle of Cadzow.

At the hour of seven, the king, Douglas, and their retinue sat down to a banquet, or rere-supper, in the castle-hall. It was sumptuous, and what it lacked in genuine hilarity was made up in rude and antique splendour. At that banquet friends and foes seemed united for the time—though like Scotsmen in general, the moment it was over, and while the hall yet echoed with the flourish of trumpets as the king rose, they drew into cliques and coteries, who talked and scowled at each other. The king, Crichton, and Livingstone earnestly desired a compromise and coalition with Douglas.

On one hand the latter wished to scare them by a display of his power, and on the other to fathom their ulterior plans without revealing his own; thus during the banquet he carefully avoided the perilous subject of his rebellious *bond*.

Gray, as he leaned on his partizan, at the back of the king's chair, kept the visor of his helmet half closed, to conceal the emotions of his heart, which his face might have betrayed. Not even the image of Murielle, pale, gentle, and sad-eyed, could soften at that time the bitterness that burned within him. His long separation from her; his wounds inflicted by the hands of the earl and his followers; his many wrongs; the snares of Achanna; the long captivity in the Flemish castle of Bommel; his kinsman's murder, and the terrors of that desperate flight from Thrave, all swelled up like a flood of fiery thoughts within him, and he actually conceived the idea of smiting Douglas on the face with his iron glove in the king's presence, and challenging him to mortal combat in the hall.

Night had set in—a dark and gusty night of February, when the wind howled loudly and drearily round the towers of Stirling, and when the moon cast its fitful gleams with the shadows of the fast-flying clouds, on the wide vale of Forth, and the mighty masses of the Ochil Mountains. The pages were lighting the sconces and chandeliers in the great hall, while the yeomen of the cellars were supplying the guests with more wine, when James, impatient to broach the subject of the bond, privately invited the earl to accompany him into a closet, which is still shown in the north-western corner of the castle—the same quarter of the royal residence in which he first saw the light. In golden letters, on its cornice, may yet be seen his name:

Jacobus II. Rex Scottorum.

Its walls were then covered with gilded Spanish leather; a fire of perfumed wood burned cheerfully on the hearth; but the poker and tongs, though each surmounted by an imperial crown, were chained to the jambs, as if in the house of a simple citizen.

After trimming the lights, the pages, on a sign from the king, withdrew backwards, bowing at every step, and he was left with the earl, who found himself alone, or unattended, and in the closet were the Lords Crichton, Glammis, Sir Patrick Gray, a gentleman of the bedchamber, named Sir Simon Glendinning, and one or two others, who were the chosen friends of James.

Aware that their sovereign was about to take the earl calmly but severely to task, they all drew somewhat apart, and Gray, with soldier-like instinct, leaned in silence on his partizan near the door. On perceiving these little movements, a smile of disdain crossed the earl's swarthy face, and he played significantly with his jewelled dagger.

James resumed the subject of his general conduct, and if Master David Hume of Godscroft, the historian of the house of Douglas, can be credited, the earl answered submissively enough, and craved the royal pardon, often alleging that the slaughter of Sir Herbert Herries of Teregles, Sir Thomas MacLellan of Bombie, and others, were *not* acts against the crown, but lawful raids against his own personal enemies.

"But how came you to slay the Gudeman of my mills at Carluke?" asked the king." ——Carluke—ha! ha!"

"The death of a good man is no laughing matter," said James, with a frown on his handsome face.

"He was accused of having weeds on his land."

"Weeds!" was the perplexed rejoinder.

"Yes, your highness—weeds. It was statute and ordained by Alexander II., that he who poisoneth the king's lands with weeds, especially the corn marigold, was a traitor."

"By my faith! that should make clean garden-work in the realm of Scotland," said the old chancellor, bitterly; "but the law says, that he who hath a plant of this kind found on his lands may be fined a sheep, or the value thereof, at the goul-court of the baron; whereas the miller died, or was found murdered—hewn to pieces by Jethart axes, within the Holy Gyrth of Lesmahago—a crime against the Church as well as State."

"I came not here to talk of peasant carles and their modes of dying," said Douglas, with a terrible frown at Crichton, his hatred for whom he cared not to conceal; "and since when, my lord chancellor, has a slaughter, committed in the form of *Raid*, been termed a *murder* in Scotland?"

"Enough about the poor miller," resumed the king, with growing severity; "my lord, I have another complaint; you have lawlessly separated a faithful subject, the captain of our guard, from his wedded wife, and thus have torn asunder, for many long years, those whom your own father-confessor united before the altar with every due solemnity."

"I hope to separate them yet more surely," replied the earl, with a glance of unutterable hate at Gray.

"This, in my presence?" exclaimed the king; "thou heart of iron!"

"In any man's presence, and to any man who mars or meddles with my domestic affairs; but I beseech your majesty to change the ungracious subject."

"Be it so," replied the king, with a gentleness he was very far from feeling, as his temper was fiery in the extreme. "All these are matters for after consideration; but what say you to that most treasonable confederation, into which you have entered with the earls of Crawford, Ormond, Ross, the lords Hamilton, Balvenie, and many others? By that bond you seek to array one half my kingdom against me—a kingdom over which my dynasty has ruled in strength for so many generations."

"So much the worse," sneered the insolent peer; "for all dynasties begin in strength and end in weakness."

"I pledge my royal word," continued the king, trembling with suppressed passion, "that when I first heard of your league, and of its terrible tenor, I could scarcely give it credence."——"Possibly, your grace—but what then?"

"Simply, that bond must be broken."

"Must!" reiterated the earl, incredulously.

"Yes must, and *shall*, by the soul of St. Andrew! No such leagues can be tolerated in a realm, without the express sanction of its sovereign; and by abandoning this confederacy, Douglas, you will remove every suspicion from my mind."——"Suspicion!—of what?"

"Secret motives, whose aim we cannot see."

"Sire!" began Douglas, loftily, but paused.

"Notwithstanding all that has passed, I am unwilling to believe the evil which men impute to you," said James, with a most conciliating manner; "but you must expect neither favour nor mercy from me if you continue to show such examples to my people, and teach them to live as if there were neither law nor justice in the kingdom."

Douglas heard this bold remonstrance (in which we follow the words of history) with surprise; but recovering himself, replied plausibly; and in the pauses of this conference the sounds of laughter, hilarity, and the clinking of cups and goblets came from the adjoining hall, with the notes of the harps in the gallery.

"Your Majesty's favour I shall certainly endeavour to preserve," said the earl. "You are aware that I have the honour to command many who obey me faithfully and fearlessly, and I trust you are also aware that I know well how to render dutiful obedience to you. None of your subjects in Scotland possess higher rank or greater power than I, the Earl of Douglas, do; nor is there one who will more freely peril life and fortune in defence of your majesty's throne and honour. But," he added, suddenly relinquishing his adopted suavity, and glancing malignantly at Crichton, Gray, and others; "*those* who lay snares for my life—even as they snared my kinsmen in 1440—are now your majesty's constant attendants, friends, and advisers, so that I dare not trust myself in your royal presence, without a letter of safe conduct, as if I were an Englishman, or any other subject of a foreign king."

"And without an army of followers," added the chancellor, who, remembering the ambush in which he had so nearly perished before his own gate, was confounded by the stolid effrontery of his enemy.

"But the bond," said the king; "the bond, my lord!"

"As for that league of mutual friendship, formed by certain nobles and myself, I can assure your majesty, that, for any purpose which pleased us, we should adhere together quite well *without* its existence."

"Did friendship alone produce the bond?" asked James with an eagle glance in his keen hazel eyes.

"No—we were driven to seal and sign it,—not with intent to attack our enemies, but to defend ourselves against them."

"Lord Earl," said the king, gravely, "deeds, not words, evince the affection and submission of a subject; and there can be no greater security for him, than the justly administered laws of the realm. Such men as you, my lord of Douglas, have ever raised those factions which have subverted the authority of your kings and the laws of your country; and now I am resolved to tolerate no subjects of any rank or condition who dare to form leagues, offensive and defensive, against all persons."

"My ancestors——" began the earl furiously.

"Oh, my lord," said James; "what is all your mad pride of ancestry, when compared——"

"With yours, your majesty would say!"

"No," replied the king, with a bitter smile, while growing pale with rage.

"What then?"——"With *personal worth*."

The daring Douglas gave his young monarch a glance of profound disdain; and during this species of altercation, it was with difficulty that Crichton, Gray, Glammis, and Sir Simon Glendinning restrained the desire for falling on the earl sword in hand. "Proceed," said the latter with a sigh of mock resignation.

"The objects of your bond are to disclaim all rule, to do what you please, to commit treason, and by your own swords to justify your ultimate views, until you rush upon the throne itself. So I, as a king, whose power comes direct from God and the people, demand that this most dangerous league, with Ross, with Crawford, Ormond, and Balvenie, be instantly broken!"

"The bond was formed with the mutual consent of many; and unless they meet for consultation, which they may do on *a day's notice*, it cannot be renounced without dishonour by any one of us."

James, who knew their boast, that "on a day's notice" they could array forty thousand men in their helmets against him, gave the crafty peer a withering glance as he replied, "My lord, the first example of renunciation shall be set by *you*. No man—not even though earl of Douglas and lord of Galloway—dare disclaim my authority, and you shall not stir a single pace from this chamber until, in presence of these loyal lords and gentlemen, you retract your adherence to this treason."

"Your grace must remember that I came hither upon the public assurance and letters of safe conduct."

"No public letter can protect a man from the punishment due to private treason!"

Then, says history, "as this last reply of James implied a threat of personal violence, the native pride of Douglas betrayed him into the most imprudent passion. He broke into a torrent of reproaches, upbraiding the king for depriving him of the office of lieutenant-general of the kingdom, declared that he cared little for the name of treason, with which his conduct had been branded; that, as to his confederacy with the earls of Ross and Crawford, he had it not in his own power to dissolve it, and that if he had, he would be sorry to offend his best friends to gratify *the boyish caprices* of a king. James, naturally fiery and impetuous, became furious with rage at this rude defiance, uttered in his own palace by one whom he regarded as his enemy." He drew his dagger, and, animated by a gust of temper far beyond his control, exclaimed, "False traitor! if thou wilt not break the bond, THIS SHALL!"

With these words he drove the weapon into the earl's breast—the keen and glittering blade passing between his cuirass and the gold espalette at his left armpit. Choking in blood, the fierce and fearless earl fell back for an instant. Then, maddened by pain, and perhaps by the prospect of immediate death, he unsheathed his own poniard, and was rushing upon James, when—as we are told by Buchanan—Gray interposed and struck him down by a blow on the head with his partisan. "This for MacLellan!" he exclaimed, in a hoarse voice.

"Villain!" sighed the earl, as he sank on the rush-covered floor, and struggled vainly to rise again.

"I struck but to save my king, lord earl," said Gray, bending over him, "and for no private wrong of my own, nathless my words, so Heaven be my judge! but say, shall Murielle, my wife, be surrendered to me?"

The earl gave Gray a ghastly smile as the blood flowed darkly over his bright armour, and a livid pallor overspread his swarthy face.

"Speak, I conjure you," urged Gray; "speak, ere it be too late— Murielle—"

"Shall never be thine," muttered the dying earl, with quivering lips and uncertain accents; "for when this news reaches Thrave, Achanna—James Achanna—has—has my orders—orders to—to— —"

"What?" implored Gray, bending low his ear; "what?"— —"*To strangle her!*"

These terrible words were scarcely uttered, when many who were the earl's enemies rushed in with their swords and daggers, and, holding back the king, Gray, Crichton, and Glendinning, who—now that their first gust of fury was over, would have saved him—speedily ended his life by the infliction of six-and-twenty wounds.

They then opened the window, and flung the yet warm and sorely mangled corpse of that mighty earl, who was the rival of his king, into the nether baillerie of the castle; and from the terrible deed of that night of Shrove Tuesday, the 20th of February, the apartment in which it took place is still named the "Douglas Room."

As a sequel to it, the Edinburgh newspapers of the 14th of October, 1797, have the following paragraph:—

"On Thursday se'nnight, as some masons were digging a foundation in Stirling Castle, in a garden adjacent to the magazine, they found a human skeleton, about eight yards from the window over which the earl of Douglas was thrown, after he was stabbed by King James II. There is no doubt that they were his remains, as it is certain that he was buried in that garden, and but a little distance from the closet window."

CHAPTER LIII
THE SIEGE OF THRAVE

> Well, then, to work; our cannon shall be bent
> Against the brows of this resisting town;
> Call for our chiefest men of discipline
> To cull the plots of best advantages:
> We'll lay before this town our royal bones,
> Wade to the market-place in Frenchmen's blood
> But we will make it subject to this boy.—King John.

The unfortunate Sir Patrick Gray knew the atrocities of which the castle of Thrave had been the scene during the late earl's lifetime; and he also knew the cruelty of which Achanna, his tool and minion, was capable; thus the dying words of Douglas made his soul tremble with terror for the safety of Murielle, in such butcherly and unscrupulous hands. But how was she to be saved?

All the vassals of the crown were not numerous enough to penetrate into Galloway and storm Thrave, amid a land of pastoral wilds and pathless forests, swarming with freebooting lairds, fierce moss-troopers, and half-savage Celts. Of venturing there *alone*, like a knight-errant, his recent expedition had fully illustrated the danger, and after the last terrible deed in Stirling the peril would be greater than ever.

That stern deed of the young king filled the Douglases with rage; but it was not without a salutary effect upon their adherents, as it evinced that he would no longer brook their insulting and rebellious conduct.

Posterity can have little sympathy for the fate of Douglas, "whose career from first to last," says Mr. Tytler, "had been that of a selfish, ambitious, and cruel tyrant, who, at the moment when he was cut off, was all but a convicted traitor, and whose death, if we except the mode in which it was brought about, was to be regarded as a public benefit."

His friends and his adherents, however, were not disposed to take this calm view of the matter. His younger brother succeeded to his titles and estates, and was styled "Earl of Douglas and Duke of Touraine;" and he, with the earls of Murray, Ormond, Lord Balvenie, and others, all Douglases, proposed to storm the castle of Stirling, and put all within it to the sword, not even excepting James and his young queen, Mary of Gueldres; but a little reflection convinced them of the peril of such an enterprise, and, moreover, that they were without cannon or other resources to attempt it.

However, six hundred nobles, barons, and gentlemen, of the house of Douglas, mustered in full array, with all their vassals, within the town of Stirling, on the 25th day of March—the feast of St. Benedict—and dragged through mud and mire the king's safe conduct, which they nailed on a wooden truncheon, and tied to the tail of a sorry old jaded cart-horse. They then burned it publicly at the Market Cross, where after four hundred horns and twenty brass trumpets had proclaimed defiance, they stigmatized "the king, the lord Crichton, Sir Alexander Livingstone, Sir Patrick Gray, and all who adhered to them, as false and perjured traitors!"

They bade formal defiance to the royal garrison. Then, after completely pillaging the town, they set it on fire in every quarter, and, leaving it in flames and ashes, retired through the adjacent country, which they filled with tumult and outrage. Having thus expended their fury on all that came in their way, they retired each to his own fortress, to prepare for what might follow.

Not long after this, the new earl, with his brothers, friends, and kinsmen, daringly fixed on the doors of the parish churches a document, in which they solemnly renounced their allegiance to the king "as a perjured traitor, a violator of the laws of hospitality, and an ungodly thirster after innocent blood."

The parliament now resolved to aid their justly-incensed monarch in punishing these contumacious nobles, and in a short time he found himself at the head of thirty thousand carefully-selected men, who assembled on Pentland Muir, and with them he resolved to advance against the Douglases. Sir Patrick Gray and the royal guard, of course, accompanied him on this expedition.

The king had with him, William, the lord high constable, whom he had just created earl of Errol, and leader of feudal cavalry; Lord Crichton's son, whom he had created earl of Caithness and lord high admiral of the kingdom; the lords Hailes, Fleming, Boyd, and many other loyal nobles, with all their followers.

He had a fine train of artillery (as artillery was viewed in those days), under Romanno of that ilk, the principal cannon being *the Lion*, a great gun cast in Flanders and shipped at Bruges, for Scotland, by order of his father, James I., in 1430. It was of polished brass, covered by beautiful carvings and ornaments, and bore the following inscription:—

"Illustri Iacobo Scottorum, principe digno,
Regi magnifico, dum fulmine castra reduco,
Factus sum sub eo, nuncuper ergo Leo."

The white or gaudily-striped and bannered tents of the royal army covered all the great tract of land known as Pentland Muir, and clustered by the margin of lonely Logan Burn, which flows through a green sequestered vale, the solitude of which was now broken by the hum of the camp, the hourly din of horn and trumpet, the clanging of the hammers and anvils of the farriers and armourers; thus, the shepherd on the Pentland slopes could see the red glow of many a forge and watch fire reddening the sides of the hills by night, and in his shealing he could hear the unwonted sounds, that scared his herds and hirsels from their pasture, the eagle from its eyrie in Torduff, and broke the silence of the pastoral waste:—

Piercing the night's dull ear; and from the tents
The armourers accomplishing the knights,
With busy hammers closing rivets up,
Give note of dreadful preparation.

The wiry music of the harp might also be heard at times amid the camp, for many minstrels accompanied the king's army. The *last* time its notes were heard in a Scottish host was when Argyll marched to the battle of Benrinnes, in 1594.

After hearing solemn mass said in the old rectory kirk of Pentland, where whilom was a settlement of the *Gillian Chriosd* (followers of the Lord)—whence comes the name of Gilchrist—the order was issued by James to strike the tents, and then the whole army marched against the Douglases. The king wore at his helmet the glove of his beautiful Mary d'Egmont, and a knot of her neck-ribbons decorated his lance. The task his troops had undertaken was somewhat arduous, as they had to penetrate into wild districts destitute of roads, where every laird and peasant, every yeoman and hind, felt it his duty to defend his chief against all mankind, even the king, if he came in a hostile guise.

With the ghastly smile of the dead earl yet before him, and the terrible words he had uttered yet lingering in his ear, Sir Patrick Gray longed to be at Thrave; and his heart sickened with impatience during the tardy passage of the king's army through Ettrick Forest and Annandale, the home of powerful and predatory Border clans, into Galloway; for malcontents and marauders were to be punished on every hand; the growing cornfields were swept by fire; towers were stormed and castles dismantled, by having their gates unhinged and their battlements thrown down.

Many of the Douglas adherents, on seeing the determination of James and the number of his host, implored forgiveness; and he, being by nature too fiery and impetuous to be vindictive, pardoned them; but the young earl had fled, no one knew whither save his own friends.

At last the king approached the banks of the Dee, and saw before him the famous stronghold of Thrave. The vanguard of his army, the vassals of Lord Glammis, gave a shout when they first came in sight of it, and that shout found an echo in the heart of Gray, as it did in the hearts of the Douglas garrison; for in Thrave, at least a thousand men, under Sir Alan Lauder, prepared to defend themselves to the last, and literally to fight with ropes around their necks.

When the vanguard halted, and the army began to encamp, the king, accompanied by Sir Patrick Gray, Lord Crichton, and others, rode forward to examine this strong and spacious castle, on which the Douglas banner was waving, and all the ramparts of which, from the outer barbican wall to the summit of the keep, seemed full of armed men, glittering, moving, and instinct with animation, all save one who hung from the gallows knob, and he was still enough.

The mighty fabric, with its moat and bridge, its grated windows and battlements bristling with steel pikes, brass sakers, and long arquebuses, was as grim, as gloomy, as dark and stern as ever, and its shadow was cast by the evening sun far along the surface of the Dee. A white puff of smoke floated suddenly from the keep in the sunshine, and with the sharp report of a culverin, souse came an iron ball, which struck the earth beneath the forefeet of Sir Patrick's horse, causing it to rear wildly.

"A narrow chance of death," said he, with a dark smile.

"There are some chances that do not happen *twice* in a man's lifetime," said the king laughing; "so we had better change our ground."

As they rode towards the three thorn trees at the Carlinwark (one of which still survives, though gnarled, knotted, and old, with the lapse of, perhaps, ten centuries), a shout rose from the half-formed camp, and the soldiers began to rush to their standards, for now a large body of troops were seen debouching from the woods in their rear, and a rumour instantly spread that they were English forces under the young earl of Douglas, advancing to raise the siege. But the momentary alarm was soon quelled on the return of Lord Glammis and the Master of Crichton, who, by the king's order, had advanced to meet them and reconnoitre.

"They are fresh troops from Ayr, who are come to join your highness," said Glammis, "the men of the three Baileries of Kyle, Carrick, and Cunningham."

"Under whom?"

"The Lord Montgomerie of that Ilk and Sir Robert of Kilmaurs, who request permission to kiss your hand."

"Good—'tis well."

"And better still, there have come in with them, the three Wards of Etterick, Yarrow, and Tweed."

"The archers of our old Royal Forest of Selkirk! Thank Heaven, despite this Douglas war, there are loyal and true hearts in Scotland yet!" exclaimed the king. "And now to summon this devil of a fortress. Who will ride forward with the sign of truce?"

"That will I, readily," said Gray.

Others who were of higher rank might have claimed the perilous service; but all knew how Sir Patrick was situated, or connected with the family then in rebellion against the throne, so none came forward to dispute the errand with him.

"I thank you my faithful friend," said James. "You know the terms I offer; instant surrender, and that if the garrison resist, every man found within the walls shall suffer by the edge of the sword."

CHAPTER LIV
THE DEFIANCE

Thou a young king art, Alfonso,
New thy sceptre in the land;
Establish well at home thy power,
Ere thou drawest forth the brand.—The Cid.

Sir Patrick Gray laid aside his helmet and gauntlets, and with a freshly peeled willow rod, the old Scottish symbol of peace and truce in his right hand, rode boldly forward, and while scanning every window with eager eyes for one beloved face and form, he found himself before the formidable gate of Thrave. No faces but those of armed and helmeted men were visible.

At his approach the drawbridge was lowered and the gates were unclosed; but the portcullis, which was composed of iron bars welded together in harrow-fashion by the ponderous hammer of Malise MacKim, remained closed, and within, or beyond it, he saw the Lairds of Pompherston, Cairnglas, and Glendoning, with James Achanna, and Sir Alan Lauder, who was governor of Thrave, and as a symbol of that office wore a silver key suspended at his neck by a chain of the same metal. All were in complete armour, but wore their helmets open. Anxiety and anger, but also resolution, were expressed in all their faces.

"In the name of his majesty the king!" exclaimed Gray, reining in his horse.

"Well—what ware bring you here, sir, in the name of his majesty the king?" asked Lauder, sternly but mockingly.

"I, Patrick Gray, of Foulis, knight, commander of the royal guard, summon you, knights, gentlemen, and others, adherents of the umquhile and forfeited Earls of Douglas, Murray, Ormond, and of the Lords Hamilton and Balvenie, to yield up this strength unto the king, or otherwise to abide our cannon, and the fate in store for all who are guilty of treason and rebellion!"

"Sir Patrick Gray," replied Lauder, a grim old man with a long silver beard and a severely knitted brow, "you have come to the wrong quarter to offer such hard terms. My name is Alan Lauder, of the Auld Craig o'Bass; my shield bears a double treasure, to show that I and mine have been faithful to our trust, and my motto, as the monks have it, is *Turris prudentia custos*, and by it shall I abide. The garrison of Thrave believe in their patron, St. Bryde of Douglas, and, perchance, rather more in their arblasts and arquebuses; and this house shall we defend to the last, so help us God!" he added,

"Reconsider your words, rash man! The wise may change their minds on reflection, but fools never."

"Begone, lest a ball from an arquebus end this parley," replied Lauder, whose grey eyes sparkled with anger.

"Be it so," said Gray, gathering up his reins and turning his horse; "but the king desires me to add, that the Countess of Douglas, the Lady Murielle, their ladies, and all women and children now here in Thrave, may depart in peace to Tongland Abbey, or the College of Lincluden. If not, that they should repair to the quarter of her bower-chamber, whereon, if a white pennon be displayed, our cannon shall respect it."

"Good — for that small boon; as I have a fair daughter, I, in the name of my brother outlaws, thank this most clement king," said Douglas of Pompherston, bitterly.

"Is the Lady Murielle with the Countess?" asked Gray, with too visible anxiety.

They all exchanged cold smiles, but no one answered. Then a page, a pretty boy, to whom Murielle had frequently been kind, was about to speak, when Achanna suddenly put a drawn sword across his mouth, saying sternly: "One word, ye false gowk, and it is your last!"

Gray was about to address Sir Alan again, when a voice exclaimed: "Place for the Countess of Douglas!"

Then, through the rusty *grille* of the portcullis, Gray saw the countess approach, attended by the fair-haired daughters of Sir Alan Lauder. His emotion increased on seeing this twice-widowed dame — widowed so young and so prematurely; she who was whilome the Fair Maid of Galloway, the sister of Murielle, and *his* most bitter enemy; yet, withal, he instinctively bowed low at her approach.

Full in stature, and magnificently formed, she was a woman whose natural grace and the tragic character of whose beauty were greatly increased by her dress, which, though all of the deepest black, was richly jewelled with diamonds, and the same stones sparkled on the hilt of a tiny dagger that dangled at her girdle. Her dignity was enhanced by the amplitude of her skirts, the satin waves of which filled up the eye; but her pale and lovely face, her short upper lip and quivering nostrils, expressed only scorn and aversion for poor Gray, while with one white hand, after throwing back a heavy braid of her jet hair, which she knew well to be one of her greatest beauties, she swept up her flowing train, and with the other pointed towards the camp of the king, as a hint for his envoy to begone, and as she did so, her bright black eyes flashed with latent fire.

"Countess of Douglas— —"

"*Dowager* Countess," she interrupted Gray, with a derisive bow, and with a voice that almost hissed through her close white teeth.

"Madam, King James has now assumed the sword—"

"Of *justice?*" she asked bitterly, interrupting him again; "you should say the dagger of the assassin, Sir Patrick Gray, as it better becomes his hand; but we hope to test the temper of both his weapons. Twice has he widowed me—"

"He, madam?"

"Yea, even he; this James Stuart, who comes hither to waste our lands, to dishonour our name, to raze our castles, and to quench our household fires," she continued, in a voice which though piercing was singularly sweet, and reminded Gray of the gentler accent of Murielle. "Not content with slaying my husband cruelly and mercilessly under tryst, he has sworn by his royal crown and the Black Rood of Scotland, that the plough-share shall pass under the ground-stone of Thrave, and that the place where it stands shall be salted with salt."

"I came not hither to threaten you, madam, neither was I desired to confer with you, but with Sir Alan Lauder and those misguided men who are now in arms here; and my answer— —"

"Shall be this—from *me*, Margaret, countess dowager of Douglas, umquhile duchess dowager of Touraine, and lady of Longueville, Annandale, and Galloway, that James Stuart and the Gueldrian his wife may reign where they please, but I shall be queen on this side of the Nith, and woe to the man, be he lord or loon, who says me nay!"

Her glance of flame, her lovely little lip that curled with hate and scorn; her proud face, with its unearthly wrath and beauty—so fair in its proportions, yet so fearful in its aspect of passion—haunted the Captain of the Guard long after they had parted.

"Enough of this," said old Sir Alan Lauder, coming brusquely forward and taking her hand; "away, Sir Patrick—back to him, or them who sent you, and say, that though our lord the earl was foully slain under tryst in Stirling, his spirit is with us here in Thrave, and shall inspire us in resisting to the last of our breath and the last of our blood, a king who has falsely wronged us!"

"And in every particular *shall the earl's last orders be obeyed*," added Achanna, with an malignant glance at Gray, whose head grew giddy with rage, while his blood ran cold at the terrible inference he drew from these words; and the bars of the portcullis alone prevented him from cleaving the wretch to the chin. So ended the conference.

In this exasperated mood he rejoined the king, who, with many of the nobles, awaited him at the three thorns of the Carlinwark.

The siege now began with great vigour.

On the 8th July, James wrote to Charles VII. of France, announcing that all the fortresses of the Douglas family had surrendered to him except Thrave, which his troops were then besieging; but August came, and still the defiant banner with the bloody heart waved from the vast keep that still overshadows the Dee.

The season was a lovely one.

The oak, the ash, and the beech were still in full foliage of the richest green; the white blossoms of the hawthorn were past, but the bright scarlet berries of the rowan hung in thick bunches over the trouting pools of the Dee in many a copsewooded glen. The grain, where not burned by the king's troops, was ripening on the sunny upland and lowland, contrasting in its golden tints with the dark-green of the thickets, the purple of the cornflower, and the gaudy scarlet of the poppies. The gueldre-rose and the sweet-briar filled the air with perfume; the wild pansies and wallflowers, the pink foxglove and bluebell, grew by the old fauld-dykes on many a Galloway muir and lea; and the gorgeous cups of the long yellow broom waved on the wild hill-side, and by the wimpling burn that gurgled through the rushy hollows, and under many an "auld brig-stane," in farmtown and clachan; but still the brass culverins of King James, from the three great thorns of the Carlinwark, thundered against Thrave, while old Sir Alan Lauder and his garrison replied with carthoun, arquebuse à croc, and crossbow bolt; and now the black gled and the ravenous hoodiecraw kept high aloft on the blue welkin, watching for the inhuman feast that usually followed such unhallowed sounds.

The troops of James had invested the castle on every side; tents covered all the vicinity; trenches and mounds, where spears and armour glittered, crossed all the roads and approaches. Supplies, succour, and hope, seemed all cut off together. More than a month had elapsed since the siege began, and still the vigour of the besieged was undiminished; and in the royal ranks the loss of life by their missiles was very great.

The balls of the king's artillery—even those of the boasted Lion of Flanders—were rained in vain upon the solid face of that vast donjon-keep, for they were too light. The great art of projectiles seemed yet in its infancy, and Sir John Romanno of that ilk, the general of the ordnance, rent his beard in despair.

CHAPTER LV
MOWAN'S MEG

Seven orbs within a spacious round they close,
One stirs the fire, and one the bellows blows;
The hissing steel is in the smithy drown'd,
The grot with beaten anvils groans around.
By turns their arms advance in equal time;
By turns their hands descend, and hammers chime.
They turn the glowing mass with crooked tongs,
The fiery work proceeds with rustic songs.
Virgil, *Æneid* viii.

For many days salvoes (*i.e.*, discharges of heavy ordnance fired in concert by sound of trumpet) were sent against Thrave without success, and yells of triumph and derision, when the balls of iron and whinstone rebounded from the massive walls—the *triple yells* of the Galwegians, the same terrible war-cry which their forefathers raised amid the heart of the Saxon host at the Battle of the Standard, were borne upward on the wind to the king's battery at the Carlinwark.

"This devil of a tower is invulnerable!" said Romanno, casting down his truncheon in anger; "it is a veritable maiden castle—strong in virtue and unassailable."

"Virtue, said ye?" growled the old chancellor, under his barred aventayle; "ah, but our court-rakes aver that even the most virtuous woman has always one weak point, if we can only find it out."

"Out upon thy white beard, chancellor!" said the young king, laughing; "what mean you to say?"

"That, like a fair court lady, this castle of Thrave may have a weak point too."

"But, unless we attempt an escalade, the capture of the place is impossible by battering," said the general of the ordnance.

"Impossible!" reiterated the young king, his face and eyes glowing together, while the red spot on his cheek assumed a deeper hue.

"Pardon me, your highness," said Sir John Romanno; "but I humbly think so."

"Think; but you *said* impossible."

"Under favour, yes."

"There is no such word in a soldier's vocabulary," replied the spirited monarch; "and while our hearts beat under our breastplates there is hope."

"But the idea of an escalade," said Gray, "with the Dee to cross, and a wall to mount, exposed to a fire of cannon and arqubuses à croc, with long bows and arblasts to boot, and thereafter mauls, lances, and two-handed swords in the *mêlée*, is not to be thought of—at least until, by dint of cannon, we effect a breach."

"A breach!" exclaimed Sir John Romanno; "by my forefathers' bones ye are little likely to see that, sirs, when the shot of our heaviest culverins, even those of the Lion, our chief bombarde, rebound like silken balls from the stone rampart, and our cannoniers seem no better than court-ladies at palm play."

A loud and somewhat hoarse but hearty laugh close by made all turn towards the offender. They perceived a man of vast and herculean proportions, with a shock head of black hair, which the absence of his scarlet hood (as it hung down his back) displayed in all its shaggy amplitude, a swarthy visage, with lurid black eyes, and a long beard. He wore a doublet of black bull's hide, a rough kilt dyed with heather, and he leaned upon the shaft of a ponderous iron mace, which, with a long buck-horn-hilted dagger and fur pouch or sporran, formed his only appurtenance.

"Art thou the knave who laughed?" asked Romanno, furiously, with his hand on his sword.

"And in this presence!" added the chancellor, whose wrath was also kindled.

"Dioual! I did laugh," replied the man, in a strong and guttural Galloway accent; "is it a crime to laugh at the folly or bewilderment of others?"

"Thou base varlet!" began Romanno, in a towering passion, clenching his gauntleted hand, when Sir Patrick Gray interposed, saying, "By my faith, it is my friend, the strong smith of Thrave, who saved me from the white sleuth-bratch. Come hither, carle, and remember that you stand in the presence of the king."

Malise MacKim was too much of a primitive Celt to be abashed even before a king, though he had frequently quailed under the eye of Douglas, and the tongue of his own wife, Meg, who was proverbial in Galloway as a fierce virago; so he came boldly forward and stood erect, with an inquiring expression of eye, as if waiting to be addressed.

"Whence is it that your king's perplexity excites your laughter?" asked James, gravely.

"Speak quickly, carle," added the chancellor, pointing ominously to a branch of one of the thorn trees under which they stood.

"Threats will not force me to speak; but I answer the king, *not* you, my lord," replied the unabashed Galwegian.

"We are not used to be laughed at, sirrah," said James; "therefore, if you do not give us a fair reason for your untimely merriment, by the holy rood! I shall begin to threaten too."

"I am Malise MacKim, surnamed the Brawny, and I am the father of seven sons, each a head taller than myself— —"

"Thou art a lucky dog, would I were the same," said the king; "but is this a reason for laughter?"

"What the devil is all this to us, fellow?" asked Romanno.

"This much; they are all smiths, and can each wield a fore hammer forty pounds in weight, as if it were a kettle-drum stick. Ochoin! Mhuire as truadh! Ochoin! There was a time when we never thought to swing our hammers in the service of mortal man, save Douglas. But vengeance is sweeter than bread in famine; so, if your grace will give us but iron enough, I will be content to forfeit my head, or to hang by the neck from that thorn tree, if, within the space of seven summer days, my seven brave bairns and I fail to fashion you a bombarde which, at the first discharge, will pierce yonder wall like a gossamer web, so aid us Heaven and St. Cudbrecht?"

"This is a brave offer," said the general of the ordnance, mockingly; "and what weight may the balls of this proposed cannon be?"

"Each one shall be the weight of a Carsphairn cow," replied the smith slowly, as if reflecting while answering; "and if each fails to shake Thrave to its ground-stane, the king's grace may hang me, as I have said, on that thorn branch, as a false and boasting limmer."

"You speak us fairly, good fellow," said the king, who seemed pleased and amused by the burly smith's bluntness and perfect confidence. "We are not in a position to reject such loyal offers. Fashion this great gun for me, and if it does the service you promise, by my father's soul! you shall have a fair slice of yonder fertile land between the Urr and Dee."

As he spoke, James drew off his gauntlet, and presented his hand to the gigantic smith, who knelt and kissed it respectfully, but with the clownish air of one alike unused to kneeling and to courtesy.

On MacKim requiring material, each of the principal burghers of Kirkcudbright contributed a *gaud* or bar of iron, in their anxiety to serve the king, and to have the death of Sir Thomas MacLellan more fully avenged. As a reward for this contribution, King James made the town a royal burgh, and in memory of it, his gallant grandson, on the 26th of February, 1509, granted the old castle of the MacLellans as a free gift to the corporation.

At a place named the Buchancroft, a rude but extensive forge was soon erected, and there, stripped to their leathern girdles, the brawny MacKim and his seven sturdy sons, like Vulcan and the Cyclops, plied and swung their ponderous hammers on great resounding anvils, while welding the vast hoops and forming the long bars that were to compose the great cannon which was to demolish the famous stronghold of Thrave.

Seven days and seven nights these muscular smiths worked almost without cessation, and the lurid glow of their great forge was nightly seen from the doomed fortress to redden the sky above, the waters of the Dee below, and the tented camp of the besieging army; and only a few years ago, when the new road was made past Carlinwark, a vast mound of cinders and ashes, which formed the *débris* of their work, was discovered and cleared away.

Meanwhile, a band of artificers, with hammer and chisel, were fashioning the balls, which were quarried on the summit of the Binnan hill; these when finished were permitted to roll thundering to its base; and it is remarkable that the great stone-shot for this gun, which yet remain in the castle of Edinburgh, are of Galloway granite from the same eminence.

At last the vast bombarde or cannon was complete in all its bars, hoops, and rivets; it weighed six tons and a half, exclusive of the carriage, and measured two feet diameter in the bore.

During its formation, Sir Patrick Gray endured an mount of mental torture and anxiety which temporary inaction rendered greater.

‗ Would Achanna dare to put in execution the terrible order of the ferocious earl? Would her sister, unrelenting as she was, permit it? He feared that the deed might be done when the castle surrendered, and his feverish and active imagination pictured the gentle, timid, and delicate Murielle writhing in the grasp of an assassin.

But if some dark deed had not been *already* done, why did Achanna place his drawn sword across the mouth of the page, who was about to speak of Murielle, during the parley at the portcullis.

Had knighthood and common humanity fallen so low among those outlaws, that her life would be no longer safe in her sister's household; or were the last words of the dying earl a falsehood, merely meant to sting and embitter the soul of one whom he hated with a tiger's hatred?

Gray afflicted himself with thoughts and surmises such as these, and while the siege was pressed by the king and his troops, his days and nights were passed in misery.

On viewing the great piece of ordnance, James II. promised again that if it proved more successful than the Lion and his other culverins, he would nobly reward the artificer, who, with his seven sons and the royal cannoniers, dragged Meg—for so MacKim named the gun, after his own wife, whose voice, he affirmed, "her roar would resemble"—to the summit of an eminence which, unto this day, is named from that circumstance Knockcannon. Royal heralds with their glittering tabards, and pursuivants with their silver collars of SS, marched in front, while trumpets were blown and kettle-drums beaten; pipers blew, and minstrels played upon their harps; the king's jester swung his bladder and cracked his jokes; and thus, amid music, merriment, and acclamations, the mighty cannon was dragged up the slope and brought into position.

It was then loaded with an old Scottish peck of powder and one of its granite balls, and thereafter was levelled at the fortress of the rebellious Douglases.

"Now—now," exclaimed Malise MacKim, in grim triumph, as he wiped the beads of perspiration from his swarthy brow; "unless my lady of Douglas can fly through the air like an eagle, or swim down the Dee like a grilse, she and the false brood who slew my kinsman and stole his daughter shall exchange their steel gloves for steel fetters!"

All in the king's host were eager to observe the effect produced by this mighty engine of destruction, the first discharge of which, when Sir John Romanno applied the match, seemed to split the welkin, and the recoil of the wheels tore deep ruts in the turf, while many averred that they could trace the course of the ball like a great globe of stone in the air, through which it hummed and whistled.

Be that as it might, when the smoke was blown aside, a great breach or opening (now called the cannon-hole) was visible in the face of the keep, where the side of one of the windows was partly torn away. The masonry was seen to fall in a crumbling mass into the barbican, and the shout of consternation which arose from the garrison was borne on the morning wind to the king's camp, and far beyond it.

The cannoniers now cast aside their helmets, cuirasses, and cuisses, that they might work with greater facility at the laborious task of reloading this great gun, which was discharged several times with equal success; and Sir Patrick Gray watched with agony the result of every shot; for the deep, hoarse boom of each explosion that seemed to rend the hills and sky found an echo in his heart. They seemed like the knell of her he loved.

The warlike James II. was in ecstasy with the success of this new piece of ordnance, and summoning the fabricator to his tent, he then, in presence of the chancellor, the constable, and the principal nobles, granted to him and his heirs for ever, the forfeited estate of Mollance, which lies between the rivers Urr and Dee.

Mollance was locally pronounced Mowans, hence the name of the great gun which he fashioned, and which is now in the castle of Edinburgh—*Mowan's Meg*; though unsupported assertion has assigned her origin to the town of Mons, in Flanders—an origin of which there is not a vestige of documentary proof.

Hastening from the king's tent, Sir Patrick Gray arrived at Knockcannon in time to see another mass of masonry beaten down; and this time the feeble shout from Thrave was drowned in the tumultuous cheer that rang along the slopes, which were covered by the camp of the royal army.

"*Cor Jesu, in agonia factum, miserere morientum!*" prayed the voice of one beside him.

He turned, and saw his old friend the abbot, who had just left his secluded abbey of Tongland and arrived in the camp.

"Ha, father abbot," said Sir John Romanno, while six of the sturdiest cannoniers, bare armed and all begrimed by perspiration, smoke, and gunpowder, swung another granite ball into Meg's capacious muzzle; "how are you? By the mass! if he you wot of were in Thrave, this would make him shake his horns and cry *peccavi*."

"He—who?" asked the abbot, in a tone of displeasure.

"Thy old friend—Mahoun—the fiend himself."

"Shame on thee, Sir John."

"I am but a plain soldier, good abbot," replied Romanno, who was in excellent humour with himself and every one else; "each man to his trade: thou to thy massbook and missal—I to my lintstock and quoin."

"A truce—a truce!" cried a hundred voices, as a white flag was displayed at the summit of Thrave, where a man waved it to and fro, though the Douglas banner was not yet drawn down. Then came the faint and distant sound of trumpets craving a parley.

The abbot immediately offered himself as a mediator; and, on obtaining the permission of the king, who was now weary of this protracted and destructive siege, and was anxious to return to his beautiful Fleming at Stirling, he left the camp for Thrave, accompanied by Sir Patrick Gray, whose anxiety for the safety of Murielle was now irrepressible.

CHAPTER LVI
THE PARLEY

Peace, lady; pause, or be more temperate:
It ill beseems this presence to cry aim
To these ill-timed repetitions.
Some trumpet summon hither to the walls
These men of Angiers; let us hear them speak,
Whose title they admit, Arthur's or John's.
Shakespeare.

Of this interview, during which there occurred one or two painful episodes, the old abbot has left a minute account in the MS. records of Tongland Abbey.

As he and Sir Patrick approached the castle-gate, they could perceive a great circular breach yawning in the face of the keep, where Meg's shot had beaten in the masonry. In many places the corbelled battlements were demolished or mutilated. The barbican wall had suffered considerably, and many dead bodies, with their armour buried or crushed by the cannon shot, were making the place horrible by their ghastly aspect, while great purple pools and gouts of blood indicated where others who had been removed had fallen, or where the wounded had crawled away.

For the first time the terrible gallows-knob was without a victim, the cord which had sustained the last having parted during the concussion of the ordnance.

Through the open gate of the fortress the abbot and captain of the guard were able to see all these details. The grating of the portcullis was raised, and in the archway beneath it stood Sir Alan Lauder, the lairds of Pompherston, Cairnglas, Glendoning, James Achanna, and others, all as usual in their armour, which was dimmed and dinted now by daily and nightly wear. The soldiers of the garrison, who crowded about them with their pikes, axes, crossbows, and arquebuses, seemed hollow-eyed, wan, and pale. Hunger appeared to have become familiar to them as danger and death; thus it was evident to the captain and abbot that the famous larder of Thrave, with its twenty-eight cattle, contributed by the twenty-eight parishes of the surrounding stewardry, was becoming exhausted; for the garrison and other inmates had far exceeded a thousand persons at the commencement of this protracted and destructive siege.

"We have come in the name of mercy and humanity," said the abbot, pausing at the gate.

"It is well," replied Douglas of Pompherston, in the hollow of his helmet; "we feared you had come simply in the name of the king, and we consider him a poor representative of either."

"In whosesoever name you have come," said Sir Alan Lauder, "I can treat but with my lord abbot alone."

"And why not with me who am captain of the king's guard?" demanded Gray haughtily, while throwing up his barred visor.

"Because the blood of Douglas is on your hands, as on those of your master."

"To save whom that blood was shed, else your earl of Douglas had died a regicide, as well as an outlawed traitor. But, whatever terms are given or accepted, I, Patrick Gray, of Foulis, here, in my own name, demand, that the ruffian named James Achanna be excepted therefrom, for I have resolved to slay him without mercy, and, I hope, without remorse, at kirk, at court, at market, or wherever I come within sword's point of him, so help me the holy Evangels, and Him who ever defends the right!"

Achanna grew pale at these threatening words, and on seeing the fierce and resolute aspect with which Gray spoke them; but recovering, he resumed his malignant smile, and uttered a scornful laugh.

"Thrave has not yet surrendered," said Sir Alan Lauder; "and while that white flag waves on its wall, even Achanna's life must be respected. He has been loudly recommending a surrender for some days past, if the young earl, our new chief, came not to our succour," added the white-bearded knight with an angry glance. "Perhaps he may be less eager now, when he learns that the avenging sword of Sir Patrick Gray awaits him."

"Sir Patrick Gray's hostility is nothing new to me, neither are his injustice and falsity," replied Achanna through his clenched teeth, while darting one of his covert glances full of hate at Lauder; "so be assured that I value his wrath as little as you may do, Sir Alan——"

"Then, as old Earl Archibald of Douglas said of Crichton and the Regent, 'twere fair sport to see a couple of such fencers yoked together," interrupted the old knight bluntly, "so please you to step forth six paces from this gate, and meet him hand to hand, on foot or horseback, and I shall be your umpire."

"Thanks from my soul, Sir Alan!" exclaimed Gray with stern joy; "for these words I pledge my honour that your life, fortune, and family shall be saved and protected, tide what may with Thrave."

Achanna bit his nether lip, and without advancing a pace towards Gray, who had reined back his horse and drawn his sword as if inviting him, replied doggedly:

"I have not forgotten the last orders of the earl, ere he rode to Stirling; among *others* we were to defend this stronghold to the last, should it ever be attacked, and to be wary how we risked our lives; but I can now see that if yonder devil of a great gun continues to pound and punch us thus we shall be forced to surrender, lest the roof of stone descend upon us."

"Well, and what then?" asked Lauder bitterly.

"To surrender is to hang."

"Well?"

"By my soul thou takest it very coolly, Sir Alan Lauder," said Achanna, glad to change the subject, and elude Gray's unanswered challenge.

"I do so, Master Achanna, because I foresaw that when King James entered Galloway, with the royal banner displayed, it would end in hanging for some, and beheading for others—hanging especially for thee."

"And beheading for *thee*, so I care not whether we surrender to-night or a week hence."

"You play but ill the jovial desperado," said the Castellan with contempt, as he turned from him.

"Yet he fights for his own hand and commoditie, as Hal o' the Wynd fought," said the abbot of Tongland.

"I am weary of this," exclaimed Sir Patrick Gray; "coward, will you not advance to meet me?"

"And fight with a flag of truce flying; I am not so ignorant of the rules of war," replied Achanna, who felt that the crowd of brave and reckless men about the castle-gate viewed him with derision; "My courage has never failed me, sirs, though I knew the fate in store for me, as—as——"

"As what, fellow?" demanded Lauder.

"A follower of the conquered Douglas and his outlawed adherents."

"Conquered—outlawed!" muttered those who heard him.

"Well, sir, doth not that breach in the castle wall look as if we shall soon be the first, as surely as we are the second."

"Jibing villain," exclaimed Lauder, "beware lest I spare the doomster all trouble, by passing my sword through thee!"

The Scots of those days had but vague ideas on the subject of homicide, so Achanna became alarmed, and said:

"Sir Alan Lauder, remember my years of faithful service."

"And what have those years done for you?"

"Converted me from a boy to a man."

"From a rascal of one age to a rascal of one more mature; but thou shalt hang, if Sir Patrick wills it," said the castellan, with growing wrath; for in fact Achanna, perceiving that matters were going against his friends, had found Thrave less comfortable for some time past, and was anxious to escape or make his peace with the king.

"Enough of this, sir," said Sir Patrick, sheathing his sword; "let us resume the subject of a capitulation."

"The countess—here comes the countess!" exclaimed several voices, as the crowd of armed men divided and drew back; and Margaret, leaning on the arm of Maud Douglas of Pompherston, approached. Eagerly and anxiously Gray looked beyond them, but in vain.

"Oh," thought he in his heart, "where is Murielle?"

The hateful Achanna seemed to divine the thought; for a cold smile curled his thin white lips, and a colder still as he surveyed the countess, and remembered the proud derision with which she had long ago repelled his boyish affection. The lovely face of Margaret was deadly pale—white as the ruff or tippet of swansdown, which guarded her delicate throat and bosom. She was muffled in a long black dule-weed, or mourning habit, the folds of which fell to her feet, and on the left shoulder of which was sewn a white velvet cross. In many places this sombre garment was spotted by blood!

Her beautiful black eyes were bloodshot, and an unnatural glare shone in them. She seemed scarcely able to stand; thus old Sir Alan Lauder hurried to her side, and tenderly placed a mailed arm around her for support.

"Well, Monk, thou who forsook, in his sore extremity, thy chief and master," she sternly said to the abbot, "what seek you here?"

"Douglas was my chief, but *not* my master. He is in Heaven," replied the abbot calmly, pointing upward.

"Well, shaven juggler, who hast added his precious prayers to the cause of the strongest," continued the imperious beauty, "say what you would, and quickly. What errand brings you here?"

"Peace and good will. Oh, madam—madam," exclaimed the meek old abbot, stretching his withered and tremulous hands towards her, "in the name of Heaven and of mercy end these horrors—an aged man, a priest of God implores it of you! James and his soldiers have sworn to take the keys of Thrave at the point of the sword; but our young king is a knight, alike gentle and generous, and from your hands I am assured he will take those keys in peace, if peacefully bestowed."

"From *my* hands," she reiterated, in an unearthly voice; "alas——"

"What *can* she mean?" thought Gray, as a dreadful idea flashed upon his mind; "is this sad, this wild and stern bearing the result of remorse? can she have attempted——"

He thrust aside the thought, and listened attentively.

"From my right hand—never!" added Margaret, with bitter emphasis.

"From the hands of whom, then?"

"My youngest bower-maiden; she deserves the honour, for her father, Sir Alan, has made a valiant and vigorous defence."

"The king would prefer them from the hands of the Lady Murielle," said Gray, with more anxiety than caution.

"Speak not to me of Murielle!" exclaimed the countess, with a shriek, as her head drooped; and she fainted in the arms of Lauder.

"What has happened—speak for mercy, sirs! what horror do you conceal from us?" exclaimed Sir Patrick Gray and the abbot together.

"Look here," said the old knight, in whose keen grey eyes there mingled a curious expression of commiseration and ferocity. He drew aside the countess's dule-weed, and then the Captain of the Guard and the abbot perceived that her white neck was stained with blood, her shoulder covered with hideous ligatures, and that her right hand and arm were gone— *gone* from the elbow!

"Who—what has done this?" asked Gray, as his sun-burned cheek grew pale.

"See you, sirs, what the first shot from yonder hellish engine hath achieved?" replied Lauder, reproachfully.

"The first," reiterated Gray.

"And I would give the last blood in my heart to have the seven makers of it hanging in a bunch from yonder gallows knob!"

Local history records that this terrible mutilation occurred when the countess was seated at table in the hall, through one of the windows of which the great bullet passed; and some years before the battle of Waterloo, when Thrave, like several other Scottish castles, was undergoing repair, as a barrack for French prisoners, a favourite gold ring which the countess wore upon the forefinger of her right hand, inscribed Margaret de Douglas, was found among the ruins, with one of Meg's granite balls beside it; and the old peasantry in Galloway yet aver, that in this terrible mutilation "the vengeance of Heaven was evidently manifested, in destroying the hand which had been given in wedlock unto two near kinsmen." [5]

By a strange coincidence, or an irresistible fatality, at the same moment that the countess was borne away, it came to pass that the man-at-arms who held the white flag let it drop from the summit of the keep into the barbican below. Then Sir John Romanno and his impatient cannoniers, perceiving that the flag was gone, and that some commotion had ensued about the gate of Thrave, supposed (in those days there were no telescopes), that the parley was broken, and that violence was offered to the envoys, so a shot was fired from the great brass bombarde named the Lion of Flanders.

With a mighty sound, between a whiz and a boom, it passed betwixt Sir Patrick Gray and the abbot, entered the archway, and, by a singular combination of retributive justice and fatality, struck James Achanna just at the girdle, and doubling him up like a crape scarf, literally plastered his body, armour and all, a quivering mass of blood, bones, steel plates and splints, upon the wall of the keep, into which it was imbedded.

The white pennon was again hoisted; but this terrible episode and appalling spectacle hastened the conclusion of the truce and the siege.

"Bid King James ride to the gate of Thrave, and a woman's hand shall give him the keys—withered be mine in its socket ere it shall do so!" said the sturdy old laird of the Bass, as he broke his sword across his right knee, and cast the glittering fragments into the moat, just as he had done after the seizure of Earl William, in the castle of Edinburgh.

"What terms seek you?" asked the abbot.

"The lives, the liberties, and fortunes of all."

"The king is merciful, and in his name we promise these shall be given to you," replied the two envoys, as they returned with all haste to Knockcannon, where the king was still on horseback, attended by Crichton, Glammis, and the principal lords of his council and army.

"You have promised over much, my good friends," said he, on hearing the terms and the relation of what had passed at the castle gate; "yet it would ill become me to bruise the bruised. I cannot restore this gallant dame's dainty right arm; but by the Black Rood of Scotland, I can wed her to a more loyal husband, with the hand she still possesses!"

And King James kept his word.

FOOTNOTES:

[5] This ball is still preserved by a gentleman in the neighbourhood, and corresponds exactly in size and quality with those shown in the castle of Edinburgh, as appertaining to the celebrated Meg, which are of Galloway granite (from Binnan Hill), the component parts of which, as geologists are aware, differ in several particulars.

CHAPTER LVII
THE FALL OF THRAVE

Song sinks into silence,
The story is told;
The windows are darken'd,
The hearthstone is cold.
Darker and darker
The black shadows fall;
Sleep and oblivion reign over all.
Longfellow.

"When your majesty's ancestor, Malcolm III., of valiant memory, received the keys of the castle of Alnwick, remember what occurred," said the wary and suspicious old chancellor.

"Malcolm was slain," replied the king.

"By foul treachery. The Saxon garrison yielded, and the keys were to be presented on the point of a knight's lance; but at the moment of doing so, the knight, like a mansworn traitor, pierced King Malcolm's eye and brain with his weapon and slew him on the spot. He escaped, but from the deed assumed a name—hence comes the Pierce-eye of Northumberland."

"But what of all this? I do not think I have much cause to fear our poor countess now."

"She has one hand left, and it can hold a dagger, I doubt not."

"Oh, good my lord, I shall not be unprepared for any emergency," said James laughing, as, accompanied by Sir Patrick Gray and fifty selected men-at-arms of his guard, he rode forward to Thrave, the earl of Errol following closely with at least a thousand knights and gentlemen, mounted and armed in full panoply.

The armour of the young king was beautifully engrained with gold. He wore a casquetel, which in lieu of visor had two oriellets, or oval plates, to protect the ears. It was encircled by a gold coronet, and had a crenel, or spike, in which a plume of scarlet and yellow feathers waved, and to which the queen's glove was tied. The hanging sleeves of his surcoat were richly embroidered by Mary's hands; and his whole arms, costume, and horse-trappings glittered with singular brilliance in the sunshine of the evening, as he caracoled over the green sward towards the embattled gate of Thrave.

On his breast sparkled the collar and jewel of the Golden Fleece of Burgundy, which Duke Philip the Good had just sent to him, in charge of Messire Jacques de Lalain, Dyck Graf of Bommel, who with his train had reached the camp only on the preceding evening. This order had been instituted by Philip himself in 1429.

When the king was within twenty paces of the gate of Thrave, it was unclosed, and a lady, attended by a group of the countess's bower-maidens, the tall and dark-eyed Maud of Pompherston, the Caillean Rua, and the fair-haired daughters of Sir Alan Lauder, the castellan, all clad in dule-weeds of black cloth with white crosses on their breasts in memory of the late earl, and all wearing hoods and veils, came slowly and timidly forward, like a procession of nuns.

On seeing them, James at once sprung from his horse, the reins of which he gave to the Master of Crichton, his page. Gray, and other attendants, immediately dismounted, and leading their horses by the bridle, kept near the king, before whom the principal lady, after advancing a pace or two in front of her companions, knelt, saying in a low and broken voice, "In the name of mercy and St. Bryde of Douglas, receive these keys."

She bowed her graceful head, at the same time upholding, with hands of charming form and whiteness, the three great iron keys of the castle of Thrave.

"And in the name of good St. Bryde, and of gentle mercy, sweet lady, we accept of them," said the king, handing them to his master of the ordnance; "and once again we pledge our royal word for the promised terms—life, liberty, and fortune—to all who have withstood our cannon here in Thrave. But rise, madam," added the king, "it ill becomes a gentleman to receive a lady thus."

With one hand he raised her, and with the other lifted up her long black veil,—for James II. was not devoid of that admiration of beauty, which was one of the chief characteristics of his chivalrous family.

"Murielle!" exclaimed Sir Patrick Gray, starting forward on beholding her face.

"Your long-lost wife?" said James, with surprise.

"My wedded wife—Oh, Murielle——"

"Then to your wardship, Sir Patrick, I must consign this rebel Douglas, but on one condition——"

"Oh name it, your majesty!" said Gray, who was almost speechless with emotion.

"That you keep her for life, either at court or in your tower of Foulis," replied the king, laughing, as he placed Murielle's hand in that of Gray, amid murmurs of applause and satisfaction, in which all the knights, nobles, and even the grim old chancellor joined.

Murielle Douglas was beautiful as ever; but the pure breeze of early autumn that came down the vale of the Dee, the exciting scene, and the great presence in which she stood, alike failed to impart a red tinge to her pale cheek, and even her rosebud lip had lost its usual carnation hue.

In short, poor Murielle had evidently suffered much in mind and body; for the years of blight and anxiety she had spent in gloomy Thrave had not been without a natural influence upon a spirit so timid and gentle; and now, as she wept upon her husband's breast, she neither heard nor heeded the acclamations which rose from the king's camp, with the roar of culverins from Knockcannon and the Carlinwark, as they greeted the appearance of the royal standard which Sir John Romanno hoisted on the great keep of Thrave, the now humbled stronghold of her forefathers, the mighty lords of Galloway.

EPILOGUE

Not long after these events the new earl of Douglas was reconciled to James II., and though both parties were insincere—their mutual injuries being too deep and too recent—there was peace in the kingdom for a time.

Inspired by a sentiment of revenge for the death of their chief in Thrave, the MacLellans long refused to lay aside their swords, and for years continued to commit such dreadful outrages upon the Douglases and their adherents that James outlawed the new laird of Bombie and all his followers; but during his reign they re-won their possessions in the following remarkable manner.

A band of outlaws or wild rovers, said by some authorities to have been Saracens or Moors, but who were more probably Irishmen, as their leader was named Black Murrough, landed in Galloway and committed such devastations that the king, by a royal proclamation, offered the forfeited lands of Bombie to any knight or man, however humble, who could kill or capture this terrible stranger, of whose stature, strength, and ferocity the most startling stories were told, for the marvellous was a great element in those days.

In a wild place, near where the old castle of Bombie stood, there is a spring which flows now, as perhaps it flowed a thousand years before the epoch of our story. The bare-kneed and bare-armed Celts of Galwegia, and the helmeted and kilted warriors of Rome, have drunk of it. With its limpid waters, St. Cuthbert, whose church was built close by, baptized the first Christians of the district in the name of Him who died on Calvary; and in later and less-peaceful times, the fierce Lag and Claverhouse have drunk of it, with their gauntleted hands, when in pursuit of the persecuted Covenanters, by hill and loch and the shores of the Solway.

It chanced that Sir William, the outlawed nephew of Sir Thomas MacLellan, was wandering near this well, on a day when the banks of the Dee were changing in tint and aspect under the genial sunshine and warm showers of spring, when the trees were putting forth their young and fragrant blossoms, and when the blackbird and the rose-linnet sang among the thickets that overhung the river.

Full of those sad and bitter thoughts which were naturally induced by the outlawry and proscription of his family, the young heir of Bombie approached the spring to drink, and lo! near it there lay, fast asleep, a rough and gigantic man, whose form exhibited wondrous strength and muscle, and by his side lay an Irish war-club, the knotty head of which was studded with sharp iron spikes. He was the leader of the strange devastators,—he, for whose life King James had offered the castle and heritage of Bombie.

MacLellan drew near, and by a single stroke of his double-handed sword, shred off the great head of the terrible sleeper, and grasping it by its thick black locks of matted hair, he conveyed it without delay to the king, who, in terms of his proclamation, immediately restored to him the forfeited lands of Bombie, and from that day the MacLellans assumed as a crest, the head of a savage on the point of a sword, with the motto—"Think on." The scene of this episode bears to this day the double name of Bombie's Well, and the Wood of Black Murrough.

Broken in spirit, the proud Countess Margaret, whilom the Fair Maid of Galloway, condescended at last to seek the forgiveness and protection of King James II., after which, as she was still the loveliest woman of her time, he bestowed her in marriage upon his half brother, John, earl of Athole, son of the late Queen Jane and of the Black Knight of Lorn, who perished so miserably in Flanders.

Robert, duke of Albany, died in exile, and no man in Scotland ever knew where he found a grave; but Sir Patrick Gray and Murielle lived long and happily. We know not which survived the other. He was created a peer of the realm by the title of Lord Balronald, and received the captaincy of the royal castle of Lochmaben, which he defended valiantly against the English in the year 1460, during that war in which James II. perished by the bursting of a cannon at the siege of Roxburgh, when standing by the side of Sir John Romanno, near the old Thorn Tree, at Fleurs.

William Lord Crichton, the wily and somewhat unscrupulous old chancellor, died in peace in 1455, at his own stately castle in Lothian, and lies interred in the old church near it.

His aged compatriot, Sir Alexander Livingstone, died about the same time, after securing a peerage for his son, the captain of Stirling, who was created Lord Livingstone of Callendar, and Great Chamberlain of Scotland.

We need scarcely inform the reader that the worthy abbot of Tongland never succeeded in his great project concerning the Master of Evil, whom he wished to destroy as an enemy by making him a friend; though in after-years a poor Capuchin of Venice revived the idea, by petitioning the states of that republic, and also the pope, on the same subject, and had the reward of being viewed by both as a—madman.

The beautiful young queen, Mary d'Egmont of Gueldres, only survived her husband three years.

It was our strange fortune to behold her remains, previous to their re-interment at Holyrood, in May, 1848, when nothing remained of those charms which she inherited from the houses of Cleves, Burgundy, and Gueldres, save her teeth, which, after having been three hundred and eighty-five years in the grave, were singularly white and regular.